KT-501-708

The Indian Widow

Sarah Woodhouse lives with her husband and two children on a farm in Norfolk. She has been writing historical short stories since she was eighteen.

Her first novel, *A Season of Mists,* was set in Norfolk in the eighteenth century. *The Indian Widow* is her second novel and she is currently working on a new story.

Available in Fontana by the same author
A Season of Mists

SARAH WOODHOUSE

The Indian Widow

Fontana/Collins

First published in Great Britain in 1985
by Century Hutchinson Co. Ltd.
First published in Fontana Paperbacks in 1986.

Copyright © Sarah Woodhouse 1985

Made and printed in Great Britain by
William Collins Sons & Co. Ltd, Glasgow

For Papa

CHAPTER 1

Mr Temple Purley found the relict of the abominable Francis Fletcher a tall, brisk, airy, commanding girl with a long chin and unforgettable nose. Her dress was shabbily conservative – how must her former glory be diminished! – although it was true he could not remember meeting her before in his reluctant five-year association with her husband; and sly whispering rumours had reached him, even him, most self-sufficient, lugubrious and retiring of men, that Fletcher had kept her locked up, had deprived her of necessities, had beaten her. He poured her ratafia and looked more carefully for any sign of mistreatment. To be sure she was damnably thin, the yellow-brown skin tight across the strong bones of her face, and the hand which took the glass was skeletal and wore no rings; to be sure her eyes looked dull and bruised, but Fletcher was two months dead so nothing of that nature could be ascribed to him now – she had been crying then, or passing sleepless nights. Her state was undeniably pitiable. He had only this morning spoken to her legal man, had found him dispassionate, blunt: the Fletcher fortune was squandered, the debts mountainous, the widow so much flotsam on a general tide of disaster.

Temple Purley was an unimaginative man, had done business with Fletcher as infrequently as possible, and was concerned only with the very large sum outstanding, the very large sum, which his widow was obviously unable to pay.

It was July, the hot season; outside Calcutta baked and steamed. Purley fanned himself languidly with the paper that told, in a neat spidery hand, the exact sum in rupees Francis Fletcher had owed him. And across the low table Mrs Philadelphia Fletcher regarded him with a stark sort of bravado from under a hellishly old-fashioned hat ornamented with tarnished silver lace.

'The house is sold,' she said at last and then, as if by any chance he did not know: 'Everything is sold. I have two bags of clothes and enough to pay for temporary lodgings until I can arrange a passage to England.'

'Yes. I have spoken to Price.'

'And naturally he told you the desperate state of my finances. He has told the whole of Calcutta, I assure you, just as he informed all Madras and half the country between there and Seringapatam. Oh, he is unflaggingly loyal, optimistic, and discreet,' and she turned the glass round in her long bare fingers, looking down into it for a moment and then up again. 'I cannot imagine why you wished to see me, Mr Temple, knowing I have not the means to settle your account.'

She looked straight at him, a manly, almost ferocious look, as if daring him to come to verbal blows. So she knew all about the shortcomings, the iniquities of her husband's attorney. But she spoke in the same firm tone she had used since the interview began. It was almost as if the man's flagrant indiscretions meant nothing to her. Of course, she must be used to gossip, to being the object of sideways looks, the centre of scandal. Had he not heard she had had an affair with Fletcher's brother a year or two back, that she had been alone with him when he died of the cholera and had taken jewels and money from the house? She had been accused by the wife, he remembered dimly, there had been a lawsuit threatened, and Fletcher had seen to it everything was returned. It had been a sensational, pyrotechnic week, every ear in Madras singed by listening to the hottest news.

'Did you hear me, Sir? I have no means to pay you.'

'Hmm, yes. Five thousand pounds perhaps, a little less,' murmured Purley, lifting the paper he held to his short-sighted eyes. 'What are we to do about it then, Mrs Fletcher?'

He had not meant to see her. What was the point of it? He could have had her taken up for debt but what was the point of that either, except to serve a childish sense of revenge? Some money had been paid after all, and she had made valiant efforts – so he had heard – to settle where she could. His five thousand was the last hurdle in a desperate race and she could not rise to it, her resources were done.

But she did not look as if she was about to lie down and die.

'If it is ever within my power . . .' she began, downing the ratafia with an even fiercer look from her abused eyes, 'but I do not have great hopes, do you?'

Was it humour? He thought he saw a glint, a flash in her light eyes, a spark of some long-suppressed hilarity. He stood rather stiffly, not at ease because he had no idea how to take her, was even a little afraid of her. He could not guess how deep her self-possession went, but she did not appear on the brink of hysteria, and made no appeal for pity. The glint had gone. The hat dipped as she drew on her gloves. Then she glanced up again into his unimpressive, kindly face.

'Why did you ask me here, Mr Purley?'

Out of ardent curiosity, he might have said, he who was seldom curious and never inquisitive; out of a nagging sense of responsibility, wholly absurd, that had grown imperceptibly at every fresh rumour of her distress; out of the weak promptings of his businesslike mind which had quickened at Price's insinuations about missing jewels, a ranee's rubies concealed perhaps in a pair of whalebone stays . . .

Mrs Philadelphia Fletcher stood up. She was about five feet nine, which seemed a prodigious height to a man six inches shorter and did very little for his courage. She stood as straight and slim and upright as any woman he had ever seen, and if there were rubies beneath her tight silk bodice they were surely of a size invisible to the human eye.

'Why, Mr Purley?' she demanded again.

'To wish you a safe journey, Mrs Fletcher,' he managed, an arrant lie but a brave one, as he held out his hand. 'To assure you I consider the debt written off, irrecoverable. I have put it down to the unfortunate lapse on my part in doing any kind of business with your late husband. He was a man of sagacity. I would not normally allow such credit.'

A cheat, a charlatan, a rogue; sagacity be damned! He had

heard Fletcher called a cardsharper, a whoremaster. And could this creature be his wife, could she indeed? How old was she? Twenty-seven, -eight? She looked imperious. Well, so she might. All she had left was pride, though pride would scarcely feed and clothe her and keep her from the wolves. Mr Temple Purley, who was an honest and wealthy man, a man of sense and scruples, found himself wishing he might give her twenty pounds, or ten, a trifling enough gesture. He felt so sorry for her. But it would be misunderstood, and in any case her hawkish look was a great deterrent, her hand strong and painfully thin in his.

'Your servant, Sir,' with a cool nod and a hush of her skirts as she turned away. We both know what my husband was, said her eyes, and we were both forced to give him more credit than he deserved.

'May I ask where you are to settle in England?' Purley asked at the last, gazing miserably out at the dust beyond his door in which no chair, no servant waited; she had come alone then, and on foot.

'I am going home.' It was said with assurance, a strong determined inflexion, as if it was necessary to convince herself home existed anywhere now. 'A place called Lingborough on the Norfolk coast. I was brought up there with my aunt.'

'I do hope . . .' But he did not know what he hoped. His imagination failed him. He felt only that faint persistent pity. And in any case she did not wait to hear what he hoped, she walked away with a long, graceless stride, her skirts flicking the dust and all the tarnished silver lace winking in the pitiless sun.

It was her stubborn courage that moved him. He wished her well from the bottom of his heart but wishing would not help her, nor conjure a single anna in her name. He watched her out of sight and then sighed, mopping the perspiration off his flushed skin with a large kerchief, and went in.

She had the two bags of clothes, some few tattered books, a turquoise ring that had been her unknown, long-dead

10

mother's, and Phee. She had enough money for the passage home, and that paying the lowest price for a malodorous hole somewhere in the bowels of the ship, and she had two pairs of good whalebone stays and no rubies; most particularly she had no rubies.

Sometimes she would dream of rubies, rubies she had once held in her hand, rubies that had been her passport to freedom. In the hot hot dark of those last nights before the rains she would lie awake while Phee snored and remember the rubies. Was it really three years ago now, all that terrible business? Three years ago Francis had abandoned her in that house where all the servants who had not fled were dead of the cholera and where George Fletcher his brother lay dying. How glad she had been to see him go, that frantic, hysterical Francis, scarlet from drink, exertion and anger, who had raged at her to leave and when she would not, had struck her again and again.

'You will die!' he had cried in a high, terrified, savage voice. 'Leave him. He's a dead man already. Don't you understand, you fool, if you stay with him you'll die too.'

'I do not care,' she had replied, and at that moment it had been the truth.

So she had been left alone, and George sinking and sinking, wasting to death before her eyes. She had done what little she could, and at some point he had said brokenly: 'Take the rubies, the Sarawar rubies. Dear girl, take them. They are all I have to give you here and I always meant them to be yours . . . If you get out of here hide them, hide them very well. Francis will take them from you if . . .' And later, much later, in the middle of an incoherent jumble of words: 'If they help you leave him, help buy your passage home, I shall . . . I shall be happy.'

He had always taken the trouble to be kind. He was middle-aged, gouty, his face pitted by smallpox. As Purley was to do so much later he admired Lally's courage, her dogged resistance to an adverse fate and Francis Fletcher, merchant of Madras. He felt fatherly towards her, responsible. He

11

might have done something to prevent the marriage but had not, even when he had found out Francis intended to marry a young frightened virgin fresh out from England. No, he had not. He felt overwhelmed by remorse. Belatedly he had tried to help, sustaining her in the first terrible months of her marriage, giving her patient sympathy after she had lost her little girl, easing the wounds of her ten catastrophic years in India. Now, on his deathbed, he was giving her her freedom.

It was not to be, of course. If George's wife had not been acutely conscious of every rupee, every silk coat, every shirt, cravat, wigstand, snuffbox, IOU and uncut gem in her husband's possession Lally might have eventually sailed, disgraced but liberated, to wherever she had pleased. But the fuss – the Sarawar necklace alone was worth a fortune – and Hester's natural suspicions falling on Lally, could mean only one thing. Lally was no brazen liar, even after ten years of close observation and occasional practice. In the space of a morning Francis knew the whole truth. The rumours, the intervention of cohorts of lawyers, the adulterated versions of what had happened as George lay dying, Hester's outraged and ill-advised statements, ebbed and flowed about Lally where she sat behind her locked bedroom door, all hope of escape gone. Her morals and her sanity had been called in question – and who now did not believe Hester's spiteful accusation that Lally and George had been lovers? – and in the end she avoided arrest for theft by the narrowest of margins.

When, finally, she emerged into the world again, the very narrow world of Madras society, she found more doors than ever closed against her. Now it was not only because she was Francis's wife but for her own sake: she was a loose woman and a thief. But it seemed somehow not to matter so much. She had grown used to being cut dead, being whispered about, being shunned. She went to those few social gatherings to which she was invited and behaved with chilling propriety, making full use of her height which was all the advantage she had. And they all said how proud she was, quite the Jezebel,

12

and how perfectly fitted to be the wife of the appalling Fletcher.

Mrs Stritch still spoke to her; Mrs Stritch had nerves of steel. In the face of overwhelming opposition, even from her own husband, she continued to believe Lally the victim of grim circumstance and always had a place for her at her own table. It was to the Stritches Lally took Phee, her little maid, that day three years later when she left Temple Purley's office after her strange interview in which he apparently wrote off her enormous debt. To the rest of Madras and to all Calcutta Lally might be 'that Fletcher woman' but to Amelia Stritch she was always 'poor dear Philadelphia'.

The Stritches were in Calcutta for the same reason as Lally: they were there to arrange a passage on an Indiaman, one of their sons going home to England to school. Amelia received Phee with misgivings for the girl looked tearful and mutinous, and within ten minutes confirmed all suspicions by having a hysterical fit on the verandah, shrieking she would stay with Lally or die. There was very little they could do but douse her in cold water and lead her, sobbing, to the most out of the way corner. Lally stifled pity tinged with exasperation, appeared completely unmoved, and retired with her hostess to drink tea.

'It is so foolish of you to leave her behind,' was Amelia's mild reproof from behind the urn.

'I cannot afford to take her. I could not pay for her to eat.'

'My dear, I did not realise things were so difficult. I have heard . . . They are saying . . .'

'Think nothing of it. I know everything they are saying. They have resurrected the story of the Sarawar rubies and it is commonly believed some are still in my possession, that even now Hester is duped, cheated out of her inheritance. If only it were true' – a sudden furious, perfectly human, savage look across the tea cups – 'If only it were true!'

Two days later Phee was returned, with thanks, the note explaining she had refused to work, had sulked, had hidden herself in cupboards, had tried to run away. Amelia thought

13

perhaps it was for the best, and enclosed, without comment, the sum of ten pounds. Lally was touched but did not show it. The emotional, wayward Lally of the past had been transformed in India to this severe, unsmiling woman who now supervised the packing of her two remaining bags as if they were crammed with precious articles, when in point of fact they held nothing of any significance to her except a lock of her dead baby's hair. The rest, excepting the last of her money, she could have tossed into the Hooghly without a qualm.

So it was that Lally Fletcher, widow of a man who had rivalled princes in wealth, left India as poor as she had arrived. The lack of baggage and the tiny half-Indian maid caused no comment on the ship but Lally herself, the renowned Mrs Fletcher of Madras, caused ripples of curiosity and speculation. She did not appear to have one friend to wave her goodbye until, at the very last minute, Temple Purley was brought on board, clutching at his wig in consternation, crying her name out loud.

He had brought her a fine cashmere muffler. He presented it shyly but had the satisfaction of seeing her flush very slightly under her sallow skin. She was not immovable then. He said awkwardly: 'For the colder regions, my dear Mrs Fletcher. For the northern seas.'

'How very kind of you.'

It occurred to him dimly that a blue cashmere scarf might seem less than adequate as a parting gift from a country that had robbed her of so much, but there was nothing but gratitude in her face. He bowed over her hand.

'If there is anything I can ever do . . . If you have any unfinished business, any worries. Write to me. I am at your command.'

'You are very generous, Sir.'

'Oh, do not take me amiss, Mrs Fletcher, I am too old to waste time flattering young women. It occurred to me simply that your husband being the man he was there might be . . . complications, shall we say, unfinished deals, maybe other

14

creditors, hopefully other debtors. I do not trust your legal hack Price. I tell you straight, the man's a vile piece of work. You might find it less easy to cut free of India than you suppose.'

'I do hope not.'

'For your sake so do I.'

'Mr Purley' – a fleeting smile that did not light her eyes, a straight, cool look – 'I am fully conscious of the fact I owe you five thousand pounds. You may say it is written off, I can never forget it.'

'It *is* written off. That matter is closed. I had no motive coming on board today but to wish you Godspeed, and to warn you . . . There is a rumour beginning that your husband was well known to – I dare not say on intimate terms with – Hyder Ali.'

They were standing side by side at the rail on the poop deck. Behind them were crammed the various cages and crates of poultry, pigs and goats, and somebody's furniture not yet struck down into the hold, and great coils of rope thick as a man's arm. There was a cool breeze off the river and the rippling sunlit water was reflected in Lally's face as she bent over to look down.

'It is quite possible,' she said quietly, as if in reply to some commonplace remark. 'Francis would have financed the devil so there was some advantage to himself, but rest assured he would at the same time have been selling ammunition to the angels.' She gave a wry smile, a very small, very wry smile, but even so her face changed, grew a little softer. It was the merest shadow of her vanquished humour but Temple Purley saw it and felt comforted and bowed again before putting on his hat.

'I never doubted,' he said, 'you were a lady of acumen and resource. I knew it when I first met you. I wish you a safe journey. Your servant, Ma'am.'

He left her on the burning deck, shading her eyes to watch him diminish and diminish until he was no more and she was quite alone again. Two days later, watching the sun come up out of a quiet sea, she thought of him, and of the huge, unhappy house in Madras, of people and places, of the sights, sounds and tastes of India, and already it seemed such thoughts had a dreamlike quality, as if it had all never happened, just as all that was left of the land itself was a flashing glimpse of a great lateen sail away in the north-east, where a coastal trader plied along the rays of the sunrise.

CHAPTER 2

The sea voyage was remarkably swift but also remarkably stormy. Lally was the only woman on the ship apart from Phee, which was also remarkable. She was eyed speculatively and askance and from all angles, but a stiff widow and a haughty-looking one at that was not inclined to set any hearts aflame. Rather the crew came to see her as a Jonah, such contrary winds for the time of year, two deaths from a mysterious fever and one man overboard before ever they had reached the Cape. She walked the deck in all weathers – an energetic, elastic walk – and with a tenacity they might have admired her for had not the sight of her day after day begun to strike a chill in them; sailors are deeply superstitious souls and Lally's long face and profound reserve brought out their worst. Perhaps she brought out the worst in their captain too, a stolid, plain-thinking, plain-speaking, plain-eating, misogynic sort of man. He did not approve of her: for being a woman, for having been married to a notorious libertine, for being aboard his ship and taking it all in her stride, the rolling and pitching, the sickness, the boredom. Once she slipped on deck and hit her head on a barrel, had been scooped up and borne below in disorder, bloody but conscious – too conscious for the captain, who felt her grey accusing eyes on him.

No, he did not approve of her but he accorded her a grudging respect, the kind a soldier might reserve for the more obdurate of his enemies. She gave him frights. It was almost impossible to make conversation with her, she replied in monosyllables or not at all. She would not be drawn, she would not be merry. He divined little by little that her self-confidence was, in fact, a kind of withdrawal: she had retreated within herself, there being nowhere else left for her to retreat. He could not be expected to show sympathy

17

however; his was not a sensitive nature, and he could not forget she had been Francis Fletcher's wife. Besides, he did not like her, he felt overpowered by her keen, intelligent gaze. If he had been asked, afterwards, what he remembered about her, he would have said only that she had had freckles, a great host of the damn things marching across that hawkish nose, and a cool boyish way of speaking as if he was a servant, as if he was of no consequence whatever, and that she was tougher than any nabob's widow he had ever met to survive five months of that stinking little hole beneath the waterline which she had shared with her maid and quite a few of the ship's rats.

He would have said, without a moment's hesitation, he would not have her travel in his ship again, not if the Company was to pay him double and buy him a palace for his retirement.

London was first glimpsed romantically under a rainbow, for it was a passionate April, now sun, now wind and rain. The storm just over had done wonders in suppressing the obnoxious stench of the place; for a bare half hour everything was fresh and damp. Then the sun came out more strongly and the city steamed, a revolting putrid steam. Lally did not find it overpowering, scarcely noticed; it was nothing to some of the darker corners of the India where she had survived the last ten years. Phee, fathered on one of Francis Fletcher's housewomen by a very young English soldier of predictable weaknesses, found the place a potent mixture of the miraculous and the disappointing. Yes, the houses were splendid, but there was so much mud, and so many poor people: she had not expected the barefoot and ragged in her father's beloved city.

They travelled on to Twickenham, leaving the worst smells behind. At Twickenham lived Lally's oldest, her only friend, a sweet and charming girl at school and now a sweet and charming lady with a cheerful indolent husband and three children, another expected any moment. Her house, her servants, everything was at Lally's disposal; and did Lally know she had kept every one of the letters Lally had written her these ten years? No, Lally had not known, she trembled at the thought. And perhaps Caroline Pascoe trembled too when she opened the door to this tall thin person, yellow as buttercups and regal as the Empress of China. Could this apparition be the reckless, laughing Lally she had once known so well? She was no fool, had read between the lines of all those letters, had suspected a great deal, but now she saw she had suspected only a hundredth part of the truth.

Her husband, that dear easygoing man, was less shocked by Lally's appearance but was equally bewildered. Was this the wild, mischievous girl whose spirited rebellion at Miss Porter's School for Young Ladies his wife had so admired? He found her an angular, unprepossessing woman with faded light brown hair and an unattractive skin. The nose was unfortunate, he thought, so too were the freckles. More unfortunate was a total lack of animation in a face designed by nature for more positive use. He did his best by her, took her for walks, showed her the sights of the neighbourhood, and was rewarded with a cordial, muted interest, no enthusiasm at all. It was strange, for she walked with a great galloping stride, he was sometimes hard pushed to keep up, and she would throw up her head, one hand to her hat, and charge straight and true at whatever distant object he set her. But her face … It was as if the soul had been quenched, he thought, the spirit extinguished.

In the middle of May, Caroline's baby due any day, Lally sat down with pen and ink. The task was disagreeable but it must be done. But what could she say? And what was Anne like now, married to a prosperous parson, a mother of five? Of course, Anne was not all her family: there were ten other cousins at least, two uncles, an aunt, a great-aunt, but they had not written to her in India, she expected nothing from them now. She wanted to go back to Norfolk because once she had been happy there and she remembered it with a quiet joy and a subdued longing. It was the place alone that drew her, not sweet little cousin Anne in Lingborough parsonage. For years she had dreamed of it, had clung to the memory as to a talisman: one day she would return. She had only to close her eyes and she could see it: the great wild hump of the Heath, the wind-bent thorns, the tracts of heathery waste, and then the abrupt descent to the coastal marshes where the rushes and coarse grasses flattened under the sharp cold wind, where the wild geese flew over and the snipe tumbled in the white sky.

Lally Fletcher opened her eyes again and the yellow May sunshine flooding in through the tall windows nearly dazzled her. Then she bent to write. She wrote a gossipy, sprawling letter quite out of character, the lines peppered with casual references to the house in Madras, the vast retinue of servants, the unnumbered luxuries taken for granted. As she signed her name she felt the weight of her machinations and was ashamed. She had told no lies but hinted at a hundred. Her only excuse was that despair had driven her to it; she and despair had kept close company these ten years and she had often been brought to such sorry contrivances. Besides, she wanted to go home. In an unsettled life Lingborough was the only place she had ever thought of as home. She wanted to go back, to see perhaps if she could rediscover the person she had once been, and with her a new peace of mind, a sense of purpose. She had forgotten what peace of mind was, or content, or happiness. Where was the Lally now who had swum the moonlit dykes for a dare, leaving her petticoats on the bank and parting the ripples with brave, cold hands? And the Lally who had ridden that terrible horse, so strictly forbidden, going full tilt across the Heath with the wind taking her breath away? Was she quite dead? Lally felt she must be, that whatever Francis had not killed had gone with little Susan to the grave.

The letter to Anne was finished at last and despatched, not without misgivings. What kind of stir would it cause at the parsonage? But in remote Lingborough, mewed up with four small children under seven and a fretful baby, domestic crises abounding, a maid with child, the gardener sent to the Assizes for smuggling, Anne Glover was in no mood to resist shameless curiosity or the temptation to renew her acquaintance with the incorrigible Philadelphia, scourge of her childhood. If Lally now was only a mature version of Lally then, there would not be a dull moment in the parsonage for the next six weeks. So a letter had come back to Lally in Twickenham inviting her for the summer, the whole summer if she cared, she would be unreservedly welcome; Anne only hoped the house would not seem too small amd cramped after the splendours of Madras.

Lally kissed Caroline a fond farewell, truly fond, though as restrained as everything else she now said or did, and Caroline, who loved her, choked on all the witty and light-hearted remarks she had been going to make and kissed her back with tears in her eyes.

'You have not told them you are poor,' she accused, as they waited for the carriage to be sent round. 'That was a silly pride.'

'It was sound common sense. They would not have invited me had they not thought I was gloriously rich.'

'How cynical you have become.'

'Have I not? But I am not past saving, am I; or would you still be my friend?'

The carriage took her to the great inn where she and Phee took a coach to Norfolk. Robert Pascoe hung on the door a moment with all the comical anxiety of a spaniel, wishing them a safe journey, all the other polite, parrot phrases. He was genuinely sorry to see Lally go, would far rather have had her astringent company while Caroline was giving birth than that of his voluble mother-in-law and her two unmarried daughters.

'I wish you all joy,' he cried, as he was forced to let go and the coach began to move, and he meant it; her head with its dilapidated, outrageous old hat bobbed out of the window a moment and he saw her eyes, a blaze of gratitude.

But the journey was no joy, it was a nightmare, Phee sick as a dog, the rain endless. There were tales of floods, fallen trees;

the miles between London and Norfolk might prove as difficult to cross and possibly as wet as those between Calcutta and The Downs. At Colchester Phee was so ill Lally was forced to abandon the coach and take a room overnight, a shabby, rancid sort of room which was all her funds would run to, and there, fireless and beset by fleas, she dreamed of India, of peacocks, of Francis's fat, stubby fingers grasping at her dress, handing her the jewels: 'Wear these tonight. Thank God at least you have a decent long neck to show 'em off.' The jewels choked her. They seemed to tighten of their own accord, or was it Francis pulling, pulling ... She gasped and struggled and cried out weakly. And woke.

It was a chill, misty dawn. The rain had eased. The first coach of the morning was below already and someone along the passage was shouting for cocoa and hot rolls. Lally dressed, dragged on her cloak, went down into the yard. It seemed to her a long time since she had stood alone in an English inn yard amid the scrambling tumult as a coach got under way. She stood swaying a little, the cold breeze striking through her thin dress under the cloak, her hair a great mass of uncombed curl. They had run out a chaise, were putting to the horses; there was a squabble about baggage going on. A child dragged at Lally's skirt whining for a penny and she looked down, detached its tiny hand firmly, said she had no pennies, and glanced about in case the mother was about to pick her pocket. A round little face framed in filthy curls gazed up at her, not more than three years old. Susan, Lally thought suddenly, Susan. The colour drained from her face.

An ostler at her elbow: 'Mind yer toes, ladies. All right, Charlie, get 'em away.'

The chaise lurched forward. Lally saw the child whisked to safety, a thin rabbity girl howling at it in annoyance. And then there was another face in front of her, a little above, a cadaverous, saturnine, despotic face. It was thrust out of the window of the chaise.

'God's death, you'll be under the wheels, woman! Get away! Get away!'

CHAPTER 3

The man in the chaise stuck his remarkable face further out and shouted. His furious commands took a while to penetrate the din but at last, already into the road, the horses were pulled up. He leapt out, ran back, his black coat flying, his wig adrift. And there she was, retreating now through the crowd of nagsmen, drinks sellers and general opportunists who packed the yard. When he caught at her arm, roughly, impolitely, she turned and gave him a startled stare, a look of horror tinged with reluctant recognition. She had a long, strong face, a singularly large nose, freckles, and a grave, even stern expression. No beauty in the least, he thought, only a sort of gangling awkwardness charged with suppressed energy. She was so tall he felt a distinct chagrin, tempered by hilarity, to find her eyes on a level with his own.

He said: 'Forgive me, but you were within an inch of your life. My carriage . . .' They were knocked together, torn apart again; another coach came in behind them, the sweating, steaming horses vanishing into a mob of orange-girls, quacks, pot-boys, and a diminutive sprat with footwarmers. 'Take care, take care. You will be run down for sure. Dear girl, back, back! Inside at once. This is no place for civilised conversation.'

This last remark caused her to look him up and down, as if wondering what he and civilised conversation might have to do with each other. This time her horror was mitigated by a trace of wry amusement, the very slightest glow in the depths of her eyes. Certainly he was a strange sight, a rusty old coat flapping open over a staggeringly flamboyant waistcoat – green silk trimmed with silver – and a full-bottomed wig, and spectacles half way down his nose.

'I am travelling to Norfolk,' he was saying as they beached

on the quieter reaches of the inn's interior, a smoky dark hole given over to worm-eaten settles and portraits of dead patrons and prize cattle. 'If you are bound in that direction pray let me offer you a seat. I would be honoured. I would be overjoyed.'

It was improper, it was not to be tolerated; he had nearly run her down, had shouted at her, and now stood all smiles and false humility begging her to treat his carriage as her own. He was a complete stranger, and a disagreeable sort of stranger at that. Of course she must refuse him. She looked straight into his pale grey eyes. They were good eyes, clear and bright, and behind them lived a substantial intelligence, a prodigious acuity; his was not a brain nor a nature to trifle with, the eyes declared.

Two thoughts came to her: the eyes were at variance with the clothes, the wig, the spectacles – and she had not done anything truly reckless for years.

'Yes,' said Lally Fletcher, 'I would be so obliged. Will you give me a moment to fetch my maid and my baggage' – a quick, unsmiling look from beneath her level brows – 'and my hat.'

The post-chaise had no springs and the post-boy was the worse for an illiberal quantity of strong cider. Progress was erratic, the horses generally in charge, and the three passengers were feeling sea-sick.

Lally leaned weakly in one corner and gazed stonily at the dull countryside, wan and unattractive in a squall of rain. It was Suffolk – or perhaps not. The last ten hours had seen the destruction of her sense of time and place. During all the long voyage from India – and in a ship as crank and unseaworthy as any that had ever cleared the Hooghly – she had never felt so unwell. A covert glance beneath her lashes at her suffering companions showed her Mr John Glory Lovatt in a position of utter resignation, his eyes closed at last, Phee huddled miserably into a huge shawl, moaning gently.

The weather was turbulent, a capricious June promised. The may blossom had been ruined in the bud, the chestnut flowers torn asunder. The fields past which the chaise rocked and jerked were sodden and dank, here and there morose cattle in a huddle or a clutch of vociferous, dispirited sheep. Lally looked out and sighed. She wriggled her toes in her shoes and found them numb. There were stray raindrops on her skirts and a fringe of mud to her petticoats.

'We are there, surely to God we are there,' cried Mr Lovatt suddenly with a wild stare. 'We have been on the road a full week since the last change.'

'An hour perhaps,' said Lally mildly. 'I heard your watch strike.'

He pulled it out. It was a pretty timepiece, quite obviously French. The exquisite enamelling winked as he turned it in his hand.

'My grandfather acquired it after Malplaquet,' he said as if he read her thoughts. 'As a boy I used to think there might be a romantic story attached to it but age has taught me the tale is probably sordid and dishonourable. Still, it tinkles the hour prettily, and as an oddity has other merits: I once had a lightfingered gentleman in the Colonies steal it and then hand it back to me for he feared he could not fence it, it was too remarkable.'

'Have you been in America then?' It might account for his tanned face in which those light eyes shone so mysteriously.

'I have indeed. Ten years and more.'

'Throughout the war then.'

'A sorry business on the whole, the usual inglorious confusion. The common soldiers get all the hurts, the fools at home the glory. I am only thankful I could observe from afar.'

'You took no part in the fighting? You have no interests in the country?'

'Neither monetary nor landed interests, dear lady, no!' A harsh laugh and he pocketed the watch again. 'I am what you might call a natural philosopher. Birds, above all things, birds are my passion. I have tramped about the New World discovering strange birds for my delight and edification – and that of others, I hope; yes, I do hope so. An education in itself

25

simply to journey to the more inaccessible places, what with snakes and Indians and dumb guides who spoke the wildest approximation to the English language I have ever heard and even more execrable French. And I have never ridden so many disobliging mules nor slept so hard in my life.'

Lally sank back in her corner. Had he worn that preposterous wig on mule-back, and if not what else? She was fast being overcome by chill and nausea, a green, clammy state. Poor Phee had abandoned herself to both and had buried her head entirely in the shawl hoping only, with the dying flicker of coherent thought, not to be violently sick before a gentleman; especially such a gentleman. Lally could see her raising a pained and watery eye to look across at him, repelled yet fascinated, as if he were a toad. And Lally remembered how low Phee had been brought by the journey, how ill she had been at sea: dreadful, distressful retching for days and days, a damp pale staring face, and then a sort of stupor, a suspended animation; at one point she had really believed the poor simple girl might die.

How long ago the ship seemed now, and the heat and dust, the Calcutta waterfront and Mr Temple Purley handing her the cashmere scarf. How long ago.

Mr Lovatt was looking at her. He had pulled the spectacles down from his eyes again. Could his eyes lie? A more elusive character belonged to those eyes than the man who had crossed the Colonies by mule in search of birds. And it was that elusive character who had offered her the seat in his carriage and offered it to the old Lally, the vanquished, devil-may-care Lally – and offered as if he knew her, had known her in the past at Lingborough, thundering up over the Heath on the black pony, a man's hat rammed down tight on her ruined curls.

Yes, he had spoken to the old Lally – and the old Lally had replied.

The rain had ceased at last. Tumultuous grey cloud flung over the darkening fields. Lally shut her eyes and thought of clean linen, and a bed without fleas. When she opened them the slight wiry gentleman opposite was leaning forward to touch her arm.

'We have arrived. If you look out you will see buildings. Pray God it is not illusion. Your maid is asleep, bless her; how she has suffered. Lord, I shall be glad to get down to stretch my legs.' And then, with a penetrating look: 'You must regret your decision to travel with me, Mrs Fletcher. Even the slowest coach would have been more comfortable.'

But not as cheap, said her bold, steady eyes. He was looking at her with affection, she thought suddenly, as if . . . As if they were very old friends.

'You are a tigress,' he said. 'You would overcome anything.'

She blushed, not because of the mockery – she had learnt even in this short time that he was always mocking, meant nothing by it – but because of the irony. She felt that whatever courage, whatever stoicism she had once possessed had been drained out of her long ago.

The chaise pulled up in a yard, a rowdy, crowded inn yard lit by reeking torches and crammed with two outgoing coaches, any number of horses, chairs, men and boys in a hurry, and whores. Mr Lovatt stuck out his head and surveyed the scene, sliding his glasses down his nose and jerking up his wig in order to do so. There was a brief and pointed difference of opinion with a man crying hot pies and then the chaise lurched to a complete standstill. Mr Lovatt opened the door.

'So this is Norwich,' he said gloomily as he handed Lally down.

She stood behind him on the wet cobbles watching the light spraying over the shouting pot-boys and the steaming horses, the painted door of a coach, a slinking dog, a skinny child, a woman's hand raised to wave goodbye. And she saw herself, at seventeen, standing in just this place waiting for the coach that would take her to London – to the ship, to Calcutta, Madras, to Francis Fletcher.

'Come, come,' yelled JG, seizing her elbow – all his friends

27

called him JG, she must certainly do so – and propelling her indoors: 'Dear girl, you look cold. If this is June, God's love what is January like in these parts? No, come, we must eat.'

There was a mean fire, food, tolerably clean linen, and a bed without fleas. It was a respectable and comfortable bed, and though Phee snored at its foot and sometimes cried out in her mother's tongue which brought the terrible memories tumbling back, Lally found some kind of refuge behind its thick curtains. Towards dawn she rose from a shivering and uneasy sleep and, pulling round Phee's shawl, went to the window and peered out. There below was the cobbled yard, deserted now but for some chairmen playing dice, an old woman sitting asleep on a basket of geese, and the hot-pie seller piping an old army tune on a cheap whistle. There was a thin sour rain falling and all the lights were out but one.

She had stood there, Lally remembered, by the ticket booth, in the rose-coloured cloak that had been her aunt's parting gift, a tall shy girl, still smiling though she was leaving all she had ever loved, still eager for adventure though she must cross half the world for it. Well, India had destroyed that Lally down there in the rain and had made this other woman, the one who watched tonight from this high window.

She wept silently, mindful of Phee, but the tears ran between her fingers and down the cold glass.

Below her two of the chairmen had got up and were dancing to the highpitched pipe, a shuffling, ungainly pattern on the cobbles, their arms linked, their drunken faces glowing with delight.

The tiny mirror showed her a pale indistinct blur in which the nose looked more dominant than ever and the eyes were simply tired. In reality her skin was uncommonly sallow, a combination of the Indian climate and those massed freckles; it was the pallor of defeat she saw, an outward expression of her inmost feelings. There was her face, narrow and drained of colour, a ghost in the glass. In it, quite clearly as far as she could make out, were the marks of ten years in Madras, a

28

dreadful marriage, a lost child, the suppression of all the spontaneous humour and affection she had ever possessed, and the knowledge that she had nowhere to go, no one, apart from Caroline, who cared a toss for her.

But this morning there was sunshine on the dipping boards of the floor and the curtains were blowing in a striking breeze; the weather was on her side. The world smelled of wet earth and new leaves, hot horses and bacon cooking. She prodded her tangled hair. She was determined to arrive at the parsonage in style, as much style as was left her. What would Anne think? Caroline had been profoundly shocked, had not known her in the first few seconds. And Anne had never loved her, sweet, silly, gentle Anne. What would she say when she knew the truth of Lally's situation, that Francis had owed lakhs of rupees here, there and everywhere and that she had paid the debts to the point where she was reduced to little more than her shift and Amelia Stritch's ten pounds? It seemed to Lally too, however she viewed it, that Temple Purley's five thousand would haunt her forever, that she could not consider it written off, and that until she paid him in full she would never be free of India and all it had meant.

She had an unfortunate face for a girl without money. Money and influential relations would have transformed it to a face of character, that nose commanding attention. But she had neither so could claim no distinction, and the freckles on her nose made it ridiculous: it was an emphatic nose and the freckles re-emphasised the point already made. Even the blue of her eyes was a stormy, troubled blue, green or grey according to her mood. She had a good mouth, that was all, full and wide. It was not a smiling mouth any longer, simply an acceptable shape. She studied it minutely for a moment but no, it did not smile.

At last she stood up and began to dress. Poor Phee, still so unwell, even her sleeping face a dirty livid colour. It would be no good waking her for breakfast. So Lally sorted out her clothes silently on the far side of the room, putting on the severe blue riding habit with the gilt buttons which seemed to suit her come-hell-or-damnation mood, and the bold hat trimmed with silver lace she had last worn to Temple Purley's office in Calcutta.

Phee woke as she was putting the last pin in place and cried because Lally should have shaken her, should have made her get up and attend to her duties – and as an afterthought: were they going in any more carriages today, could they not stop another night at the inn?

A little later a knock heralded a diffident, blushing boy to say that Mr Lovatt had breakfasted and was on fire to be away – had she not said her destination was Holt? He was setting out for Holt directly. Was Mrs Fletcher ready? Could Mrs Fletcher be downstairs in five minutes, five minutes and not a minute more?

Mrs Fletcher gave up the thought of tea and toast and adjusted her hat with a last despairing glance in the mirror, tucking her dull brown hair behind her ears. Then she sailed downstairs, Phee in tow. She had a determined, practical air. Two unknown gentlemen bowed to her, struck by her bold advance. Out in the yard by a decent chariot stood JG, beaming.

'You have eaten? You are quite ready?'

She nodded, said yes, she was quite ready. His eyes gave her such a look she thought he must guess the sad truth but he only smiled, held out a hand, helped her up. It was a fine morning and they had less than thirty miles to go. He had shaved for the occasion.

'I have a basket of "necessary wittles" as the landlord put it,' he said cheerfully as they passed through the marketplace, assailed by the whiff of stale fish, 'and a whole bottle of brandy.'

Mrs Fletcher, he was thinking, looked as if she might need both.

After a while Lally began to stare out at the countryside as if waiting for some landmark, some familiar bend or pond or huddle of farm buildings. The colour came into her face and there was a softer, eager look about her.

'How long did you live up here?' JG asked, busy lighting one of his foul cheroots. Smoking was a habit he had acquired abroad, he said. Lally had noticed that he always pulled down his glasses when he indulged in it; once or twice they had fallen off the end of his nose.

'Twelve years.'

'Your cousin will be glad to see you, I trust.'

'I doubt it.'

'Surely you are mistaken? Will they not be overjoyed to meet you again after so long an absence? And you have such adventures to recount: the voyages, the perilous climate, the elephants, the princes. In so remote a corner of England you will be an undeniable attraction. Have you any intention of settling? What will you do?'

'I shall probably outstay my welcome. When they discover I am penniless they will be glad to put me out of doors.'

He grinned and puffed a vile cloud at the roof. She had turned to look out again. Yes, there, there was the farm where she and Charlie had sheltered the day the pony had bolted with the trap; there, crouched behind the sheltering elms, its casements wide to the singing wind. And suddenly the deep unexpected joy returned and a piercing delight.

'I loved it here,' she stated with abrupt, disarming candour.

'Indeed. I have not travelled in these parts before though I know the shore, the terrible shore. I came to grief upon its sandbanks long years ago. Will anyone meet you in Holt?'

'I sincerely hope so.'

A pause. He was brushing ash off his not very white stockings. Phee opened her eyes, groaned, her waxy face apparently as bloodless as a corpse. Lally opened the sash to let out the smoke and when she shot it up again and turned back she found JG's considering eye on her.

'You did not like India,' he said.

She did not reply. Her expression was remote and chill. She bent forward to look out again and her hat obscured her face.

They made exacting progress; Holt appeared just as they

felt they could not endure another minute. Lally scarcely dared look at it but found when she did it was all much the same, that she might only have been shopping in Norwich rather than away ten years in Madras. JG squinted sideways at it and said ha, how alike were all these damned country towns with their one or two good inns, their score of pot-houses, their few genteel shops, and hogs, invariably hogs, sometimes geese, making a quagmire of the main street. He declared his intention of lunching, at his leisure and in comfort, for he would not eat his beef at the gallop for any man, he told Lally, and he was heartily sick of pestilential post-chaises. He flung open the door and sprang forth.

'Where is the house you have rented?' she demanded as they made for the open door of the favoured inn, JG whacking about him with his basket of necessary wittles in order to clear the way of hens, small children, and a snapping terrier.

'A few miles to the north of here. God preserve us, I had hoped the country was more civilised, more elegant hereabouts. I am to study the birds on the marshes. Did I speak to you of the marshes? Migration? No? There is a theory, dearly held by . . . Ah, do I smell our beef?'

He did not. There was no beef but five-year-old mutton, the best in the county, the landlord assured them. Would they care to step along? No, there had been no message from Lingborough parsonage. The parsonage coachman was a weak, bow-legged fellow called Bested; there had been no sign of him nor of the parson's bays.

'What shall I do?' Lally pecked at the strong mutton and left her wine.

'There is no question . . . I must take you there.'

'But of course you must not. I must hire a chaise of my own.'

'A ridiculous expense. If my reckoning is not faulty my destination lies half way to yours. It will be no trouble to drive you two more miles to your parsonage and perhaps will shame them into an apology.'

'By careering up to the front steps in your chaise? I am sure they would consider it exceedingly improper.'

'Then you must present me as an old friend, a London friend, perhaps an acquaintance of your late husband's. We might have been in correspondence about the varied birds of Asia, might we not?' A grin, that wide elastic untrustworthy grin. 'I am always willing to lie in a good cause.'

'It is very kind of you,' she replied stiffly.

'Kind be damned!' The cheroot tilted in the corner of his mouth. 'Kind! It would be a shabby fellow who would abandon you here when his own house was but a mile or two from yours. Here, give me your arm. Where is Phee? They dragged her off to the kitchen for her mutton, I suppose. Phee!' A shout that brought the landlord, a pimply boy, the terrier, and Phee at the run. 'Well, and have you eaten? Come. Come my dears. I have a great curiosity to see this parsonage. It is many years since I met a parson of fortune and taste. Come.'

Now there was glorious burning sunlight and a fresh wind. Though they were far from a main road the going was good, dry upland tracks. The countryside was rich and kind, and in a while they dropped down into a little river valley, passed some mellow old farms, a scatter of cottages – Ledworth, said Lally, to whom the sight was achingly familiar – and then turned right-handed abruptly and bore down to a ford.

'There,' cried JG, rapping the glass, 'there I believe is the house I have rented.'

Lally caught a glimpse of the low windows behind the trees, and, as they splashed through the river, of the mill itself. She had fished in the mill pool once, her hair in a sailor's queue and Charlie's breeches on under her skirt for warmth.

'The Ship House? The old miller lived there when I was a girl.'

'Long underground, poor devil. They tell me it has been empty three years at least, and the mill derelict. I have rented it off a man called Brotherton, a man of consequence locally, a breeder of hounds, a Justice of the Peace.'

'Horses. He bred trotting horses.'

'Now I have not heard tell of the horses, I must confess. But I formed a mental picture of him from his name: Horace Nathaniel Brotherton. Rubicund, I thought, rubicund and shaggy, country manners and . . .'

'The Brotherton I knew was Valentine. This is his younger brother. Cookhams, the estate is called, a lovely house in a workmanlike sort of park, very fine but nothing pretentious. I went to my first ball there and slunk about the garden all night in misery because some heartless boy had called me clumsy. And he was quite right, of course, and I knew it.'

'Then Valentine is dead. My dear, I fear you will find great changes.'

Lally put her eye to the misted glass and smiled, a brief indication of deep relief. 'The place has not changed,' was her quiet comment.

They were climbing now through sparse woodland faintly hazy with bluebells and all of a sudden came out upon the level. JG wiped his window and stared out. There was an astonishing wilderness, vast reaches of gorse and heather and young bracken, windy shoulders of land where the plovers cried into the clear blue of the sky. The chaise rattled on, and JG let down the sash, sniffing at the honey scent of the gorse bloom and looking out over the top of his spectacles. Then he yelled to the post-boy and they came to a shuddering halt.

'I believe this is the spot for a picnic,' he said, climbing down. The post-boy climbed down too, pathetically anxious, and asked if the gentleman knew that the Heath was infested with highwaymen, that every day, yes, in broad daylight, poor weary travellers were mugged and stripped. He was not at all surprised to hear it, replied JG without the least sign of terror, for it was a desolate, lonely place. Pray be so good, he said genially, to fetch the little basket out of the boot.

They sat out in the vivacious wind to eat, Lally with her skirts in an arc about her and dropping crumbs down her tight blue bodice, her ringlets blown into a haystack. Phee, huddled

34

in the carriage more sick than ever at the though of food – she had only just survived the ordeal of the inn's greasy kitchen – heard her mistress's fine strong voice, Mr Lovatt's low, amused murmuring. It was a remarkable picnic. The two principals talked birds for the most part – there were plenty in view though all of them distressingly ordinary, said JC – and ships – he knew a great deal about ships, it was somehow unexpected. Lally, glancing up from a chicken wing, thought she saw deep laughter only half hidden by the spectacles. What was he then? Naturalist or mariner or both?

There was a very old rusted military pistol in the basket under the pickles and the pasties. 'To frighten the highwaymen, my dear,' explained JG, seeing her wondering eye on it.

'It would certainly frighten me. When was it last fired?'

'At Fontenoy perhaps. I do believe it is a relic of that battlefield.'

'Another spoil of victory, like your watch. Do I take it all your family were soldiers?'

'Alas, I believe it was a glorious defeat. But yes, I spring from a line of military heroes. I am the changeling.'

She was not insensitive to a dozen hidden meanings, a deal left unsaid. But his look was vacuous and charming. He smiled and chewed and shifted closer under the shelter of a gorse bush, braying imprecations at the wild wind.

The wind was nothing to Lally. She had waited ten years to feel it on her cheek again. How could he eat so much, she demanded, after his two liberal helpings of that rank mutton? She stood up, brushed off her skirts, and was away across the tough grass like a doe – or not like a doe, for Lally Fletcher resembled more nearly a leggy and graceless horse, uncollected, possibly uncollectable. In two minutes she had unpinned her hat and lodged it precariously, not to say humorously, on a spoke of gorse. The sun did nothing for her leaf-brown hair except show up its deficiencies. She practically cantered out of sight and JG, abandoning his hamper, set off in pursuit with a wild shout.

He pounded between the gorse bushes taking great breaths of the streaming air. As he breasted a rise a sudden gust made tears come to his eyes but he could still make out Lally Fletcher a little way off by a stunted thorn, her hair a mess, her hem muddy, her hands clasped together. In front, deeply deeply blue and flecked with foam, was the chilly expanse of the German Ocean.

'Lord,' said JG, putting a hand to the stitch in his side and heaving air into his lungs with a pained expression, 'I somehow never thought to look on that particular stretch of sea again.'

Lally did not take her eyes from it. 'Nor did I,' she said.

CHAPTER 4

Lally had been sent to Lingborough Hall at the age of five. Her parents and two small brothers recently dead, she was pitched willy-nilly into the growing crowd of her cousins on the remote Norfolk coast, for only her mother's youngest sister Fanny had the room and inclination to take her in. And if she had not grown into the kind of child or young woman they had expected and hoped for, none the less they had been generous, mildly affectionate, remarkably forbearing. Until that day they had arranged for her to go to India there had never been any suggestion she could not stay at Lingborough for the rest of her life.

She had been no kind of threat to her five pretty cousins for they had portions to augment their looks; her own reputation was as a harum-scarum who rode a horse like a man and could fall off in a ditch and come up smiling. The expected accomplishments were beyond her: she played badly, hardly sang, and dancing was a mystery. It was not that she did not try, she was dutiful and diligent; in her aunt's forlorn attempt to turn her out a lady she was all co-operation. But it would not do. She was made for action and the outdoors. Her uncle found her an oddity, but a pleasing oddity: she was not interested in fashion, domestic economy or handsome young men, in strawberry jam, hoops, or washing her face in the May morning dew. She gave him her full attention, understood him when he talked fishing or horses, and did not mind the weather. It had struck him once or twice she would be the ideal comfort of his old age and was quite sanguine about the likelihood of her remaining a spinster. He also disagreed with his wife that she had a bad influence on Charlie, if anything it was the other way about, and as to the boy falling in love with her . . . No sane young man of his

37

acquaintance had ever fallen in love with his sister, which was what Lally always had been and always would be to disorderly young Charles.

Uncle Windham's sudden death in 1770 began a year of disaster. Aunt Fanny was ill after a complicated childbirth, an unlooked-for late addition to her growing family, the poor little child soon dead too. Julia, the eldest daughter, chose this moment to elope with a cavalry captain – a rank all at Lingborough Hall might have expected to show more sense of responsibility. Two weeks later Pippa, all set to make a brilliant marriage with one of the county nobility, threw over everything for the son of a neighbouring farmer. And then Charlie had been involved in a farcical escapade with cousin Philadelphia that had ended in bloody catastrophe, disgrace, and the rousing out of the local constables. In this case, seeing something positive could be attempted, retribution was swift: Charlie to the army, Lally to India.

It had been a crazy plan. Even at the time Lally had had misgivings. They were to hold up the Lingborough Hall coach – in which Edward, the elder brother, would be setting out to Norwich – and, masked, cloaked, and armed, give him the fright of his life. It had all gone according to the plan too except that by mistake they had pointed their unloaded pistols at Sir George Stapleford's coach, returning home to Luffwell Hall from Lingborough, and in the dark and confusion finding that mistakes are not always easily righted. Thus Lally had careered into the stableyard at Cookhams in the early hours, in breeches and bloodstained shirt, dizzy from the wound in her arm, while Charlie galloped home without her, abandoning her to fate. It had seemed a shabby, shameful episode afterwards, though perhaps the acute sense of Charlie's betrayal made it seem more so. But had it been bad enough to warrant transportation? Or had the adults concluded Lally's relationship with her cousin was no longer innocent, that he and she . . . No, no, surely not. She had rebelled against the thought then, had done so ever since. There had been nothing between her and Charlie. They had been close, always close, planning, contriving, adventuring – Edward had always thought her unspeakable, forward, ungovernable – but it had been the closeness of brother and sister, nothing more. The debacle on the Heath was to change all that, was indeed their last innocent meeting, for the adult suspicions, only half understood at first, made Charlie look at Lally with new, critical eyes and made Lally shy of him to the point of being tongue-tied.

So to India, to Calcutta and the marriage market, then to Madras and the great pale splendid house. The only letter she had ever received – apart from Caroline's – after leaving England was from Charlie himself to tell her, with his usual ill-spelt dash and trace of humorous self-pity, that he could not abide life in the army, he missed Lingborough, dammit he missed her. Was she happy? Was she truly happy?

She was in despair, expecting Susan by then, miserable and ill, but the old bravado took hold of her: she could not bear to tell him. And something else too, the little bitter memory of how he had left her to bleed to death on the Heath. Of course he had not known she was badly wounded, had galloped away regardless thinking she would follow … Of course he had not known. But a dull small pain remained. She wrote back that she was happy, was with child, that in Madras she was a great lady, so grand he would not recognise her – which was probably true, for he had never seen her painted and powdered and in such remarkable décolleté, and never would. A year or two later word came, as word comes eventually even to far-flung trading colonies, to say that Charles Windham had died wretchedly of a festered wound received in an ignominious duel with a fellow officer.

Lally sat down and wrote a brief, reserved letter of condolence to Aunt Fanny. Words could not convey how she felt so the words were respectful, polite, and meaningless; in any case she had learnt by now not to show what she felt. Apart from her shadowed eyes, a momentary inattention, no one could guess how deeply she might mourn.

The letter may or may not have reached Lingborough. She

did not expect a reply, nor did she receive one.

'Are we there?' asked JG as the chaise turned between high gates.

'I suppose we are' – Lally gave a forlorn look through the window – 'Anne's husband must have a great deal more money than I supposed. There used to be a lovely old house here, brick and flint, covered in creeper. The parson was a dear old man with a squint.'

The house had been rebuilt in a rather ponderous classical style and was still, even after seven years, baldly new; JG pranced up the steps crying, 'Such changes! My dear, such changes!' and whipped out his spy-glass to take a closer look at something on the roof. And Anne Glover's parson turned out to be neither dear nor liable to squint but he was much older than his wife and wore his own silver hair loose about his melancholy face. Lally hid her surprise creditably, he could not manage to suppress his own. Introductions were awkward. JG was passed off as an old friend of the Pascoes who, most fortuitously discovering Lally in Colchester, had offered her a seat in his chaise. The explanation seemed plausible, certainly to everyone but Lally and JG, who did not look at each other. Anne, swallowing forebodings, asked him to stay the night, was he really pressed to go? She was most kind, he said with a charming bow, but yes, he was pressed to go indeed, was expected elsewhere; his servant would be waiting, there were books and specimens to unpack.

In the parlour lengthy silences and more awkwardness: Anne ordered tea with the voice of the dying calling for water. Was this gawky woman in atrocious clothes – a decade out of date and shabby, quite sea-stained – really Cousin Lally? And this Mr Lovatt, what was he? A gaunt wiry man in a black coat, an emerald waistcoat, a red bandanna. A red bandanna! He was stooped and ill-looking, sniffed a great deal, and carried his wig – a large verminous wig – tucked under his arm. He was wearing a sort of nightcap on his head, greasy black hair falling on his collar. When he spoke it was only to remark

40

on the great numbers of swallows' nests under her eaves and to add something unintelligible about his journey, the dangerous Heath, and *Caprimulgus*.

'Who is he?' the parson demanded of his wife before dinner. 'He speaks like a gentleman though I cannot understand two words in ten, but he dresses like a vulgar clown. And why does he not wear a decent cravat and put his wig on his head?'

'He has been in America some years, I believe.'

'That may account for some oddities to be sure. I cannot imagine what these Pascoes might be, tolerating such a fellow.'

'Perhaps you might put his eccentricities down to genius. Remember Dr Johnson,' said Anne. 'You did not think much of his appearance either.'

'And I find your cousin less than agreeable,' he was continuing without paying her the least attention, 'an extraordinary woman.'

Anne smoothed her cream silk bodice. 'Oh, I think Lally was always extraordinary, now she is ... more so.'

So much 'more so' that poor Anne could not make her out. She had a memory – an imperfect memory she thought now – of a vital, laughing girl with wind-blown hair, a springy walk, bold, merry eyes; the devil to go and live now, pay later, Charlie had once said of her in admiration.

The Lally who sat at her dinner table, however, was a stranger. Anne tried not to stare at her. Lally, sensing a covert scrutiny, put up her chin at it and succeeded in looking coolly at ease. Inside she felt ... She felt lost, defeated. In India she had been sure she belonged to England, now in England she felt an outcast. Perhaps she had always been an outcast, never fitting the space allotted. Looking across an acre of polished wood and the winking silver and bushel baskets of flowers she met Anne's wondering dark eyes. How changed you are, they said, how very, very different: how yellow, how strained, how grown old. Conversation was painful, like extracting teeth. Only JG tried to charm and that in his own, his very own way which stunned rather than enraptured his audience. Any minute now, Lally thought, he would lean back, light a cheroot, launch into an absorbing description of *jinx torquilla*, and then end up with a sailor's lament for the ladies of Portobello.

But at last the meal was over and JG was bowing his goodnights. She must visit him, he said, he was only two miles away, two miles were nothing to a tigress. He did not bow or take her hand but, in the manner of old friends, kissed her cold cheeks. He said something else at the door, something like 'Lally, dear Lally, take care' but she did not hear it, she was distracted by Anne's questions about India, and in a moment he had gone.

Stapleford had peacocks, the parson was saying, they made a dismal howling noise. Had Lally ever been to Luffwell Hall?

Lally and Anne looked at each other, and away. Stapleford was a mild, pleasant man, continued the parson, unaware he trod the verges of quicksand, very honest and considerate. Anne's pretty mouth gave an involuntary little smile. Her eyes met Lally's again. Under Lally's tight silk sleeve was the puckered scar of her last encounter with Sir George Stapleford.

'I would rather know about the family,' she said, in that calm, imperious manner that had so enraged the captain of the Indiaman. 'Are all my cousins married?'

They were, and Julia had always been perfectly happy with her captain who had bought himself out of the army and into Parliament, and Pippa had never regretted throwing up that spindly viscount for Hugh Uffington, and … and …

The bed was noble, the linen fragrant. Lally's head ached with the histories of her six cousins and their numerous children. She slept badly and cried a little, quietly and to no purpose. She could not remember when she had last wept passionately, perhaps not since Susan died. Dawn came, beautiful and cool. Lally took pains with her face and hair but they seemed past saving, the one stamped by brutal experience, the other blasted by every contrary wind. She crept downstairs, anxious not to meet anyone, anxious to escape. On the back doorstep – the only door that yielded to her silent, frantic efforts – sat a small cat waiting to be let in. She picked it up, buried her face in its yellow fur. A memory rose in an instant, a memory of the young, young Lally and the tabby cat at Lingborough Hall, a neglected but contented Lally and a morning that smelled of sun and clean linen and lavender. And: 'You are going to India,' they had told her at breakfast.

She put down the parsonage tom and he fled inside. She closed the door. There was a pearly greyness, a smell of rain, but the eastern sky was already brightening with the rising sun; there would be an hour or two of fine weather at least. She began to walk towards a little shrubbery. And then footsteps, the ominous scrunch of gravel. It was far too early for callers. A servant then. She swung about, shading her eyes against the first shaft of sun, and there was a tall fair man coming briskly round the corner of the house, head up and hands in pockets.

'Good God!' and more cheerfully, coming closer, 'I beg your pardon. I am not used to finding anyone up at this hour.'

He was a lean man, big-boned, dressed in breeches and a country coat. There were two pointers at his heels, equally lean and big-boned, and with the same pleasant, amiable expression.

'Have you come with Mrs Fletcher from Madras?' was his apparently innocent enquiry, as he stooped to command the dogs to leave pushing at her skirts. 'I know she has been expected this last week and more.'

He had taken her for a servant, she thought, quite unoffended. Who would expect the rich Mrs Fletcher to be walking about the gardens in a tired old dress and no shoes so early in the morning?

'I *am* Mrs Fletcher from Madras,' she said.

He looked suitably contrite but only for a moment. 'How unpardonably rude you must think me then.'

The dogs pushed at her hands, their dark eyes glowing,

their thin tails beating the grass. Lally looked down.

'You have me at a disadvantage, Sir. I am not dressed to receive callers. And I do not know your name.'

'Sam Uffington. I farm at Rooks Hill. I do believe we must have met years ago, at least Anne assures me of the certainty; I confess I don't remember it. I do recall hearing you had been sent to India.' To avoid a scandal, said his brown eyes. They were very fine eyes and very dark, unexpectedly so for his hair was a dull pale gold.

'Would you care to see the gardens?' he asked suddenly, offering his arm.

'Do you always call so inconveniently early?' as she took it, 'and always round the back?'

'I came to see if Edward could go fishing.'

Edward was the eldest child, an engaging though over-serious six-year-old with his father's long bony face.

By now they were striding down a gravel walk beneath high walls clothed in peach trees, plums, strange vines. Every here and there was an elegant little niche with a statue and round a corner through an arch was a pool, a very little pool by aristocratic standards but thick with waterlilies and inhabited by gross, lurking carp. A few yards further and there was a formal herb garden, intricate little hedges, a sundial. Sam veered away, still with Lally on his arm, and plunged down a yew avenue, damp and earthy. Her skirts blew out, a wide flow of sapphire blue. It was an old, old dress but it suited her, delicate lace at the elbows, tight and low across her nice freckled breasts.

'I suppose I should ask you whether you had a good journey and whether you are staying long at Lingborough,' said Sam.

'I suppose you should. The answers I think are no, and no.'

'Polite conversation is not my strong point,' and he turned left under a wrought-iron arch and hurried down another wet walk. 'Are your feet not cold? Why have you no shoes?'

'I have no shoes because I wished to creep out unobserved.'

'And did you?'

'I trust I did. If not, what will they make of my vanishing

into the thickets with a gentleman before even the sun is up?'

Sam laughed, and bore on without hesitation.

'My brother Hugh married your cousin Pippa. She sank a viscount on his behalf and he has never been allowed to forget it. They moved to Bath, for she is quite absurdly delicate and your Aunt Fanny held out for it so long that poor Hugh was brought to agree to it for the sake of peace and quiet. I have been allowed to assume the role of uncle to Edward, a devilish difficult undertaking since his father insists he stick at his books, poor shrimp, and his mother believes too much fresh air will kill him. No wonder the child's pale and fractious. I do what I can. The nurse is on my side. Sometimes I whistle under the window and if he's awake she sends him down and we go fishing.'

He had slowed the pace a little in deference to her bare feet, for they had reached more gravel paths, but she seemed unconcerned so he pressed on. She said nothing but looked about as if trying to get her bearings.

'I understood,' he said at last, 'your aunt sent you to India to stop Charles...'

'Marrying me? He had no such intention.'

'Well, that might account for a great deal. Dishonourable intentions would have been the more frightful. He was a wild boy, Charlie. If I recall correctly he only ever took notice of his father and then only if he was beaten into a receptive mood. But it was cruel to send you to India with the express intention of ... To a sort of foreign marriage market.'

'It was a little like a horse fair,' Lally agreed without expression, 'except we were not asked to show our teeth.' It was about all, she might have said, not positively displayed. The humiliation still haunted her. She tried not to remember it, and failed.

'Had you no choice?'

'None. It was expected to be settled before we left the ship. It was not done to refuse the man who offered first. His would be the only offer – do you understand? There are polite ways of going on even in hell, it seems.'

He hardly had time to take in this bitter comment before a last frond of dripping beech was elbowed aside to reveal the lake. It gleamed pinkly in the strengthening sun, ornamented with a great many ducks and gulls far out on the choppy water, noisy and convivial.

'It seems excessive for a parsonage,' began Lally, gazing about her at the disfigured landscape. On the hill opposite were the scars of felled trees and the bricks of a long-demolished building. 'But that is the Hall!' she cried. 'Of course, this is our lake from the other side. But what has he done? The park is ruined and the bridge gone too.'

'Oh, Parson Glover has a considerable fortune, and an interest in architecture and gardening. I dare say he knows a thing or two about the theory, noble prospects and the like, the latest thing in fountains and statues. Your aunt sold him the Hall when she went to Bath and he had grand designs, refused to let it, pulled it down. I am not sure Anne has ever forgiven him but she don't speak of it now, never walks this way. In twenty years Nature will have mended what she can, Mrs Fletcher. Of course, I have no taste in these things, and sometimes it seems to me a parson with three livings to attend to ought not to have the time for it.'

For the first time his cheerfulness faltered, his voice altered, took on a forbidding tone. He was not unfailingly genial then, she thought, but she said nothing, only looking sadly out over the newly-dredged lake to the ruins of her old home.

'Were you happy here?' asked Sam.

'Yes. Up on the Heath on a pony, yes.'

'The Heath? A nest of highwaymen and smugglers.'

Yes, the lake would mend, she was thinking, and the trees would grow. 'As for smugglers, Lingborough is full of them. I once saw every able-bodied man in the village mustered on the beach to bring in a large cargo.'

'I trust Aunt Fanny, bless her, did not know you were abroad?'

'I trust my aunt was unaware of all my nocturnal adventures, except the very last.'

46

'You were shot, were you not? It was all over the district. But you must have been a fool to expect anything less, making a sorry mistake of that kind; Stapleford always travels well-prepared. I'm only surprised he did not kill you.'

Lally had scooped up her skirts to cross a boggy place and he caught sight of her long and shapely legs dirtied to the knee.

'So he might have done, had I not reached Cookhams before I bled dry.'

'And where was the infamous Charles all this time?'

Her look was inscrutable. She appeared to be studying the gulls bobbing from shadow to sunshine out on the dimpled water. There was the splash of a bird landing and all the sucking, trickling noises of the lake edge. A baleful-looking moorhen ran between the sparse reeds. After a significant pause Lally remarked: 'Rooks Hill is in the valley not far from Ledworth mill, is it not? A big old house.'

'Big, old, and dashed inconvenient. I love it dearly.'

Her smile, the first she had given him, was fleeting and restrained. He returned a grin and offered his arm again; it was time to be walking back. The servants would be up. But Lally halted him with a sudden tightening of her fingers on his sleeve, leaning sideways a little. There was a little brown bird on a willow twig a few yards away.

'At this distance,' she said with a lift of her pale brows, 'only JG could tell if it was a sparrow or a nightingale.'

'It's a dunnock,' said Sam after a casual glance. 'Who is JG?'

'Perhaps you will meet him. He is staying at Ledworth, at The Ship House.'

They retraced their steps. In the knot garden was a fragrance of lad's love and rosemary and box. Sam kept up a tremendous pace, as if he was afraid he might not get her back in time for breakfast, and she half ran, tall as she was, her skirts brushing the aromatic hedges in great sweeps.

At the door of the house he took his leave with punctilious formality. The dogs rolled in the gravel. A spirited little

47

breeze had sprung up and was flattening Lally's skirts about her bare ankles. Sam Uffington stared very hard at her bare ankles as he bowed low, wishing her good day.

'How absurd it seems,' she said, 'to be treated like a lady when I am quite aware my hair is on my shoulders and my lack of footwear is a disgrace.'

His ready smile shone out for her. 'I am so glad you left your shoes behind. At least without them I have an inch or two advantage. How I would tremble were you able to look me straight in the eye.'

How sorry poor little Edward would be to know he had missed his fishing, she thought, watching Sam walk away to recover his horse, the dogs trotting quietly at his heels. Heaven knows the boy must have few pleasures of that kind in this opulent but stifling house.

She went indoors, and left damp footprints on the polished tiles and a pattern of muddy smears all up the stairs.

CHAPTER 5

'Rot my soul,' exclaimed a voice, 'there's a damn peculiar-looking fellow.'

The damn peculiar-looking fellow was standing on the saddle of a browsing donkey and looking over a hedge with a spy-glass.

'It's Mr Lovatt,' said Lally, craning from the carriage window. 'But who is the gentleman on the brown horse?'

Anne sighed. 'Oh dear, Jack Brotherton, how I detest him. He is Brotherton's only son.'

'A bachelor?'

'Oh yes, though to be sure he is a father several times over. I have heard the gossip. And I believe there have been bastardy bonds too.'

'And I thought you such an innocent, shut up in your parsonage. Gossip! You should not be listening to gossip!'

'Oh, Lally. John may treat me as a child, there is no need for you to do so. Why, one of the poor girls who swore he fathered her child was one of our own maids. And I would swear Jack Brotherton did it on purpose because she was a good girl and lived with us – John is very strict with the maids – and it made me so angry . . . But of course I could not say anything, and the poor girl had her baby and it died and John would not have her back. There was a great deal of . . . trouble. So you see, I hate the sight of Jack Brotherton. It may be foolish but there it is.'

The carriage had come to a standstill, for the narrow lane was blocked by JG's amiable donkey and Jack Brotherton's unamiable horse. Suddenly that horse's face appeared at the window, a flaring nostril, a suspicious eye, and a broad white blaze flecked with foam where the poor beast had tossed it from his mouth.

'Mrs Glover, good day.' An insolent voice and a harsh, insolent face, a bad complexion, raw, red, perhaps a tendency to boils. All this Lally noticed while Anne made the reluctant introductions.

'You shall be on your way, Mrs Fletcher, the moment I have cleared this rascal from your road,' said Jack Brotherton, his foot on the carriage step.

'The rascal is a friend of mine,' said Lally in return, her eyes wide and dark. 'I would be obliged if you could lend him your assistance. He has the donkey in the ditch.'

Damn you and your airs, said Brotherton's look, but there was a reluctant admiration there too. Or perhaps, as he dragged his temperamental mount round in that hand's breadth of space, jerking cruelly at the bit, he was remembering the late Mr Fletcher's fortune. It would not do to take offence when a fortune might be in the offing.

The donkey was extricated from the ditch where it half stood and half lay chewing vegetation with infuriating unconcern. It was not an easy task. Jack Brotherton's whip accomplished it at last and his loud unpleasant voice could be heard giving pithy and gratuitous advice to the dumb naturalist, who stood with the donkey's reins looped over his arm looking suitably chastened.

'Dear ladies,' JG said when he could reach the carriage window, 'I apologise most sincerely. Ah, Mrs Fletcher. I was going to call on you this minute, this very minute.'

'Standing on the back of a donkey?'

'Oh that!' He adjusted his spectacles, returned his wig and hat to their proper place, and beamed vacuously at them. 'That was a woodlark, *alauda arborea*. Nothing out of the ordinary, I assure you, but I hoped to come at a better view of him over the hedge top. Mrs Glover, good morning. Are you returning to the parsonage?'

There was a moment's silence. Then Anne said in a small voice: 'We have been shopping in Holt. If your donkey will tie on behind, Mr Lovatt, you are welcome to a seat inside.'

The donkey would tie on but only after expressing forceful

views to the contrary.

'Such a mild creature, so good natured, and so impressively stubborn,' said JG getting into the coach. 'I am sure I could never have managed without Mr Brotherton's help.'

Mr Brotherton, who had been about to make his farewells at the far window, glared and said nothing. His eyes rested on Lally for a moment as they might have done on a horse he had not seen before, a horse of repute, one which he did not much like the look of but which he could not ignore.

'Your servant, ladies,' he said at last, 'I hope you give us the pleasure of your company at Cookhams before long.'

He had ridden out of sight before anyone in the carriage spoke again. It was as if he had cast a blight on ordinary conversation. Then JG fished in his pocket and brought out a snuff box, some string, a tattered book, four half cheroots, some small change, a few feathers, and what looked like the bones of a mouse. Anne shrank back. He gave a squawk of satisfaction and opened the book.

'I have made a note' – a bland look through his glasses here – 'Do you think your husband would allow me in his belfry, dear lady? There are owls, a family of owls, in the tower. I have observed them going in and out.'

Of course he could see the owls, Anne said, but of course. Her husband could not take him up himself but Mr Hayes the curate ran up and down the ladder quite like a boy for all his grey hairs and she did recall, though vaguely, that Mr Hayes had some passing interest in owls himself. Or was it bats? She gave a helpless look but his smile of gratitude was swift and disarming. Anne blushed. She found him a most difficult man, erudite, alarming, an uneasy combination of the scholar and the highwayman; with a minor alteration in appearance he could have passed for either. Still, she could forgive him almost anything for that wide ingenuous smile, the particular attention of those fine eyes.

The fine eyes were lingering surreptitiously now on the face of the other woman in the carriage. How reserved she was, he thought, far more so than on the journey, and how subdued;

51

how dark was that insufferable stare of hers, her eyes a stormy grey.

'How are you enjoying the parsonage?' he asked as he handed her out at the steps. Anne was lingering to give copious instructions to the driver and the timid girl who had come out for the baskets from the boot.

'I have only been here three days.'

'For my part three hours would be enough. What brought such a pretty girl to marry a man like that? Incomprehensible woman, how strange thou art!'

'No doubt it is true,' was the dry answer, 'that some of us can be faulted in our choice.'

'Why, what choice had you? A child of seventeen thrown among wolves.'

'Do you know the circumstances then?'

'I imagine you were put on public display much like a pig in a crate, that like the same poor animal your opinions were not consulted, and that at the end of an hour you were labelled Fletcher and sent up to his house. Am I right?'

'For the most part. I believe I should object, though, to being compared to a pig.'

'I meant no offence. Oh, I have seen women bought and sold by sober and respectable men in much the same way and for much the same reason as it is done in Calcutta.'

They had mounted the steps, were inside. JG hurried Lally to an open door. He peered inside, said yes, it would do, quiet, private, not too chill.

'Are they kind?' he demanded, shutting the door behind Lally and gazing about at the books with a knowing eye.

'Very kind. But I believe this room is the parson's sanctuary. We will shortly be ejected like common burglars. Yes, Anne is kindness itself, and I have spent happy hours with the children.'

'Ah, children. You had a child once, did you not?'

'How did you know?' A quiet, quiet voice. Her eyes looked more tired suddenly, smudged and lined with fatigue. He had touched some deep, abiding grief.

52

'Your cousin mentioned it at dinner the evening we arrived. She spoke as if I knew. A girl, was it not?'

'She was three when she died.'

He let the subject drop and his voice changed, his eyes indistinct again behind the glasses. 'I do not mean to pry, my dear. I have called on you simply to keep up the pretence of being your Mrs Pascoe's friend; to live two miles away and ignore you would surely be thought suspicious. In any case, I covet the owls, my love, I do indeed. Though the parson be thoroughly disagreeable I must gain access to the owls.'

'I am sure they must be perfectly ordinary barn owls.'

'But everything repays study, repays a little attention. And who yet is truly familiar with the domestic arrangements of the barn owl? We are so very ignorant, Lally Fletcher, so disgracefully ignorant about all manner of things.'

The door opened. A distracted Anne put in her head. 'There you are! But why are you in here? Why are you not in the parlour?'

JG smothered Lally's reply with a shout of surprise, a great whoop of delight, and he sprang to throw up the elegant sash and lean out, his glass to his eye. 'Do you see? Do you see it? On that branch over there. *Loxia curvirostra*. It must have been blown here by the hand of Fortune. I have not seen one so close for many years. Quick! There it goes!' He swung the glass about, trying for a last glimpse of the elusive prodigy.

'Oh,' said Lally, trying to look intelligent, 'I did notice something. A reddish sort of bird. I had no idea it was so famous. I took it for a chaffinch.'

The parsonage was a well-regulated house; the parson liked his life orderly. His wife was allowed to dispense comfort and charity to his parishioners at a distance, so to speak, and she had never crossed the threshold of one cottage in ten. Her life was divided into time with the children and time without, the time without occupied in morning visits, occasional shopping, and needlework. The parson did not encourage her to read and did not listen to her opinion. It was no wonder she had

53

hoped Lally might provide her with some diversion, and she still clung to this hope, for all Lally was not at all what she had expected.

'I find her so changed,' she confided to Sam Uffington when he called not two hours after JG, replenished with an excellent cold dinner, had been persuaded to leave. 'She was such a naughty little girl, always in scrapes – Papa whipped her twice, imagine it! She took one of his hunters because Charlie dared her and rode it quite ten miles, across the Heath and nearly to Holt. The fuss! And she was quite unrepentant. What could he do but whip her? She and Charlie used to steal the garden pony, pretend to be smugglers, savages, bareback riders, and failing the garden pony there were always the donkeys. But now . . .' – a blank, bewildered look – 'I do not recognise her. She is a stranger. She is . . . so stern.'

All this time Sam had been gazing down a broad stretch of emerald grass where the children were shrieking and scrambling about some stumps with no less than three cricket bats and obviously more than one ball. In the middle of the melee the crane-like figure of Lally Fletcher leaped and twirled, her skirts apparently looped up with string so that an indecent, charming length of white stocking was on show. Wild shouts of encouragement and congratulation wafted to the watchers at the window. It crossed Sam's mind that the old Lally would have relished such a battle, that the old Lally had probably hit every ball as far as the village if not into the sea beyond; that the old Lally was not entirely extinguished.

He looked at Anne. She was very fetching in a dress of flowered cotton, and the plain pink underskirt matched her flushed cheeks. Wisps of soft dark hair blew against her cheek as she moved to look out.

'I am afraid Lally and John do not see eye to eye,' she announced sadly. There was the tiniest frown between her brows.

'It would not surprise me.' Why was she always worried these days, Sam was thinking, always a little nervous? She made him uneasy. He was deeply conscious of the fact she was

54

unhappy, not simply under-occupied and bored but unhappy, and it made him exasperated and guilty.

'And then there is Mr Lovatt,' she was saying tremulously, assailed by the terrible memory of Mr Lovatt only attached to the church tower by the crook of one knee, dangling in space to come at a better view of the owls' domestic arrangements. 'John says he has a fine mind, is evidently a learned man, but . . .' The but said it all.

'I must meet this Mr Lovatt.'

'Do you really wish to?' She raised an eager face in which, he thought, the blush deepened. 'Well, you might escort us to The Ship House, he has bombarded us with invitations. Lally is keen to go' – indeed, Lally would be keen to go anywhere so long as it was away from the parsonage – 'and I am afraid that if I don't go with her she will go alone, she will steal the pony.'

Anne had vivid memories of past devilment on horseback, of Lally returning stuck all over with briars and generally flayed and muddied and looking like a gipsy. Although the Lally who paced up and down her fine summer drawing room like a restless beast and who strode furiously round the whole gardens twice a day was not the Lally she remembered so distinctly from her childhood, she was still afraid of the hideous consequences of letting her loose near a horse.

'Would John not take you?' Sam asked.

'He and Mr Lovatt would fall out at once. But he would not forbid *you* to take us. I think,' said Anne with desperate candour, 'I think he is afraid of you.'

'You are mistaken. But I hope he respects my opinion.'

Sam was not a good liar, he was not that way inclined and besides, he had so little practice. He did not look at Anne as he spoke. He would have found it painful to think she knew in what ineffable contempt he held her husband, the man she had chosen, after all, in place of himself. She kindled a strange desire in him to protect her. She was not unintelligent, was perhaps not even unworldly in her own way, but she was sweet and shy; he would help preserve some few of her illusions if he could for the sake of that sweet, shy girl. He had once been in love with her, long ago.

Lally came flying through the french windows, face flushed and dirt on the bridge of her nose. She halted abruptly at the sight of Sam but he held out a hand immediately, took her own cool strong one, and smiled his pleasant smile. What a contrast she made with Anne, he thought.

'You are very brave to risk your life with that parcel of rogues, Mrs Fletcher.'

'Ah, but I have the advantage. I am so much taller than they are.'

Was it a reminder of his remark in the garden? If he had not always found her extraordinarily grave he might have suspected she was making fun of him.

'Sam is to take us to The Ship House,' said Anne.

'He is? How noble! Have you warned him how insufferable Mr Lovatt can be, how deplorably messy, impolite and uncouth?'

'Oh, Lally, John meant nothing by it. He is so correct himself and he thinks others should be the same. You must not mind it.'

'Were those his exact words?' demanded Sam in an undertone as he stood side by side with Lally in the window.

'Exact.'

'What a ponderous, dull, puritan fellow he is,' and he stared out at the cricket match, adding aloud: 'For your sake, Mrs Fletcher, I will hazard my life in that brawl and hit a few balls before I leave.'

They left Anne to organise nursery tea and strolled down the lawn, Sam taking off his coat and waistcoat and rolling up his shirt sleeves.

'I'm sure I would hate to think you were risking your life for my sake,' said Lally.

'Let's say for the children then.' Good God, that clear, fine, emotionless voice of hers. 'I feel so deuced sorry for them, cooped up here, never allowed to run about and get dirty or climb trees or fall off a pony. To be sure it's no business of mine but I hate to see it. I try to come over when I can to give

56

them some fun. But I need not worry any more, it seems. They have Cousin Lally to take care of them.'

She put her head on one side and looked at him through a muddle of curls and lace; her cap as askew, dipping over her forehead. 'You should have married her yourself, Mr Uffington.'

He was crimson, his eyes fell. She had hit the mark at the first attempt. He looked remarkably stubborn and disgruntled and then, his blush receding, mildly furious.

'I am not hankering after an old love, if that is what you mean.'

'I mean . . . No, I mean nothing. I am only glad she has you for her friend. You see, she reminds me of the little gold and brown birds I used to watch years ago on the Heath, flitting in and out of the gorse, so pretty and restless. Does that sound insane? They were so sweet, but they never stayed still a moment, never seemed to know where they wanted to be.'

'You feel sorry for her.'

'And so do you.'

Sam acknowledged the excited shrieks of the cricketers with a wave of his brown arms. 'Are those really Anne's children? Why, they are never allowed outside, have to sit starched and solemn indoors all in a row.' He gave a shout of laughter, catching Edward's bony shoulders as he ran at him, yelling a greeting. 'By God, you have reduced them to a horde of savages. You have my undying respect, Ma'am, my hearty congratulations.'

It was after they had exhausted themselves searching for the balls he had knocked with quite prodigious strength into the shrubbery that he said, coming to stand beside a panting Lally: 'To return to Anne, the birds on the Heath – your Mr Lovatt should be interested, for is he not some kind of naturalist?'

Lally was busy capturing wisps of hair and securing them under her cap. The wind snatched at her skirts and revealed yards of draggled petticoat.

'You are not very good at being unpleasant, Mr Uffington.

And it would be ridiculous to be jealous, would it not?' And then, plunging to catch a ball before it should knock the smallest member of the party on the head: 'I believe you and he could become good friends.'

The purpose of the trip to Holt had been to buy material for Lally, to make her at least two new dresses. Anne, who had never known privations of any kind, except the emotional, had been astounded at the contents of Lally's two bags.

'But everything is so old,' she cried before she could help herself and found Phee's rebuking gaze on her at once. 'Lally, there is nothing new at all.'

'I suppose not.'

'But is there . . . Was there . . . Oh, Lally, have you no money at all?'

Lally hung up her only ball gown, brocade and parchment silk, expensive lace. It was still a beautiful dress. It brought back memories, yes. Even the faint perfume that clung to it brought back the memories. But it was a lovely dress and it lent her a sort of splendour, a dignity unsurpassed.

'No, I have no money. I will have to owe you for the flowered damask.'

Anne sank on to the bed, bit one of her nails. 'But your husband was rich, the house in Madras . . .'

'The house in Madras was a palace' – and here Lally gave her a straight, hard, challenging look – 'I have never lied to you.'

Anne drew up her knees, leaned her elbows on them, cupped her chin in her hands. Her smile was very sweet and kind.

'No, you never have.' And then, more softly: 'How very cruel they were to banish you to India.'

CHAPTER 6

The mill at Ledworth spanned the river, though it was no kind of feat for it was a very little river. The Ship House, though attached to it, was planted solidly on the bank, half obscured behind a thicket of birch and hazel and young oaks that had grown up where the road turned to plunge down the last few yards to the ford. Sam, tying his horse, rapped on the front door.

A small boy with bare feet answered it. The gentleman was in the garden, he declared, he had brought the eels, that was all. And he dived under a sway of oak leaves and was gone. Sam turned to Lally, descending from the pony trap.

'D'you think we're expected?'

The house was low-ceilinged and dark. The gentle creak of the trees beside the door sounded indeed like the noise of a ship at sea, though maybe a more seaworthy craft than the one Lally had suffered from Calcutta. The one main room opened off a wide hall with a tiled floor and newly whitened walls. An ancient oak side table displayed the large rusty pistol last seen in the picnic basket, a vase of pinks, overpoweringly fragrant, and the eels, charmingly entwined.

It was very quiet. In front of them was another door, a latched country door even lower than its counterpart, set wide to the blowy day. A shaft of sunlight struck in to light up the gloom. From beyond came the sound of a low voice, coaxing, charming.

'It is Mr Lovatt,' said Anne.

They stepped out. A triangular lawn, edged by weedy borders full of peonies, the heady pinks, poppies and tall daisies, ran down to the river. There was some kind of landing stage, a jetty of rustic poles. On this JG was standing, and sometimes peering, hanging out over the brown, swift-running water.

'There he goes,' he cried, the flimsy poles giving with his weight. 'There, there. See him?'

Sam stared dutifully and saw nothing but by careful manoeuvring Lally glimpsed a ripple of silver low down between the weed.

'My pike,' explained JG. 'I feed him every day and he waits here like a dog.'

'What if you catch him one day by mistake?' asked Anne.

'Impossible. But I should put him back at once. Why, we are almost friends.' The pike was exceptionally good company he explained sweetly, was silent, uncritical and unfailingly punctual.

Sam was introduced. Lally saw his eyebrows jerk and a smile lift one corner of his mouth when JG's coat opened to reveal, inevitably, another waistcoat fit for a fairy prince. But almost at once they had fallen to talking fish – where the dace spawned, how greedy the herons were – and there was murmured agreement, and laughter, and some gesticulating up river.

'The sun is hot,' said Anne, joining Lally by the water's edge. A trembling paling separated the lawn from the swirling mill pond. If they leaned over just a little they could see the dark water vanishing under the brick arches of the mill. There was a dank, green, decaying smell. A gust of wind took Lally's hat and blew it back, the new straw hat Anne had persuaded her to buy in Holt – and had leant her the money for, raspberry with embarrassment. It was tied with a large blue silk bow under her chin and the sudden pull nearly strangled her. She plucked it undone and took it off.

The sun was indeed hot, but the wind was frolicsome. Lally stood in a cloud of rebellious skirts and frizzy ringlets. Anne exclaimed, laughed, and put up anxious hands to her own head.

'How do you like my retreat, Mrs Glover?' JG was coming across the grass at a lope. 'Lally, my dear, the habit is charming, you would pass for Diana. But the hat ... The hat is too roguish for a nabob's widow.'

'You mean it is undignified?' She turned on him calm but sparkling eyes.

'Mr Lovatt . . . Mr Lovatt, there are cows in the mill pond,' cried Anne, jumping up and down to see. 'There are. Look.'

'No. They have come down to drink, poor loves.'

They walked even closer to the bank. JG looked ruefully at the mill. 'It is gone to rack and ruin. They say it has not ground corn in twenty years. It is on Brotherton's land but he cares nothing for it.'

'The river is very tiny here. Perhaps in a dry summer there would not be enough water to turn the wheel.'

'Dear Lally, what an eminently practical way of looking at it. Far better than to suppose, as I had done, that Brotherton was an indifferent landlord.'

'I have not met him. I am invited to take tea at Cookhams tomorrow.'

'Tell me,' JG asked as they strolled back to the house, 'do you know its history? Are there any ships in the case?'

They stopped to gaze up at the little leaded panes crammed up under the eaves, at the old, old pantiles covered in moss.

'Oh yes, there was a ship,' said Anne, 'the *Belle Jeanne*. There is a local legend that says she was carrying gold.'

Where the gold went was anybody's guess but the miller at Ledworth had sent carts for the wreckage, had built himself this eccentric little house next to his mill. Even in a countryside where every farm had a barn or stable composed entirely of ships' timbers and each storm brought enough ashore to construct a village, The Ship House was unique.

Indoors the living room was wide, windows looking at the river. There were a great many books, several dark pictures of horses and dogs, a gate-legged table, two dining chairs, a hard sofa, a peculiar old loveseat, and a birdcage with no bird in it. There were boots flung carelessly in one corner and several pipes scattered over the table along with the remnants of some scores of cheroots. There was also a box of fish hooks and a handbill about smugglers.

JG neglected his guests and lodged himself in the window seat looking out at the unkempt triangle of garden. The sound of flowing water, hushing under the brick arches, came to them through the open door, and every few minutes the shout of a cuckoo, somewhere up the valley, and the low crooning of turtle doves.

'I like this place,' said JG. A little later: 'If you yell at the outer door you might get old Rush to come. He'll bring you something to eat and drink.'

Rush had his own ideas on refreshment, bringing them a plate of gooseberry tarts and a bottle of brandy on a tarnished tray. He was a small man in a loose, greasy coat and with his grey hair in a pigtail. JG seemed to find nothing unusual in the offering and wandered out, tart in hand, to deal with the eels.

'What an extraordinary man,' said Sam.

'JG?'

'JG. That wig must have seen service in Charles II's day. And that waistcoat! But he is unquestionably knowledgeable about fish, and birds, and a great many other things. And he is interested in ships. We have planned an expedition to Yarmouth.'

'You are to be congratulated on your courage,' said Lally. 'He is a terrible traveller and usually keeps his pistol – that very large rusty pistol – in a picnic basket.'

At this point they were interrupted by a loud voice from the back regions protesting it was more than human flesh could bear and another, spiked with cold command, that replied: 'God damn your eyes, you do it or I string you up.' Neither voice was instantly recognisable, though the first might have been Rush.

Anne's look of blank consternation was followed by another of shy anxiety. 'Do you think we ought to leave?'

'Leave? Dear lady, why must you leave?' and JG burst in, his cravat all anyhow. A more than usually dank draught of air came in with him and Lally, who had a glimpse of the retreating Rush through the closing door, suspected he had been in the mill; there were cobwebs on his stockings. He

brought Anne a cordial, handed it to her with a seraphic smile
– false, thought Lally, watching closely. As if she had spoken
aloud and he had heard her he turned and looked at her over
his glasses, a long, cool look.

'Has Rush been with you long?' She would not be stared
down, would rally, would challenge him.

'Oh, years. You must forgive his odd manner. He was
pressed into a man-of-war at a very tender age. It marks a man
for life to be sure. Ah, Mrs Glover, you are admiring my little
owls. They are not the native species. An acquaintance in
Virginia …' and he and Anne moved apart to admire them
and scraps of conversation floated back to Sam and Lally: how
lifelike … knew nothing about stuffing birds except for the
table, of course … flamingoes? Had not heard of such things
… yes, yes, an illustration most welcome.

'What is it about him that takes her fancy so?' Sam asked
morosely, following Lally out into the garden again. 'Do all
women find him attractive? He has a damned piratical face,
he is not young, and the wig and the spectacles ruin all.'

Lally stood on the landing stage and poked a long thin stick
into the weed. Sam was like a larger sort of kind-hearted dog,
she thought, unfailingly friendly when approached without ill
intention, always tolerant until kicked. Now he was behaving
as if someone had trodden heavily on his tail. He smarted but
was too well bred to show it; he growled softly but did not bare
his teeth.

'I am sure Mr Lovatt is simply a novelty,' she said carefully.
'Anne leads such a dull life. You cannot blame her for finding
a passing interest in flamingoes.'

'You are laughing at me.'

'Not at all. But I think you are wrong if you suspect JG of
misconduct, of flirting.'

They stood side by side. Lally's stick disturbed nothing
more than a very small frog who plopped into deeper water.
She felt that Sam knew very well JG was not flirting, that he
was simply being his usual self: irritating, intelligent,
distracted. It was debatable whether had he been shaved,

bathed, got out from under that appalling wig and inserted in a suit of decent clothes, he would have made a greater impact; Anne had never met anyone like him and was fascinated. Wary, vaguely terrified, nevertheless she felt the attraction, much as she had felt the attraction of inviting the dread Philadelphia to the parsonage. She was bored, bored, and deeply discontent.

In a little while Sam went in and Lally stayed on the river bank. The wind had dropped a little and there was a kingfisher busy further upstream, she could see the streak of colour beneath the alders. Above the sound of running water came the periodic bursts from the cuckoos and once, just once, she heard the whistle of an otter. If she closed her eyes, she thought, she could pretend she had never been away.

Sam had gone to raid the kitchen for more gooseberry tarts. He found Rush greasy, chicken bones on the table. There was a piquant fragrance of strong ale, lard, and woodsmoke – the fire was fit for devils, a great leaping conflagration – and something else, something rancid, corrupt, chemical.

'Can you snuff it, cock? His Lordship was stuffin' a stoat. Poxy old smell, aint it?'

'Stuffing a stoat?'

'Why, yes. That's it over there, poor tortured hanimal. I only hope it don't go orf like the weasel.'

'Well, I can tell it is a stoat,' said Sam kindly, not getting too close. 'I suppose it will serve. Did it have the one eye in life or is it not finished?'

'Ho, a humorous gentleman, I see. His Lordship aint partial to stoats, he was only a-practisin'. And eyes is fiddly. Did you want something, Capten?'

Sam expressed an interest in more tarts. Rush winked, drew them out from the bread cupboard. Was His Lordship still close with that Mrs Glover? Ho yes, and hadn't they both known just such a dark little woman, sweet and helpless, in San Salvador. Old John G would have to watch his step, women like that were the very devil, appealed to a man's tender feelings, and from what he'd heard the parson was the eye for an eye sort, a puritan type. Oh, go ahead, Capten, eat the whole plateful.

Sam, bemused, made himself comfortable at the table and ate steadily under the bright false eye of the experimental stoat. He had been out in the fields at dawn, had ridden over to the parsonage after a meagre breakfast – they had been sweeping the chimneys at Rooks Hill and the fire was out – and he felt now as if his strength and cheerful temper had quite wasted away.

'That Mrs Fletcher,' cried Rush, cramming his head and shoulders through a small back window, 'she'll drown. You'd best go bring her down, there'll be the devil to pay.'

Lally was visible at one of the broken windows of the mill, leaning out carelessly over the turbulent water.

Sam crashed dramatically through the low door that led from the kitchen into a musty sort of stable and then into the mill itself. No doubt she could swim, he was thinking; she was a capable woman, had probably learnt the strokes in this very mill pond. But still he called loudly and repeatedly, leaping across the rotten boards and swinging himself vigorously up the perilous ladders. On the floor where Lally had been there was nothing but spiders and vague patterns in the dust. Sam called again.

She was on the very top floor now, looking out over the valley. The wind had played havoc with her hair and she had chalk and flour and soot all over her skirts.

'You will fall,' he admonished, rather foolishly.

'How chivalrous of you to come after me.'

'No one has set foot in this place for years. If you miss your footing on those ladders you will break your neck,' and he stooped to look out at her view and found it simply green: green meadows, green trees, the green-brown water. 'The flies are after the cattle,' he remarked glumly, watching them stamp and shift.

'Are they yours?'

'No, Tom Truelove's. They are all bad doers. They belonged to one of his tenants, a poor, mad fellow they took away to Bedlam. Tom helped the wife, gave her a big dry cottage, bought the stock at a fair price. But his generosity will be the undoing of him, those beasts will never fatten.'

Lally watched him stoop again, saw his practised eye run across the cattle, saw the telltale flicker of a nerve by his mouth that showed her how he disparaged them. But he grinned, said he hoped if the day came he ever had to call any man master he would call Truelove by that name, soft-hearted fool he was.

They descended by degrees, hampered by Lally's skirts and the fact that one rung in three of the ladders was unsound. The ground floor gave the impression of cleanliness, though it was still thick with flour. Sam cast about for a minute, curious as to why he felt the place had recently been in use, and then stood at Lally's side to stare over into the wheel pit.

'A foul dank smell,' he said, wrinkling his nose. 'Take care. My chivalry may not extend to rescuing you from that slimy hole.'

'There is a little iron ladder, see.'

'For the unfortunate miller to get down among the workings of his wheel, no doubt. See how the sluices have rotted away. Come, Mrs Fletcher. Come back into the house.'

He held the door for her. She brushed past him and halted abruptly, head up.

'Oh, you smell the stoat,' Sam said. 'JG has been trying out the arts of taxidermy. Look, there he is. He has a sort of criminal leer, as if he was only fit to be hung.'

Anne's laugh drew them to the living room. She was sitting at the table poring over a book of bird drawings, primitive, artless things done, JG was assuring her, by a lowly seaman on a Boston schooner. He was bending over Anne's shoulder, his finger on the page.

'I think I shall put the pony to the chariot,' Sam said, but neither of the two heeded him, went on about swamps, herons, and lowly seamen.

'All your feelings are showing in your face,' said Lally gently, finding him hooking up the traces.

'You must think me a great fool.'

'Not in the least. I sometimes wonder if old hurts ever heal or whether we only tell ourselves they do. Were you very disappointed?'

'I suppose I was. It was not a grand passion, you understand, but she gave me every encouragement.'

'And what was the objection?'

'My income. It could not match John Glover's.'

He spoke without bitterness. For the most part his was a sanguine temperament, and although he suffered a slight no better than the next man he had been brought up on the idea that marriages should not ignore the rules of good business. He knew himself outclassed, hoped it would not matter, and found that it did; there was little he could do, for Anne was not deeply in love with him and Aunt Fanny had pushed very hard on Glover's behalf. How could he blame her? It would obviously be a comfort for her to know her daughter's welfare would not be entirely at the mercy of the weather. So Sam took it philosophically, though perhaps not as philosophically as his friends imagined he did.

Anne emerged, still laughing, on JG's arm.

'Such a pleasant visit. I do hope we may call again,' she said.

JG smiled, handed her into the carriage. 'Have you been along the beach?' he asked Lally. 'But of course you must know it well. My donkey takes exception to the waves, so loud, so furious. Is it always like this in June? Such a heaving and boiling would do credit to December. Ah, Mr Uffington, you have a noble horse. I have seen none like him hereabouts.'

'Oh, Jack Brotherton could show you half a dozen as good, but not,' he added as an afterthought, stroking the animal's nose, 'as kindly, as sweet-tempered.'

'That is because brute beasts grow like their masters.'

Sam grinned. 'Pray do not forget our trip to Yarmouth.'

'I shall not indeed.'

Lally turned to say goodbye, her foot already on the step, the reins in her hand. JG squinted amiably at her. She was

67

about to speak, the pony moved, her foot slipped, and she toppled backwards. He smells of cheroots and soap and snuff, she thought absurdly as JG righted her, and himself.

'You must be more careful,' he said, very low, 'not to fall into bad company.'

'Is that a joke?'

'If it was it does not seem to have had the required effect.'

'It was a very poor joke.'

'I acknowledge it.'

'If that is the best you can do I think you should leave making jokes to those of keener wit.'

'I believe I must agree with you. However, it is consistent with the character of Mr Lovatt that he makes poor puns and lamentable jokes occasionally. It is only to be expected. He is a man of whimsical eccentricity, his wit is far from keen.'

His glasses had slipped. She looked directly into the blaze of his pale eyes.

'Lally, Lally have you hurt yourself?' came Anne's anxious voice.

'No, not in the least. I must try to be more ladylike in future.' And, as she took up the reins again, and the whip: 'I do believe I should have been far happier as a man, do you not think so?'

Sir George Stapleford thought so, being obliged to talk up to her while she ramped all round him in the saddle of a tall and disagreeable horse, the wind fretting the feathers of her daring hat and momentarily a great froth of white petticoat on view. He had been to look at the poorhouse they were building on the common behind Ledworth church, and he had left his carriage in the lane and had stumped dutifully across to where the workmen were finishing off the timber frame. He knew perfectly well thay would work the better for a daily visit from either himself or the overseers. The poorhouse had been his idea, he had provided eight tenths of the capital, and he felt obliged to see it completed on time. He gave sixpence to the boy driving the old horse that was treading the clay, asked some sensible questions, and retreated towards the carriage.

A thud of hooves, a crash, a woman's low, clear command to 'Jump it, damn you, you great brute' had heralded the re-entry into his life of the wayward Philadelphia, whom he had last seen stretched out dishevelled and bloody on a particularly fine brocade sofa in Valentine Brotherton's parlour more than ten years ago. He did not recognise her, needless to say. He only knew he was in danger of being run down. He was a very short man with the looks of a friendly little terrier without any of the inquisitive intelligence and snap. For a second of absolute terror he looked up as the huge horse lumbered over the churchyard wall and landed feet away, dodging sideways on seeing him with a snort of simulated fright and stumbling in the soft, poached ground.

'I do beg your pardon,' said Lally, drawing up. She was flushed – from exertion, from guilt – but she sat straight and true and gave him a long stare. He was older, even more shrunken, but she would have known him anywhere. What had he said that night years ago? 'No, of course I will not bring charges. The foolhardy business is best forgotten. But the young desperadoes should be whipped. Cracknell might have killed her.'

'A fine morning, Ma'am,' and he swept off his hat quite cordially as if he was often surprised by ladies galloping in churchyards and taking the flint wall like a bank, changing feet on top.

'Sir George Stapleford, is it not?' She had circled him twice by now, keeping out of range in case the horse took it into his dull head to kick.

'You have the advantage of me.'

Lally persuaded the horse to stand still a moment. She could see the line of deep hoofprints leading back across the churchyard and a small figure in the distance tracking them in a vague, bewildered manner.

'We have met before,' she said. 'My name is Philadelphia Fletcher.'

It meant nothing to him – and then everything. He looked

up, astounded, his mild little eyes scanning her face for any sign of the Philadelphia, the bold Philadelphia, the bloody Philadelphia, of Cookhams. He did not find any. He found nothing he recognised, save her nose and her seat on a horse.

'My dear Mrs Fletcher, how could I forget? When it was my own coachman nearly shot you dead. But how long since we have seen you in these parts.'

'I am staying with my cousin at the parsonage.'

'Lingborough. Well, bless me. I do believe Sam Uffington mentioned you were widowed, were coming home, but I didn't think much of it – what is there for you here, after all? Well, and you arrived and the news not reached us.'

Lally suddenly dismounted. If he thought to find her less formidable on foot he was mistaken. She towered above him, and in a severe habit and a rather military hat she looked somehow de-sexed. He could not recall Lally Blackwell had ever looked so damnably grave either. And then she said, in a voice that did, unexpectedly, touch a chord: 'You must forgive me for skulking behind these trees. You see, I have stolen the horse.'

He started. 'From the parson?'

'Just so. I bridled and saddled him in the greatest secrecy and escaped unseen. But he is a great insensitive, uneducated brute and he ran away with me as we came past Bennet's Farm. I fear he came across the churchyard like a cavalry charge but then he saw the wall and would have stopped. I told him he would not, he had got me in, he would get me out.'

Stapleford leaned on his cane and smiled. 'And here was I thinking you so changed or else an old man's memory was playing him false. My dear, will you not walk with me a little way. Give that disgraceful object to Beech – Beech! – and come give me your opinion of my poorhouse.'

The coachman Beech led off the horse and Lally strode across to gaze earnestly at the heaps of clay and straw and the stark frame about which half a dozen men banged and tapped and pegged.

'There will be room for twenty poor souls,' Stapleford said, catching up. 'Uffington has been pressing for something of the kind for years; it has been discussed and put off, discussed and put off. Brotherton is JP, chooses the overseers – this year Truelove shares with Sam, six months apiece and a damned unpleasant task. Funeral expenses, fuel, food ... All have to be found for the poor wretches. Bastardy bonds, squabbles over settlements, apprenticeships ... And all the usual muttering when the poor rate rises by so much as a penny. Well, Sam came to me, asked outright if I would have a house built, a homely sort of place for those too old or too young or too infirm for outdoor relief. What do you think of it?'

She said polite, appropriate words, but she walked all round the place twice, holding up her skirts, and wondered whether it was not built too close to the beck. The beck ran down to meet the river a little way above the mill and was a notoriously temperamental stream, now dried to a trickle, now a torrent. Yes, agreed Stapleford, but the site was the best on the common and Sam Uffington had plans for the beck ... He cocked a bright little eye at the pensive lady standing on the brink, her keen expression undeniably daunting.

'Your cousin at the parsonage,' he began cautiously, 'I hoped ... I hoped she might take an interest. The women here are to be set to spinning, and we are to find a teacher for the children. Could you ... May I ask if ...?'

'I have not heard the parson mention any poorhouse.'

'No.' He checked, looked irritated, helpless, disappointed. 'No. The least said about the parson the better perhaps. We have pinned our hopes on the new curate, Hayes, for, hmm, spiritual guidance. There will be looms for the men, you see, a vegetable garden, a few acres of arable, grazing for a cow or two. The plans are very sound. No, no, Mrs Fletcher, I fear the parson's interests lie elsewhere. But Mrs Glover, Mrs Glover could exert such influence. I have always found her sweet and obliging. And Mrs Brotherton, who is our staunch ally, entertained strong hopes she might agree to teach here once or twice a week.'

Lally had not yet met Eliza Brotherton; she descried Sam's

contrivances.

'I fear I have no influence over my cousin,' she said.

Stapleford sighed, was politely resigned. He escorted her back to the truculent coachman and the sweating horse.

'It has struck me,' said Lally suddenly, half way to the saddle, 'that if you had not enclosed seven hundred acres of common land many of your paupers would still find it possible to support themselves with some dignity – at least the dignity of a cow and some roots and enough firewood for the winter.'

Stapleford stepped back hastily as the horse cavorted. 'You must speak to Brotherton then, for he has enclosed, not I. He is a great man for progress. He has ridden about the country scrutinising enclosed land from Weybourne to Diss, has the answer to every problem. And he would tell you there will always be poor wretches who cannot get a living through indolence or ill health, common land or no, and that by turning these acres to corn he is contributing to the wealth of all.'

'I begin to form a picture of Mr Brotherton. He is not a man of charm and openhandedness like his brother.'

'Like Valentine? No, indeed. I trust this will go no further,' and he moved as close to Lally's side as the moody horse would allow. 'Horace Brotherton likes to think he is a man in the vanguard of agricultural science.'

'And is he?'

'Well, his land grows no more corn than mine and his sheep are not noticeably fatter, but he has a decided grasp on the theory. Occasionally he is led astray by the extravagant claims of eminent scientific gentlemen who have never set foot in the true country all their lives.'

A distant holloa came to them on the mild air. The horse backed off, breathing with dragonlike intensity. 'I believe I must leave you,' said Lally.

He made a leg, smiled. He liked her. By God, he liked her. He could remember that arch, fleeting grin as she had struggled to rise from the couch at Cookhams.

'You will not breathe a word?'

'About the horse? My dear, I have not seen you.'

Nature had endued the horse with all the worse faults of his race. Lally sat strong and true but he galloped away with her nevertheless, rocketing over the common with the action and indefinite purpose of a snipe. He skimmed the lowest furze clumps and got himself out of a boggy place with a herculean thrust of his vast quarters, but he was a coward at heart, and worse, he had no sense at all, so that he half fell over a hedge into one of Truelove's fields and half fell out over another, quite beside himself with equine hysteria. The hard knock he gave himself scrambling back on to the common sobered him however and Lally, whose single object had been to stay in the saddle, felt his speed slacken. She immediately drove in her heel and applied her whip: he would run until he was exhausted, too exhausted to get the better of her again.

Now that she was in control he ran like a tired horse, pecking and stumbling on the tussocks. She sent him on mercilessly, facing him at the beck. He thundered down towards it, saw the wink of water, swerved, and pitched on his nose.

It seemed a long time afterwards that she could sit up and look about in the certain knowledge she was not yet dead. A voice was speaking from very far away. It was not her own. It was a masculine voice, she had heard it before. A face swam into sight, momentarily, mysteriously disembodied.

'The devil might have killed you,' said the voice. 'Can you move your arm? Can you walk?'

She did not appear to be able to do either of these things, but then she was not trying. The face had become hideously familiar, the face that now bent close to her own, brick-red, grinning strangely with relief. It was Francis's face.

Arms lifted her. 'The workmen are coming,' said Jack Brotherton, 'I'll send one of them for a carriage.'

'Put me down,' said Lally. 'Put me down,' and struck him, as hard as she could, across the cheek.

CHAPTER 7

'Madam, your conduct is deplorable,' crowed the parson, abandoning toast, eggs, chops, bacon, everything, and rising to his feet with the deliberate movements of a man about to pontificate at length.

Lally closed the door behind her and leaned back against it, entirely unmoved. If he intended to pitch insults at her, said the bold angle of her head, he was welcome to try, their effect might not be quite what he supposed. Perhaps the gleam deep in her eye dissuaded him – the very light of battle if he was not mistaken. And she stood bathed in the early morning sunlight, glowing with regal splendour. His voice faltered, died away.

'My dear, do be kind,' said Anne tremulously from behind the chocolate pot. 'Lally has apologised already. It was all an unfortunate mistake.'

Certainly it had been a mistake on Lally's part to purloin the only horse in the stables capable, under normal circumstances, of throwing her down. That he had achieved this in the end by the expedient of throwing himself down and trying to roll on her was all to her credit, but he had done it, and had left her to Jack Brotherton to bring home in a country cart.

'An unfortunate mistake! I declare I can now understand what prompted your mother, Anne, to send Mrs Fletcher to India. But have neither of you any shame? There is Brotherton – generosity itself, such noble assistance – forced to borrow a cart from a gang of rough labourers, and there is the horse, lamed and grazed, running wild over Ledworth common, and then Madam' – a withering look at Lally which she greeted with a toss of her head and a dangerous sparkle in her eyes – 'then Madam you are carried in for dead, give your cousin a profound shock, and seem wholly unaware of any

74

'. . . of any breach of convention.'

But he saw he was making no impression. Her face was impassive, impenetrable. At last she moved to the table, sat down quite calmly, and began to eat.

'Does he never smile?' she asked Anne when the door had closed behind the indignant parson.

'Oh, Lally, must you provoke him so?'

'And must he treat me so like a child? I admit I stole his horse, but had I not fallen off it would have been returned to its stable as quietly as it left it and no one but old Salter would have known.'

'Poor Salter. He came to me when you were so long overdue and was so worried . . . He said he would never have let you go out but he knew you from the old days. He said he had warned you about the horse and you laughed.'

'How unsympathetic of me. Well, he was perfectly right.'

'Are you sure you are not hurt anywhere? You looked so pale yesterday when Jack Brotherton brought you in.' Pale and dangerous, she thought; there had been a glitter about Lally's eye that suggested the tigress roused. Anne felt it had had something to do with Jack Brotherton but no explanations were forthcoming and none suggested themselves. Lally, on being put to bed, was found to be stiff and bruised, nothing worse. It had been a lucky escape.

'I wish you would not worry about me' – a pause, a pregnant pause – 'You must think more about yourself. You ought to go out more. Why he imagines you must be cooped up in this place from week's end to week's end is incomprehensible.'

Anne rose, walked to the window. 'Well, we are invited to Cookhams this afternoon, if you recall.'

But Lally would not go to Cookhams, pleaded exhaustion and aching limbs. A bruise on her cheek and a graze on her chin lent, quite literally, an appropriate colour to her excuses. Anne resigned herself to going alone. Of course, Lally thought, getting out of bed the moment she had left the house, there was probably only the remotest chance of meeting Jack

Brotherton at Cookhams, by all accounts he was seldom at home. On the other hand she knew that if she did every shred of her composure would be stripped from her, that she would not be able to face him, and that his voice and his face would provoke all the old memories and reduce her to a shivering, anguished wreck. And he was not the kind of man to forgive her that blow, had scarcely spoken a word to her on the crazy journey to the parsonage yesterday. Well, she had hit him hard and he had already been staggering; he was forced to put her down. She supposed she had humiliated him thoroughly.

If only Sam had been passing at that moment, or the unknown Truelove, or benign little Stapleford. Why, oh why had it been Jack Brotherton? She began to dress, calling for Phee to help her, and Phee, who rather liked the parsonage, which seemed to her a comfortable, orderly house, took a great deal of trouble brushing out her hair, asking hopefully: 'Shall we stay here long, Mem Lally?'

'I think not.'

'Then where will we go, Mem Lally?'

Lally looked up into the smooth little brown face, into the dark trusting eyes.

'I do not know, Phee,' she said.

Two days later Lally met Horace Brotherton by chance in the dripping shrubbery and was offered his arm back to the house. He was a large man, lumbering, gouty, high-coloured, with the purple nose of a drinker and a great many pretensions to grandeur. He kept a good stable, an enviable cellar, and took his position as a magistrate seriously, priding himself on what he fancied was his stern magnanimity. Behind his back he was called Bull Brotherton, which described his person and his manner of going on adequately enough.

He had heard all about the Fletcher woman from Jack, who had not described her in glowing terms: a thin, leggy female, a dashed big nose, a cold manner, as he had put it. His latest encounter with her seemed to have left him speechless but it would take a rum female to put him off, his father reasoned, especially when there might be money in the case. Thus a niggling curiosity had drawn Bull Brotherton to the parsonage, which he found deserted, only echoing faintly to the wailing of babies, the one noise certain to drive him out again at once. The glimpse of a pale skirt in the shrubbery drew him in pursuit and he rounded a holly bush puffing and spluttering just as Lally strode from the other side.

He learnt nothing from the encounter except that the nabob's widow had that kind of blue eye which changed rapidly with any change in her mood and that it was fixed on him as furiously as his was fixed on her. She was not exactly fashioned, he decided, for amorous pastimes; and yes, she was uncommon willowy, yes, a noble nose, and yes, a cool, dismissive way of speaking. He did his best to make conversation but it was heavy going; she seemed disinclined to smile and more than disinclined to linger.

At his departure Lally ascended two at a time to the nursery. There, in the awful confusion of three howling small children and a howling baby, she repeated Brotherton's invitation to a supper dance at Cookhams. Anne, swathed in white aprons and a white cap, reeking of the foul preparation they were pouring liberally into the children's hair, lice having been discovered on Tommy and suspected on Rosa, gave a feeble cry of disappointment.

'There will never be time for a new dress to be made,' was her wistful comment.

The formal invitation came the day after and by some misadventure Sam Uffington's was delivered to the parsonage. On any other day it would have been handed to old Salter to take to Rooks Hill when he went to Ledworth church with any messages for Hayes the curate, who lived in a tiny cottage next door to that crumbling place. Today however the house was in glorious disorder for the Glovers were going to Norwich for three days to stay with friends, to go to the theatre, a concert, a grand supper. Sam's invitation fell Lally's way and she seized it, glad of any excuse to fly the house. Even in the parson's absence she felt oppressed, confined. Perhaps, she thought, the ride from Lingborough to Ledworth would clear her head; it was time she made a decision about her uncertain future.

Every horse was forbidden her, the pony too; she was reduced to the lowly donkey carriage, the children's plaything, which had no springs, no upholstery, and crooked axles. The donkey trotted through Lingborough cheerfully enough but the climb up to the Heath dampened his spirits: he dropped to a walk and tried to turn round and go home. At the gibbet on Tuppeys Hill, that high point where three roads met, he crabbed and sidled though nothing hung there, though there was nothing more sinister than the gorse and heather and the soft, harsh calls of a partridge. He dropped down by degrees from the heights where the plovers tumbled like leaves and there was always the cool breath of the sea, and by degrees came to the ford by the little mill.

There was a cart, tightly tarpaulined, drawn up under the trees. The door of The Ship House was shut; there was the blank look of the uninhabited. Lally felt a twinge of acute disappointment and drove past.

She was in a strange mood, half desperate, half determined. She had thought yesterday she could not bear the parsonage another minute, thought so now, would think so again tomorrow; but where could she go? Where? Here in this dear familiar country she had expected to find purpose and courage, instead of which she simply felt lost and confused. The memories of India refused to fade, the deeper memories of Charlie had been revived.

The donkey, driven with passion, took umbrage and retaliated by shying violently at a flock of geese in a pasture. At this the nearside trace snapped clean in two and the donkey turned round slowly and looked at Lally with glowing eyes.

'Should he not be driven forwards? Or is this the latest fashion?' asked JG, ambling up on a leggy and fleshless horse with cropped ears and hardly any tail. 'Do you not find progress deplorably slow?'

'Perhaps instead of trying to be jocular you could get down and see if it's in your power to mend the trace.'

'Splice it, you mean? I would if I could, dear girl. But where are you off to in such a lather?'

The donkey looked blown, to be sure, and reproachful too. Lally brushed at her drooping curls and sighed. 'I am taking an invitation to Sam Uffington at Rooks Hill. I suppose my best plan would be to ride the donkey.'

'You will do nothing of the kind. You will ride pillion with me.'

'The parson . . .'

'Since when did the parson govern your actions? Look, let us push the poor cart out of the lane and you take the donkey's rein, so. Do you see this horse of mine stands like a statue when his reins are pulled over his head? He has a great many vices but some convenient tricks too. He comes to a whistle.'

'I had a pony once who did the same. It is very useful in the dark.'

A pause, the gleam of an eye in her direction, what looked like a suppressed grin. Then JG was in the saddle again and she had to scoop up her skirts and climb behind him, balanced precariously sideways. She had often travelled like this in her childhood, put up behind servants on a proper pad, in the days when the lanes had been impassable for wheeled traffic eight months of the year, but this was different, for she was in a dimity dress with precious new petticoats beneath and the horse's rump was smooth and slippery. She had to clutch indecorously at JG's coat and, when the miserable donkey threatened to drag her off backwards, abandon all shame and put an arm round his waist.

Between the steep banks the sun was warm on their backs. The country now was very far from wild: little rolling hills, woods, the tiny meandering river. The cottages in Ledworth were sunk behind drifts of faded cuckoo flowers and cow parsley, and there were ducks squabbling on the pond. Everything seemed deserted though Lally was conscious of at least one pair of curious eyes following her eccentric progress down what passed as the village street. They got by the tiny church where, if she craned to see, the hoofprints of the parson's idiot horse were still plain among the tottering headstones, and then they turned right-handed down the track to Rooks Hill.

A wisp of blue smoke rising was their first glimpse of it, a weird and crooked chimney above the trees. They had to ford the beck here, the beck that eventually wandered across the common and ran down to the river. It was a swamp, a noisome swamp. Men and carts had passed through it, across and back, across and back. JG urged his horse over with cheerful oaths and the donkey sank to his girth.

Then there was a shaggy piece of grass on which half a dozen more moth-eaten donkeys browsed and slept, and a very large flock of geese were in the iron charge of a tiny boy with a stick twice as tall as himself. There was no sort of hill in evidence, with rooks or without. The farmhouse was set back from the road by a short sweep of grossly overgrown carriage drive and a half moon of rank grass behind some palings. It was at least two hundred years old, had massive and crazy chimneys, and had been capriciously repaired and renovated and knocked about. But it was a fine house, an east wing added in Queen Anne's time and boasting sash windows and a handsome sundial on the red-brick wall. It was a big house too. JG raised his eyebrows at it, riding up to the front door to let Lally down and then dismounting himself with a shout that brought no response, inside or out.

'They are all from home,' he said. 'They are gone to cut the hay.'

He stood in a flowerbed to peer through the windows. Dark panelling met his eye and at least two lots of backstairs opening in chimney corners, and worn tiles and flagstones, a roomful of good old furniture, and a lugubrious, smoky atmosphere.

'The place is deserted,' he remarked after an age of this sort of unsatisfactory spying.

'There must be someone, servants, a gardener . . .' Lally

looked round hopefully but gardeners were there none, nor had been for some time by the look of the lush grass the horse and donkey were tearing up with undisguised greed.

She and JG ventured round the back to find a large enclosed yard full of hens, ducks and pigeons. The door to the house was set wide but all was silent.

'There is no one here at all.' Lally stared about her, saw a milk jug and pail abandoned by the dairy step, a dog's bowl and chain by a stable door. There was the clucking and crooning of the poultry, the fresh breezy quiet of a fine summer morning, and that was all.

Then a woeful howling reached them, and shouts, and muffled curses.

'The horse!' exclaimed JG, setting off in great leaps. 'He is an abomination! Someone has been kicked for sure.'

In the rank drive was a brown-suited old man in the act of chucking a clod of earth at the miscreant. The skinny roan horse, with an angry rattle of the bit, trotted straight up to JG through a bed of young nettles and put his nose against JG's glorious waistcoat in a confidential way.

This, thought Sam, coming through the gate at that moment, and looking with loathing at that outrageous creation any decent man would keep well hidden, only went to show that horses had defective eyesight, something he had long suspected.

The house proved dark, draughty and inconvenient. JG sank under his huge wig and drank off half a bottle of mulberry wine 'for fear his blood should become sluggish'. But Sam was an ardent host, pointing out the quaintness, the peculiarities of the place with obvious pleasure and pride. There was a priest's hole behind one of the fireplaces, he told them; and certainly the fireplaces were big enough for a convocation of cardinals just so they did not mind being well-sooted. JG mused on this a while and then stated that he would rather believe the space had been intended for smuggled goods: had not the crypt in Lingborough church been used for such a purpose before John Glover routed out the barrels? And every building in the district had its false walls, false floors, double ceilings, suspicious bacon lofts.

Sam had no traffic with the smugglers, though he bought his tea and gin by night, so to speak.

'They rule all hereabouts,' he said, when they had returned to the panelled parlour with its polished oak furniture. The two pointers sat on the rug by the cold grate following every word he spoke with their loving eyes and soft, cocked ears.

'And so they will while the duty is so high. What can you expect?' asked JG, doing a round of the gloomy portraits on the walls. 'I hear there is one local riding officer and an assistant and both of them the enemies of their own Revenue cutter – the contempt of the landsman for the sailor, you might say. But rivalry be damned! What use are they with or without a cutter? A score of men against hundreds. Smuggling is good business. Why, even your Indiaman traded stocks to some questionable gentlemen before you sailed within limits, I'll lay my life – eh, Lally?'

She nodded. The memory of the Indiaman was one of distant discomfort and distress. She sat in a high-backed chair and watched the two men lighting pipes from an unreliable flint, laughing at it. How different they were, and yet both brown-skinned from the outdoors and much of an age. She did not believe JG was any older than thirty-five, for all he put on ten years with the wig. She would have to warn him, she thought with a brief, secret smile, that he took the ten years off again when he smoked his cheroots. Now a pipe … Yes, a pipe was the part.

His eyes slid from Sam to her. He looked through a cloud of smoke but he looked very keenly.

'Oh, 'twas Lally who had business with you,' he was saying, 'I rescued her from an impasse, a difference of opinion with her donkey. "Some put their trust in chariots, and some in horses: but we will remember the name of the Lord our God."'

'Yes,' said Sam, with a lively glance in Lally's direction, 'I see. No doubt it is an apt quotation.'

'In Lally's case doubly apt,' replied the irrepressible JG, regarding the bowl of his pipe with a mischievous look. 'Rush trotted home yesterday with an unbelievable tale of bolting horses, duckings in the beck, and our Mrs Fletcher laid out on a hurdle and wept over by none other than bonny Jack Brotherton.'

Sam removed the dogs from the hearth by the simple method of waving a booted leg at them. They wagged their tails in a low, sweeping, conciliatory gesture and departed.

'It is not true?' he demanded, stepping to the door to shout for his housekeeper Mrs Hirtle, and failing her, for old Cushion, the brown-suited man bitten by JG's horse.

'Well, the horse bolted and I fell off, that much at least is true. I regret to say Jack Brotherton did not weep.' He had some cause, she thought, being struck in the face by a woman he had sought to rescue. The memory of it stabbed her again, and another memory, of Francis, Francis in blue, corpulent and unhealthy, swaggering down a room to bow to the prettiest woman he could see.

'Are you cold?' Sam was stooping by her chair now.

'No. I have to give you this and then I must leave.' The invitation to Cookhams changed hands.

'But you must have something to eat and drink. Why, JG is to stay and dine – no, I insist. You should be properly introduced to the curate and he is coming this afternoon to go over some church accounts. I will stop that roof dripping if I have to visit the bishop to get it done.'

'I fear the curate, were you to seek his opinion, might express the wish that I had drowned in the beck when I came off the notorious horse. I left great gouges all across his churchyard and knocked some flints out of his wall.'

The two men laughed. Mrs Hirtle entered on the crest of it as if she feared some devilry was afoot: she and Cushion had some very old, very racy memories of Miss Philadelphia. She looked and looked but, like Stapleford, recognised only the nose, though Miss Philadelphia had always had a dry way of speaking and had been known to reduce a score of sober gentlemen to unbecoming hilarity.

'Mrs Hirtle, you are just the same as ever. You used to visit the Hall to call on your sister.'

'Yes, Ma'am,' said Mrs Hirtle, whose sister, the Lingborough Hall kitchen maid in those days, had supplied endless stories of Miss Philadelphia's perfidious way of going on.

Now I can see, thought the housekeeper, why poor Mistress Fanny was half afraid of the girl. Why, she might be a duchess, sat there with her shoulders square and her chin up; and she hurried away to tell her underlings and prepare some tea.

Lally refused an invitation to dine; apart from considerations of propriety she could see the men would be happier left alone. So Sam offered to escort her back to Lingborough himself – JG was advising Mrs Hirtle on clearing the bats from the attics – and ordered a saddle put on a ponderous grey mare with huge feet. Then he looked ruefully at Lally's pretty, crumpled skirts and waved the horse away again, calling for a pillion pad to be put on his own chestnut.

'He is not used to carrying two,' was his only comment as they skirted the grazing donkeys and the geese. For all that the horse floundered through the quagmire at the beck willingly enough, and they went through Ledworth at a dignified hand canter, Lally's skirts blowing in the wind. She found that Sam knew every field and covert and carr and could describe them, what they grew and what game they harboured. He knew his neighbours intimately, their foibles and prejudices, their ability to plough straight, to weed, or to breed cattle. He asked her if Jack Brotherton had been chivalrous and when she said yes, yes, she could not fault him, Sam laughed a harsh humourless laugh and said she must have reformed him then, for he was a notorious loose rake.

They crossed the ford and began to climb. The lane was deep going, ploughed by heavy waggons and a great many of them, and a great many horses, and not a few men on foot.

Every rut and indentation might have made a Revenue man's heart bleed. Then they were up on the heathery wilderness where the thickets of thorn trees bent inland with grotesque deformities and the white scuts of rabbits bobbed away among the gorse.

'It's no kind place when the wind hurls in from the north,' reflected Sam, remarkably conscious of Lally's arm about his waist. 'There have been several robberies up here lately, the same man each time Brotherton thinks, a cunning devil, he must have good local knowledge. What with that and the smuggling a lawless coast indeed.'

A vision came to Lally of a slender young girl in boy's breeches and a mask dashing from under the trees on a rangy black pony shouting, 'Stop! Stop! Your money or your honour!' at a laughing young gentleman on a grey.

'Did you know my cousin Charles?' she asked.

'Not very well. Our paths crossed now and then. I had a meagre social life in those days, my father ill, my youngest brother Joe playing the devil at cockfights and race meetings. I took charge of the farm at eighteen and I doubt my best coat came out of the cupboard for the next ten years.' A pause in which he felt her light, supple weight shift and a drift of faint perfume – rosewater? – came to him. 'You and Charles were very close.'

'Yes. Yes, I always thought so. But perhaps he brought out the worst in me. His brother Edward was very cautious and correct, he would never have taken me fishing or lent me his breeches; he would have died before doing so. Charlie was only too glad to have a partner in crime, didn't even stop to consider I was a girl.'

'He was very dear to you, I see that.'

'I have sometimes wondered if he was the only one who ever really cared for me. As a boy might care for his favourite dog, you understand,' and her softened voice took on its more familiar dryness. 'Nothing more.'

They rode on. Lally leaned more heavily on Sam's back as the chestnut swerved from something that might have been an adder and might have been nothing, and she closed her eyes to listen to the thud thud thud of hoofbeats. This was freedom of a sort, a muted unsatisfactory freedom, but better by far than being shut up in the parsonage with those chattering women and the wailing babies that reminded her so heart-achingly of her own.

'It has occurred to me,' Sam said as the gibbet came in sight, 'it seems to me …' How was he to put it without offending her? He wished he could see her face. 'Am I wrong in believing you chafe to escape the parsonage but …'

'But I have no money. Exactly, Mr Uffington.'

'I did not know how to broach the matter. Rumour has it you are tolerably rich.'

'Rumour lies.'

'Do you wish to remain at Lingborough? In Norfolk? Well, we are building a poorhouse with Sir George Stapleford's money, a small place, somewhere to send the most distressing cases. Mrs Brotherton and Mr Hayes have joined forces over it, are keen to set all the poor devils to reading and writing, have even spoken of stirring up old Mrs Greeves who has the dame school in Lingborough. But Mrs Greeves is dropsical and quite the better part of seventy-five if my memory serves me. Tom Truelove and I, being overseers this year, hoped to get someone younger, someone like …'

'My cousin Anne.'

'Yes. How did you know? Do you not think it would do her so much good? It would give her an interest and God knows it's time either she or the parson had some interest in the parish. No, forgive me. That sounded cruel. But anyway, old Stapleford approached the parson months ago and he refused to let her attempt it, grew quite heated. These last few days though I have been turning it over in my mind. How would it suit you, Mrs Fletcher? There was talk of a small salary and a cottage in the village.'

Lally was silent so long he began to feel anxious. He could not see her face at all, even if he screwed round to look over his shoulder; all that was visible was the brim of her hat and the light brown clusters of her loose curls. 'I know it is nothing after … In India you must have … Your husband was a wealthy man,' he finished lamely.

But he felt her arm stiffen, the hand at his waist clenched.

'Dear Mr Uffington, I do believe you have just saved my sanity,' she said.

CHAPTER 8

The weather turned sultry, too sultry to be borne. Anne returned from Norwich pale and exhausted and languished behind drawn blinds; iced tea was called for at all hours; even the babies were too stupefied to cry. Only Lally, who had endured far worse, appeared unaffected and continued, to everyone else's chagrin, her ritual daily circumnavigation of the gardens, stalking through the drooping greenery until the beads of perspiration sprang out above her freckles. In the very early morning when there was the remotest chance of coolness she walked out in an old cotton dress, no stays, no petticoats, no decorous fichu at the neck. Her straw hat was always on the back of her head where she liked it best and skewered there with a pin for she could not bear ribbons under her chin in such heat. She went barefoot, and sometimes sat for an hour, a blessed, peaceful hour, with her toes in the waters of the lake, gazing across at the ruin of the Hall.

Towards the end of that unbearable week the curate called to discuss the poorhouse project and brought with him Mrs Greeves who was most decidedly dropsical but apparently immortal. For forty years she had been stuffing some minute knowledge of literature and elementary mathematics into the heads of such children as she could get; a few paupers posed no problem. But how was she to travel? Her condition was perilous. Dr Milton warned her about overexertion. So here she was at Mrs Brotherton's request merely to relay to Lally the basic requirements and to wish Lally well.

It was too hot to discuss anything seriously. Only Lally was alert. Mrs Greeves wilted on the sofa and the curate, a strange, bow-legged, warty little man, exceedingly kind and harassed, drank several pints of iced lemonade and mopped his brow over and over. Was there any objection from Parson Glover? It seemed not. The parson had compressed his mouth, changed colour, and been struck dumb certainly, but only for a moment, a brief moment. He had not been able to think up any rational objection and he knew better by now than to make any irrational one to such as Lally Fletcher. In any case, he believed her a lady of independent means. How could he stop her? And he was happy and relieved to see her doing something useful: a charitable act, noble intentions, unquestionable benevolence of spirit.

'I am afraid the salary is only twenty pounds a year,' said Mr Hayes. He had discovered who had uprooted the bulbs in his churchyard but he found he could not hold it against her, he felt rather obscurely that she was too fine and dashing for rebuke.

'And I really doubt Mr Truelove's cottage will suit at all,' added Mrs Greeves. She was thinking that Lally was not the sort of girl to marry again, that she was not pretty, not voluptuous, and there was some doubt about money. Why should she care about a cottage and a salary if she had been left well provided?

'I have not had the pleasure of meeting Mr Truelove yet,' said Lally, fetching a fan off a side table and handing it to the uneasy lady on the sofa.

'He is a widower, a good, generous sort of man, takes his obligations seriously,' the curate told her. 'He farms alongside Mr Uffington.'

Mr Uffington was the curate's hero, Lally found, though a rather fearful respect was mingled with the adulation. Mr Uffington was to have the church roof mended, and the windows, and the tower. His ancestors had kept it in good repair, he would not see it fall down in his lifetime. The two ladies suspected Sam had used strong and biting language on this point. Mrs Greeves smiled surreptitiously at Lally behind her fan.

When her two suffering visitors had gone Lally went out into the garden. She loved the garden. Its scents and colours reminded her of Lingborough Hall. It was there that Sam found her after riding over to bring young Edward home after a riding lesson. He had found the house as dark as a tomb though nowhere near as cool, the servants torpid, Anne indisposed and unavailable. There was no sign of the parson. Sam wondered disconsolately into the garden with his dogs at his heels. How was he to tackle this infernal matter of the church roof? His gaze swept upwards: there were great clouds massing over the beeches, the weather would break soon and there would be a deluge. And just when they had got the hay cocked.

He turned the corner by the carp pond and there was Lally, sitting sideways on a white garden seat, her legs up, a book on her knees. She was in a delicate sprigged blue, no shoes or stockings. She had a slender waist, he saw again, but its effect was somewhat diminished by her height; there was, as JG had remarked to him over dinner, rather too much of Lally between neck and knees. But now Sam fixed his eyes on her firm and freckled bosom and was aware of a sudden and distinct change in his own breathing. It was a very nice bosom and it was ill-concealed.

For a moment she did not seem aware of him, and then she looked up and her eyes clouded shyly: his thoughts were probably quite plain upon his face. She snapped the book shut, swung down her legs, and lifted the low bodice of her dress a fraction.

'Forgive me,' said Sam, 'I had no idea anyone was in the garden.'

Lally smiled, begged him to sit down, not to mind her dreadful old dress, her bare feet – did he not remember her bare feet the first time they had met? Her voice sounded a little uncertain, not at all as bold as usual, and she did not look at him directly, which was unlike her. He sat by her side with his coat off and his cravat loosened. How much hotter would it get before the storm broke? Why, they had been sweltering like this for days and no real sunshine, only heat, heat, and a louring, overcast sky.

Lally was very quiet. She did not remember any man ever looking at her like that before. It was a sobering experience at twenty-eight. And she had not intended to play the wanton, had come out here to be alone and away from the vapid atmosphere of the house, had hoped to remain undiscovered in this remote corner.

There was the clap of pigeons' wings from the beeches, the buzz of bees in the lavender border, the plop, plop of the carp rising. The light – it was not sunlight, rather an evil glare – beat down, and the dark clouds gathered and gathered. Swallows hunted low across the grass and as the light lessened, lower still.

'It will rain tonight,' Lally said confidently.

'My wheat will suffer for it. And the hay.'

'I thought you were downcast. Perhaps Rooks Hill will miss the worst of it. Perhaps it will all fall on the Heath.' And then, seeing he was not disposed to being cheered up: 'Mr Hayes told me this afternoon that you and JG are away to Yarmouth shortly.'

'At the end of next week. He is going to ride that bony nag he bought from the gipsies for ten shillings. It is no beauty but it can gallop, and stay all day, and jump like a deer. How strange. I never imagined he knew very much about horses. Or is he simply lucky, do you think?'

'I have often thought he is most mysterious, and that he has a great many faces,' Lally said slowly, gazing down the grass to the pleached plums on the hot brick wall. 'And I am not sure I have ever seen the real one.'

'All that clownish innocence simply a pretence? You may be right. When he set that horse alight on the Heath the other day, sat tight as a monkey, outdistanced me without the least trouble and pulled up hardly blowing, well, I did wonder if he knew what he was about all the time, if he had bought a queer-looking brute on purpose to keep up the part. And this passion for ships. There is something odd about it, unexpected. But I like him. I do not think I have ever liked a man half as much before.'

'And Anne? Is Anne safe with him? Have you got over your reservations on that score?'

Her face was as grave as ever but yes, she was teasing him. He knew it. He gave a good-natured grin.

'Oh, Anne,' he said, 'do you think Anne would be safe with any man who wooed her conscientiously?' And in another moment: 'Damn! You must forget I ever said it. I was ... I was thinking aloud.'

Their eyes met. Her eyes were really rather beautiful, he thought, so troubled and expressive between those brown lashes. To his surprise she blushed, flicked through her book with a rather false unconcern. 'Do you know,' she said, 'I owe Anne fourteen guineas? Is that not disgraceful? It means that three quarters of my teaching salary is already pledged.'

'You do not look particularly cast down.'

'There comes a point,' she said with a tight, sardonic little smile, 'beyond which there is nothing to be done but shrug and carry on, like a dismasted ship in a storm.'

'Are you really desperate? Anne thought you might ... remarry.'

She drew back. They were so close on the narrow old seat that he could feel the warmth rising from her bare skin but as he spoke it was as if she became chill, numbed. What had her life been like with this unknown Fletcher? What?

'I must go,' he said, getting up. 'You will give my regards to Anne.'

But Lally took his arm back to the house, matching her stride to his as they passed along the gravel walks, the two dogs slinking behind, tongues hanging out, tails down. Sam kept his gaze well away from her breasts, deliberately admired the few remaining roses, the obscure statuary. He had no time for gardens, he said a trifle wistfully, and Rooks Hill had been going to ruin since his mother died. And then, with a touch of understanding pique: did she not think that stone bench by the shrubbery had cost half as much again as the mending of the hole in Ledworth church roof?

He was not given to pettiness, however, nor envy: the

92

parson could have as many stone seats as he liked provided the churches in his care were tolerably sound, the babies christened, the dead buried. He thought to strike a lighter note and as they came in sight of the house remarked: 'I hope this scheme of mine to make you teacher at the poorhouse will not bring you to battle with Glover.'

'Oh, he is overflowing with enthusiasm. He was beginning to be afraid I would never leave his house.'

They stopped together at the edge of the shrubbery. The dogs came up to sniff her hands and stand looking lovesick while she caressed their soft ears and crooned at them.

'I hope I may introduce you to Truelove soon,' Sam said, looking down on her curls, the damp tendrils round her brow. 'I hope you will deal kindly with him.'

'You speak as if I were generally unkind.'

'I have never seen you so. But he is a blighted, moody man; he lost his wife to consumption and he has no child. He is ... a little difficult sometimes. He is easy to take amiss. And you exhibit ...' Exhibit his symptoms, the symptoms of old pain, old grief, disappointment, wrecked hopes.

'Yes, Mr Uffington, what do I exhibit?'

'I believe you have been desperately unhappy, are not recovered from it yet.'

She straightened but she did not look at him. She put up a hand to her damp cheek and pushed back the hair.

He said: 'He has been a good friend to me in difficult times. It is only that his outward appearance is ... deceptive.'

'Dear Mr Uffington, is that not true of everybody?'

'No, no. The Brothertons, every one of them, are precisely what they appear, so is the parson, so am I, come to that.'

She looked at him now. It was a challenging look.

'Are you?'

He laughed it off, said he must go or his dinner would spoil, whistled to the patient dogs. He did not make a leg, nor take Lally's hand; she had the strangest feeling that he would have liked to kiss her cheeks the way JG always did but that he felt uncertain how she would take it.

'Was that Sam?' Edward demanded, meeting her on the stairs. 'I wish I could live at Rooks Hill. I like it so much better there. You had better come up quick, you know. Phee is crying, and when I asked her why she said she was in love. Isn't that funny?'

JG had declined to appear at the parsonage for some time though he was, it seemed, in communication with the church owls. He called again at Rooks Hill, spent several days on the coastal marshes with his spy-glass, rode to Cromer and back, and had been seen crabbing off Lingborough. Then Lally received a terse and almost indecipherable note, delivered into her hand by a panting Rush, inviting her to take a dish of tea at The Ship House. Rush hovered for her answer, ill at ease on the parsonage steps, while Lally read and re-read the lines with a tiny frown of concentration.

'There is no date,' she cried, 'no time.'

'Which is today, Ma'am, my life on it,' said Rush.

He indicated the trap waiting below, a shaggy brown pony between the shafts.

'I will be back directly,' said Lally and ran indoors.

She was back directly with her hat, a jacket, and a book. With no backward glance at the windows of the parsonage she climbed up and arranged herself on the seat. The pony woke up; Rush spoke and he sprang forward, shaking his mane from his eyes.

At The Ship House Lally was greeted by a coolness that smelled of soot and dank water. The chimneys had been newly scoured and a fine film of black dust lay over everything. There was no one there.

She stepped across to the window to look out at the water meadows across the river, at the heavy willows moving in the breeze. She put down the book and threw her jacket across a chair. It would be just like JG to invite her to take tea and then forget all about her. For a while she browsed among his books, for the most part learned treatises on rare turtles or obscure apes. In a dim corner was a heap of what she took to be chicken feathers but which turned out to be the moultings of several stuffed birds, one still recognisable as some kind of owl. A faint, unmistakable whiff told her the stoat was at hand, and sure enough there he was on the table under a nightcap. Lally backed away, went outside through the front door. There was no sign of Rush. There were signs though, quite obvious signs, of great activity near the old mill entrance: hoofprints in the baked and crumbling mud, and the mark of a cart, heavy laden.

A familiar deep, sonorous voice reached her, singing about the mermaids down below, and when she looked up there was JG riding his roan horse through the ford. He was stooped to avoid the dripping branches of the willows and alders and the crooked little thorn bushes that grew right down to the water's edge, and he had tied his wig to the saddle, and his coat, and had rolled his shirt sleeves up to the elbow.

'Lally, my love, you are early.'

'I rather fear it is you who is late.'

'Late? But I left the curate at ten; he has lent me his honey buzzard, the generous man. It could not possibly be more than half past.'

'Your clock has struck half eleven.'

JG looked unrepentant. 'Perhaps it was the snake kept me. I found a vast hatch of grass snakes by . . . Is Rush not about? Rush! Rush!' and he let the reins fall on the horse's neck, sliding from the saddle and turning to pull a suspicious oilskin package from the saddlebag. 'Look, they are a present for your cousin, for refusing her invitation to dine this week. Are they not magnificent?' Three very small and far from fresh trout were disclosed.

'You have been fishing,' accused Lally, 'fishing as well as catching snakes.'

'No, no. I bought them from a child along the river bank.'

She smiled. How like him. And then . . . She became aware that he had left off the spectacles, that it was his own dark hair curling on his brow, that though it was the same haggard face, the same nose, the same grey eyes, yet this was a different JG altogether.

'Rush you old devil, pox on you, come and take the horse,' he yelled, and there were noises of a reluctant approach from within and Rush's head poked out at last. 'Come, Lally, come, we have something to celebrate.'

He led her to the parlour, clapping his wig on his head and searching for the spectacles. The pile of feathers had been his short-eared owls.

'The cat has been in,' he said. 'Or Sam's dogs.'

'Sam's dogs are too well behaved.'

'Let us hope so. What is it, Rush? Oh, the punch. We are going to try Rush's famous punch. Do not ask where he learnt to concoct it, it owes a great deal to the West Indies and something to a Jersey smuggler called Roquier.'

'But I thought I had been invited for a dish of tea.'

'Is that what I said? Did I write tea? Now why should I have done that? Here, take this glass and taste it and tell me if it's not the most intoxicating witch's brew you ever put your lips to in your life.'

She did so; it was. When the fiery flush had subsided and she was able to speak she said: 'To what ... do we drink?'

'My ship. I have bought a ship.'

'A ship?' She choked on another mouthful of spirits, her watering eyes blinking after the disappearing Rush. A stray thought: who *was* Rush? Not a gentleman's servant, discreet, biddable. He still walked and spoke and swore as if he were at sea.

'A cutter,' JG was saying, 'a beautiful lithe cutter. Mind you, I have bought her unseen. She lies at Yarmouth where Sam and I go tomorrow. She has lost her mast in a squall, is beached, looks only fit for firewood they tell me. But she will live again, will fly. Yes, yes, when I have finished with her she will fly.'

'Was it advisable to buy her unseen?'

'I paid so little I would recoup the price if she were chopped up and hawked round on a barrow. But she was recommended. She was the sweetest, fastest, most seaworthy little ship off this long coast before her sad accident.'

Lally could feel the blood rushing to her face. It was the effect of the rum, or of those grey eyes looking at her with such sublime certainty she knew exactly what he was talking about, that every shade of meaning could be perceived.

'I brought you a book on penguins,' she said. 'I found it in the parson's study.'

'I know next to nothing about penguins. How kind of you.'

'But a great deal about very fast cutters.'

'Oh, a very great deal.'

'I suppose you know what it is to be dismasted, to be wrecked.'

'I have been dismasted countless times but only wrecked twice, I think.'

'If you are not careful you may be wrecked again. This coast has been the graveyard of many good men. Will it not seem strange for an eccentric naturalist to go to sea in a racy sort of cutter?'

'I hope this eccentricity may account for it.'

'I think you hope in vain.'

They looked at each other. Then he came to where she had sunk on to the window seat and he sat beside her and took her hand, turning it palm upwards within his own.

'Do you think I intend to run Geneva and Bohea?'

She felt his hard warm fingers close over her own. 'But of course,' she said.

He laughed, let go of her hand. 'I knew I could never fool my Philadelphia. You smoked a trick right at the start, in Colchester, when I offered you a seat in the chaise. Do you know why I took you up? Because your face seemed familiar. There, is that not an admission from a man who is neither introspective nor superstitious? I was in half a mind to turn back and then there you were and I thought, here is a girl who loves adventure, who will not whine at discomfort, who will take the world as it comes. Had you said no, you would travel on the stage, I do believe I should have returned to London on the instant.'

'So it is my fault you came to Norfolk to be a smuggler.'

'I forgive you.'

'How magnanimous of you.'

He grinned. He turned to look out of the window and ran a hand through his short hair, tossing the wig aside. 'Look, a perfect summer's day. Shall we go out and see if my pike is come to dinner?' And in a while, seeing her distress: 'My love, I came here because I was asked to come, to take over the organisation on this stretch of coast. The local leader was dead, a strong, clever, savage man, and everything ahoo, as Rush would put it. Internecine squabbling, imperfect communications, botched runs – and cargoes being lost for want of care and forethought. There seemed no natural successor to the dead leader so a committee voted I should be asked to step in, reorganise.'

'Your reputation must be second to none, they do not take kindly to strangers hereabouts.'

'I think I may safely say I have an extraordinary reputation. And are you considering alerting the riding officer?'

She did not answer. His eyes scanned her face. And then he smiled his charming smile and reached for her hand again, uncurling her fingers and bending to kiss her palm.

It seemed to Lally as she paced beside him to the lush river bank that either the sunlight was more dazzling than before or she was very slightly tipsy. The sun-dappled water swirled away past the rickety landing stage, and there were twigs and leaves caught in the current, and petals, and pieces of weed. Then a sudden flash, a flicker of turquoise.

'Did you see him?' asked JG. 'The kingfisher.'

She could see him now, away upstream, perched on a willow stump. Then he dived again, was gone. There was only the water, the heavy, green summer smell, and the singing of some little bird hidden in the rushes. Lally leaned forward and looked down, down where her face rippled on the swift water. All the old longing and restlessness returned, but longing for what she did not know, except to be free to choose, to make something of her life before it was over and all the chances gone. She had felt this longing on all those foolish escapades with Charlie, and each time had been a little more deeply disillusioned.

'Never eat a kingfisher,' JG remarked. 'They are disgusting. They are like Jack Brotherton, rogues in velvet coats.'

Where have you come from, she wanted to ask, and where will you go when you leave Norfolk? You read books on apes and penguins, quote the Bible, love the sea. She looked down at his hand resting beside hers on the warm wooden rail, the square roughened hand of a man who is no stranger to physical labour; he had been fastidious about his manicure but the signs were still there.

The breeze lifted her ringlets, such fluffy, disobliging ringlets. She said nothing, though a hundred questions clamoured to be answered. And suddenly across the water meadows came the melancholy cry of a peacock – did not Sir George Stapleford have peacocks at Luffwell Hall? – and the sound, so unexpected in the blowy perfection of an English summer day, made Lally start back.

JG noticed but made no comment. And presently the little frown cleared from between her slim brows and her mouth relaxed, and she looked up with sudden pleasure as the kingfisher darted back across the rippled water.

'How do you know,' she asked, 'that the poor things are so terrible to eat?'

CHAPTER 9

The day came for dinner at Cookhams, cards and music promised afterwards. Mrs Brotherton found herself oppressively burdened with unattached males none of whom would be averse to a handsome widow with a cheering allowance. She looked forward to meeting Lally at last, discounted the forebodings of her husband and son, and spent half a guinea with the frisseur to ensure the top of her head at least came to the level of Lally's chin.

Cookhams, standing in the Ledworth valley between Rooks Hill and Luffwell Hall, was a square Queen Anne house facing south across a beautiful well-wooded park. It looked exactly as it had the night Lally had galloped into its stableyard on the black pony and collapsed so dramatically on the cobbles, except instead of a friendly chink of light at the library window the whole front of the house was ablaze, the door thrown wide, and carriages at the step.

They were to eat at five, the state of the roads after the heavy downpour and the very real possibility of highwaymen on the Heath dictated it. The company was large: three Brotherton offspring, Jack, Kate, and Cecilia; a couple of substantial local farmers, Chewton and Turner, one with his daughter, the other his wife; Sam Uffington, Truelove, JG, and an attorney called Simmons, a rare, exquisite young man who clearly wished he had stayed safe in his snug Norwich office; and the parsonage party, the parson already in expansive mood.

Mrs Brotherton first glimpsed Lally from the back and was taken with the thought that the woman was beautiful, that proud brown head, long neck, striking elegance. Then Lally turned and looked at her. Such a pity about the nose, Eliza decided, moving forward with her hand outstretched, but it was not the nose that gave her greatest pause, it was the artificial cheerfulness in that countenance, the quick, obligatory smile.

'My dear Mrs Fletcher, how I have longed to meet you. Are you quite recovered from your fall? Jack declared he did not know how you survived unscathed. Now I must introduce you to everybody here; we are missing only Sam Uffington and he is never punctual.'

So Lally passed about the room, aware of a remark here and there behind this fan or that, aware of being marked down as extraordinary, dominating, haggard even. But she forced herself to smile, leaned down to catch the commonplace remarks, gave a general impression of subdued ferociousness and devil-take-you, and eventually found herself brought to a halt by Eliza's hand on her arm and: 'Mrs Fletcher, have you met Mr Truelove? He is a paragon among men, the very backbone of my poorhouse committee – I call it a committee though we are only four; I do not count Sir George. Tom, Tom, here is Mrs Philadelphia Fletcher from Madras.'

A lean, unexceptional man of middle height turned round and made a leg. Lally looked into a dark face frightfully pitted by smallpox; the mouth was hard, the eyes challenging. He had obviously heard about her from Sam and had not liked what he had heard. Across the room she was aware of another dip and flutter of the fans.

'I have long wanted to meet you,' she said with a graceless but touching courtesy. 'Mr Uffington has sung your praises.'

'Sam so rarely speaks ill of anyone it is hardly a commendation.' An abrasive sort of voice, a hard, level look.

'You are unjust, sir. He told me you were a good, generous man who takes his obligations seriously.'

He was startled by the direct attack, tried not to show it, and fetched her a small glass of punch, standing morosely at her side to drink his own.

'I see you are inclined to be forthright, Ma'am.'

'You disapprove?'

'You must give me leave to reserve judgement until I know you better.'

There was a movement in the doorway and Sam entered, pink and sparkling, a sort of ardour about him as if he had just this moment left breastplate, lance and dying dragon in the hall.

'You may hear screams shortly,' he said, coming up to Lally and Truelove after greeting his hostess with distinctly chilly charm. 'I have left the dogs in the hall. It is forbidden but I have done it. Tom, you are spry and fit, I see. Have you told Mrs Fletcher about the cottage?'

'I find it extraordinary you suppose Mrs Fletcher would be interested.'

'But I have explained it all,' Sam cried and then, glancing round, lowering his voice, 'Do I have to go over it again?'

'I cannot believe Mrs Fletcher truly wishes to live in such a place and support herself on twenty pounds a year.'

'I do indeed,' said Lally. 'I have no money of my own, you know.'

So he had been told but he had not believed it. For proof he gazed at her intently yet again but found nothing to substantiate her claim, for her dress was very fine – not exactly new but very fine – and her hair, though unpowdered and simply dressed, was prettily done, unquestionably becoming. She was very thin, and her face was pale, the only trace left of India a kind of jaundiced shadow, but there was nothing there to indicate despair, extreme poverty, or anything else along those lines.

'JG is here,' she was telling Sam, nibbling the end of her fan.

'No doubt he will enliven the evening. It will be like letting off a firework in church: no possibility of his not being noticed. I do hope he will not mention bustards again. Do you know, he has been up my chimneys like a sweeper's boy prodding and poking and has found a barrel of spirits my father must have hid there forty years ago. We broached it and it was tolerable, a rum smoky taste. But I told him to stay on the ground in future, there were soot and jackdaw nests all over the house. He even had the effrontery to bang out his wig on my dining-room chairs.'

Truelove laughed at this and slapped Sam on the back, and said for sure it was well known in Lingborough and Ledworth and all points between that Mr Lovatt was a rare cove, a diehard eccentric, that his donkey had been seen wearing his wig, the wig was quite famous.

'He has a horse now,' said Sam, 'a skinny mean toad of a horse. He bought it from the gipsies down the Pightle. It runs like a deer, stands like a rock when you drop the reins, will even lie down on command. I reckon that horse has been on the road, been out by night, so to speak.'

'A highwayman's horse?' asked Truelove.

'Or a smuggler's,' said Sam.

There was something in the way he spoke that made Lally look up at him, but he smiled, perfectly amiable, the very picture of a man who did not know the meaning of devious, who had never heard of Machiavelli. When Truelove moved away to speak kindly to young Cecilia he said to Lally: 'Has JG told you about his purchase, his latest purchase? Well, I know nothing about ships, can row a flat-bottomed cockle on the river, that is all. No, and I know nothing about cutters, can only just tell a lugsail from a gaff. Lally, he has bought a hull; in truth, there is nothing else left of her. There we stood gazing at this wreck while he beamed and crowed and said what lines she had, how fast she would go, how this rigging or that would serve her best. There were a great many sly looks from all the men on the beach, knowing winks, that sort of thing. And yet ... Lally, that man knows everything there is to know about ships. What was he about?'

A voice at his elbow, a drift of perfume, a sweet face. Kate Brotherton stood smiling up at Sam with a wide, lovely smile. Sam's answering look was direct and approving, he could no more conceal his delight than a baby. She was very conscious of his admiration, nervously touching her dark ringlets, using her long lashes to their best effect. She was also conscious of

Lally's interested scrutiny, and she bore that less well, startled by such a calm, disinterested appraisal.

'The eldest Miss Brotherton is exquisite,' said JG, bringing Lally more punch a little later. 'Sam is confounded. Do you smell a match? Mrs Brotherton has a wary eye on him. She is sticking out for a better catch, I fear, though what better could there be? He comes of a good old family, has land, is the soul of integrity.'

'Integrity is all very well but it does not pay the bills. It is common knowledge Sam is hardly solvent.'

'Hmm. Yet I like his coat. *That* is new and he must have gone to some expense: it is most fashionable and the best quality.'

JG himself was respectable tonight in a coat of brown figured silk. He had brought himself to shave with more care than usual and his chin was only pardonably blue above the folds of his cravat. He hitched up his glasses and gazed about the room.

'I cannot pretend to admire Brotherton Junior; look how he admires himself. And what high colour, what sly eyes. He has inherited all his father's physical defects and none of his good humour. Rush told me he is only just holding his own against the creditors and his father has paid out thousands already to avoid a scandal. It is the talk of every pot-house from here to Lynn. Yet still he gambles and lays huge wagers as if he were a nabob. I should keep out of his way, dear love, he is not fit company for ladies. By the by, who is that lean dark fellow with the pocked face and fiery eyes?'

'You mean Truelove. I believe he counts as a neighbour of yours. The cattle who drink at the mill pond are his. He and Sam are overseers of the poor this year, and he owns the cottage I am determined shall be mine.'

'You say that with a martial grimness. Is there some doubt you will be appointed to teach at the poorhouse?'

'No; and yet . . . I suspect Mr Truelove does not like me. He is a puritan; look at his clothes, that grave face.'

'Your own is equally grave upon occasion and you are very

far from puritan. But dear girl, lead me in his direction, I shall do my best to charm him to your cause.'

Lally did so with misgivings but whatever passed between them must have been discreet and innocent, for Truelove offered his arm to lead her in to dinner, thereby cutting out by a fraction of a second Brotherton Junior and the curious Mr Chewton.

'I believe I have irritated poor Jack,' said Truelove as they sat down.

'I believe he is always that dangerous colour.'

'Sam told me he was fortunately at hand when your horse bolted.'

'Most fortunately.'

'And was he all solicitude, all charm?'

'Do I detect a note of mockery, Mr Truelove? Are you giving me your opinion of the man?'

'I am sure you know my opinion.'

Lally's mouth lifted at the corner. She turned to bend her ear politely to some remark of poor Simmons on her other side but she was still conscious of Truelove's gaze. She did not think he liked her at all but he was intrigued; she was quite certain he was intrigued.

Dinner was splendid: content and presentation could not be faulted. But it was clear everyone was going to take more than a civil interest in the tall girl at the end of the table, the girl who had once been married to one of the richest men in Madras. Even in Holt they could tell you about her, though there was inevitable disagreement about the extent of her fortune: were there not rubies in the case, purple rubies, uncut, with which she had fled Calcutta, creditors in droves lining the waterfront behind her? That Philadelphia had nerve, a saucy disregard for law. And if the inhabitants of Holt could see her now they might have believed anything, for the dress she was wearing had once been very fine indeed, gold brocade, expensive lace, and she wore it like a queen, there was no doubt of it, not gracefully but with an attractive bravado, a damn-all defiance in the angle of her head, the set of her slender shoulders. She might be worth ten pounds or ten thousand, it was impossible to tell.

A cataclysm of questions, intended to solve this mystery once and for all, drove Lally to take refuge in her wine glass, which proved no refuge at all, only a quick way to a very light head. She was aware of Sam's dark intelligent stare across quite half a mile of table and the wreck of the best meal she had eaten – and not tasted – in ten years, was aware of Jack Brotherton's bovine interest, the covert looks of his two sisters, his father's hearty friendliness, and of Mr Simmons being conspicuously attentive at her left elbow while Truelove was conspicuously silent at her right. This was worse than anything she had ever imagined.

Then suddenly she remembered Temple Purley, his touching gift of the cashmere muffler, his deep and genuine concern; and she remembered Sam's look of pure lust in the parsonage garden, and his surprise, as profound as hers. For some reason these two memories gave her the courage to lift her glass again, to study them all quite coolly over its rim and, catching JG's eye, to smile with unaffected delight.

'And her husband squandered the entire fortune?' Horace Brotherton said confidentially to Sam, filling his glass and spilling a little on the table for he was a clumsy man and had already drunk more than was good for his gout.

'So I believe.'

'All of it, God dammit? It's hard to swallow, man. He was worth something, they tell me, quite a prince in Madras. Are you sure it's all gone? You ought to snap her up, do yourself some good. Who knows, there might be a grain of truth in this ruby story Eliza brought home t'other day. I may not know a frill from a flounce but dresses like that one don't come at twenty guineas.'

Later he took the trouble to speak to Lally, took great pains in fact – and had some success. The awkwardness of their encounter in the shrubbery was not to be repeated. She did not blossom at his attention but she unbent, smiled gently on him, was quietly civil, and asked intelligent questions about the portraits on the walls – he knew nothing about art but he appreciated her interest. As for Lally, she recognised in him a bumbling, heavy-handed wish to please, the last vestige of childhood innocence: he would like her if he could, said his expression, though he was aware of her chequered history, her youthful misdemeanours. He could not help his bulbous features and huge hands; they were a trick of nature, like Lally's roman nose.

After dinner too there were cards, at which Lally confessed herself an idiot. How could she explain the sight of cards made her feel ill, the memory of Francis's endless parties, of the drinking, the debauchery, rising to choke her?

'You need some air,' was JG's blunt comment. There was a great deal of it outside, she only had to ask. But she shook her head, strands of pale hair blowing across her forehead. She said: 'You were right, Sam is captivated. Kate has a lovely face.'

JG cast an affectionate look in that direction. Why so he was. And yes, the girl was perfection, look at those dark curls, that adorable nose. But for his part he would rather have the younger sister, only eighteen and plump, unformed; in five years she would be charming, in fifteen beautiful. There was character there, strength of will, humour. Sam was welcome to Kate, she was too tender.

Lally put up a hand to her damp cheeks and felt the perspiration trickle beneath the tight lacing of her stays. The heat of the candles was overpowering. And there was something else: if she turned her head a little she could see herself in a vast gilded mirror, the light shimmering on the skirts of her dress, the cream lace cascading at her elbows. It was the Lally of Madras who sat there, except that her hair was unpowdered and she wore no jewels; and there beside her in the mirror was the shadow that was Francis, bending to speak softly in her ear: 'I beg, Madam, you are pleasant to my friends.'

She closed her eyes. It was hot, hot. The room stank of pomatum and spilled wine and candle grease. If she looked again in the mirror she would see the rubies round her neck, George's rubies, would see Francis stooping to lift them with a fat, covetous finger: 'Such a shame we have to give them up. But you could be hanged, my sweet, for stealing them.'

'I did not steal them.'

'But who will believe you?'

'My dear, are you unwell?' Eliza Brotherton was there, a large lady in pink.

'Mrs Fletcher has a headache,' said JG.

'Perhaps fresh air will cure it after all.' And Lally stood up, gathered her skirts, and departed in search of some.

Mrs Brotherton watched her go, perplexed. 'A most unaccountable young woman, so abrupt. So aloof.'

JG offered his arm. 'We must let India take the blame. They tell me it is hot, unbearably hot at certain times of the year. And they also tell me Mrs Fletcher's marriage was not a happy one.'

Mrs Brotherton sighed. 'That would certainly account for a great deal,' she said.

The terrace was occupied: Sam walked there in close conversation with Kate, and Chewton's daughter Fanny with bored Mr Simmons. The tuning of a viola within made both couples step back inside, and a moment later there was a muffled clapping, some exclamation, and the first bar of a popular melody. Lally, who had already reached the lawn, kept walking.

There were no large gardens at Cookhams, nearly all the land close to the house was given over to the park where Brotherton's prize cattle roamed and browsed. There were only a couple of grassy levels that passed as lawns and some grassy avenues between great oaks and beeches. It was down one of these avenues Lally was accosted by a greasy little figure with a pigtail and a clerical hat.

'Ho, and is it you, Mrs F? I thought it was one of them statues come alive.'

'What are you doing lurking in the bushes?'

'Them as asks no questions et cetera, et cetera, as His Lordship would say. If I was you I would trot back indoors, my lovely, and forget you ever saw me.'

She would not have obeyed, was summoning up a galaxy of protest, but just as suddenly as he had appeared he slipped back into the undergrowth with a distinct hiss, the branches swayed together, and he was gone.

'Mrs Fletcher, why are you not dancing?' asked a voice, a dread, well-known voice. Lally turned and there was Jack Brotherton brushing snuff off his velvet sleeve and smiling at her through the moonlight.

'I came out for some air.' Had he seen Rush? It would be difficult to tell if such a face was suspicious, even curious. She would not underestimate him though.

'Then may I escort you back to the house? You have been missed, Truelove has been asking for you, and Uffington, and your cousin' – here a grin that was intended to be both friendly and arch, and failed in both – 'perhaps she fears you have gone for a moonlight ride, come to grief again.'

Lally did not take his arm, walked apart, head up. 'I am sorry you find it necessary to remind me of my past iniquities, Mr Brotherton.'

They had reached the terrace. He turned, reached out, and captured her hand, raising it to his lips. 'Oh, I have forgiven you. You were half senseless at the time. No doubt you feared an attack upon your virtue.'

She would have snatched back her hand but he held it so tightly. His look was ludicrous, his intentions blatant.

'Should I fear one still?' she asked in a low, furious voice.

'Would it displease you?'

She got her hand away at last, took the steps two at a time in a maddened rush, fled the terrace like a gazelle, scarcely touching the ground. In the doorway she collided with Sam, who shot one look at the pursuing Jack Brotherton and took Lally's arms in an unconsciously painful grip.

'He has not insulted you?'

'No, nothing serious: a childish exchange. I do believe he

was trying to play the gallant, had no evil intentions at all. When he looks at me all he sees are rubies. Oh Sam, Sam, please don't step out! You must not be so fierce. Quick, come in.'

She had not called him by his first name before. She saw his face soften. But then, hearing the footsteps on the terrace, he hurried her away into the next room on the excuse of a glass of wine. In the next room were the card players, the more elderly among the party, and beyond were the musicians, well into their limited repertoire, and the dancers.

Lally would not dance. She had not been noted for her grace, she said in Sam's ear, agility yes, but not grace, in the old days at Lingborough Hall. 'It takes a man of courage to stand up with me,' she said, 'a man of quite foolhardy courage and very well shod.'

Sam laughed. He had a large, unaffected laugh and several faces turned in their direction. Kate, dancing with Simmons, looked slightly reproachful. What could that unattractive Indian widow say to make him burst out like that? And she herself was only smiling that faint, careful smile.

'Where is JG?' Lally was asking, peering about.

'I last saw him talking partridges to Turner, who had never previously considered the wretched things except to eat them. Sit down and I will fetch you that wine. Look, there is that minx Cecy Brotherton gazing soulfully at Tom Truelove. She has some most unbecoming habits.'

But Tom Truelove, unaffected, strolled across to Lally and made a courtly leg. Would she dance? He was not a great hand at a minuet but she was welcome to try him in these sort of country dances. Lally shook her head and then, remembering Sam's stricture to be kind, asked if he would not sit beside her and tell her exactly what it was to be an overseer of the poor. He was cornered, could not refuse, was reluctant to accept. He sat down with bad grace and cleared his throat. Sam returned with the wine, exchanged a few words, and was snatched from them by the parson who had incontrovertible evidence someone had been in the crypt again.

110

'Smuggled gin has been in his crypt again, I'll wager,' said Truelove to Lally in an undertone. 'He may lock and bar the place as he likes but he will never get the better of the smugglers.'

She drank the wine a little quickly. Her eyes sparkled. She was aware of his stealthy glance as if, even now, he did not know how to take her, as if she astonished him.

'Where is JG?' she asked.

As if in answer the dancing ended, the few couples left the floor, and there, on a little gold sofa just big enough for two at the far end of the room, sat JG and her cousin Anne, their heads close together and their obvious enjoyment visible to all.

'By God,' said Truelove, 'the parson must watch out.'

'The parson seems more worried about his crypt,' said Lally lightly.

She had a bewildered, empty feeling. She could not identify it: jealousy, disappointment, fear? A combination perhaps. Surely though, he meant nothing serious by it? But even as she thought it she saw his hand move to rest on Anne's bare arm, saw Anne's look that was the return of that caress, and heard a voice deep inside herself cry no, no, I love him, I do ...

And Tom Truelove, looking up, surprised the tears in her eyes.

CHAPTER 10

The dismal hoot of the peacocks made Lally pause half way up the long avenue to the house. It was cool under the beeches, cool and pleasant, and up until that moment there had only been the soft crooning of the wood pigeons and the distant bleating of sheep to break the heavy summer silence. There it was again, that strange, haunting cry.

After a minute she forced herself to go on, though the spring had gone from her step and she looked about with a bleak, incurious expression as she came in sight of Luffwell Hall at last. It was grandiose, a dark, inhuman pile set down in this lovely place a century before and looking what it was: gloomy and cold. The trees grew too near the house and the land fell away too steeply from it down to the river which, unsuccessfully dammed to make a lake, had spread into a rushy marsh.

Sir George was out. His wife was effusively welcoming, said there was nothing she did not know about Lally's contract, she had been primed by Mrs Brotherton – at length – by poor crippled Mrs Greeves, by the curate. All the details were written down here and here, and there was this ledger and that, and how was it that Lally had come alone, where was her cousin Anne, surely business could be combined with pleasure?

Lally was perhaps even more stately than usual, sobered by the hoot of the peacocks, and there was a high, becoming colour in her cheeks: Luffwell was three miles from Lingborough parsonage and she had walked briskly. Harriet Stapleford allowed herself to be impressed.

'How long it is since we last met,' she said when the more tedious business of the morning was disposed of. 'Why, you were quite a child. I remember your aunt was so upset by all that silly gossip, oh, you remember … The whole neighbourhood talked of nothing but you and Charlie for a month after you were shot on the Heath. Nothing so exciting had happened for years.'

Lally sipped her tea. 'I do not remember. I did not leave my room for a fortnight and then was not allowed out of the house.'

Harriet, who was a gaunt, grey, sensible woman of fifty, sighed and shook her head. 'It was a wonder to everyone you even lived. George has never forgotten his first sight of you on that sofa at Cookhams, he often speaks of it. He said there was a pool of blood upon the carpet. I trust he exaggerates – if not, that would explain old Valentine's seizure. But that night has gone down in history, my dear, and will be remembered and embellished until it can be remembered and embellished no more. For myself I always held it against your cousin Charlie that he left you quite alone to face the music; no, I never thought Charlie came out of the business very well. Of course the poor boy was a hothead, not like Edward in the least. Edward was such a … such a pudding' – an amused lift of slim grey brows and a tilted smile – 'but to leave you like that … And afterwards he did not acquit himself at all honourably.'

'He did not want my aunt to send me to India.'

'Well, of course he did not. And nor did I. I had been her friend for many years and I told her openly I thought it was a mistake, that I did not think it proper to treat you differently from her own daughters. Windham had never done so. But she was set on it, the idea was in her head. Vane might have put it there – do you remember Vane? – for his youngest child went into the Company, did very well in China for two years until he died of a fever out there. Still, the more we tried to dissuade her the more determined she became. She was afraid Charlie was going to run away with you, you know.'

Lally knew. Her eyes had lost their colour, were sea grey, and there was a pinched look about her lovely mouth. How strange, how very strange the past should be so clear, so close;

it was not even as if the intervening eleven years did not have their own sharp memories, even more terrible. There was an old lacquered clock on the shelf, the same broad Turkey carpet on the floor. She had come here long ago with the girls, the belles of Lingborough, her adopted sisters: Julia, Maria, Anne, Pippa, Jane. But that had been before … Before India.

You are going to India … Imagine how pleasant it could be, the constant sunshine, the sights … What opportunities must be there … Her aunt at the breakfast table: how bright the sunshine had been on the white cloth … Pass the marmalade Lally, oh how lucky you are, I wish I could go … And later, much later, Charlie, grasping her hands until the slender bones cracked, crying: 'Don't go! Never go! Come away with me. I won't let them treat you so shamefully. They want you out of the way. They want you to marry some nabob, some poxy pontificating nabob old enough to be your father. You will die out there. I shall never see you again.'

'My dear,' said Harriet, 'I have distressed you, talking about the old days. Forgive me. Come, we must put the past behind us. Have you time to walk in the orangery? George will be disappointed not to see you. He admires you so much, you know.'

'I did not know.'

'Oh, but yes. He is quite as much your champion as Sam Uffington.'

'I do not consider Sam Uffington …'

Harriet ushered her through a door into the sweet, damp, warm world of the hothouses. Lally looked about in amazement.

'Oh, it is George's passion – he has grown pineapples, the most remarkable melons. He has become a recluse because of it. You were about to say … Ah, yes, dear Sam is your champion. He has moved heaven and earth to make sure the parson raised no objection to your teaching, has wrangled with Tom Truelove, his old and cherished friend, over that disgraceful cottage, and has lauded your virtues to Mrs Brotherton until she is giddy.'

'He feels sorry for me.'

'I dare say. He has a kind heart. But perhaps there is more to it. Even the heart of a confirmed bachelor cannot help but be moved by the promise of rubies.'

'There are no rubies in the case.'

'I thought there might not be. How sad! We lead such dull lives here, we were so depending on the rubies.'

Lally, who had momentarily become entangled in a damp, clinging swathe of greenery, said in a muffled voice and with no attempt at subtlety: 'Why did Anne not marry Mr Uffington? She is not happy in her glorious parsonage.'

'My dear, she would not have been happy at Rooks Hill. As to why she would not marry him, she would not marry him because Fanny pressed for Mr Glover. She treated Sam shabbily, everyone said so, for certainly there was an understanding between them, but there, she did not return his love and could never have borne Rooks Hill which he would die for. I often think that no affection at all is better than affection on one side: nothing so bitter as unrequited love.'

They moved on. Harriet was as active as Lally, forged through the jungle. In due course they had admired all there was to admire in the way of fruit and turned about.

'Mr Truelove does not like me,' said Lally, as if thinking aloud.

'He is very wary of women, they have brought him nothing but pain. I expect he has never met anyone like you.'

'You are laughing.'

'I was thinking how he might have behaved had he been obliged to pluck you from the beck like Jack Brotherton.'

'He would have behaved perfectly correctly.'

'So he would. What a shame it was not Sam then. He would have shouted at you.'

'Are you certain?'

'Quite certain. Do not be fooled by his easy manner. I have always suspected he would make the most terrible enemy, quite ruthless.'

Lally looked back over her shoulder, gave a direct, devilish look between the moist leaves: 'You like him very much.'

Harriet swiped the plants aside. 'For heaven's sake, let us go in the house. Yes, I like him. He has been a good neighbour to us. And do you know, I do believe he is in love with you.'

Lally came over the brow of a shingly bank and there was the stony beach, the sea a deep blue, swelling and roaring. She sat down and looked out across the water and saw the patched lugsails far out, and gulls, gulls high up and leaning on the everlasting wind. The summer peace and stillness of the Ledworth valley was far inland; she had left the last of it at the shingle bank. Here there was somehow always rushing air and movement and noise.

After a while she took off her shoes and walked down to the edge of foam and stood, watching the bubble and hiss at her feet. She was blinded by the sun dazzle, and the intense blue, and the salty breeze. She was blinded by tears too. She cried passionately at last, as if only now she could own to the horror and revulsion and anguish. She thought she would choke on the tears, on the great deep sobs like a child's. After a while the frantic wiping of her face left huge streaks and blotches, and her hair fell down a little to hang on her cheek, and the water poured over her feet and soaked her hem. Heaven help her, she was a fool. And all this brought on by an innocent visit to Luffwell Hall and the cry of a peacock.

She began to scramble back up the beach, panting, sliding, the soft determined wind whipping her hair across her wet face. There was a man coming towards her. He limped – a distressing limp.

'Are you all right?' was his shouted question.

Lally's anger at her own stupidity, mixed with a certain shame anyone should see her so reduced, made her look at him with sceptical disfavour. The wind played havoc with her hair. She could not see him properly. She put up her hands, clearing her field of vision. What must she look like? She had been weeping furiously, had ruined her face, her clothes …

116

'May I walk with you back to the village?'

Did he think she was lost? Insane? 'No, I thank you.'

'But you are crying. How can I leave you here alone?'

She fought her hair, stared out at him. He was a stocky man, had a wrestling physique. He wore his own hair in a long queue and it was auburn streaked with grey, yet he did not look very old and the lines on his face had been put there by wind, weather and concentration, not time. He was in brown country clothes, plain, decent, conservative brown, and his hat was clamped under his arm. He looked respectable, he looked almost comically concerned, and he looked completely at a loss.

He bore her scrutiny well. He gave a quirky smile at last and said cheerfully: 'I have forgot my manners, Ma'am. Forgive me. My name is Bensley Vernon, captain of the Revenue cutter *Spaniel*.'

And he fell into step beside her as she turned to walk inland.

'Are you in pursuit of Miss Brotherton?' JG demanded as he and Sam gazed down from their hide amidst the bracken and gorse to the coast road and the marshes.

'No. No, it would be hopeless if I were. I am too old now to caper about after a pretty girl in the company of men ten years younger and ten times as eligible. I need a good plain country woman who knows how to cook dumplings.'

'My dear Sam, don't give yourself away for a dumpling.'

'As for Kate herself,' continued Sam, having fallen into a reverie, plucking savagely at the heather stems, 'I have been thinking how much like Anne she is, that perhaps seven tenths of the attraction is nostalgia.'

'How commendably precise you are. For sure they are both small and dark.'

Sam turned on his back, closed his eyes, and listened to the larks.

'God dammit what a business, just to get a wife,' he said.

'You could advertise – I have seen it done. You co ld buy a

117

poor woman from a husband who does not want her. You might, by devious means, buy a virgin. Just so, with some trifling lip service to civilised behaviour, Lally Fletcher was bought and sold on the Calcutta waterfront.' And then, dropping his voice as if musing on some inner vision of his own: 'A noble bosom, noble.'

But his eye, his keen, experienced eye, had been caught by two figures down below, a short vigorous man and a tall gipsy woman. It was Lally herself, by God, he declared, leaping up and running down the hill, flailing his arms and shouting.

Sam's first thought was that there had been an accident. Now, looking closely as he came up, he perceived a very mutinous, very scarlet Lally under the disordered hair. And she tipped her head back as if daring him to comment. A mass of curls fell down about her face, a blotched face, indescribably grubby. She had been weeping, weeping a great deal. And her hem was wet.

'I am quite all right,' she said, strikingly cool. 'This gentleman was seeing me back to Lingborough.'

Bensley Vernon, having been introduced, gave no sign he was going to abandon his self-appointed task. He regarded Sam and JG with a rather blank, good-natured expression, perhaps not surprising in view of their state of undress: no coats, no neckcloths, no hats – in JG's case no shoes or stockings, and the tanned, piratical look of them. Lally found herself assuring him again that the gentlemen were her friends, but when they set off the last half mile to Lingborough Vernon was still with them, the very picture of a puzzled and good-natured sheepdog.

Sam offered Lally his arm. Would she rather walk with JG? JG was inconvenienced by the loss of his boots, he was walking tenderly, keeping as far as possible to the close-cropped turf. The boots had been left behind a gorse bush on the Heath, but which bush who could say?

They walked on towards the parsonage two by two, JG and Bensley Vernon slowly dropping behind. The Revenue man turned out to be acquainted with Linnaean theory, with dotterels and shrikes and any kind of warbler. A rarefied, intense, elliptical conversation pursued Sam and Lally, stepping out with a false heartiness in front. Once, unable to resist it, she turned to look at him and met his shining eye.

'They seem to have found common ground,' he said in a low voice.

'Yes indeed.'

'Well, if it preserves me from these pestilential forays through the undergrowth with a spy-glass, always being told to hush, and keep flat, and then when I do being roused out immediately to look at some perfectly ordinary brown bird fidgeting in a gorse bush – if it means I am let off to start shearing my wheat, my blessings are on Mr Vernon's head. Dear God, how I have suffered!'

'Ah.'

'Now you are laughing at me.' It was true. A delighted, ludicrous grin blazed from her ravaged face. All the humour she had once possessed and he had never seen flashed across it, so that for a heartbeat she was another person entirely. And then it was gone, the light and the dancing laughter, and her face was closed again, and secret, and all he could see as she bowed her head was the wild flight of freckles over her nose.

They turned in at the parsonage gate. A feeling of being watched overcame them. There was the muted clamour of barking dogs. Behind, some way behind, JG and the animated Vernon toiled on at a snail's pace, and there were several shouts, gleeful exclamations, and JG's distinctive crowing laughter blown on the mild breeze.

'Will you dare sail in JG's cutter?' Lally asked, coming to a stop at the steps. She looked back, shading her sore eyes, and wondered at the sight: a Revenue man and a smuggler practically arm in arm.

'In *Snipe*? It would not make me feel guilty to refuse the invitation. Tossing up and down on the sea don't appeal to me, especially in a cutter. I could endure something the size of your Indiaman now.'

'Is it called *Snipe*?'

'I believe so. And I believe JG would thank you for referring to it as she. In my experience on this coast sailors grow marvellous crotchety if you neglect their customs; there is no one to beat their sticking to custom except perhaps the farm labourer who does this or that simply because his grandfather did so and his grandfather and so forth. Now what are they at?' and Sam made urgent gestures at the two gentlemen deep in problematical quotations from some noted authority. 'Oh, infernal . . . Are they to stand there yapping about ruffs and grebes all day? Look, you must go in, Lally. Leave them to me.'

'But they must come in. Anne would . . . Anne would be so disappointed to miss JG.'

Sam's brows snapped together. 'He is barefoot.'

He had forgotten it in his enthusiasm for declaiming Brisson, but he walked crouchingly upon the gravel, looking for all the world like a large ape. Lally, who had passed through so many moods since setting out in determined cheerfulness for Luffwell Hall, found all the grief and suffocating self-pity of the beach drained away, and in its place the strangest desire to laugh and laugh. Since laughter had ceased to have any place in her life this made her oddly light-headed.

'I agree,' said Sam heavily, 'they are like something from a low comedy, the very lowest comedy.'

'But how happy they are.'

'JG is never happier than when talking birds. Or ships. Wait until they discover their mutual interest in ships.'

This happy moment still seemed a long way off: they were arguing a point about plovers, what plovers could not be made out by the watchers on the step, but definitely plovers, a living demonstration of their flight and a recognisable whistle were included. This last, creditably performed by the Revenue officer, signalled the end of Lally's self-control. She swayed sideways and grasped Sam's convenient arm, turning her face into his sleeve with a broken murmur of: 'I cannot bear it – no boots, and flapping about on the gravel like a monkey with wings, and whistling . . . Oh Sam, take me in. I shall die.'

He did so. In the hall she detached herself, aware she had overstepped the bounds of ordinary friendship. He was laughing himself and did not seem to mind it, however. His look was as amiable as ever.

Looking back, long afterwards, she knew that moment was a turning point, that nothing was quite the same again. The touch of his hand on hers as he had moved to lead her through the door, that crazy laughter bubbling up in both of them, had sent a message, whether he knew it or not: desire, deep affection, esteem. She remembered what Harriet had said, and blushed, and her heart, which had slowed and quietened, raced away again foolishly. She shook out her stained skirts and poked at the wreck of her hair, and walked with a calm assurance she did not feel to the parlour door.

Inside Anne and Kate Brotherton sat at a small table playing cards.

'I have brought you some visitors,' said Lally.

CHAPTER 11

'Perhaps she was abroad too long,' Anne remarked tentatively to Sam at a musical evening in Holt a week later. 'She's so . . . so unsettling.'

That Lally Fletcher was unsettling, would be unsettling in all but the most broadminded household, Sam acknowledged. But then, what had her life in India been like? She was stiff with everyone except children, except JG, and even there lately she had seemed reserved. Only that once by the parsonage lake, and once on the parsonage doorstep, and perhaps up on the Heath when he had asked her about the poorhouse, had he caught sight of the Lally she must once have been.

'She says nothing about the past,' sighed Anne. They were seated side by side in complementary tedium, listening to the grating of the local chamber orchestra, three gentlemen with more enthusiasm than ability and a staggering facility for choosing all the longest pieces ever written. Sam, who was bored to death, sat with a fixed expression of polite attention, his eyes glazing over. And then across the room he caught a glimpse of a blue dress, of a bent, attentive head. She was listening, drumming her fingers on her knee; ringless fingers, she never wore jewellery. She had an attitude of fierce concentration, the arpeggio was hardly worth it, and Sam fancied she had strayed far away in place and time.

It seemed to Sam suddenly that it was a cruel twist of fate that would seat him next to one woman he had lost and opposite one he might long to possess in vain. But his good humour never deserted him for long. He beat out the rhythm on his buckled knee and half closed his eyes.

'Kate is here,' Anne was saying, sinking her voice to the almost inaudible. 'She has talked nothing but Mr Vernon ever

122

since Lally introduced him.'

'Well, I hope the young man does not entertain false hopes, at Cookhams a man of his calling must be classed lower than a toad.'

'What a curious way of putting it.'

A general shushing in their vicinity put an end to the conversation. Anne blushed prettily and hid behind her fan. Sam, glancing down at her pink ear, her sweeping lashes, wondered if it was true she had a *tendresse* for JG. She had certainly grown wonderfully solicitous over his bare feet that day, had been in a strange, heated state. He had never seen her like it. It had come to him then that she might be suffering, though unconsciously, those same desires he felt for Lally Fletcher. He found it a sobering thought. He had nothing but affection for JG but he did not underestimate him in the least. It would not be out of character for him to seduce the parson's wife. No doubt the thought he might, and the hope he would not, was the cause of Lally's unease. And what of Lally herself? If she did not love JG then Sam did not know what love was, though to be sure it was a simple, immutable love, he had seen it between twins, as if they could share sensation and thought.

Such complicated reflections, sinking more and more into the abstruse and philosophical, began to make his head ache. He was not in the mood for it, and besides, he cared too deeply for all concerned. He should not have come to this damn concert, he decided, it was too much after a day in the fields. The room was hot, painfully hot, and the scraping and plucking hurt his ears. No, he should not have come. He would have to be out in the Folly Piece at dawn to greet the reapers. He sank down in his chair and his eyes closed. When he opened them again, it was because the music was finished and the applause was dying away. Anne was shaking his arm.

'Were you asleep? It is over. Sam?'

He blinked like a cat, resisted the overpowering urge to stretch, and stood up. Out of the corner of his eye he saw Lally standing too, cornered by voluble Mrs Brotherton and joined in a moment by the parson, a look of unyielding disapproval in every feature. He said something; Mrs Brotherton started, Lally bridled. Sam, pushing his way towards them with poor Anne in tow, caught the tail end of a remark about horn books and catechisms. He was two paces from them when Lally looked up and gave him a queer, burning look born entirely of her unspeakable longing to strike the parson dead.

Shock, unsteady breathing, crazy desire: all these he felt and all together, so that the room receded, he was left with nothing in focus but her eyes, wide and blue, staring straight into his.

'Lord,' said Eliza Brotherton, 'how sour you look, Sam Uffington. Was the music not to your taste?'

He murmured some profound lie, did not look at Lally, declared his intention of returning to Rooks Hill at once, he must be up in the morning before the men were abroad. In spite of this he found himself some moments later in a stuffy back room where refreshments were being offered, and not only that but next to Lally, who was looking hot and distracted.

'That last piece,' he remarked, having secured her a lemonade. 'You did not like it.'

'You slept through it.'

'Not all of it.'

'It brought back memories. I am afraid so many things bring back the memories of Madras.'

'How quiet a backwater this must seem to you after being mistress of a great house.'

'I do not complain.'

They retreated from the crush. They were very formal with each other. Whatever her life had been like, he surmised, she had had some bad experiences with men; or one man, by whom she now judged all others. It was quite clear she was frightened by what she had read in his face and his touch, she who, until now, had not seemed frightened of anything. He would have to step carefully if he wanted to bring this business to any kind of conclusion. But did he? She was not a light, careless girl he could take on his own terms and leave without regret, and in any case the matter was more complex, more tangential than a purely physical attraction. Did he then want to strike out into the deep water he had avoided so diligently?

'How thoughtful you are,' she said, with a shy, puzzled look. He noticed she kept just far enough away to avoid contact, buffeted as she was by the press of concert-goers. She would never put her head on his shoulder and laugh again: the consequences were too dire.

'Thoughtful? Oh, something came into my head. What was it? "What is life but a vale of affliction?"'

He saw the spark in her eye, that dear, troubled blue eye. 'Good heavens, who said that?'

Sam thought a while. Then he smiled his slow pleasant smile and was rewarded by a flicker of response in her face, a trace of the trust and mild affection she had had for him until a little while ago.

'I forget,' he said.

The weather stayed fine. The air was full of the rhythmic swish swish of the sickles in the cornfields, and Sam rose early and worked late, sometimes until the moon was riding up over his tattered copses and the last of his men had been home in bed an hour. He worked with a concentrated energy, leading, driving, rallying the harvest gangs or taking up a spare sickle himself when a man dropped out. He drove hard certainly but there were no complaints, for he swung and sweated with the least of them, asked no man to do anything he would not try himself. Rather they wondered at him, for his stubborn endurance on so little sleep, for all his unstinting effort. Still, it was well known the harvest would make or break him. A good year this year and perhaps the farm would begin to pay. He deserved it, they said, he was a fair master.

The day came when the last sheaf was carried home triumphant and JG came to share the customary feast, and Sam went to bed with an aching head and slept for ten hours. He woke with the certain knowledge that ten days' hard labour had done nothing to change his feelings towards Lally Fletcher. He had thought he had paid the penance for lust; it seemed it was not so.

Two days later he met her, something he had been putting off. He had ridden down to The Ship House to see JG and had found him from home, Bensley Vernon in occupation. Vernon had been slashed in the leg with a cutlass in some minor brush with smugglers off Lynn and was on shore till it mended. The process was slow, the wound had been deep and complicated, but he was due to go back to sea in a week or so. Until then, tiring of his raucous and grasping landlady at the Lingborough Plough, he had taken lodging with JG and was now, as he explained to Sam, up to the ears in *Vegetable Statics*, Ray and Adam Smith thrown in for light relief. He seemed remarkably cheerful even though his host had vanished, had already been missing twenty-four hours. Oh, it was nothing, said Vernon, Rush said he often spent two or three days on the marshes.

Sam was about to ask, in what he hoped would be a convincingly roundabout way, if Vernon had dared show his face at Cookhams, if he had paid his respects to Kate Brotherton – there was no question he was smitten – when the drum of hooves on the baked ground and the splash of water made him look up.

'I do believe it was Mrs Fletcher' – Vernon had been by the open door – 'She will come a real tumble if she carries on like that. Don't she give a damn for broken bones?'

'Not that I have noticed.'

'Well, she was riding JG's roan. She will not enjoy a toss from that. It has wicked long yellow teeth.'

The real possibility that the roan horse had been bolting came to them both at the same time. 'I'll go after her,' said Sam.

It was no easy task. The lady had two fields' start and was riding like the devil. He could not gain on her at all. He only came up with her at last because she had pulled up to look down at the homeward-bound harvesters on the wheatfields of Brotherton's land. She was in her old riding habit and her hair was all swept up under her old, lace-trimmed hat. The speed, the physical effort of staying in the saddle – a man's saddle with a pistol on it – had brought colour to her cheeks. She looked, he thought, as handsome as she could ever look.

'You have come to reprimand me,' she said at once as soon as she saw who it was.

'Of course not. I thought you were being run away with, would come to grief. But where is JG? And how did you come by his horse? Bensley Vernon is at The Ship House and told me he disappeared early yesterday.'

'He is often away,' she said, rubbing the hogged neck of the roan with the butt of her whip. 'I met him in the lane by Cookhams and borrowed his horse for a moment in exchange for the parsonage pony. I was on my way to badger Mr Hayes about the catechisms.'

'That man is not to be allowed out. What possessed him to put you up on an animal unfit for a tinker let alone a lady? You ought to get off before he pulls your arms out.'

Her look was the old challenging one, her seat was indisputably firm. At any moment, he thought, she would laugh at him. 'It is far too hot to argue,' she said. 'Will you ride back with me to find JG? Then you may ask him yourself where he has been. Until a few minutes ago he was at Cookhams, taking Mrs Brotherton a gift of some exotic fruit he came across in Holt. He said she was overwhelmed.'

The likelihood of exotic fruit in Holt seemed so remote the idea alone might overwhelm lesser ladies than Eliza Brotherton. The thought of JG presenting it solemnly to that statuesque lady, having first hitched up his glasses and pulled down his wig, made Sam laugh out loud.

'I do believe he was at Cookhams on Mr Vernon's account,' Lally remarked, turning to ride beside him. 'Mr Vernon has been mortally stricken by the lovely Kate.'

'You introduced them. It happened under our noses if I remember correctly.'

Lally remembered too. Bensley Vernon had bent over

Kate's hand, wished her good day, and fallen in love.

'Do you hold me responsible?'

'How could I? He may have found you on the beach, or you found him, it hardly matters; but it was JG invited him into the parsonage, almost thrust him through the door.'

'He intends to make a match, you know. He told me just now he could not bear the sight of poor Vernon moping about, knowing full well it was ten to one Kate was doing the same.'

There was a silence. A week or two ago it would have been a companionable silence, but now it was a little constrained, a little too long. The roan horse jogged a little and misbehaved in a mild way as they passed his stable at the mill, and Rush's unmistakable voice could be heard cursing someone or something in the back regions. The silence lengthened, lengthened.

'Do you suspect JG of an underhand motive?' Sam asked when he could bear it no longer.

'In pushing Vernon's suit? I could not say. But did not Mandeville say that the mainspring of human actions is selfishness?'

They were approaching Ledworth when they saw in front of them a long-legged man in blue on a fat docile pony with a lady's saddle, singing a bawdy piece about bosoms and legs ho ho, pull the something. The apparition looked up at the thud of approaching hooves and gave a shout that might have reached from one ship to another some way off in the midst of a battle.

'How well she rides. Do you not think so, Sam?'

'Did you not think she would fall?'

'Fall? Why should she? And being Lally she would get up again at once.'

His knee was crooked round the nearside pommel, some mysterious packages were dangling from the offside one, and his wig was on the back of his head. 'I fear I have eaten a good half of your apricots, Lally dear. I do hope they were not intended as a present.'

128

She dismounted and came to look in the basket. 'Those were given to me by Mrs Turner for the parson's dessert. I believe Mr Uffington is right, you are not fit to be in society and should be closely confined in future for all our sakes.'

Her remark seemed to strike JG as wryly amusing. A look passed between him and Lally that Sam could not interpret, nor perhaps did he want to, being stabbed by blunt, irrational jealousy. There it was again, that silent, amicable question and answer between them, not even the lift of a brow, simply a look, each to each, and complete understanding. He scowled, was moved by an imp of irritability to say: 'You could always replenish Lally's basket at Luffwell Hall. Was that not where you stole the "exotic fruit" I have heard about?'

It had been a shot at a venture, a sour little calumny, not at all premeditated, but Sam was not too slow to see the flicker of a nerve, the involuntary tightening of JG's mouth, the minute signals that his words had found a mark.

He looked at Lally but she was busy with the pony's girth.

'I see you are still suffering the effects of your harvest supper,' said JG, getting up on the roan. 'You are crabbed and out of sorts. Rush has a sovereign remedy, it never fails. Ride back with me and we shall see if we cannot cure you.' And then, after a pause to gather his reins: 'Vernon is there, you know, that ruddy, good-natured fellow. He is reading all my books systematically, beginning with the first one on the top shelf. He has no conversation but birds, ships and smuggling, drinks like a sailor, eats like a sailor, and no doubt in a tight corner can swear like a sailor, but oh, oh my dear Sam, how tedious is a man in love! I have resolved to bring him and his love together simply for the sake of peace and quiet, and he is so perfectly right for her: solid, dependable, realistic, cheerful. What does it matter he has no money, she has enough. So I am set up as match-maker. I have poured honey into Mrs Brotherton's ear an hour or more, have agreed with her every statement on every subject from plums to parlour curtains, and I have her promise Kate may come to tea at The Ship House if little Mrs Glover comes to chaperone. There!

What do you think of that as a stratagem?'

Sam saw Lally's eyebrows lift, her slim figure stiffen slightly. She might have been appalled, she might have been trying not to laugh.

'Mrs Glover?'

'And Lally, it goes without saying. What do you think? Vernon and Kate may sit on my loveseat, may whisper what they will without let or hindrance.'

'And you and Mrs Glover will sit in the window seat and do the same, I suppose?' growled Sam in a voice he prayed Lally could not hear.

'How crabbed you are indeed, what have I done to deserve it? Are you accusing me of making love to Mrs Glover?'

'Hush. I am not accusing you of anything. It was only something …'

'Something?'

'Something Mandeville wrote,' said Sam, wheeling his horse alongside the parsonage pony and asking with a false smile whether he could not escort Lally to the curate's cottage. She answered his false smile with a falser one, but assented, woke up the pony, trotted on. It seemed to Sam a gulf had opened between them, that he would never cross it now unless he wooed and won her, a hazardous, doomed venture.

They rode on, side by side, JG trailing behind, his spy-glass to his eye.

The party was fast deteriorating into a brawl.

Sam, JG, and Bensley Vernon were at the fire, the curate was at the table dismembering the loaf, the children playing hide and seek beneath it, and Anne, the two Brotherton girls and Lally banished to the far corner with the jam pots.

It was late on an overcast afternoon. A small chill wind was lifting the fronds of willow and ruffling the river water, and in the meadows the cows were chewing the cud with the resigned look of those who sense a deluge in the offing. The low room with its smoky beams was warm but gloomy, and growing gloomier as the light faded and faded outside. By the noises that came from the hearth it seemed the fire was being mean-spirited, the muffins would not toast.

'Will it never draw? Damn it! Pass me the poker!' cried Sam.

'Did you know that I have filled two notebooks with my observations on the owls?' said JG.

'No, I did not. I would not expect the subject to warrant two whole notebooks.' A heave of the poker and a volcano of sparks, then nothing but the angry glow of defeat. After another minute there was an inch of flame, an inch and a half, but at Sam's sitting back on his heels it settled again and the damp wood hissed miserably.

'This will never do.' Vernon was nibbling at his uncooked muffin. 'Can't we use the fire in the kitchen?'

'Rush is exceedingly jealous of his furnace. Besides, the kitchen stinks of corruption. JG has been embalming again.'

Sam lodged another beech log across the others with considerable precision but the fire rejected all blandishments, sank lower and lower.

There was a rustle of skirts. 'Let me do it,' said Lally.

She knelt on the rug, fearlessly destroying what they had taken a painstaking half hour to build, and covering her hands with ash. A great deal of trickery with old handbills, the Norwich newspaper, some dry twigs and judicious blowing began to take effect.

'There,' she sat back on her heels and looked at the steady flames.

'How competent you are,' said JG with a gleam of his usual mockery. 'Next you will tell us you have built fires outdoors, have cooked rabbits on spits.'

She looked up into his dark, devilish, mobile face. He was laughing at her. Every feature was composed, but he was laughing at her. He knew as well as Anne, who was darting troubled glances from the background, that a whole warren of rabbits, and some few pheasants and partridges, had been cooked over secret fires under the direction of that mountebank Charlie.

'I dare say I could do it if I tried,' she replied, and without thinking she turned to smile at Sam, still kneeling beside her. He returned the smile, serious but kind; he was not going to join in any banter. He made to help her up but she shook her head, ignored his offered hand, shook out her skirts and smoothed them down as if that was the most urgent thing in the world.

Then Edward and three-year-old Rosa came up with two of JG's pipes clasped between their teeth. It was a welcome diversion. Lally was shaken, quite as shaken, she thought in a wry attempt to bring herself to her senses, as if he had kissed her. Only Francis had ever kissed her on the mouth; that too was one of the experiences she had hoped to put behind her. Thank heaven Edward was asking her something, she would have to stoop to listen, and take his hand.

'Let's ask Rush,' she managed at last, and they went out and into the back regions like conspirators. Rush was not there but the door to the mill was half open. They swung it wide and called.

He came at once, pattering across the wooden boards. He was flustered, even deranged, and he had dust and meal flour all over his breeches. Still, he smiled his gappy smile when he saw who they were, was restored to something like his usual self, said no, there was no milk whatsoever, but there was ale, cider, small beer and gin. Lally repeated that Mrs Glover wished to drink tea and besides, the children must have milk. Why? demanded Rush. He had drunk Geneva as a nipper. No, no milk in the house, but the goat was on the river bank yonder. Then where was a bucket? A pan? A jug?

Lally and Edward picked their way to the goat's browsing place beyond the willows, and Lally milked a pint into the cracked blue jug while Edward fed muffin to the obliging nanny. There were great purple clouds massing over the hill and the cold, heavy, draughty prelude to a storm. Above their heads the leaves shivered and there was a strange light to the river, a lurid, metallic glow.

'Here's Sam,' said Edward, and Lally's nerves turned unreliable in an instant. She released the goat, peered dourly into the jug. It would only just be enough and the tea would taste.

'I think perhaps you should return with all speed,' said Sam. 'It is not so much JG's atrocious exhibitionism but the glowing promissory looks between Kate and Vernon. Anne does not seem to be taking any notice.'

Rush was more forthright when he detained her in the kitchen to suggest she strained the milk through some muslin, the jug had been none too clean.

'Have you noticed' – with a leer and a poke of his head – 'which way the wind is blowing? Little dark women! A little dark woman'll be the death of him. Never could resist 'em. Here, hold it steady, Mrs F, or we'll be a-swimmin' in it. Mark my words, no good will come of it. No good ever comes of playing tomfool with another man's woman even if she is flying all the right signals. Does that look better? Muddy sort of colour, aint it? Never touch the stuff, give me gin and strong ale any day.'

The curate met her in the hall. 'Ah, Mrs Fletcher, how opportune. Mrs Brotherton told me ...'

What Mrs Brotherton had told him was drowned in the high-pitched shrieks of Cecy and baby Rosa playing tag round the table, and Sam's bull-like roar at one of his dogs who had crept in from the stable to see if any of the muffins might come his way. Lally, poised on the threshold with the dread milk, found a scene of homely chaos. Anne was on the window seat looking out at the first large drops of rain, JG bent beside her, studiously attentive. Kate and Vernon were on the sofa dragged up to the hearth, just far enough apart for decency's sake. Mrs Brotherton would have her work cut out to repel that particular young man, Lally thought, he was undoubtedly tenacious – a very terrier in tenacity. He would have to be, of course. He had nothing to recommend him: he was thirty, had only his low salary to live on, suffered the daily chance of terrible wounds, and would admit to few prospects. His hopes of surviving to forty while still remaining at sea were practically nil – he did not, like some fellow officers, keep safe in port on the excuse of weather or repairs – and no help would be forthcoming for his widow.

'What have I done?' Lally said aloud.

The curate had already plunged under the table to extract a howling Rosa, Cecy was flushed and guilty, Sam was busy ejecting the dog. No one heard her except JG, who rose from the window seat to relieve her of the jug and look tenderly into her face.

'I rather think you have been the catalyst in a pot of hitherto inert chemicals. How is that for a fancy metaphor?'

She smiled. She could not help smiling. And then she wondered what Anne would do faced by the real JG, no wig, no glasses, no elderly, eccentric manner. She was not a passionate girl, and her discontent did not include any complaint about the parson's strictly limited physical demands. To have an admirer was a pleasurable sensation, but a lover … Lally would be surprised if she had ever considered JG as a lover.

'What deep thoughts,' said JG, 'what frowns.'

'I was only thinking how unprincipled you are.'

'I expected you had grown used to that long ago. But in what context? Your sweet cousin?'

'Hush, she will hear you. No, your making a friend of Mr Vernon. I suppose you find the irony amusing: the smuggler and the Revenue man under the same roof.'

'My dear, he is safer here than on the deck of his own ship. He is a dutiful, foolhardy young man, else he would not have been walking alone on the beach where you met him. It is not unlikely certain loutish, undisciplined locals would prefer he disappeared into a marl pit or a quicksand. Here with me he comes to no harm and can get up to no mischief.'

'It is a shame. I like him.'

'Ho, ho,' and he put a cool hand over hers, smiling, 'you have a soft heart after all, Lally Fletcher.'

'Only for Mr Vernon. I do not like to see him duped.'

'And what about Sam? Is he not duped?'

'His life's work is not catching smugglers, he has the choice to feel abused or not as he pleases.'

JG backed her out of the door, let it close behind them. He took her face in his hands and smiled, and leaned to kiss her mouth gently. 'How belligerent you are when you smell an injustice! How I love you for it.'

'As a sister,' she said, and her voice hardly shook.

'The strongest, purest love is often between brother and sister, you must not belittle it.'

The kitchen door opened. Steam, smoke, stoat and gin fumes wafted out.

'Ha,' cried Rush, resolving genie-like from this smog. 'You butterin' her up, are you? She's no fool. Knows her Hyson from her Singlo, keeps those big eyes wide open. You want to watch it or she'll have your neck stretched lovely.'

CHAPTER 12

'You must allow,' said Sam, circumnavigating the choked pond at the back of Truelove's cottage and staring gloomily at the windy expanse of Ledworth common – a nipping, autumnal wind today, and streaked with leaves – 'you must allow it is decent enough. We have done our best. At the very least it has a homely look about it. I can't abide the mentality that forces poor broken wretches into Houses of Industry.'

'Surely they are a laudable attempt to achieve a happy state where the poor pay for themselves by honest labour? Do you not approve? You are always saying how your good folk grumble about the poor rate.' JG relit his cheroot which the wicked wind extinguished every few minutes.

'Have you been inside one? I went with Truelove ... Oh, it's of no consequence. But it hung on my conscience somehow. I hated to see so many beds to a room, such lack of privacy, of ordinary common dignity. And if you want my opinion I do not believe they will ever pay for themselves. Not to speak of such cheerless regimented ways of going on dampening the most optimistic spirits – and how many are optimistic who apply for parish relief?'

'Perhaps you are too paternal in your outlook. Why, reason demands . . .'

'"I laugh at reason, give me ocular demonstration" as somebody said. Who was it? Well never mind, he had the right of it. There is a damnable gulf between theory and practice – and I learnt that long before I was an overseer.'

JG studied the poorhouse, twenty yards away the other side of the swollen beck. It looked a little new yet, but essentially the same as the other cottages in the village, owing a great deal to some noble second-hand oaks, some ninth-hand Roman bricks, several hundredweight of flints, and a good ton of reeds. It looked homely. A curl of smoke from the central chimney was torn away into the freezing air.

'And this is the dreary habitation Lally will make her home?' JG demanded, swinging about to peer with disfavour at the damp and sway-backed building behind them.

'Oh, it will look all the better for some paint and curtains at the windows. It has gone to ruin. Old Cushion – my Cushion's late father – sat it out till ninety in that cottage, grew more and more squalid. Tom Truelove hadn't the heart to shift him, he was perfectly happy there so long as he had his pipe and his fiddle to hand. He died two years ago and the place has stood empty since.'

'I understand Truelove's reservations. I have never seen such a roof. Any loud difference of opinion might make it slide off altogether.'

'So long as the parson is not in it Lally will not mind in the least. And it used to be a decent place, could be so again. It has a fine little square parlour and a dairy and two tolerable bedrooms.'

They tramped across the short grass, crossed the beck by the footbridge, and fetched up by the low door – why so low, enquired JG, were paupers in general stooped or squat? – of the poorhouse. But the paupers inside in the pleasant whitewashed room where they were eating their dinner of bread and cheese – it was a banyan day, no soup, no porridge, no meat and vegetables – were uniformly normal in every way: three women with babies, six other children, four very old women, five old men. They looked at JG with a flicker of curiosity but greeted Sam with a respectful familiarity that said a great deal for the esteem in which he was generally held. The couple in charge, a large woman Sam called Peg and her very small husband, seemed cheerful, competent and domestic. Sam cast a glance at the spinning-wheels, the looms, the pork tubs, the hideous smouldering range, asked half a dozen pointed questions, and bid them all a hearty good day.

Outside again he said reflectively: 'Perhaps the range was a mistake. Stapleford quibbled the cost, of course. I put great store by it, felt a proper range would serve their purpose better than an open fire, but it looks a sulky great thing, and eats fuel, they say. You see how it is? Theory and practice again. Mark my words, that range will cost God knows what amount, will blot my books, cry Extravagance on every page, and all Stapleford's miserly fears will be justified.'

JG considered. 'Perhaps they have not come to grips with the brute yet. Perhaps you should let Lally loose on it. It may turn out an unqualified success.'

Sam laughed, and turned at the sound of a carriage. The parsonage bays jingled into sight, the wind furrowing their coats. A familiar head poked out of the window.

'We must stop here, Bested, or we'll never turn in the mud,' said Anne. She climbed out with an agility and an air of purpose the two watching men had never seen in her before. On her arm was a large covered basket and behind her, loaded with blankets, bundles of clothes, and what looked like an ale jug of heroic proportions, came Lally.

'Oh, pray make Bested help Lally with all that clutter,' said Anne, walking up to Sam with a sweet smile – a smile he remembered well from a very distant past. They had come to meet Truelove, she told him, had made an appointment to view the cottage. This – and she indicated their burdens – was the first stage of the long-awaited removal from the parsonage.

'The parson makes no further objection then,' asked JG, as she took his arm to cross the beck, 'none at all?'

'Lally defeated him. It was not so much there was a row – she simply sat there and said she was moving to the cottage. Only she said it in that kind of voice – you know. And of course it is much more sensible for her to be so close to the poorhouse, for she teaches the children every morning, and the donkey has become so stubborn and disagreeable. She has walked here several times, which does not seem fitting, and besides, she will not be able to do so in the winter.'

'My dear, in the winter, in that cottage, she will surely die.'

'I do hope not' – a warm sideways look, a smile – 'I never thought I would say it, but I will miss her very much. I believe she gives me courage, for I have none of my own, not the twentieth part of a shekel as Mr Hayes would put it. I would not be here now if Lally had not brought me.'

It was not quite true. The chance of JG walking out to meet the carriage as it passed The Ship House, the chance of an exchange of harmless pleasantries, had lurked somewhere at the back of her far from devious mind. He knew it. He grinned, bent to kiss her small clenched hand. She blushed at the mocking gallantry, and at the look in his eyes, from which the spectacles had slipped. It had never occurred to her to look properly into his eyes before. Her blush deepened considerably. She let go of him and ducked in through the poorhouse door.

'I'll wager you everything I have,' Sam said, as he rode up and waited for JG to cross back over the beck, 'that Glover has no suspicion his wife is consorting with the lowly or meeting strange gentlemen by arrangement.'

'Surely Truelove is not a strange gentleman? Surely he is respectable enough? A widower, a man of blameless character?'

'Any sane man might think so. But Glover entertains very little and in no way would consider Tom a neighbour. I think on occasion he has exchanged civilities with him at the church door – that is Ledworth church, and he has not taken a service there now for several years – and once at my own harvest supper, for I will not tolerate ill manners at my own table, but it would surprise me to know Tom has ever put the toe of his boot over the parsonage threshold. So you see, Anne had made an assignation with a strange gentleman in a manner of speaking.'

'Was not Lally the moving force?'

'Oh, Lally,' said Sam bitterly, and rammed down his hat, and laughed, a forced, humourless laugh, as he cantered away.

Lally remembered that afternoon afterwards as one of unallayed chill, awkwardness, and unfinished sentences. From the moment Tom Truelove bent to poke the unwieldy key in the oversize lock to let her in to the moment of his doing so again having let her out, a frosty and glum silence prevailed. To begin with Truelove himself was in low spirits, the mood of a man who thoroughly disapproves of what he is doing but must carry on, with gritted teeth, to the certain end. Then there was Anne who, having exchanged the parsonage for the boundless, blowy common, felt light-hearted and frivolous and was apt to cast Truelove amused and roguish glances he did not appreciate. As for the cottage itself, it was much worse than they had expected in spite of several times peering through the windows in the preceding weeks.

'When we were children,' Anne remarked lightly to Lally as they descended from a terrifying tour of the upstairs, given over entirely to the worm, the mice, and an array of fungus that would have enraptured a scientific committee, 'do you not remember how we used to come here to see old Mrs Pegg? She had been Julia's wet-nurse when Mama was so ill.'

Lally remembered, but that was the dim past, the very distant past before she and Charlie had joined forces.

'It needs a new roof,' she said to Tom Truelove, reaching the bottom stair. The absence of tiles where tiles should surely be and the rottenness of the thatch where thatch still clung made it imperative.

'You do not need to tell me, Ma'am. And you are fully aware I do not consider this cottage suitable for you to live in. I doubt we could get a new roof on before the spring.'

'A decent gale will take off what little is still there,' said Anne, brushing dirt and cobwebs off her skirts.

'I confess I have been a bad landlord. But old Cushion liked it as it was. He was a singular old man. And I had no heart to . . .'

'Your heart does you credit,' Lally snapped, 'but I do not see why he should have liked his roof full of holes.'

She regretted it as soon as it was out. She had schooled

140

herself to make a good impression on this difficult man and here she was making his hackles rise. In the little parlour, already dark because the afternoon light, tentative itself, could make no impression through such small and dirty windows, his face looked gloomier than ever; she suspected his dislike of her was more intense.

'Mr Uffington has promised me a tub of whitewash and a dozen scrubbing brushes,' she said, trying to sound pleasant, 'and one of the women from the poorhouse is to come and clean and cook. Then there is Phee. Phee has always wanted to keep house. In a week or two when you visit, Mr Truelove, you will not recognise the place.'

His face opened and closed with pardonable incredulity and barely concealed horror. Lally drew herself up, ready for the attack which would surely come.

'I had hoped you might reconsider.'

'But the place is enchanting. I have always wished to be on closer terms with the stars.'

'You mock, Madam. What am I to say?'

'Say nothing, simply entrust the key to my keeping.'

He did so. He let her out, locked the door, and turned to drop the huge key on her palm. She stood looking at it, her slender body swayed by the gusting wind, and he thought she could not have looked at it with a more fixed intensity had it been the key to heaven. He made a leg, said good day, and received a distracted, peremptory smile. He thought he would like to know what the key meant to her. He found her quite as eccentric as her friend Lovatt, if not more so: women had no business being eccentric. Literary women, political women, he abhorred them. If there was any point in the world on which he and parson agreed it was that women should not have opinions.

'I hope you will be happy here,' he said, and it sounded rather more ill intentioned than it was.

The whitewash and the scrubbing brushes put in an appearance, so did some dilatory workmen and two strapping girls from Rooks Hill in whom Mrs Hirtle had nurtured a passion for cleanliness. Indeed, it was soon obvious Sam was bearing the cost of the improvements, that it was possible this was the only way he had persuaded Truelove to let Lally have the cottage at all, and that it was to him and only him Lally must direct her thanks.

She moved in on a moist autumn day when the beck was a furious torrent, and the new hens, brought up on the cart with the furniture, were half drowned before they were put in the run. No one greeted her except the inmates of the poorhouse, who had put flowers in the parlour, and Mary Ann, the maid servant, and Phee, who complained the beds were streaming damp, they would have the ague. Phee had not liked leaving the parsonage, not least because she was in love with Bested's underling, a tall lanky genial boy called Tod. Anne too had cried. Lally had not expected her to, had put her arms about her and felt her tremble, small and light, the tears running down through the lawn collar of her gown.

Sam did not appear at all. He was not there to greet her on moving day, though some of the furniture had come from Rooks Hill, turned out of the capacious attics. He did not call afterwards, except one morning to the poorhouse while she was teaching. Everyone else called: Mrs Brotherton and her girls, JG of course, the Turners, Miss Chewton, several unknowns from the village, Mr Hayes with hymn sheets, Anne almost every day with one or other of the children, and even the parson himself. Tom Truelove came, standing shame-faced on the polished floor by the roaring fire, and had the grace to commend her on her transformation of the place. Bensley Vernon called, limping over from The Ship House where he was spending the night – a rare night of leave – before rejoining his ship.

But Sam did not come.

He sent a note, a brief, kind note, hoping she was well and the cottage comfortable. He said he would call when he could.

'Sam has been exceedingly busy on behalf of your paupers,' JG told her, calling very early one morning. 'He has surprised me yet again. Here I was believing him no analytical thinker, no innovator, and lo and behold, he gallops off to Norwich, exerts his influence – according to him only geniality and good manners – on his bank, and Stapleford's bank, and several deep-pocketed gentlemen whose business acumen is not in doubt, and we are to have great improvements, this swampy expanse turned into a flat, kindly meadow, the beck dammed and cleared, and a cold bath built. Imagine it! A cold bath. He spent all yesterday driving learned doctors up and down, was all charm, all affability, said the most obliging things – most of them lies – and never turned a hair at the objections, the quibbles, the mean spirits. My dear, I was astounded. A trained diplomat could not have done better. And there was I sure he was a blunt, retiring, honest man of the soil.'

'You do not mean we are to have the sick and infirm disporting themselves in the beck?'

'I am unsure of the method, but yes, I suppose the purpose is to immerse oneself – otherwise why call it a cold bath? But it will not be up here on the windy heights, no, no. Sam has some land that runs down to the beck further upstream, a salubrious, sheltered spot. He has struck some shrewd bargains and he means, if Brotherton allows him to, to use the money from rents and suchlike to get this blasted common in order so that what is left to the poor may at least be of some use to them.'

They stepped across that part of the blasted common outside Lally's door, and across the beck, which certainly looked cold if nothing else, and reached the poorhouse.

'Your ship,' Lally began, 'Anne said . . .'

'She is at Cromer, beached. I am having her painted. Soon we shall try her out.'

Peg was opening the door in front of them. 'Oh, Ma'am, step in, step in. They are a-waiting you this half hour. And Mr Glover coming at noon to hear their catechism.'

JG swept off his hat, bowed. Peg dimpled and stood aside, and Lally ducked in, smiling, her ringlets tossing.

'How shabby of him,' she said in her strong clear voice, 'not to have informed me of it before. Well we shall give him something to think about, I hope.'

So they all hoped. The parson was naturally not very popular, for he was not seen to do his duty, something that rankled in a society where some at least of the landowners were still conscious of almost feudal obligations. The bishop might think a great deal of him but that was as nothing in a parish where he might not even be recognised on foot, he came there so seldom. Lally's hopes were more fervent than anyone's, for she had often felt she would make a success of this venture or die, but there were certain problems.

Her charges were not promising material, apart from the six children whose minds might be said to be blessedly virginal, though even that was a little in doubt; they were indubitably innocent of book learning at any rate. Of the three women lately delivered of babies two were amenable, one not, and the old woman and the old man who made up the class were both very deaf.

There was a silence as Lally entered, pulling off her hat without ceremony and untying her cloak, kicking her pattens beneath the table they had given her as a desk. She had been teaching now for four weeks, had made some progress, but what a mutinous crew, what disaffection, mumblings, inattention. The mix of adults and children was unsatisfactory, and one of the women was a determined troublemaker. Early on Lally had seen her only hope in strict and unrelenting division: the children under Molly Flood, Hannah Clarke the widow natural spokesman for the rest. Thus and thus they achieved a fair competence with their letters, progressed to scratching their own names, and were in the process of making further monumental and breathless steps up the road of Education. The catechism Lally drummed into them till they had it by heart, feeling this was the easiest way of discharging her duty to it. She then procured through Anne – a dashing, daring Anne – a packet of broadsheets from Holt, several well-known old catches and songs, and some of the children's books from the parsonage. With these she kindled their imaginations, to the extent that more ballads and more tracts were ordered from the secret courier.

'If John knew about these wretched songs he would cast us in the pit, you and I,' said Anne when she delivered them. 'It is enough they know their ABC and the catechism.'

'There is not a baby here that does not know the catechism.'

Nor was there. At noon, the parson sour and lofty at Lally's desk, there was not one mistake, not one moment's hesitation. And Lally, standing ramrod by the door, her long hands folded in front of her, her head unnaturally high as if she would repel all boarders by sheer strength of personality, felt a great surge of warmth, a bursting light, a joy.

'Well, well, such progress after so little time,' was the comment after half an hour. 'But tell me, how is the reading, the writing? Can they' – and he swung a large, cunning face in Lally's direction – 'can they write anything yet?'

You do not have to speak as if they were not here, she wanted to say, but her face, though fierce, gave no hint of the anger rising on the heels of her deep, deep satisfaction. She said calmly: 'Hannah, come write your name for the parson.'

Hannah did so, handing her thin pale baby to one of her older children to nurse. She was a short, tough little woman probably no older than Lally herself, but a husband pressed to sea and now drowned there, eight pregnancies of which five had resulted in living children, all this had made her old, her coarse brown dress hanging shapeless on her wasted body. She seized the pen in front of the parson without a qualm and signed her own name in a great welter of ink.

'Hmm,' said the parson, and rose abruptly.

He stalked into the other room where Peg stood at the fire keeping the dinner from spoiling. Everything seemed in order, he said, but it distressed him to see some of the inmates, especially the children, so slovenly in dress. Could nothing be done?

'Oh,' said Peg, wiping her hands, 'Oh, Mr Uffington and Mr Truelove are to provide something. The children grow so fast, sir, and have never had anything but rags.'

145

Behind him, among the scholars, a distinctly audible exclamation: 'Mean old bugger,' and Lally's whispered cry of 'Hush!' several times over. The parson plunged out through the open door, pink to the ears.

Immoderate laughter followed him across the footbridge to his cob, and the delighted squawks of the children at the window.

CHAPTER 13

The sun had gone long ago, what sun there had been. The thin damp air of an autumn night had thickened and thickened to a foul mist that hung ghostly in the hollows and under the great trees. There was no moon.

Lally walked quickly, keeping to the edge of the road and away from the boggy ruts where men and horses had passed and repassed. If she stopped to listen she could hear the distant roar of the sea on the shingle, for the wind was northerly and brought with it a smell of salt and snow. Now she was past the gallows, half running, her skirts lifted up, and the mist was thinning. Up here was a more sinister, shadowy dampness.

She should never have walked so far, it had been madness from the start. But today something kept so strictly under control for so long had broken, as it had too that day on the beach when Bensley Vernon had found her, and she had had to escape . . . Escape the poorhouse, where the two oldest boys had taken their leave of her in solemn misery for they were being apprenticed to local tradesmen; escape the parson, for he had called to speed them on their way with a lecture; to escape Mrs Brotherton, who had descended on the cottage to drink tea and impart the latest gossip about Kate's unlucky love affair. At last, at last Lally had run out and set off across the withered common with a tigerish spring that carried her away from Ledworth, skirting the little ruinous church, and up to the Heath. Then on, on to the marshes and the sea.

She had walked with purpose though she had none, did not even notice where she was, as if only by walking could she ease the memories that crowded up. It was October, the leaves wet and yellow, the wind blustery and keen; it was October and Susan's birthday.

147

She had cried enough for Susan, that was for sure. And she did not want to cry today, only walk, walk, her eyes dry and burning, to rid herself of thoughts of the dead past and of what might have been. Thoughts of India, of that tiny bundle she had relinquished to be buried in that remote place. She had never told anyone about it, not even Caroline Pascoe, as alone in her grief as she had been alone in that village, abandoned by Francis while he paid extensive compliments to a local ruler up river. They should never have brought the child with them, he had said, and now the brat with a fever and so much important business still to do. That it was strictly private and dishonourable business Lally was sure, but all that was nothing now to the fact that Susan was ill. And there were no white doctors for miles, no one but a holy man and an old woman: a midwife and a witch. In the cool, pearly, beautiful dawn Susan had died, a sweaty wasted thing at her breast, not really Susan at all, and Lally had opened her mouth and howled. Then the women of the village had howled with her in a strange, ritualistic compassion, but they were understandably suspicious and more than anxious for their own babies, and when Lally refused a bitter concoction the witch-midwife tried to make her drink, they all melted away into the heat and an unnatural silence. Long afterwards some men had come and had prised Susan away from her, had wrapped her in a cloth and had carried her out.

After that Lally had gone back to Madras, travelling alone with the distraught ayah and the silent bearers, leaving no message for Francis and filled with a terrible determination. It was as if grief gave her the courage she had lacked before, not the courage to endure – she had proved that already – but the courage to act. From that time she had locked her door to Francis, ordered the house how she liked, refused to meet any of his friends. And Francis, used to contained and smouldering discontent, could not cope with open rebellion, feared scandal, and kept out of her way. Only once or twice after that, by words or blows, had he been able to reduce her to her former state of servitude; only in the matter of George

Fletcher's rubies did he feel he had scored any kind of lasting victory.

Lally had nursed him the last week of his life, dutiful but detached. She had done everything necessary with a quiet deliberation; it would be wrong, she had thought, to hate a dying man. God knew he must have sins enough on his conscience, she wanted none on hers. But she could only just bring herself to touch him, and when he called out she could not comfort him, could barely speak. She felt sometimes she could forgive him everything except his callous disregard of their daughter, his public assertion the child might not be his, his lack of any sort of grief when she died. Then she felt no, she could forgive him nothing, the wounds were still too raw and painful. The cold, hard, silent Lally who had been left to cope with the debts, the terrifying legal intricacies, the voyage back to England, had been a person she despised but could do nothing about.

And all this was why she was going full tilt down the smugglers' road on the Heath, her hair down her back and her boots muddied and her face wet with mist; that was why she was an hour overdue for dinner and Phee and Mary Ann would have roused the poorhouse, got up a search party.

There, there through the pale shifting air was the steep track down towards the valley. Another half hour if she could keep up the pace would see her at the cottage. She put a hand to the pain in her side and walked on, past the thickets and clumps of dripping trees. This was a haunted, lonely place but she did not mind it, never had minded it, had come here almost every day on foot or on horseback for years and years. She was not afraid, though it was very dark, and the mist rose and streamed about her. She began to go down, carefully, avoiding the mud.

The sound of hooves came to her, hooves in the yielding ground. She stopped, she did not want to be seen. Suppose it was Sam, Truelove, even the parson? It was almost too late to duck aside and find shelter for just here was only bracken and bramble, but she turned, sweeping up her full skirts, ready to make a plunge away from the road into the black wilderness.

A voice cried: 'Who's there?' sharply from a little distance and the hooves stopped, then trampled in a circle; she could hear the creak of leather and the soft blowing of the horse's breathing. She stepped into the bracken and floundered, caught her cloak in a bramble, dragged it free, and then fell forwards into space with a little scream of fright.

'Damme, I thought you were dead,' said Jack Brotherton, bending over her.

She was lying among the sour old bracken stems and her hat had come off, but her hat was the only casualty. Apart from a bruise on her shoulder and one on her forehead she had come off lightly. She sat up, pulling down her skirts, and he put out a hand – she could barely see it – to help her to her feet.

'So it's you,' he said, 'I took you for a gipsy.'

For a moment she could not reply, she was only glad she could not see his face.

'Where are we?'

'You tumbled into a pit. You were lucky it was not full of barrels awaiting transport. And you were lucky I found you, the night's so dark.'

The pit; how could she have forgotten it. Charlie's mocking laughter rang in her head. There were several on the Heath, used by the smugglers when a cargo had to be hidden in a hurry. It was a wonder she had not broken her neck, Lally thought. She pulled herself slowly up the steep side, her clothes catching in the brambles, her face whipped by a thorn branch, the bracken stalks pulling away in her hands. At the top the shadow that was Jack Brotherton loomed near and his arm went about her shoulders, drawing her close.

'Poor girl, are you sure you have not hurt yourself? It seems I am fated to be your rescuer. First the beck, now this. Where next, I wonder?'

She withdrew, twisting her arm from his grasp. 'Thank you for your assistance. I believe I can get home by myself.'

'You have a poor opinion of my chivalry, dear Lally. You

do not mind if I call you Lally? I notice that fellow Lovatt is very free with your name.'

There was an insult underlying the words, a suggestion she might allow other more intimate freedoms. She stepped back. If there had been any chance of melting away into the foggy darkness she might have done it; primitive instinct said run. Instinct also whispered it was not what he was but what he lacked that frightened her, for perhaps if she were to appeal to his better nature she would find he did not have one.

He was in dark clothes, a pistol in his belt – well, who would not have pistol and sword up here in the territory of vagabonds and robbers? His hair was tied back under a plain hat and no white showed anywhere, no white at wrist or throat, no lace, no shiny buttons. And when he whistled his horse and it walked up out of the furze it too was black or dark brown, no white marking to be seen. She had seen him on a brown horse before, she remembered, the very first time they had met, but that had been a lean racy sort with a broad blaze.

'You have not yet told me what you are doing up here this time of the evening,' he was saying, catching the reins. 'Do married ladies in India go out alone after dark?'

When she did not reply he finished lengthening a stirrup leather with an angry slap. 'Can you get up? I'll walk you to the common.'

'There is no need.'

'Get up.'

She put her foot in the stirrup, somehow got her leg over. The horse sidled. Jack Brotherton swore at it and jerked it in the mouth.

'Perhaps,' he said after a while as they began to drop down into the valley, 'Mrs Fletcher of Madras feels free to do exactly as she pleases. Such a history of playing the game to your own rules, eh? I have been making enquiries. I asked about among my friends and oh, dear Lally, the stories, the gossip. What a small world it is to be sure. The name of Fletcher is almost as well known as that of Clive, I do declare.'

It occurred to Lally she could drive her heels into the horse and put an end to this; the sobering thought that Jack Brotherton had the reins and that should they be pulled out of his hand the horse would surely fall on them before she could reach them followed immediately. She sat helpless. In a minute they would drop among the sparse woods, come out behind the church. The track petered out there. In days gone by the barrels and oilskin bags of tea had been stored overnight in the huge cellar under the tiny cottage now given over to innocent Mr Hayes.

'I think you mean to frighten me, Mr Brotherton. Why should you want to do that?'

'Frighten you?' He checked the horse, stepped up, groped for her hand on the pommel. Before she could pull it away he had crushed it, had put his lips against her palm.

'I was only thinking how disappointed certain people might be if they knew you and your late husband had been on such bad terms, that you had had a child by his brother, that you had stolen a prince's ransom in rubies and only saved your long and elegant neck by giving them back. How bitter that must have been. I am sure I would have done anything to keep them.'

She could not pull her hand away but the horse, uneasy now, gave a jump forward and she was suddenly free. As quickly as he could she dismounted, on the wrong side so that all Jack Brotherton grabbed was an empty stirrup.

'I meant no harm,' he cried but she did not wait to hear, she set off at a run, sliding and stumbling between the trees. She heard him bringing the horse to a halt, heard him mount, heard the thud of hooves. By the grassy space where the track ran up to the churchyard wall he cornered her by some ash saplings, riding the horse up close. Perhaps her pale face gave her away, or perhaps he could make out the draggled white petticoats as she kilted up her skirt to go faster.

'I meant no harm,' he repeated. She did not wait for what he had meant, she struck at the horse's head and the poor beast snorted and ducked sideways.

'Damn you!' cried Brotherton, and brought him back,

plunging and blowing.

'You have pluck, I give you that,' he said as the animal quietened. 'I admire you for it. Come, can we not be friends again? You are not really frightened I would run you down?'

For answer she brushed out of the young trees and began to walk quickly but calmly along the narrow path that led to the common. She did not look behind. She heard the chink of the bit, the soft tread of hooves as the horse turned full circle, but he did not come after her and in a while, without hearing him leave, she knew she was alone.

'My love,' said JG, kissing her cheek, 'you look . . . remarkable.'

She was in dark blue, a dress cut from some old silk discovered in the parsonage attics, the fine white lace from a discarded dress of Aunt Fanny's, both given her by Anne. Why, she could not go to a ball at Cookhams in any old thing, Anne had said.

And now the wine had gone to her head, or Brotherton's solicitude, Cecy's gaiety, or Tom Truelove's deep, respectful bow. She danced. She had never expected to dance at Cookhams and enjoy it. The mirrors showed her an elongated Lally, her curls falling over one shoulder and one freckled breast, caught up in combs and adorned with audacious feathers. She had powdered her hair tonight, had let Phee loose on it, Phee who was worth more than the most expensive frisseur in the county. The ladies of Madras, the dissolute ladies of Francis's court, had often asked to borrow Phee, she could dress a head so beautifully. The ladies of Madras . . .

How Lally remembered Madras tonight, but the memories were bearable, she could smile and pay attention to JG. She could smile and pay attention and still, in her head, see herself at the first ball she and Francis had given after they were married. She had been so young, so frightened, so alone. She had known almost nobody, had been too bewildered to recall the names as she was introduced, and then, very early on,

153

Francis had left her to play cards in another room, a private little room where he could drink with his friends. She, the hostess, had found herself quite alone. She had been eighteen, slim as a reed, absurdly tall, absurdly vulnerable. Someone had come up and asked if she were cold, or tired, and she was both those things inside but pride would not let her admit it. And the gentleman in red brocade had asked her to dance so she had, pathetically grateful for his kindness, and she had danced badly, just as she was doing now. Only now it did not seem to matter. Was that the wine too, or JG's hard warm fingers closing over hers every other moment, or the strange mood she had been in ever since she met Jack Brotherton on the Heath?

JG was not in red brocade but in brown velvet, and he was washed and scraped and apparently perfumed, though he still wore the great old bob wig with its yellowing curls. His spectacles slipped down and he shoved them up again, asked her pardon as he missed his cue and caused a sensation by turning left instead of right. Lally sensed in him a desire to be outrageous tonight, at the very least tactless. It was as if some long-suppressed John Glory Lovatt was fighting for air and freedom while another, long-cultivated, opposed him. The real man, Lally thought, was well concealed. She curtseyed, turned round twice, curtseyed again, and found his hand in hers.

'You are fey tonight. You are miles from this room in spirit. Where are you, pray, or should I not ask?'

'Madras.'

'Ah, Madras. And at a ball? But not, I hope, dancing with a naturalist of advancing years.'

She smiled. Wafts of musk and brandy and hot oranges reached her. 'I danced with a very kind gentleman in red quite old enough to be my father, which you are not.'

'Not even had I fathered you at a tender age?'

'Not even then.'

'You mean I am not giving the right impression of eccentric middle age? What am I to do? I thought I had convinced everyone I am a gentle idiot come to make an innocent study of birds.'

'You may have convinced the gentlemen, they are so unsubtle in general they suspect nothing, but you have best beware the ladies . . . They are not easily fooled by lectures on crossbills and why nightingales stand upside down to sing.'

'You are really in a teasing mood, I see.'

They parted, came together. Lally looked ungainly, paced out the steps conscientiously, but her good points could not be faulted: her hair, her dress with its dashingly low neck, her long, beautiful hands. She tried to walk gracefully but nature and circumstances were against her; she saw Jack Brotherton watching from the crowd in one corner and her heart moved, missed its usual steady beat.

'A vulgar, dangerous fellow,' said JG, following her gaze. 'I would not care to meet him on a dark night without a sword.'

She swallowed. Oh God, had she forgot the steps? No. Back, forward, curtsey. It was over. She must say something, anything; JG was looking at her queerly and he had a sharp instinct for evasion.

'I have never seen you with a sword.'

They made their way to the wall and vacant chairs.

'I can use one, I assure you.'

'And I suppose you have a pistol that is not eaten away by rust, that is not kept in a picnic basket.'

'I have. I use that too upon occasion.'

There was a collision nearby, Sam forcing his way through the couples moving out to dance. He had not seen Lally for some weeks, had still not called at the cottage, and Anne, excusing him, had said he had been busy with autumn sowing, with the sheep, with the Scottish cattle.

'The curate wants a word about hoodie crows. Seems a queer topic for a ballroom. He is over by the fiddlers being cross-examined by Mrs Brotherton about some ancient charity, penny loaves or sugar buns or some such. She wants to know why it has lapsed and where is the money gone. It is rabbit and stoat, I am afraid. If you squint over there you may

155

see him cowering behind the viola.'

'I shall rescue him at once. Do not dance with Lally, she counts out the steps, lurches about like a drunken goose.'

Lally's freckles stood out in furious indignation. 'Oh, how unkind! I have never in my life been complimented on my dancing. I had so hoped you might lie for the sake of gallantry.'

JG made a leg, raised his dark eyebrows. 'Dear girl, I would never lie to you, you know I would not.'

'Why is it,' Sam asked, watching him walk away, 'that I always have a feeling everything you say to each other has another meaning?'

'You imagine things.'

Kate Brotherton was passing in a crowd of admirers, and her laugh floated back over the general hubbub. Behind, an adoring young man of her own at her elbow, came Cecy. She stopped when she saw Sam, and curtseyed very deep and low with a mocking little smile and a look from under her long curling lashes. Sam inclined his head, tried to look avuncular and unimpressed, and said: 'The little minx,' as soon as she had passed. 'She has grown up at last.'

'Perhaps you should pay her some attention.'

'Cecy? Never! And I have done with dragging about the heels of a pretty woman for a word here, a smile there, and half promises never kept. I did it once years ago. I did it for Anne. I bowed and scraped and minded my manners from here to Dereham, standing up with twenty insipid girls before I could come at her and then to have her wrenched away at the end of two minutes. I shall never forget it. Lord, the stuffy rooms, the reek! And all the elder ladies and the eatables heaped up in the corners. For all the good I did I might as well have been at Rooks Hill planting turnips.'

'Planting turnips?' cried Mrs Brotherton, precipitated into their sphere by a harassed Stapleford. 'How countrified your conversation is become, Sam Uffington. What can poor Philadelphia want with turnips? No doubt in Madras she entertained sultans, talked politics all night.'

'Alas,' said Lally, and could not help an arch look at the chastised Sam, 'I never met a sultan. Kings, princes, nawabs, yes. As for politics, I fear I never yet talked politics at a ball. Wallpaper, Paris fashion, even cricket . . . but never politics.'

'There, Ma'am, what did I tell you?' said Stapleford, 'I'll wager there aint a ha'porth of difference between here and Madras but the heat.'

Lally turned away a little so he should not see her smile. She found herself looking at Sam's hard, close-shaven jaw. Beyond, in one of the mirrors, was her own face, the long freckled face under the high powdered head. What gulf separated Francis Fletcher's house from this one, and how little they would understand if she tried to explain. What were they talking about now? She was not listening, she was remembering the diamonds in the necklace Francis had brought her from Lucknow; a stray thought: they were probably worth twice as much as Cookhams, house, woods and well-kept acres.

'. . . need more than a dame school. A disgrace. Philadelphia, do you not think it is a disgrace?' came Mrs Brotherton's urgent voice. 'Lingborough with only a dame school, and Mrs Greeves at that, confined to a sofa. There ought to be a proper building, a decent curriculum – sewing, woodwork. The parson should be pushing for it.'

Lally was aware that Sam was trying not to laugh. She agreed entirely, she said, and was it not almost a hundred years since Locke proposed the establishment of working schools in every parish? How Progress and Reform did limp along.

They all laughed then. Several heads turned nearby. So the Indian widow could be witty too, could she?

Eliza Brotherton, who was shrewd enough to know she and Sam had acquired an invaluable asset for the poorhouse, gave Lally an almost loving look. 'Oh, it is men who obstruct the advance of civilisation. If they were not for ever devising new stratagems for the economy which invariably fail for want of some minute particular, or dashing off to bloody each other's heads on some remote island the lack or gain of which makes no difference to anybody but the poor sacrificed inhabitants – if they were only to be confined, or reduced in number, or given more sense and fewer passionate parts, how well we would get on!' She spoke with a gleam in her small eyes. Her words were from one long-suffering married lady to another – how marriage had amended her romantic notions of the opposite sex!

Truelove joined them. He had intended to ask Lally to dance, vital, compelling curiosity driving him to it. He had never danced with a woman taller than himself. When it came to the point however his resolve melted under Lally's unabashed and steady gaze, and he merely asked Sam whether his bullocks had recovered from their ducking. This odd turn in the conversation assured him of their full attention and Sam was forced to explain: 'Cushion's youngest boy, great lumpish lad, should be at sea but Hovell's lugger is laid up for repairs – Cushion's boy came to help out, no more sense than a baby and no experience with cattle, for all he was bred and born at Rooks Hill. Anyway, he drives a herd of young stock in, him and two dogs and Mrs Hirtle's idiot grandson. God knows what happened. The next thing the whole shoot of them is thundering down to the watering place on the river downstream of the mill, the two boys whooping behind and the dogs kicking up the devil of a row. Well, they might have crossed over, pushed through the hedges, but the front runners swerved at the water and turned about, the rest came piling on top of them, and three were pushed into deep water, gave themselves up to panic, and drowned. I have never seen the like of it.'

'No indeed,' said Truelove, 'Cushion's boy will not forget it to his dying day. I never knew till that moment what a temper Sam kept, as Mr Lovatt might put it, so tightly battened under hatches.'

'Stuff!' Sam straightened his already straight back, looked ferocious. 'It was no worse than you have seen a dozen times before. As for hatches, when are we to venture to sea on the

Snipe? How he eulogises, poor JG, and winds us up with anticipation.'

The projected voyage in the cutter was discussed at length, Mrs Brotherton taking the opportunity to quiz Lally on the luxurious appointments of East Indiamen, the food, the daily round, the incredible expense. At last Stapleford drew her away to dance – a very subdued Stapleford, he too had had to give account of the missing penny loaves – and as Truelove stood drinking shrub and saying nothing, Sam suggested a walk in the conservatory to Lally.

It was a very small conservatory compared with the vast hothouses at Luffwell Hall, but it was pleasant after the crush of the dancing.

'I am sorry I have not seen you for some time. You have made such strides at the poorhouse. They speak glowingly of you.'

'Perhaps it has escaped your memory but you were to send me an account for the furniture.'

'Forget it. Say it is on loan. If you did not have it it would be lying in the attics still.'

Another couple passed them, smiling acknowledgement. Sam and Lally moved aside, came close together. Lally felt him throw out an arm to steady her, change his mind, support her briefly, and step back on the path. She felt hot, bewildered, and her hands shook. What was it about him that moved her, his voice, his calm, grave face, or those intense dark eyes that seemed so at odds with his pale hair?

'I heard …' she began, and faltered, feeling the heat and trembling subside. 'Did I hear a coach was held up on the Heath?'

'Two nights ago. It was an old woman from Holt on her way to Wells. She lost five guineas and a gold ring. Her driver had a blunderbuss but could not fire it and hold his horses at the same time. When he did he almost blew his own hand off and the highwayman laughed and rode away.'

'It was a foggy night,' said Lally, and then, more brightly: 'I wonder why he does not work the Norwich road? Five guineas

159

and a gold ring are little enough to hang for.'

'Perhaps the Norwich road is the preserve of another blackguard. Are you hot? Should I fetch some wine?'

'Yes. Please.' She sat on a little wooden seat half hidden in the palm fronds, and watched him walk away. She thought he had a presence, a dignity that was rare among men, that she would trust him with her life. But she was not in love with him, no. She was not in love with him. It was his kindness that touched her, his unstinting generosity.

The distant tinkle and scrape of the music, the clapping, the laughter, could have been Madras. It was not hot enough, of course, and the dresses of the dancers were not gaudy enough; no one was drunk, no one had caused a stir with a shouted insult. Madras. Madras. Why could she never forget Madras? She had been so used to danger there, to dinner parties where armed guards stood at the doors, to sudden death, sometimes violent. But here? Was there danger here as great, and perhaps more personal? Would it be wise to tell Sam about her meeting on the Heath with …

Jack Brotherton. He was a little way off, and he made a leg, his eyes searching her face. She had been wrong to think no one was yet drunk, he was.

'I have never seen you look so well,' he said.

She did not reply but opened her lace fan as calmly as she could. She was deeply afraid of him, just as she had been deeply afraid of Francis, but she would not show it, she would brave him out.

'May I sit with you?' and he was beside her, his eyes on her face and her throat and the soft rise of her breasts. She shrank back, trying not to look as if she did so. He leaned forward until she could feel his breath.

'Have you forgiven me for the other night?'

She thought she would have to stand up, move away, anything but endure him so close. He reminded her of Francis. Oh God, he reminded her of Francis. The smell of musk, pomatum, wine, was the very smell of him. Panic welled inside her and then, just as suddenly, subsided, and that cold, angry, determined courage took its place.

'I would prefer to be alone, sir.'

The conservatory was empty. A palm branch dipped against her head. Jack Brotherton put an arm about her shoulders and strained her to him, his mouth against her cheek, her chin.

'Let me go!' and she struggled to get to her feet, but he simply tightened his hold and pulled so that she sat down again.

'Are you coy, Mrs Fletcher? Surely not. You were not noted for it in Madras.'

She got away from him; perhaps she hit him but she was not properly aware of it. He had made a fatal mistake arousing the demons of Madras. She jumped up and stepped forward and it was only when he lunged after her and caught her arm, and saw the look she gave him, that he realised she could quite easily kill him.

'I suggest you let the lady go,' said a voice from behind the greenery. 'It seems all too evident she is very unwilling.'

It was JG, standing in a bed of fuchsia.

'Don't interfere,' said Brotherton. 'Go back to your damn birds.'

'It is not my nature to stand by and watch a lady abused.'

Brotherton went red, stepped forward. 'I'll call you out,' he cried. 'Remember that. By God, you insult me! I shall have your life for it.'

'Call me out by all means, but do apologise to the lady.'

'To the lady! The …'

There were faces at the door now, a hundred inquisitive eyes and ears bent in their direction. Jack Brotherton said an unfortunate word under his breath and JG swung at him the instant after with remarkable accuracy. To the prostrate Jack he said amiably: 'I trust you will apologise now.'

'I shall have your life for that,' said Brotherton, heaving himself up.

He staggered towards the doors, towards the watching, curious faces, the queer silence. Lally leaned back in the

161

shelter of the palms and breathed deeply, deeply, her heart slowing gradually and the colour coming back into her face.

JG brushed off his coat and looked round with intense satisfaction. 'My love, you are an Amazon. In another moment you would have stretched him out yourself. Where is Sam? He said he was fetching you wine.'

She pushed aside the leaves with cold fingers. 'He will call you out,' she said. 'He will say you insulted him.'

'I wager you a guinea he will not be allowed to do it. I am a guest in his father's house and besides, what joy would it be to him to fight an old man of science who does not even know how to load a pistol?'

'I see you don't care for your life in the least,' in a small, furious voice.

'On the contrary, I care for it dearly. I rather think young Mr Brotherton needs to be more wary of his own.'

CHAPTER 14

It was a small ship in all conscience. Lally sat looking green, desperately green, and once or twice ducked more or less discreetly over the side. Sam, whose suffering was no less acute but was in no way connected with the sea, suggested a pot of coffee might be welcome all round.

In the event he had to make it himself and carry it, at an angle that defied belief and gravity and with an expression of furious concentration, to the bucking bow and Lally's limp, humid presence.

'I thought this trip would be a confounded disaster,' he said, pouring a mug of the stuff and finding it thin and weak.

'Mr Vernon spoke a while ago about springing the mast. He looked very dark. JG laughed.'

'I would expect him to laugh; and not brook interference. I know nothing about ships but it seems to me he has an instinct for it. You can tell, just as you can tell a real horseman from a man who simply rides. And anyway his prime object is to see how fast he can get her through the water. He told me so. He said it was an excellent day to try her paces.'

In view of the adverse conditions, the sea running, the wind, the tide, he was getting her through the water faster than was strictly credible. She was leaning right over under as much canvas as she could carry without tearing it and herself to shreds. Clem Cushion – late Hovell's lugger and the bullock stampede – and the boy Noah, who, with Rush and Bensley Vernon, made up the temporary crew, gazed up and up with a rather witless wonder. Rush, needless to say, was unmoved. He had sailed with JG too many years, smuggling and privateering, to worry about the way this particular old lady dug her lengthy bowsprit through the green water and flying spray. Vernon calmed his own racing heart by simply not looking any more at the taut, straining canvas and staring fixedly at the deck. JG himself stood at the tiller smoking a cheroot, quite as if they were on a pleasure lake, and he drove her and drove her with a fierce but silent exultation, totally absorbed.

'I do believe he loves the sea more than his birds,' said Sam after a while, a long reflective while bent over his salty coffee. He spoke in a low voice for fear of being overheard, but he also spoke with a deepening melancholy that had something to do with the thought of Anne and Kate Brotherton dying from seasickness below.

Far away, Lally was thinking, at that place where sky met sea, there was a perceptible darkening that was possibly, hopefully, the dear green immobile county of Norfolk. The *Snipe* afforded them tantalising glimpses of it between the amazing clouds of her canvas and the great troughs of water she cast herself into every other minute. They must have been mad to set out. There was Anne, prostrate in the tiny cabin below, declaring with each faint breath she was never, never, never going to forgive JG for this. There was no way of persuading her on deck where the air might have done some little good. And beside her in worse misery lay Kate, reduced to sodden wretchedness, a bucket in her arms.

Lally, always at her best in action, kept to the deck and was sick quietly and without shame in the sea. She could not bear that fetid hole below. And in a while the nausea passed, and the swimming sensation, and the terrible desire to be dead, and she leaned back with the mug of Sam's coffee cradled in her hands and looked about her appreciatively, a faint colour in her face and her eyes shining. It was exhilarating, she thought; it was like riding a bold, difficult horse over testing country.

Sam sat close by in a vague, unspeaking intimacy. He was unaffected by the motion, scorned the sea, and looked indescribably gloomy. A great quantity of ocean seemed to have found its way into the coffee and under Lally's raffish old laced hat, tied down firmly now with a blue kerchief borrowed from Clem Cushion. And the intimacy was not really any kind of intimacy at all, seeing that Bensley Vernon, leaning over to say something to JG, was as far away from them as anyone could go and that all of thirty feet.

'He says those triangular ones at the front are jibs,' Sam remarked, feeling something was called for but at a loss to know what. 'Do you think if we slowed down she would come upright a little, stop plunging about?'

'I think the sooner we reach land the better. For Kate, I mean; for Anne. I doubt either of them will actually die but they will think they nearly did, and the parson and Mrs Brotherton will be as furious either way.'

Sam might have laughed – she intended him to – but his good humour was in abeyance. He was worried. It was a squalid and degrading business being cooped up in the bowels of a little ship, heaving and retching; there was no doubt Kate was very ill. Bensley Vernon would go below occasionally and return with a gentle smile and some encouraging remarks about first time at sea, nasty swell, only to be expected. And then there was that very solicitude: Sam had surprised him holding her, her poor lolling head on his shoulder, saying something low and tender into her hair.

'Look, land!' Lally exclaimed. He looked up. Gone was the cool remote Lally, the cynical, worldly Lally, the disillusioned, embittered Mrs Fletcher of Madras. She had screwed round to put her chin on the rail and her eyes were glowing, the ends of the kerchief flapping on her cheek.

Clem, the boy, Rush, and Bensley Vernon played cat's cradle for a while with a great number of ropes and something happened to the jibs and the other mysterious pieces of canvas aloft. The *Snipe*, coming on to her new course, shipped a sea with a cantankerous wallow, and Lally got her feet wet. There was no more talk of land. Sam hurried her below and found her a pair of outsize seaman's socks, clean but hairy. She submitted to the indignity of wearing them without a gleam of amusement, refused any further assistance although her skirts were soaked, and began to look ill. She hated it below, she confessed in a strained and hollow voice, she would die if he did not let her up. And Sam, seeing her turn pale and clammy, thrust her back into the air with a groan. Why had they come? Or why was it not a pleasant, still, golden late autumn day with a steady breeze and an undemanding captain?

Lally felt her face, slippery with spray, chased the long strands of hair. She moved to the rail, lodged herself there, and gazed across at the distant cliffs, and the green hills and the familiar sweep of a coast line she knew so well. She was acutely conscious of being watched. She straightened her back, lifted her head a fraction, tried not to mind. The wind beat into her face, stung her cheeks – cold, vigorous, glorious. She looked up at the rigging, the live, groaning sails, and then at the bow dipping into the swell and lifting again, the foam racing back. She could stay like this for ever, she thought suddenly, she would not mind if life ended at this moment; she was happy. She had forgotten happiness, the great leap of the spirit, the unparalleled sense of freedom. She turned, smiling, and met the straight, sober look of JG at the mast. He came over, and because of the crash of the sea, the noise of the wind, he stood very close and spoke into her ear, shoulder to shoulder with her, looking at the land.

'She goes like a snipe,' was his comment. 'Her trim is all wrong.'

'She's beautiful. How can you bear to come to land?'

'Ah, but ropes and sails wear out, and blocks and spars, and there are stores and stomach aches and broken chains to attend. We must all come to land in the end.'

His chin was bristling, his hair hidden under an improvised turban, and he wore an old brown jacket with bulging pockets. Instead of his usual garish waistcoat he had a plain white shirt belted over his breeches. Lally suspected the costume was a compromise between the smuggler and the birdwatcher. He was searching now for a cheroot.

'I wonder you can see where you are going through those glasses,' she said.

He grinned. He said: 'I had a ship once, a sweet lively ship

...' and then stopped, laughed, hitched up his spectacles. 'Dear girl, are you still worrying about Brotherton?'

'You have heard nothing?'

'Nothing.'

They stood side by side while the cutter forged on and the sea raced back, and the coast line dipped and wallowed closer and closer. A great sense of peace came to Lally, of finding a familiar place to rest. Then it was gone. JG turned at a shout from Vernon, and laughed, and gave an order, and left her. Lally took hold of a rope and bent her head against her hand. Then Clem, coming to offer her an oilskin, for they were going to beat up towards the harbour, Mr Lovatt said, be the wind ever so strong, and somewhere behind more orders, issued with unquestionable authority ...

'You could not possibly be thinking of Madras,' said Sam.

'What?' She looked round, startled by his tone. 'Do you think I often return there in my mind?'

'I know you do.'

She shook her head, turned round. What a strange mood he was in!

'I suppose,' she said at last, 'I have been blown all over the Bay of Bengal, and in ships very little larger than this, once for as long as seven weeks. And then there were pirates, and French privateers ... You can have no notion of the difficulties of getting from Madras to Calcutta.'

'No.'

Bensley Vernon came towards them, walking as if the deck was quite horizontal and steady, the wind whipping his long pigtail up and a grumpy, good-natured, enduring look on his face.

'We have another hour of this at least. Do you not wish you had stayed safe at home, Mrs Fletcher?'

But Mrs Fletcher, clinging to the rigging as the ship rolled, her face wet from spray and her hair down her back, simply laughed.

Sam, irritatingly robust, was feeling sharp pangs of hunger.

167

JG, who seldom thought of his stomach except when fainting from want, pooh-poohed the suggestion someone should investigate the contents of the lockers. But Vernon, Clem, and the short, roly-poly boy, looked longingly in Sam's direction. He took the hint and went below.

Anne was grey and sweating and moaning horribly but she was recovered enough to ask where they were and why they had not returned to land.

'The wind has moved round. JG calls it contrary and Rush calls it something altogether stronger. We are zig-zagging about trying to get in to the land.' He thought it politic not to remind her of the perils of navigation on this coast. Instead, to lead her thoughts away from their erratic progress entirely, he asked after Kate.

'You can see for yourself,' said Anne.

'This was an ill-starred expedition.' Sam sat down heavily on the only chair the cabin boasted and tried to adjust to the odd sensation of a room tipping and tilting around him. 'We should have known it was too late in the year.' At least Kate was asleep, he was thinking, asleep pitifully with her lovely face buried in her loose hair, a thin blanket round her shoulders.

'How is Lally?' came Anne's croaking voice.

'Talking about the Bay of Bengal. She knows all about contrary winds.'

It was sharply said, for him. Anne thought he looked older, harder, even a little forbidding. She had never been afraid of him before but this was a Sam she had not met.

'None of us can guess how unhappy she was there. She has never even mentioned her little girl.'

'You have come to care for her very much.'

'Perhaps I always cared. I think I was jealous of her in the old days, jealous of the way she behaved outrageously, flouted all the rules, and was still liked. Since she has returned I have come to see why people like her and there is no need for jealousy any more.'

He was only half listening. He was angry with a sour

168

permeating anger, and he was irritable and disappointed too. He heard the word 'jealous' but did not attend, applied it to himself at once. It occurred to him he was jealous of a dead man, that he hated the unknown Fletcher for having her ten years and making her ... this, this girl who came alive in fits and starts, this girl with the guarded eyes and serious mouth and a secret grief. God, but he was growing maudlin! He shook himself, pulled back his straying thoughts, and stood up gingerly in case he should bang his head on the very low deck beam.

He looked back before he ducked out, looked back at the two humped female forms looking for all the world like mermaids laid out down there to dry. How he disliked this solidly bachelor life. But he supposed he must resign himself to it after all, for the only woman he would ever want now was sitting up in the contrary winds with her freckles awash and touch-me-not written on every one of them.

'Anne is rallying,' he told her, emerging on deck to ask her advice about a grey irregularly shaped rock he sensed might be cheese.

'And Kate?'

'Kate is asleep. She looks like Juliet in her tomb.'

'Mr Vernon does not look suicidal. He keeps saying she will get over it, she will be a tolerably good sailor. How detestable men are when they become hearty and prone to rallying phrases and false cheerfulness.'

'You know the Brothertons will never allow the match.'

'I believe Mr Vernon means to have her fair means or foul.'

'And you admire him for it.'

'I admire him for doing all he can to win the woman he loves, yes. Is that so wrong?'

He looked quite irrationally savage, and thrust the grey rock at her: 'What is it, d'you think?'

'It is a peculiar object. What would your guess be?'

'Cheese?'

'I would not wager you on it.'

She rose from her place on the deck, fighting her swirling skirts. Her socked feet looked over-large.

'What a romantic voyage this is, after all,' she said with a lop-sided grin.

He could not resist her. He heaved the cheese over the side and laughed, glancing about for the land and finding it in an unexpected direction, rather misty now and devoid of any recognisable landmark.

Lally was looking aghast. 'You tossed it overboard,' she cried. 'Was it not for us to eat?'

'Eat that? You would be dead within the hour, that is, if you could sink your teech into it, it was like stone.' And then, rather lower and with a hangdog air as if to make amends for his boorishness: 'I have a feeling there is nothing to eat on this ship at all; JG is no epicure. Perhaps you could cast your eye about below, give your opinion, if . . .' – a pause, an appealing pause – 'if you could bear it.'

A grey misty twilight was deepening into night by the time they got ashore, and the quixotic wind blew the first rain across the cobbles. Anne protested she would not get into a carriage, she wished to go to bed. Sam felt relieved. A hired chaise, even could he find one in this little fishing town, would have to travel over treacherous roads in the pitch dark and a wind blowing up into a gale. He left JG, Vernon and the *Snipe*'s disgruntled crew on board and ushered the three women to the small inn.

It was nothing, the landlord's wife assured them on finding Wells had not been their destination at all, all manner of strange craft sought shelter there on occasion, often running themselves aground in the process. She could see they had had a rough time of it, did they want her to send a girl for the apothecary?

'Cordial and hartshorn and charge a guinea for them,' said Sam under his breath to Lally. 'The best thing would be to get Kate to bed as soon as you can.'

Rain was blown up against the windows. A shout outside

made Lally look out, to see a chair dashing for shelter, lurching drunkenly, and a crowd of little ragged urchins running up the street pelting each other with mud. It was almost dark. Links and lanterns moved about the quay but the *Snipe* was invisible; she was snug for the night.

After Sam had gone Lally rang for food and stooped to revive the fire, the hood of her cloak fallen back from the cloud of her hair. Anne arrived, murmuring that Kate was fast asleep already, was a normal colour, and had sipped some cordial. In her wake came chicken, rook pie and ale. The servant drew the curtains against the raging night and said she hoped they would be comfortable.

Lally and Anne ate silently, sparingly, their eyes meeting now and again in sympathy. The chicken was tough, the pie glutinous, the ale weak.

'I never thought I would be hungry again,' said Anne, 'but this is enough to kill the keenest appetite.'

'I wonder what they have found to eat on the ship?'

'A better supper than this.'

Anne had recovered her gaiety along with her appetite and the sufferings of the day were a thing of the past. She began to talk about Bensley Vernon, such a nice, honest, likeable young man, and how he loved Kate, there was no doubt of it. The Brothertons had not known he was to be on the *Snipe*. JG had, in effect, duped the Brothertons and brought hero and heroine together without regard for the consequences. There would be trouble; poor innocent Kate would be blamed and hounded and generally made miserable. Then there was Sam, she had seen Sam in a new light today.

'He did not even look tenderly at Kate, and I always thought he and Kate might ...' She had only known him so harsh and unapproachable once before, she said, and that was after Joe Uffington died. Did Lally not remember the youngest Uffington brother? He had kissed every girl in the county before he was seventeen.

Lally received a general picture of youthful high spirits misdirected, the usual sort of thing. The boy had been his father's favourite, much younger than his brothers; an uncanny resemblance to his dead mother accounted in part for the family indulgence, so did his natural charm. He also seemed lucky in avoiding the worst consequences of certain thoughtless actions. Before he died the father's dearest wish had been that Joe would go to Oxford, and when the time came Sam put up the cash, gave him a moderate allowance, and hoped some good would come of it. The boy immediately fell in with a rough crowd: cocks, pony racing, fist fighting, bawds, were everyday amusements. He used up his year's allowance in a month and came home – sent down, it was said – begging for more. Sam settled the debts, put him to work on the farm. A few months later Joe was away again: drink, women, a throng of local toughs and Dereham dandies – and more debts, rows, accusations, disturbed nights. Sam put up with it – how had he ever put up with it for so long? – and then, when mortgaging the farm was all that was left to him, he refused to do it and called Joe to account.

Witnesses declared afterwards that Sam Uffington had been in a flaming, frenzied, volcanic temper, the like had never been seen, Joseph had been told to pack, to go elsewhere, that money would be sent when money was available, otherwise he must shift as he could. He went to London, took to gin, they said, gin being cheap and plentiful, and blew out his brains with a pistol.

Sam had taken it quietly, too quietly. It was not a thing a man got over lightly, and he held himself responsible, there was no doubt of that. It was some time before he resumed that air of resilient cheerfulness they had always associated with him, and when he did there was a new quality about it, the very slightest reserve.

The few dribbling candles blurred and wavered before Lally's tired eyes; the musty little room was comfortable and warm. The sleet spattered against the window and from far away came hoots of laughter, the whine of a fiddle. She thought of all the dark tracts of the past where even loved ones can never come, shadows and secrets and deeply private griefs no one else can ever share. She bent her head and saw Susan there, the small head in the crook of her arm almost a physical sensation.

Above her on the wall was a picture of a grossly overfed bull paraded by a sardonic gentleman in striped breeches. The bull looked resigned even though behind him, grazing by the large turreted house of his proud owner, were at least twenty presumably amorous cows. The man in stripes reminded Lally of JG, there was the same cock of the head, the same challenge. And what were JG's intentions towards Anne, Anne whose seasickness he had treated today with such complete indifference? He had not even asked how she did. Lally wondered if he had ever loved a woman and if so what sort of woman and when, in what country and circumstances and state of mind.

The fire subsided with a rush.

'Do you know,' came Anne's quiet voice after a long time, 'of all the people ... After all these years ... I do so miss Charlie.' And as the silence lengthened again, the afterthought: 'Do you?'

'Miss Charlie?' A long considering pause.

'I shall never forget how Mama sent him away: all that nonsense about discipline and responsibility, about curbing his excesses, about an honourable career. And now he is dead, and not one of us a whit better off, least of all Charlie, and sometimes ...' She looked up. In the candlelight her tired face was pure and sweet as a child's, as she remembered childhood, the cheerful nursery into which little cousin Philadelphia had been precipitated. 'Sometimes I think only Charlie ever made us laugh. Such mad scrapes and no, no sense of responsibility at all, but he was always ready to lend you money or argue your case with Mama or talk the maids out of telling tales. Oh, Lally, there are days when I wish ... When I wish he could come careering up the drive on Polly again and crash in through the front door without bothering to ring and simply ... make us all laugh again.'

She looked up and saw Lally's eyes full of tears. It had not occurred to her the pain was any greater for her cousin.

Lally got up and walked to the window, lifting the curtain to look out. The sleet had given way to rain again, the gutter was a river, all the lanterns were gone.

When she turned again her eyes fell on the gentleman in stripes. This time it was Charlie who looked back at her, it was Charlie's stance: head at such an angle, shoulders just so. Perhaps after all her aunt had been right to part them, for surely she had loved him, innocently yes, but deeply, deeply; and surely that last night on the Heath, the wind against her cheek, the pony charged with urgency, Charlie's familiar laughing face beside her, oh surely she would have died for him and been glad to do so.

It came to her belatedly that she had almost done so after all, on the sofa at Cookhams, before the horrified gaze of old Valentine.

CHAPTER 15

Lally was not used to having an uneasy conscience. Ever since the ball at Cookhams she had had a strong, at times almost irresistible desire to tell Sam about her adventure with Jack Brotherton on the Heath. She had even hoped there might be some opportunity to do so during the voyage on the *Snipe*, but the weather and Sam's fractious mood had kept her silent. Sam himself had never spoken of Brotherton, though after the incident in the conservatory he had been seen talking quietly to Horace, and certainly nothing had come of Jack's threats over a duel. Suddenly it seemed absurd to try to lay before him her suspicions, her dread, that Jack Brotherton was the highwayman. For some reason she feared reproof, scorn, even laughter, for although the two men were not friends nor ever could have been, even had Sam married Kate, a wholesome but restrained dislike was one thing, believing a fellow a common thief quite another.

The sea trip, besides diminishing Lally's resolve to confide in Sam, did some damage in other quarters as Anne had predicted. Kate was rash enough to declare, when challenged, that she had never liked a man as well as Bensley Vernon, that she could not see her parents' objection to him, that he had no vices, excellent health and a most tender heart. In short, she was going to marry him. He had asked her, she had said yes. This proposal must have happened on the cutter, it was reasoned, although Anne could not confirm it and only described in great detail the absolute misery of those eight heart-rending hours at sea. Eliza Brotherton said very little to her eldest daughter, though her uncharacteristic restraint was due mostly to her sense of being watched by her husband and son; they were afraid she would take Kate's side against them. Her instincts were on the side of true affection – and she was coming to see this was no fleeting infatuation – and a happy outcome; her instincts were therefore all for Mr Vernon. On the other hand reason pricked her with the thought that Mr Vernon was a less suitable match than even Sam Uffington, who at least had breeding and property to recommend him, and whose mild affection for Kate might easily have been fanned into something stronger. In consequence she was rather short with Sam when she met him at the poorhouse two days after the ill-fated voyage, and certainly snappish with Anne when she called at the parsonage to ask after Edward who had broken an arm falling out of a tree. She did not really hold either of them responsible, although both had been, in theory, by way of chaperons, and neither appeared to have tried to divert the course of this unfortunate romance.

Her real distress, caught as she was between love for Kate and an implacable desire to do the best by her and a mortal horror of rousing her husband and son to unaccountable wrath, brought her to Lally's tiny parlour and a sad confession that she was at her wits' end, did not know where to turn, and only that morning a letter – a very frank, kindly, reasonable letter when all was said and done – from Bensley Vernon begging leave to visit Kate at home, to pay his respects. The rage at the Cookhams breakfast table had been considerable, she had retired with a headache to add to the heartache she had already been suffering, and what was to do about it? What was to do?

Her visit gave Lally a headache and heartache of her own. She discharged her duties in the poorhouse with a mechanical efficiency, earned no smiles for it, indeed did not seek any. Peg told her diminutive husband she feared the wind and rain had got to Mrs Philadelphia, that she was 'feeling the climate', that she ought to apply to Dr Milton for a tonic to strengthen the blood. It came to something when all the girl would do was give a frosty smile, quite the frostiest smile Peg had ever seen, and leave on the stroke of noon as if she must get outside or die.

Lally, outside, repaired first to the cottage for an hour, an hour of sober reflection by the cheerful fire, Phee coming in and out asking if she would like something to eat, tea, chocolate, and Lally replying she wanted nothing, please close the door. In a while she stood up, looked out, judged the conditions, called for hat and cloak, gloves, pattens. Half an hour later she was blown into The Ship House on a squall and found the curate already there discussing bearded tits and woodpeckers and all the arguments for and against migration. There was an awkward silence during which both he and Lally turned a little pink.

'Dear Lally, come in, come in! Your shoes! Your skirts! Surely you have not walked from the cottage?'

She said she had, she had wished to consult him on some particular, and when both he and the curate remained looking at her expectantly she was forced to improvise, to fluff out something about a boy at the poorhouse with a facility for sketching birds, such a promising gift, how to encourage it and so on. She felt damp and foolish, the small flame of bold decision that had brought her here extinguished in the draught of Mr Hayes' quite natural curiosity.

'Is there not a raw feel to the wind?' he asked her, coming to where she stood by the window and looking out at the driving rain, the riven trees, the melancholy greyness. The river was in spate, roaring under the brick arches along with the debris of some miles of scoured banks: branches, weed, reeds, even dead fish and part of a boat. The top of his head was on a level with her chin, and she had just come to the conclusion his elderly yellowed wig looked like nothing so much as a mouse's nest, when he took her arm and led her to the fire with an awkward paternal air. She steamed there gently, wet patches even on her tight brown bodice, and little pools forming under her hem. Rush came, said ha she had been a-swimming, he could tell, and brought her some gritty cocoa and a foreign-looking sticky bun. JG and the curate fell to talking birds again, and the church roof – patched up once more, God help them, no money forthcoming from any quarter – and the smallpox. More buns appeared and more cocoa. Lally's hair dried to a frizz of curls. The two men, whose cocoa was fortified with smuggled rum, rambled on at length while the rain drove against the windows and the fire hissed and roared.

Had Mr Lovatt heard that the Revenue man wished to call at Cookhams? He had met Mr Brotherton on the road this morning, said the curate, the poor man near struck with a seizure, for it would not do. In a country where five hundred men could be raised in an hour when there was a cargo to shift, Revenue men were mentioned only in jest. Even in a magistrate it would be judged uncommon ill to allow such a man to come courting his daughter. Lally, eyes half closed, the warmth of the fire penetrating at last, thought of Rush crouched among the Cookham bushes with, presumably, Brotherton's contraband tea, silk and brandy, and she smiled.

The conversation to her left grew prolix: the rum was taking effect. What a business this wedding and settlement was, continued the curate, Brotherton must thank God daily he had only two daughters. There had once been talk of taking the elder to London for a time, but the expense! And whom would she meet there? Rogues, dissemblers, a whole gang of penniless adventurers on the look-out for a simple country wench well provided. No, no, there were gentlemen enough in Norfolk. What, for instance, did Mr Lovatt think of Hall, a decent young man, a great sportsman and heir to a considerable estate? Mr Lovatt had not had the honour. Mr Uffington then; did Mr Uffington's pedigree not bear close scrutiny, and a more charitable and patient man had never lived. It was only Sam Uffington, the curate declared, who had made his life in Ledworth tolerable, the place so ruinous, the parson so unsympathetic, the stipend so miserable.

Mr Uffington's pedigree was beyond reproach, his character unblotted, agreed JG with a crooked smile of affection Lally could not fail to see. What had been in doubt was his ability to keep Kate in the proper manner. Look at the house! And Sam drove the plough himself those times he could not employ enough men to do the work.

'The smugglers pay so highly the farmers cannot get labour,' said the curate, taking out tobacco and accepting a pipe, 'and I have been told, someone did mention, that Rooks Hill is not on the smugglers' list. I do not pretend to know what that means but it suggests perhaps some kind of blight on Mr Uffington and his house.'

On the contrary, said JG, puffing a cheroot, there was no question of blights. Rooks Hill was almost the only isolated farm in the neighbourhood where smuggled goods were never stored. Sam would not have it, even though the house was purpose built. It was a measure of the respect and affection he could command that it was never held against him, even though the entire local population benefited from smuggling and anyone who was not blind could see the pack ponies and waggons going by, sometimes in daylight, down the narrow lanes from the coast.

Lally, drowsing now, contented as a cat, lost track of the talk here, heard only snatches . . . unnatural assumption . . . last bell fallen out twenty years ago . . . a seal on the beach rushed off by some Norwich gentleman who claimed to have a laboratory . . . a pretty rose when out but invincible, obstructive thorns . . .

She jerked awake at Rush's announcement that there was a small boy on the threshold gasping for the curate – he had galloped from Lingborough for the parson was from home as ever – could the curate come for a desperate quick baptism, Mary Javy's baby was having fits.

Mr Hayes sprang up, snatched coat and hat, bid Lally good day, he hoped she was quite dry now, quite recovered. He was horribly flustered for he hated riding fast, he had a dread of horses that even extended to the dull old pony Sam had lent him, a pony of such kindly disposition it would consider unseating its rider a heinous crime.

'Poor man, he has such kind intentions,' said JG, coming back in after waving his guest on his way. 'He deserves better than Ledworth, better than Glover for a master. He is quite lost here, though he is at pains not to show it, for he is not native to the county, does not understand half of what is said to him, and has no wife to keep him company.'

'He is very well liked about the village,' Lally said. 'I have never heard a word spoken against him. He is conscientious, generous, and he knows what it is to be poor.'

'Then it is a shame the natural reserve of the country prevents the poor man from knowing as much. Here, should I call Rush for some tea, some madeira? There was something particular you wished to say to me, was there not? Something you could not say in front of the curate.'

But now it had come to the point she was struck by the impossibility of it, a great reluctance to commit the folly of accusing an innocent man; and on what grounds? Her reasons, her theories, her conclusions, were as fragile as a bubble of air. The decision to approach JG which had been brooded all morning after Eliza Brotherton's visit hatched now into a rather feeble: 'Have you seen anything of Jack Brotherton?'

'He has not molested you again, dear heaven, not again?'

'No. No. I was afraid . . . I have been afraid he might know about the smuggling.'

'My dear' – coming to poke the fire – 'no one but you, Rush, and the man who asked me here knows about the smuggling. I have been little more than a desk man so far, drawing up my plans of campaign on paper. I organise through intermediaries, through lieutenants you might say. It is easy enough with a network as large, as tried as this one; it is simply a question of keeping up morale, putting down factions, making sure there are no weak men in positions of trust or command. Now the new man is ready to take over and Mr Lovatt at The Ship House will shortly be packing his bags.'

'You are going to leave?' She had never considered it.

'I must. It don't do, as Sam is fond of telling me, to labour a point. Every disguise has its natural span of success; it is time Mr Lovatt was laid to rest. I have come perilous close to losing a grip on him when your cousin looks at me with those big appealing eyes, and on the ship – Vernon is genial and good-hearted but he is no fool.'

180

'You should not have taken him. I wondered at it when I saw him.'

'He asked himself, it seemed ungenerous to refuse him. Finding a plausible excuse would have been as ticklish as having him on board, he knew I had a scratch crew and a man of his competence must be welcome.'

'He does not suspect?'

'Not yet, I think. And he is too taken up with Kate to give me his full attention yet. He has been to thank me for the voyage, has nothing but praise for my attempts to further his suit, and gratitude has tended to fog his brain a little. It will wear off, there is no doubt of it. He is an able, thinking man. I have perhaps two weeks or so, depending on what's afoot at Cookhams regarding the match, before his mind clears and he brings his native intelligence to bear.'

Lally looked into the fire. All the warmth and contentment had left her. She was going to lose him as she had lost Charlie. Why should she think of Charlie; his face was nothing like Charlie's, not even allowing for the difference in ages, condition, experience.

'Come, don't look so dark,' he said, pulling out his French watch and glancing at it, 'you knew I was but passing through.'

'The ship is to take you to new pastures, new challenges. How strange I did not think of it before.'

He knelt at her feet busy with the fire, and then when he had finished sat back on his heels, threw off the great wig, the glasses, and his coat. The firelight was gold on the white sleeves of his shirt, the ruffles at his wrist, shimmered on his remarkable waistcoat. He reached and took her hand, opened it out within his own, traced the lines upon her palm.

'You are going to tell me your mother was a gipsy,' said Lally.

'It would be a lie. She was a duke's daughter, married beneath her, so it is said, but a duke's daughter none the less. I can make out nothing from cracks and wrinkles, Lally dear, but I can tell a great deal from taking your hand, and holding it thus, and feeling the life and strength in it. If you want my

181

opinion you were made for domesticity and monogamy, for fighting injustice, championing the poor, and helping Sam quell the obstreperous medical gentlemen about to make his life a misery over this projected cold bath. Yes, I think you and he would manage very nicely.'

He had linked his fingers in hers, was smiling up into her face. His dark hair was cropped short, showed a tendency to curl, and he was imperfectly shaved as usual. She drew a ragged breath and said: 'Your success with Kate and Mr Vernon has gone to your head. Sam needs a capable, biddable wife, one with whom he will never quarrel and who will not mind coming second in his affections to his land.'

'Hmm. You conclude he has no passionate parts, that because he is generally quiet and cheerful his appetites are easily satisfied? So he had almost convinced himself, I think. And he *is* amiable, and patient, and forbearing. But not all that is nature, he exerts a formidable self-control. His real loves, his deep loves, have brought him nothing but heartbreak, that is the truth of it, and so he keeps his tender feelings in check.'

'I am not sure he loved Anne deeply,' was all she could find to say.

'Anne? Who spoke of Anne? He loved his brother, sure, and the farm, the very soil of it – he would be the best husbandman in England were the weather and money to come into some alignment – and he loved a girl once when he was still a lad of nineteen and she was drowned; oh, it may have come to nothing being first love but being cut short in such a manner it left an indelible mark.'

It was darker than ever outside. The rain fell and fell. Lally looked down at her hand in his, the long fingers, the defiantly squared-off nails.

'He reminds me of Prince Yudishthra,' she said softly, 'who would not enter heaven without his dog.'

'I do not know the gentleman.'

'The Mahabharata. It is a sort of Hindu epic. Prince Yudishthra was … Never mind. It can hardly matter now. I must go home, Phee will be waiting and I promised I would not be long, that I would be back within the hour.'

'But you have not told me what you really came about,' as they rose and she reached for her cloak, where it dried in the hearth. 'Whatever it was is causing you to acquire lines upon your brow,' and he leaned and kissed them.

Cheroots, warm skin, his lips very gentle; she wanted to stand in his arms for ever, unmolested, safe, beloved. Instead, as he turned to search about for her hat and gloves, she crowned the reality of the moment by saying bluntly: 'You will not break Anne's heart, will you?'

'I assure you a chaste kiss is all I have ever claimed from the lady.'

'How may a kiss be chaste between a rogue and another man's wife?'

'In a long adventuring life, my love, I have discovered two kinds of kisses, those that are sweetly pleasant and promise nothing – and another kind. Your cousin knows nothing of the latter. I am not about to enlighten her.'

Lally tied on her hat and covered it with her hood.

'Rush! Rush you lobcock, where are you? Mrs Fletcher is leaving. Go look in the sea chest and see if you can't find the umbrella.'

'It was sunk from mortal view in Boston harbour you being in a hell-fire hurry to quit the shore and me loaded with parcels and packets like some common scrub of a carrier. I aint seen it since. Anyway, it aint fit for a lady, heccentric sort of thing like that.'

'Go and look in the sea chest, damn you.'

'This here temper of yours isn't good for me corns. Upstairs, downstairs, cut along here there everywhere, and as much cussin' and hollerin' as'd do a pirate proud. I'm getting too old for it. I should stow my carcase in a nice warm snug and keep a bottle company, I should.'

He grumbled away, to return in five minutes with a weird object that revealed itself a sort of ceremonial parasol, place of origin unknown. It was quite large enough to shade the head of an elephant, might once have been gold silk, was heavily fringed, and some wag, at some inglorious stage in its history, had covered the outer side with a piece of waxed sailcloth stitched on with fine, even, nautical stitches. It still opened and closed, though with difficulty, but it was a mere shadow of its former self, a sad, stinking, grimy shadow.

'There,' said JG in his naturalist's voice, 'is that not just the thing to get you safe home in the wet? I would walk with you but I am expecting a call from a gentleman who would prefer not to meet you, and who would not expect to be kept waiting. But Rush will hold the rainshade for you.'

Rush cocked an eye, looked mulish, and then took the umbrella from her limp hands.

'If I 'ave to be seen with this thing in me 'ands I'd like to get it over.' And once outside the door, grappling with it in the blustering wind: 'You want to mind how you hang on to this, it's the very devil in a strong blow. Don't remember where it came from, too many years ago, but His Lordship kep' it for sentimental reasons, told me a princess had sat under it for tea.'

A half dozen princesses might have benefited from its shade all at the same time but it made an indifferent shield against the driving wet of an English afternoon in late October. Its belligerent tendencies, its swoops and lunges, were checked by Rush's considerable expertise, expertise brought to a fine pitch by thirty years at sea in all weathers. He treated the umbrella like a renegade sail and by and large kept it over their heads. The difficulty arose because Lally was so tall and her reluctant squire so short, barely five feet four. The rain beat in his face and he objected to it, and his comments were pithy and unrestrained. By the time they reached the cottage and beat their way to the door he was soaked to the skin and water was dripping off his nose and chin.

'Thank you very much,' said Lally. 'Perhaps you should come in and dry your clothes.'

'Beggin' your pardon it would not be proper, not with your household all women and me an old salt with no manners. But it was kindly said, kindly. Oh' – turning back as he beat down the umbrella to manageable proportions and tucked it under his arm where it could do no more harm – 'a word of caution. There's to be some business conducted shortly, and His Lordship itching to be out there cuttin' capers with them Revenue men like he was a boy again and not already served time for His Majesty. If you was to let on I'd told you my life'd be worth a stick of tallow. But sometimes it's as well to know which way the wind is blowing.'

'He is to sail in *Snipe*? To help bring in a cargo?' She had stepped close to him, the rain soaking her hood and running on her cheeks.

'Lord save us, what did you think he'd bought the old lady for? Stiff little weatherly thing when we've come at that rigging, sail as sweet and swift as anything in these waters. Ho, wait until we have the guns aboard. They could give us chase to Halifax and never catch us. Lookee, go in, you'll be wetter than a duck. Go in, go in. Don't you worry 'bout His Lordship, he don't care for his skin but he aint lost it yet.'

And he set off at a running shuffle through the dusk, the huge umbrella tucked under his arm and his pigtail streaming water.

CHAPTER 16

'There is nothing wrong with his sense of humour in the main, it is his sense of the ridiculous that is missing,' said JG as he and Lally watched Sam striding towards them across the bleak field, his pointers at his heels. 'Are you warm enough? Hitch up the rug a little. There. I do not think he is pleased to see us.'

But his displeasure was more general, he had fallen foul that morning of Mrs Brotherton's well-intentioned but ill-informed zeal for his cold bath project, had had to listen subsequently to a lengthy description of Kate's unhappy condition that had failed to move him except to irritability. The truth was he had come home drunk from a dinner with Truelove, something which had not happened for years and years, though he was as capable as any man of drinking deep in an age that drank to excess. It had been a good dinner, the dinner two very old friends might share knowing they had no call to indulge in small talk, to pay false compliments, to appear more intelligent than they were, or to remember decorum for the ladies' sake. It had been a very pleasant meal indeed, rambling from ribs of beef to pheasants and on to an excellent apple pie, all washed down with decent claret. The conversation had been mostly agriculture, the likely outcome of an independent America, and cold baths, until Truelove had mentioned Lally Fletcher.

'Good day,' said Sam, looking at her now with a resentful eye as he came alongside the trap. 'You look chilled. Are you paying me a visit?'

'Lally has some curious errand to do with Mrs Hirtle, or Mrs Hirtle's idiot grandson who turns out to be less idiot than you have supposed but only deaf. I passed Lally striking out across the common and offered her a seat. It did not seem fitting she should walk in weather like this.'

It was certainly cold, icy cold. There had been sleet in the night and the countryside looked blasted even now, stripped to essentials, gaunt and brown. They went on down to the house, the roan horse cheerless between the shafts of the cumbersome trap, and Sam keeping pace morosely. Rooks Hill was smoking with equal lugubriousness by the rough green, all the geese in a hissing mob about the gate.

'You live uncommon primitive here,' said JG, helping Lally down. 'No wonder Anne was not overjoyed at the prospect of keeping house in such squalor.'

'I don't think you are qualified to criticise squalor, your own is too glaring an example,' said Sam, thrusting the dogs out of Lally's way, yelling for Mrs Hirtle, startling the kitchen maid who blushed raspberry at him and skidded into the safe dimness of the dairy, and flinging open door after door until they came to the quiet parlour with its banked-up fire.

'Cushion will bring you something warm,' he said, and Cushion did so, wheezing and gasping, for the wind had got into his tubes, he said, and Dr Milton unsympathetic, expensive and all for negus and early bed.

The wind and Rooks Hill were on intimate terms. There was not a door in the place that fitted tight in its frame. Huge quarrelsome draughts came down the chimneys and sent clouds of acrid smoke about the rooms. Lally, her eyes smarting, sat well back, the dogs at her knee sneezing occasionally with soulful, apologetic glances from their irresistible brown eyes.

'Hi, Rufus, leave the lady alone. JG, look what I found in the strawberry patch.' Heaving up a box: 'What do you think of him?'

'The poor tortoise, you have disturbed his winter sleep. You are an insensitive brute, Sam Uffington. You must cover him up and put him somewhere safe.'

'Where?'

'Under the stairs? In the broom cupboard?'

'With the brooms?'

'He will not mind the brooms, my dear, he will be asleep.'

The tortoise was duly despatched to the appropriate place and Lally made her way to Mrs Hirtle and a laborious and involved conversation, sometimes at cross-purposes, about the idiot grandchild. The discussion wandered off the point several times and wandered so far that at last Lally gave up the attempt at navigation and followed the tricky, meandering course between sloe gin, smallpox, the stone, mushroom catsup, and how Polly Spragg was terribly near her time and still would not say who was the father, overseers, magistrates and her mother notwithstanding.

There was a clatter outside. 'Lord, 'tis the Brotherton carriage,' cried Mrs Hirtle, darting to the window and back. She sent a boy to open the front door – Cushion was too feeble to do it – and one of the girls to get the order from the master. Lally said firmly she hoped Mrs Hirtle would prevail on her daughter to send the boy over to the cottage, that if it was possible to do something something must be done, and the distracted woman said yes, and yes, and started rapidly for the dairy on some mysterious errand that could not wait.

In the parlour Lally found Horace Brotherton straddling the hearthrug talking awkwardly about the weather to JG. He looked as if he was making an effort to be cordial, and JG's unexceptional replies made him bluster. He turned to Lally with a look of pure gratitude as if she had only that moment descended from heaven with a personal message from the Almighty. He beamed, he grinned, and he said: 'Mrs Fletcher, how are you? And your cousin? Damme but it's cold, eh? You look thin, m'dear. You must eat well. Winters in these parts are prodigious cold. Killing winds, you know. Killing winds.'

Lally assured him she had grown up in the killing winds, did not mind them in the least. He continued to beam on her, for now he had decided to like her she could do no wrong. He had thought the voyage on the *Snipe* ill advised but he did not hold her in any way responsible, and truth to tell Kate's drowned-rat appearance had made him slap his great thighs and hoot with laughter.

Cecy, sitting in one of Sam's threadbare chairs, feared he might do as much now, for he was growing heartier by the minute. She looked helplessly at JG, whom she considered uninteresting, elderly and practically a eunuch, and to her complete surprise he drew his spectacles down his nose and winked at her. She drew back as if he had bitten her. After a moment she glanced at him again; she had on a hat with a little feather curling down over her smooth white brow and her huge blue eyes gazed earnestly from behind it, devouring him. She was still very young, a little too plump maybe and not very tall, but she would do, she would do very well. As a rule her face was lit by her merry character, her boisterous sense of humour. Now it was very grave as she looked across at the black-coated naturalist who sat curling a lock of his wig round one finger. She stared and stared, graver and graver, but he did not wink again.

Refreshments came and went, much the way of refreshments anywhere, though Rooks Hill sometimes produced them in waves depending on the state of panic in the kitchen and the state of Cushion's tubes. Cecy went to sit by Lally on the hard sofa and asked her if she had seen Mr Vernon lately, was he at sea? He had not written to Kate, he was obviously a man of honour, and Kate very much wished to know where he was so that she, by some secret means, might send a message of her own. All this Cecy murmured in an undertone, while admiring the French clock on the shelf which showed the wrong time, the worn carpet, and the gloomy panelling which had, over many years, taken on the colour and perhaps the properties of charcoal. Occasionally odd scraps of the discussion taking place at the window floated over; the men were absorbed in plans to restore the terrace.

'You mean there are paving stones beneath that grass?'

'There are, by God. My mother used to sit on them.'

'I can remember her, a fine homely woman.'

'It will be a month's hard labour to uncover them again.'

'Can't get honest labour for the smuggling,' cried Brotherton. 'Damme, some men have asked me for ...'

'It could be a very fine house,' said Cecy, looking round with a speculative eye.

A little while later she toured it with Lally, the two of them sweeping through the dusty rooms with a feeling of sadness; it was a house for a family, a large family, and it was sorely neglected and empty. When they came back into the hall, in which there was a fireplace, and in which the floor rose and fell like the German Ocean, Cecy looked out of the window at the strident wind plying the young trees back and forth, and said softly: 'If I were Kate I would marry him tomorrow.'

In the parlour a heavy, embarrassed silence had fallen again and Brotherton turned his bloodshot eyes towards the two ladies with obvious relief. He began to talk about horses, for he knew Mrs Fletcher was a noted horsewoman, Jack had told him so. He was only sorry his own two girls showed no interest.

'Was you to give them some lessons I don't doubt we would have them jumping the hedges in no time,' he said hopefully. 'And it might come sweeter from you, being a woman, than from Thomas. Not that we haven't tried. Why, Kate was held in the saddle before she turned two, I recall, but sometimes I wonder if starting them too early don't do more harm than good, puts them off before they know what it's about.'

At this moment Cushion appeared to say that Brotherton's coachman was wondering if he should stable the horses, it was coming on to rain. This unsubtle hint that it was time he returned home turned Brotherton's face the colour of vinegar.

'Damn the fellow! Yes, tell him to put them up somewhere dry.' And then, with a slinking glance at the clock that told the wrong time: 'No, no. I shall see to it myself.'

'Poor Father,' said Cecy, getting up to correct the misleading timepiece with a saucy glance over her shoulder at Sam, 'he drove here to escape one of Jack's tantrums – oh, and to discuss the threshing, though that could have waited – and now Thomas is reminding him he should go home.'

'Does your brother often have tantrums?' enquired JG sweetly, casting down the week-old newspaper with which he had been beguiling the last ten minutes.

'Oh, Jack has rages, quite as awful as Papa's. It is always to do with bills, you see. He will ruin us in the end. I have heard my mother say so. We will be turned out in our shifts to pick stones.'

Sam, who was still in an unforgiving mood, thought that Mrs Brotherton in her shift would be a sight not easily forgotten in the Ledworth valley, and grinned; but it was a mere tightening of his muscles, he did not feel humorous. He felt Cecy's levity and candour deplorable, for all she considered him a very old friend and did not feel she had been indelicate, Jack's debts, whores and questionable friends common knowledge in the district. He tried to avoid looking at Lally, she too was deplorable, or so he ought to think after Truelove's revelations of the night before. It had been those revelations that had sent Sam home the worse for too much claret, far too much port, and even too much brandy. It was a wonder he had not expired at the table. And now the cause of his headache sat calmly on his sofa with her hands folded in her lap and a soft bright eye bent on JG, who was drawing Cecy away skilfully to look into the bag of stuffed birds he had been carrying to the curate before he met Lally on the road.

The crash of breaking china came from the hall.

'That was Cushion with the tea,' said Lally. 'Perhaps I could see what's to do,' and before Sam could object she was out of the room, the door closing firmly behind her. She could not stand being frowned on, she thought, in such a surly and resentful fashion. It had not been Sam Uffington who stood there but a perfect stranger, and since it seemed she was the chief cause of this transformation she would remove herself at once, and if JG could be detached from the delights of his taxidermy and Cecy's plump prettiness, would take herself off to the poorhouse.

'It was my fault,' Brotherton was saying, gazing at the wreckage on the floor while Cushion pursed his lips and muttered ominously. 'I was out of temper with that damned fellow Thomas and charged in without thinking.'

Lally suggested Cushion fetch Mrs Hirtle, who, far from investigating the noise would have fled, no doubt, to the far reaches of the dairy, and one of the maid servants with a bucket and cloth. Her air of quiet command overcame Cushion's inevitable protest and he hobbled off, silently, to do as he was bid. Lally then bent to pick up a piece of one of the lovely tea dishes now in fragments at her feet, and turned it in the dim light of the hall so that she could see the flowers and pheasants in their glowing colours.

'How is Kate?' she asked.

'Wasting, m'dear. I have forbid her this Vernon, will not have the dog in the house, and she calls me unnatural, calls me a tyrant. Damme, I never knew she had it in her. But there you are, it must be done for her own good. She can't go promising to marry any Tom Penniless who catches her fancy. S'death, the fellow would be worse than Sam.'

'I was not aware you held Mr Uffington in such low esteem.'

'Low esteem? Well, that is to say … No, never low esteem, my dear. But he don't have a penny to spare, the whole county knows it.'

'He has a big farm and farms it well.'

'Farms it himself, you mean. Yes, yes. And in twenty years, given good harvests, maybe a foreign war or two to put up prices, an abatement of tax, he might begin to profit by it. I admire him, don't say I don't admire him, but he was cleaned out by that rascally brother of his and will live half his life in debt because of it, mark my words.'

Mrs Hirtle arrived, gabbling about that old fool Cushion and how was she to preserve the best china in such a disorderly house? Lally dropped the dismembered pheasants into her bucket and smiled and said Cushion must be treated kindly, he was old and unsteady, and in future why did Mrs Hirtle herself not carry in the tea? On this gentle rebuke she left the scene on Brotherton's arm, aware of the low rumblings that were his suppressed laughter and the tears of mirth in his reddened eyes.

'Damme,' he cried to Sam as they entered the parlour, 'Mrs

Fletcher is setting your household to rights. She has Cushion cowed and Mrs Hirtle picking up bits of china as if life depended on it. 'Tis plain as my nose she's been in charge of a great house, won't tolerate subordination. Never raised her voice and all was peace and order.'

'Indeed,' said Sam.

'Were all your servants natives?' Brotherton turned to Lally: 'Damn quarrelsome, I suppose.'

'I never found them so.'

'How many did you employ?'

'Oh, maybe ninety. The rows and riots were confined entirely to the kitchens, for we had a cook from Goa who affected to speak nothing but Portuguese when roused, which was often, and he would lay about him with a rattan and a carving knife quite indiscriminately if things were not to his liking.'

A silence greeted these words. Lally, standing quite still with the old imperious lift to her head and a faint mocking smile about her mouth, wished she had resisted the ridiculous urge to challenge that gloomy, cold, and distant man who kept by the window and showed plainly, so far as she could see, that he had come recently by some way or other to dislike her intensely. But challenge him she had. Her instinct, her quick ear, trained to catch the first elusive sign of Francis's horrendous temper, had told her that Brotherton's mention of India had thrown Sam into even darker moodiness. Well, she did not care a toss for his opinion. She had thought he was her friend, had thought indeed she stirred him rather too deep for comfort, but if his friendship was so qualified she wanted none of him. She was what she was, what India had made her, and if she did not conform to his ideal of womanhood she could not find it in herself to be sorry for him.

She found herself telling Brotherton and Cecy, who hung upon her words, about the servants who waited at table, the wig-barber, the hookaburdar, and so on, without whom no rich merchant's house could function. Lally admitted, when pressed, that the ladies enjoyed the hookah as much as the gentlemen, that there were many customs in India that would seem strange to those who had never been there. At this point she found Sam's disturbing gaze upon her and stopped, made some light and commonplace remark about Cecy's hat, and declared it was long past time for her to leave.

'How magnificent you were,' JG said as they rattled away from Rooks Hill in the drizzle. 'You could not have hurt him more with a blow on the chin. I have no notion what has brought on this fit of sullens but I might hazard a guess someone has been telling him tales of India less innocent than your own.'

'Jack Brotherton? Oh, surely not.'

'And what does Jack Brotherton know about your life in India?'

'He received some third- or fourth-hand information he was quick to throw in my face.'

JG slapped the horse's rump as he tried to turn towards The Ship House, and he whipped him up as they reached the village and saw the common ahead.

'No,' said Mr Lovatt, looking at her over the top of his glasses, 'I believe we may discount young Brotherton. Sam would dismiss any story from him as scabrous lies. I am very much afraid you must have been damned in a respectable quarter, Lally dear, and the poor man believes it is the truth. He is trying to come to terms with his conscience, he is adjusting his view of you. Never fear he will come out in your favour. It is a shocking fact we overlook all manner of vices and omissions in those we love.'

She gave a rueful smile. He laughed, yelled at the horse. They careered across the common at breakneck speed, the wheels slamming into ruts and pot-holes and sheets of dirty water rising either side.

At last they drew up, the horse with heaving flanks and JG with his hat crooked and his devilish grin broken out again. Lally did not move.

'When is the next cargo?' she asked in a low sweet voice.

'Never you mind. Oh, so Rush has been up to some tricks,

194

has he? He has told you I intend to sail for it myself.'

'I have not mentioned Rush.'

'You do not have to. He hopes you might restrain my impulses, you see. He spends all his waking hours warning me of impending disaster, telling me that I have outstayed my luck, that to bring a cargo in to Lingborough is courting death. It is just I hanker for the sea so much, for true action, none of this covert, dusty paper-shuffling by the light of candles. I did intend to sail away in *Snipe*, she was not bought to run barrels on to Lingborough beach, but the alterations to the rigging delayed me and now I have a fancy for a little night adventure. It will be tame enough, no doubt, for we could disable a company of dragoons were they to be sent in time and Vernon has so much sea to patrol he will not trouble us.'

'You are making excuses.'

'Well' – raising her hand to his lips – 'I would not like you to think the real John Lovatt as whimsical as this one.'

She had climbed down and he was about to drive off when she turned, put a hand on the shaft.

'If anyone should tell you my child was not my husband's and I stole a fortune in rubies you will not believe them, will you?'

He looked down into her serious face, into the serious and stormy eyes.

'I would not.' And with a smile: 'And no more does Sam at heart.'

Sam Uffington was not known as a man of fiery emotions, and a long apprenticeship in restraint and self-denial had given him a good measure of command over all his passions. He had always been a fair man who cared for his workers, his cottage folk, and his livestock – you could tell a lot about a man, they said, by leaning on a gate and looking over his cattle – but after Joe's death there came a slightly harsher note, a hardening of his attitudes; he had always been held in affection by his men but now that affection was tempered with awe, and his open nature sometimes struck a tone of reserve as if, like Lally

Fletcher, there were inconvenient moments when memories intervened.

He had struggled very hard for his land, for the farm. He had been born and brought up there, knew every square yard, every stump, pond, fox hole and rabbit warren; the big old house, the cow byres, the blasted garden were imprinted on his soul. He knew, though he was not a ghoulish man, that his shade would haunt it after he was dead. And he hoped, with that unconscious hope that is not really of the brain, to be laid to rest in Ledworth churchyard in the shadow of the poor crumbling tower he had tried so hard to save. He had no pretensions, wished only to lead the life, the plain, cheerful life, of a country gentleman, wished only to see his land in good heart, his barns full, his beasts fat. Whatever other ambitions he might have had Joe had destroyed. Such blows as Joe had struck, even in death, came hard to a sensitive spirit. Like other such spirits he took refuge in a kind of friendly remoteness, a smiling but determined standing apart.

Lally knew all about that, of course.

Lally knew all about that road of retreat, had paced it through scores of aching nights in the dim past, had vigilled at its outposts often and often. The Lally on the homecoming Indiaman had perhaps been Lally at the place where that road petered out into the thickets of despair. In her eyes Sam had once or twice seen with a shock his own feelings mirrored and magnified. He had wondered angrily what exactly Fletcher had done to her and how she had supported life so long in the company of a man like that: it was how he spoke of him to JG – 'A man like that'. What he thought in private, in the blazing recesses of his mind, was couched in language even Rush would have been proud to call his own.

At what moment he was consumed – it was certainly not too absurd a word for it – by the desire to have Lally Fletcher, in his bed, at his table, riding beside him across his windy acres, he could not say. He could not now remember the beginnings of this desire, try as he might to remember the finer details of their early meetings, but he knew he had always been struck by her effrontery, her frankness, her tendency to ride dead straight at every obstacle. He might have declared himself but she did nothing to encourage him and more than once he came to the conclusion she was in love with JG. An irrational envy, both of the dead and the living, put him in a bad temper, and indecision, respect, desire and chivalrous restraint battled in his breast. This was the mood that had ruined his voyage in the *Snipe* and that had threatened to make him a truculent dinner companion at Tom Truelove's.

Truelove had been to his bank in Norwich and there had met an old acquaintance, an elderly gentleman who had been a friend of his father and who had, these many years, lived quietly in London, spending most of his days in the coffee houses, and all of his evenings in his extensive library. He thrived entirely on educated talk, literary gossip, and the occasional dinner with men of standing in the banking world, his other great interest. At one of these dinners he had heard that a certain lady had returned to England, indeed, had returned to Norfolk. Perhaps Truelove had had occasion to meet her. Her name was Philadelphia Fletcher and she was the widow of the most corrupt vile dog ever to enter service with the East India Company.

The gentleman who told her story, such as he remembered it, was not devoid of sympathy for Lally. Had Francis been only moderately vicious, no more than the common run of men in a rich, pleasure-seeking society, Lally might have been dismissed out of hand as a harlot and a thief. Francis's sins being many, however, too many even for the most charitable of those who knew him, Lally was excused to a certain extent; there was no denying her misery must have been acute. It did not diminish her notoriety, of course: society in London would be justified in shunning her. It did not diminish her actual guilt. But what could one expect of a woman whose husband worshipped Bacchus to the last degree?

Perhaps Truelove related the story – the story of Lally's long love affair with Francis's brother, the story of her child, and the story of the Sarawar rubies – without the sympathy of his friend at the bank or that friend's London dinner companions. His tone had an edge of I-told-you-so about it and as more wine flowed he even became openly self-congratulatory, as if he alone in Ledworth had perceived the loose woman through the widow's veil, so much so that he failed to notice he was making Sam thoroughly miserable, that Sam's face had not only grown dark but that distress and disbelief had drawn his mouth into a hard line, a very hard line indeed.

It was not, Truelove asserted as they began on yet another bottle of the claret, that one lover constituted promiscuity or one theft cupidity, but the information showed the lady in a different light and not to her advantage. There had been monstrous debts in Madras too, quite monstrous; she had fled without honouring above half of them. This fact, and the thieving, counted more for Truelove than adultery, though he was tinged by a harsh, bigoted, dissenting puritanism, for they went against the code of honour he himself subscribed to; for the other, he was a man, after all, and in the dim past had not been strictly monogamous.

It grieved Sam to hear Lally spoken of lightly in this manner, more so because it was a friend who spoke thus. He had always found Truelove open and generous, ready to help in emergency, give sound advice and furnish an excellent bottle. The streak of righteousness which Sam privately alluded to as 'that damn Presbyterian taint' did not intrude on their friendship. It hurt him to find Truelove had always nurtured reservations about Lally. Even through the fog in his brain brought on by the wine he acknowledged it though, for had there not been continuing, dogged reluctance to let Lally rent the cottage? Had there not been a wariness, a reservation on Truelove's part?

All this was still in Sam's mind as he watched JG drive Lally from Rooks Hill, an odd equipage, and Lally trying to open a gigantic umbrella, a vast oily-looking thing with a fringe. She had deliberately thrown India in his face, he thought, had lifted her chin and given him that imperious stare and had talked sircars and palanquins, curries and tigers, quite as if she had overheard every sentence of last night's conversation and was determined to show him she did not give a rupee for his opinion of her, however low, however degrading.

And he had loved her for it. Only in that moment had he known how much and how deeply he loved her.

He sighed and looked out of the window at the wet, writhing trees, the geese – dejected geese, it wanted but six weeks to Christmas – and wondered how best to tell her so. In a little while Mrs Hirtle knocked timidly, and came in with the cheerless information that of his mother's pheasant tea service only three dishes, two saucers and one small jug were still intact. There was something else, she added hastily, finding him indifferent to the news, Mr Lovatt had forgotten his bag, the capacious bag with the drawstring neck in which were – had been – some stuffed birds. It was the peculiar whiff of corruption, a slightly stoaty, rancid whiff, that had attracted the dogs. She had swept up the remains, had put the bag in the pantry. Would Sam care to explain to Mr Lovatt?

'I think the least said the better,' said Sam brutally, turning from the window. 'His memory is none too good. If we keep quiet he may forget he ever brought them here, or if not let us hope we can convince him he dropped them on the road.'

CHAPTER 17

The following day brought Mrs Brotherton to the cottage on the common and a half hour of supreme embarrassment, acrimonious exchanges and long bitter silences to Lally.

'My dear, you should have told me,' Eliza said at last. 'Perhaps then we might have avoided this unpleasantness. I have no quarrel with you. How could I have? Of course Mr Truelove suggested you were not a suitable companion for Kate and Cecy, reminded me it was you brought Vernon and Kate together, and said you were wanting in discrimination, that you were far too intimate with Mr Lovatt, that you are overbearing and wild. I fear I was very short with him, told him I did not like his attitude, that I had my own opinion of your character and it was sounder than his. How I detest that man on his high horse. It is ungentlemanly to be so vehement when destroying another's good name, it smacks of malice. And he is so temperate, so generous ordinarily.'

'Do you believe what he told you?'

'Believe it?' Eliza raised puzzled brows. 'My dear, I had a cousin once, a shy brown dab of a thing, would not speak to a soul though the house was burning about her ears; she went to London to be companion to an old aunt. A year and a half and what do we hear? She has treated the aunt cruelly and the aunt is dead of apoplexy, she has had a child by the footman, she has gone upon the stage. It was the last particular made me doubt I had been told the truth. *I* might have treated the old lady ill – she was a female Jeremiah, praised no one, resented the least imposition – and *I* might have dallied with the footman, were he good-looking, but I would never go upon the stage, though I love all drama and have been called loquacious. And nor would that pale shrinking mouse. It turned out the old lady had died quite naturally, the baby

200

belonged to the laundress, and the stage was not the sort that actors trod upon but the sort drawn by four horses.'

Lally smiled, sank down into her chair. The ache, the sense of injustice, eased a little.

'My child was my husband's and I stole nothing,' she said.

Eliza leaned to pat her knee. 'I never doubted it. That is why I hurried here as soon as Truelove was well out of the house. Mark my words, I said to Horace, he will be hot-foot to the parson to spread the tale and poor Lally none the wiser. You see, my dear, he intends to have you removed – from the cottage, from the poorhouse. He is become fanatical, unreasonable. When I cautioned him Sam Uffington would not see it done he laughed, said Sam was acquainted with the facts, that we should but wait and see, oh, a great deal more equally childish.'

'I suppose the parson will call for my removal also.'

'He may shake the pillars but I doubt the roof will fall. But if Stapleford should come down against you then Sam and I will be hard pressed.'

'I very much fear that Mr Uffington is of the same opinion as Truelove.'

'Stuff! He is not such a fool.'

Lally gazed round the little room, clean and sparsely furnished. A sense of purpose, she thought, she had begun to find one here ... The poorhouse, the dream of the school Eliza spoke of often, the little deaf boy whose education she had barely begun. She had not found peace of mind, had not shaken off the past, but time ... time would help her. She would grow into a busy old spinster, a martial, interfering, reforming schoolmistress. But now?

Her mind ran on and on, turning over the possibilities, the brief joys, the tenacious hopes. Was this hard-won precarious independence to be snatched away? She could not return to the parsonage, she could not throw herself on Caroline's mercy: pride forbade it. In that case it was a position in a gentleman's household, a teaching position perhaps, she would almost certainly have to advertise ... And on and on.

After a little Eliza, seeing the shadowy thoughts chasing across that expressive face, sensing anguish, conflict, even confusion, reached out her plump little hands.

'My dear, I am so sorry,' she said.

And Lally slid forward till she was kneeling, her head in Eliza's lap and Eliza's arms around her.

'You must face it out,' that lady said. 'They will say in Lingborough that Truelove is a canting puritan, they will always follow Sam's lead. My dear, do not cry, do not cry. Phee will be in to see what we are about.' A moment's reflection, a glint of battle growing in her eye: 'Be damned to them! We shall build my school yet!'

Late afternoon brought a letter from the parsonage, a long, cold, angry letter setting out in detail the extent of the parson's displeasure. The boy who delivered it, dismounting from the pony by the cottage door and digging about his person for a while, produced another carefully folded sheet from a more secret place and blushed a little as he handed it over. It was from Anne, sweet, unaffected, to the point: she would call in the morning, if she had not felt so ill – sure she was with child again – she would have come today, not only that would cheerfully have dismembered Tom Truelove in front of the entire population of Ledworth. She had thought him a gentleman, not a gossip-mongering, moralising, gullible fool.

Phee drew the comb through Lally's brown curls.

'Pile it up,' said the voice of Mrs Fletcher of Madras, and watched with satisfaction as Phee lifted and twisted and thrust home the pins.

The dark blue dress was shaken out, the silk rippling in the grey light. Lally dressed with cold fingers, leaving the hooks to Phee, watching her ghostly reflection in the mirror. She reached for her cloak, drew up the hood.

'I should come with you, Mem Lally,' said Phee.

'No, I would rather go alone.'

She would rather go alone; she had fought all her battles alone. She crossed the common with her long stride, holding the cloak together, for there was a playful wind and her silk bodice was thin. She kept up the pace, did not look up, was carried on and on until the turn down through the mud to Rooks Hill, already sinking in the twilight to a strange amorphous mass, and not a thread of smoke, and no light in the windows, and only the distant, sad lowing of cattle and the sharp cry of a hunting owl. She hesitated, drawing the cloak tighter. Her resolution wavered. And then she saw there were lights, dim horn lanterns ranged on the gate posts and the low wall by the yard. She half ran towards them, the cold piercing, the wind getting under her hood to snatch at her curls. Then the door, Mrs Hirtle with round, round eyes and gasping in astonishment, and the long procession of doors within, this latched, that with a brass handle, and at last the parlour with its leaping fire and Sam writing at the table, head bent, the pen going scratch, scratch in the warm stillness.

The dogs rose to their feet, stretched, yawned, padded over to push at her hands. Their thin tails whipped side to side, their eyes glowed a welcome. Sam, who had ignored Mrs Hirtle's knock, rose slowly when he saw who it was, the pen falling on the paper, surprise, even shock, mingling with the welcome in his face. He was in a brown frock coat and breeches, a shabby brown frock coat, comfortable, much worn. Mrs Hirtle had crept away, closing the door, so Lally let her cloak fall on the back of a chair. When she turned it was to say with bold self-assurance: 'I have come to ask you to drive me to the parsonage.'

'Tonight?'

'Tonight. Tomorrow will not do' – a flash of her eyes – 'tomorrow I may have lost my courage.'

'You do not mean to tell me Tom has been to see the parson? The fool. I do not understand why he has to meddle.'

An encouraging smell of mutton came under the door on the circulating draught of cold air.

'Do not wait dinner on my account,' said Lally, 'I shall wait until you finish. I only hoped . . . I only hoped you might have the goodness to take me to Lingborough so that I can lay my case before you and Mr Glover. And Anne is ill, and troubled, and wishes to visit me tomorrow, which I cannot allow, she will be miserable and probably sick, besides which she will displease the parson by coming and I do not want her chastised on my account.'

Sam caught at the dogs' collars, exhorted them to lie down, to leave the lady's shoes. He straightened, smiled, and stepped to the fire to haul long and hard on the bellrope.

'It may ring,' he said, 'it may not. And of course I cannot eat my dinner while you sit like patience on a monument. You must join me. No, you must not refuse, I will not let you. How can you face the parson on an empty stomach?'

His black mood had left him, she saw. He was happy to have her there. She had expected him furious, affronted, sullen, anything but this, this sudden frank, smiling delight. She had armed herself against everything but this, had come prepared for rejection, censure, moral sermons, outrage. She might have guessed he would no more sermonise than a barbary ape, and that outrage was an emotion completely unknown to him. Perhaps the relief was visible in her strained face, perhaps not, she kept great care that her dignity was as absolute as she could make it, absolute. The air of damn-you-all arrogance she had cultivated in Madras served her well.

'The Heath is a heathen wilderness after dark,' he said, almost to himself, going to put up his writing things and snap shut the lid of the ink well. 'We shall have to go well armed.'

'There has not been another robbery?'

'No. No, thank God. But last night there was a patrol sent up, hoping to flush out whatever was there. Brotherton had roused out some of the Lingborough lads – he spoke about it when he was here yesterday. He feels it is his duty to scour the place for villains. Anyway, we all rode up there, armed to the teeth, damn cold, looking like banditti ourselves, and there was nothing to see, nothing, only the tinkers by Tuppeys Hill and a poor old woman turned off parish relief in Holt and reduced to beggary said there was nowhere else to go. You will see her in the poorhouse, no doubt, tomorrow.

Brotherton gave her a shilling but when he had passed by I told her to come down here, to see Peg. She was old, Lally, old, and had scarce a rag to cover her.'

His use of her name had been unconscious and he did not notice it. She did. A warmth spread through her, and her spirits rose.

It was a strange dinner though, and for all their scrupulous avoidance of the name Truelove or mention of things Indian, they were formal and restrained. Sam had never entertained a lady alone before, not at any rate a respectable lady, and felt difficult about it, not least because of the tenderness and the barely stifled desire he had kept hidden so long; Lally had never dined alone with any gentleman except her husband, and those memories were painful. Mutton appeared, astringent capers, and a sort of hearty plum pudding to follow. It was a solid utilitarian meal for a man who spent a long day in the fresh air. She must forgive him, said Sam awkwardly, he had not been expecting company, and Mrs Hirtle's cooking always left a lot to be desired. She could not come to grips with sauces and her most painstaking ministrations left any kind of fish as disintegrated as if it had been grape-shotted.

Lally found the return of his gentle humour reassuring. She picked up her wine, in which the reflection of six white candles blazed and glittered. Her eyes were blue tonight, deeply blue; the lovely dress, the exhilaration made them so. She raised her glass.

'To Kate and Bensley Vernon,' she said unexpectedly.

Sam drank, raised an eyebrow, wondered at her choice. As if he had wondered aloud she said: 'They are in love. I would hate to see them parted. I have seen too many precious things wasted for want of care or understanding.'

He saw that the shadow of India would lie across the rest of her life, but perhaps, he thought, some good might come of it in time, perhaps she would be stronger or more compassionate or more patient.

'Here's to a safe journey across the Heath,' he said, to lighten the mood. 'I am afraid there will always be desperate men up there.'

'I never saw one when I used to ride there with Charlie.'

'Charlie? He was confounded lucky he never broke his neck' – a pause to feed scraps to the dogs under the table – 'or yours.'

'He never considered it. But how ironic it seems that I am reduced to needing an armed escort over that little bit of the world I love best.'

Sam grinned, drained his glass. He would not have to drink too much, he must keep a clear head for the parson, for Lally too. She was slender, pliant, her eyes huge and dark now, she was a little drunk perhaps.

'You must think me a lout,' he said, 'a complete fool. Did you believe I would listen seriously to a parcel of gossip, that I would throw your past in your teeth? I am ashamed Tom thought I might, that he saw fit to halloo your private business up and down the valley.'

She did not reply. If he had only known it she could think of nothing to say. She was conscious of the comfortable litter of their meal, of the yawning dogs, of the quiet warm room with its ticking clock and crackling fire and the smell of soot and beeswax and camp. She was conscious too of Sam's ardently friendly attentions, the way he looked at her. When he rose and held out his hand to her she did not take it, found her own way to the hearth, afraid to touch him as she had been once before, afraid he might elicit some response in her. She did not want to love him. Francis had taught her all about lust and she wished to forget.

'We should start for the parsonage,' said Sam briskly, hanging once more upon the bell. 'If you catch the parson still at his dinner you may reduce him to indigestion along with an apology.'

'That is a wicked thought, and not worthy of you.'

The dogs came to her, pushing at her hands until she stroked their broad heads, and for a moment, a brief, scorching moment she thought that Sam was watching her with that hungry look, but then he had gone to the door and opened it, shouting for Mrs Hirtle.

'You know,' he said, coming back to help her with her cloak, 'this scheme is ill advised.'

'Of course it is. But if there is nothing to be gained well, there is nothing to be lost. He wrote a cruel letter, dashed off in a proud, uncharitable – oh, unchristian – temper. He believed the worse of me. He did not have the courage to accuse me to my face, but he believed the worst, condemned me in an instant. No, no,' and she clutched her cloak together, her head up, her eyes filled with tears, 'it is injustice. It is injustice and I shall tell him so.'

'A cut-throat place to be sure,' said Sam, looking out at what he could see of it in the blustering dark. 'There is not a house in miles and enough gorse and thorn scrub to hide any army. No wonder the Revenue men sit tight in the ale-houses and drink themselves silly. Would you venture up here to face a hundred armed men?'

'I rode up here once, remember, masked and cloaked and with Charlie's pistol in my belt.'

The thud of hooves on wet earth and the creak and groan of the elderly chaise competed with the noise of the wind. Side by side in the dark he could not see her face, and she seemed to have returned to her usual calmness, but he had no way of judging which memories were the most painful. He was a plain-speaking man, did not often think elliptically, but he pondered the possibility her love of the wild Heath, her fond inflexion, were due in part at least to the fact that this was where she and Charlie had been happy. He could just picture her, the moonlight on her martial nose, the pistol wavering in her slender hand.

'Thank God you were not up to such tricks the other night when we were scouring the heather for the highwayman. Jack Brotherton has a habit of shooting anything that moves. If I didn't know him better I would say he was nervous but the sorry truth is he would enjoy killing a poor old beggar and then telling the jury with tears in his eyes he mistook the man for a rabbit. His is that sort of humour.'

'I know.'

'Yes, of course you do. He is a wily, unpredictable, dangerous cove, the more so since drink makes him belligerent and he is so often drunk. Brotherton never seems to get the better of him, has never tried to turn him out or cut him off – though Jack is in the way of doing it for himself, he will bankrupt the family. In spite of everything the old man loves him, would do anything to reform him, is brought low every time they quarrel. It is a sad business.' His tone told Lally he knew it from bitter, unbelievably bitter personal experience. 'Jack will bet on anything, you know. He gambles everything away. He will kill old Horace in the end with his extravagance: gout, apoplexy, the stone the doctors will say, but it will be a broken heart, it is not too fanciful. The girls will lose their portions too. I see it happening already, I have walked that road myself. But there is not a drachm of pity in Jack, no, not even when he's sober. He is only less mercurial, less by a small degree, mind you. I have known him irrationally savage to a harmless, disobedient cur when he had not touched a glass for twenty-four hours. No doubt that time abstinence was to blame; he cannot live without the bottle.'

Lally, pressed close against the side of the carriage, her ear practically against the wood, thought she heard the sound of hooves in pursuit. She listened hard, but the sound had died away. With difficulty – the chaise was very old, a one-horse chaise purchased in a fit of rare extravagance by Sam's father in the days when the roads first became passable for wheeled traffic – she let down the sash, and a blast of freezing air took their breath away.

'Put it up, woman! Put it up! We shall be iced to the seats,' cried Sam, but after she had complied and had settled back, stifling a yawn, he said: 'JG is hoping to return to Virginia, and he has some plan to venture afterwards into Brazil. They have charmingly exotic birds in Brazil.'

'He will cross the oceans in the *Snipe*, I suppose.'

'Yes,' a dull, considered yes, as if his thought had strayed, as if a sombre note had been struck. 'Yes, in the *Snipe*.'

They were on top of the Heath now, rattling on towards Tuppeys Hill and the steep descent to Lingborough and the sea. Lally, opening her mouth to make some trivial remark that would lead him off the subject of JG, was shot forward suddenly as the carriage bucked to a halt, hitting her head and tumbling in an undignified heap at Sam's feet. He retrieved her, crammed her back in her corner, and stuck out his head.

'What is it, Clem?'

It was a gentleman on a dark horse not five yards away, a gentleman with a pistol, masked and sinister in the capricious moonlight, hat well down and drably nondescript from head to foot.

'Get down,' commanded this apparition, bringing up his left hand with another pistol. Sam threw a startled glance behind at Lally, shrunk rather stupefied in her seat, and opened the door.

'Put your guns in the road. Yes, just so. Throw them. And the musket. Now your valuables.'

They mustered five guineas, a gold fob, a watch between them, Lally's contribution being five shillings and Clem Cushion's sixpence. Sam stood by the coach looking ferocious, aching to do violence, and unable to think of any action with a reasonable chance of success against an armed man on a horse. Lally, recovering from the shock, appeared in the doorway.

'Get back,' said Sam, irritated. But she ignored him, struggled out of the chaise in a great billow of skirts and dragging cloak.

'Sam,' she cried, slipping in frosted mud and borne up against him by the sudden clutch of his arms: was she asking to be shot? 'Sam!'

The man on the horse laughed, and turned, and a minute later was nothing more than hoofbeats in the wind. Clem, who had been rigid with fright from the first, climbed down very slowly from his horse's back and cast about for Sam's fine pistols and the old army musket. Sam helped Lally back inside.

'Smugglers or highwaymen, the place crawls with both,' he said in a voice which, though good-humoured, still hinted at his suppressed fury.

'Have you been robbed before?' It was all she could think of to say.

'Oh, once, long ago, when old Moonshine was patrolling this beat – that was in the year the American colonies first talked of independence – he took my horse as well as my coat and my last guinea. It was a sobering experience.'

'Did they catch him?'

'Hugh went to Lynn to see him hung and they put him up in the cage on Tuppeys Hill afterwards for an example, much good it does anybody. I often wonder what he did with my horse.'

She was shivering. She must tell him, she thought, she must. He had shut the door, gone to speak to Clem. In a moment he came back and climbed in, and the chaise began to lurch round.

'I told him to go back. You are in no state to face the parson.'

'He might have been exceedingly sympathetic.'

'He might not. And Anne might be exceedingly frightened.'

They had travelled a quarter of a mile before he spoke again. He disliked not being able to see her face, but the moon swam through a heavily clouded sky, a sky torn and troubled by the wind, and even when it shone clear, briefly and hugely, all the occupants of the chaise received was a vague diffused light, the windows were so very small and dirty. Lally had been silent so long he had wondered with a start if she was crying. He had not expected her to be so shocked after the incident. True, there had been very real menace, and it would cost the robber no more to kill his victims than to let them go, the hangman settling the score for either, but so far the highwayman on the Heath had shown no inclination to shoot anyone and it would be a desperate mad fellow who would shoot an unarmed man and a woman.

She *had* been shocked. He had seen it in her face. In the moment she had sprung through the door and missed her footing and clung to him, he had seen fear quite plainly in her face. No, he had not expected it. He did not underestimate her courage, physical as well as mental, and JG had told him all about the confrontation in the conservatory, how in another moment she would have scratched Jack Brotherton's eyes out.

'Are you cold?'

'No.'

He put his large hand over hers where it was clenched on her knee.

'Dear Lally,' he began and then stopped, feeling foolish, this really was the most unsuitable time and she would reject him out of hand. 'Were you afraid?'

'He reminds me of Francis,' she said.

He was deep in tangled thoughts of his own, thoughts made less easy to follow because of his painful awareness of the scent of her hair, the pressure of her arm next to his, and the excusable impropriety of cradling her against him for comfort's sake. He scarcely heard her words, made out only 'Francis' clearly, and that stirred his pity and the familiar feelings of jealousy and frustration. He turned, eased his arm behind her, reached out his other hand to feel her cheek, and drew her face to his.

There are two kinds of kisses, she heard JG's voice say, those that are sweetly pleasant and promise nothing – and another kind. Vehement tenderness, longing, longing ... but not for Sam. She tried to draw away but could not, his hands were about her throat, she could not breathe, could not think ...

'What did you say?' He raised his head. His breath came as short as hers. His fingers slackened, held her gently now, stroking the line of her jaw. 'What did you say?'

What had she said? She had never been kissed like this; it was unjust, all her senses wakened and crying for another

211

man.

'I said he reminded me of Francis,' she said at last.

'The highwayman?'

She felt his hands fall apart and release her. 'The highwayman.'

It was for the best, she thought, easing herself away, as far away as she could get in that stuffy little interior. It must be for the best. There was no passion in his touch now, and she was suddenly thankful. I am not the sort of woman he likes, she thought, all this is something that will blow away and be forgotten, like leaves in the wind.

'I did not know the merchants of Madras rode about at night masked and armed, holding up honest travellers,' came his voice, more even now, though if the words were intended to be humorous they fell sadly flat. 'In what way did he remind you?'

She could feel the chaise tilting as they jogged carefully down the lane to the ford by The Ship House, could hear Clem's long-drawn-out commands to the horse, his sharp encouragement when the water was reached and they plunged in, rocking violently.

'Lally, do you know him?'

She had bent her head so that her words, when they came, were muffled. He bent closer.

'He is Jack Brotherton,' she said.

CHAPTER 18

Life was not worth living if one had to spend every moment warding off the ghosts of the past. So Lally decided two days later when she had woken to find the pale November sun glittering on the iced puddles outside. The wind was still keen but now it was an invigorating, kindly blow, bearable because of the sun and the sudden beauty of the brown and amber landscape revealed at long last after so many weeks of rain and fog. Phee had lit the fire extra early; the parlour was warm and pleasant, and Lally lingered over breakfast. She thought perhaps she ought to have had an overwhelming sense of anticlimax after pouring out the story of her adventure on the Heath to an anxious, subdued Sam in this very parlour two nights ago; instead she felt as if her heart was light and full of hope. He had not thought her a fool, he had not dismissed her suspicions as womanish folly, and he had asked pointed, respectful questions that showed he had listened and was gravely concerned. He had also left her in a mood of the utmost friendliness, holding her hand for a moment, telling her she must sleep sound and not to worry, that Truelove would never poison the district against her, that only Stapleford's extreme exertion could remove her from the poorhouse, and that if the parson interfered he would be seen as grossly uncharitable.

She had sent a note in the morning to Anne, begging her not to come, she would visit the parsonage as soon as she could herself; the parson's letter had not actually forbidden her the house. The curate took it to Lingborough, for he was due for one of his periodic dressing-downs, long, involved, gloomy denunciations of all the curate had achieved, had hoped to achieve, had said, had preached, or had left unsaid or unpreached during the previous few weeks. These unhappy encounters Mr Hayes took in good part, for he was too mild to object, he was under no illusion he could moderate the parson's character at this late date, and he knew he could look forward to a quiet, absorbing hour with JG, with the owls, with the ringed plover, on his way home.

It was to his cottage Lally made her way after breakfast, hoping to beg the loan of his pony. The garden boy from the parsonage had brought her yet another impassioned note from Anne, it had arrived in time to ruin her new-found content and her second cup of tea. Anne was ill; there had been rows; Sam had shut himself up with the parson for an hour yesterday and a terrible, brooding silence had chilled the house ever since. The parson would not eat, had not spoken, and had set off to Lynn on diocesan business with all the disagreeable grunting and grumbling of a mean-spirited camel. Certainly Anne did not actually write this, but Lally read it between the wild lines. She called Phee, explained, went upstairs to change into her habit and find her old hat, and then picked up whip and gloves and made off for the curate's.

She did not find him at the cottage, she found him in the church. She heard his distracted mumbling as she heaved open the heavy old door and stepped inside, sniffing at the decayed, mouldy, deadened air. Today something else was upon that air: dust. It was a choking, pervasive dust and it floated visibly in the sunbeams that fell through the plain glass windows – all the good glass had long ago been torn down or borne away – and had settled thickly over the wormy pews. In the aisle was a bucket of hedgehogs; they had been packed in straw and looked helpless and bewildered. They had been put to hibernate in the vestry, Mr Hayes explained, issuing forth from some corner in a whirlwind of motes and little falling grains and puffs of powdery plaster, but the east wall had collapsed in the night, had necessitated certain rearrangements.

'They are to catch the vermin,' he told Lally, leading her to the scene of demolition. 'But what is to be done? Where is the money to come from to rebuild? And the tower is in a perilous

state. If it falls it will destroy the nave, oh sure to, sure to ...
And where will my bats go? Where?' He rubbed sorrowfully
at his warty face and left huge streaks of white dust there. If
they had snow, he went on, peering upwards at the patched
roof, they would surely be undone, there was nothing as bad
as snow for getting under tiles. But come, come, there was no
need for despair, not quite yet. He had been polishing up the
brass, did it not look very fine? There was no plate; well, that
was to be expected, too much loot and pillage over the
centuries and the church always very poor, very poor, serving
such a scattered, rambling village, and half the Heath itself,
the barren Heath.

'I came to beg the loan of your pony,' said Lally, when he
allowed her to speak.

'He is yours for the day, I will be shovelling flints and fallen
plaster until suppertime. He is tethered in the graveyard. His
saddle hangs upon the peg in my outhouse. Now, can you
manage him or should I ...'

'No, you must apply yourself to your shovel.'

'Just so. I am very vexed ... But what is to be done?'

Through the hole in the vestry wall Lally could see the white
pony grazing between the headstones, jerking now and again
at the collar round his neck and switching his short thick tail.
The curate hopped about over the flints, giving little
exclamations of surprise and sorrow as he discovered yet
more books, sheets of music and miscellaneous treasures
beneath the rubble. How was Mr Lovatt, he asked between
gropings, how was he? The Ship House had been empty when
he had called on his way home from Lingborough, not even
that odd Rush about, and the river in full flood, terrible,
terrible. What a blow! He had so hoped to continue his
fascinated study of Mr Lovatt's observations on the owls. He
only hoped Mr Lovatt had not been foolish enough to put to
sea in his ship during the bad weather. There had been a
report of the wreckage of a Dutchman washed up beyond
Cley, nothing but odd planks, a spar or two, some barrels. He
was a Berkshire man himself, could not come to terms with

this moody sea, with the fact that the local people thought nothing of launching into it in boats like cockles. Was it this gave them their stubborn independence? In God's truth it changed one's outlook on life watching those waves swell and roar along the shingle. Oh, it was a lawless coast, humans and water alike untamable.

They went outside again by the simple expedient of stepping through the hole; the pony threw up his head in exaggerated alarm. The curate implored Lally to mind her feet, the ground was still so damp, so very damp, and wet feet were the prime cause of congestion of the lungs.

They were about to corner the pony who, at their approach, had moved to the furthest reach of his rope and strained back at it as if he expected them to flay him alive at the very least, when a shout from the distant gate floated to them on the fresh, leaping wind, and there was a post-chaise drawn up, the usual garish colour, a familiar red head at the window.

It was Bensley Vernon on his way from Wells, where he had been forced to shelter from the cruel winds of the last thirty-six hours. His ship had been taking in water, a very usual, trifling occurrence: the ship was old, always worked prodigiously in any kind of big sea, and those whose business it was to see her sound and properly caulked were parsimonious. What had caused his difficulty was the breakdown of the pump, God knows a primitive piece of mechanism, the inopportune splintering of an essential piece. There they had been left tossing in the raging dark like a pack of boobies, the ship slowly but inexorably filling.

The curate shuddered. Wild horses would not drag him from the land. He mentioned Lally's errand to Lingborough, spoke of the lung congestion, mustard plasters and port. Lally saw Vernon's face creasing more and more into lines of confusion, disbelief. He said: 'But I will convey Mrs Fletcher to the parsonage. It will not take a moment,' here ignoring the fact, a fact he well knew, that it would take him at least four and a half miles out of his way at ninepence a mile. 'If we tie on the pony the thing will be done.' He gave his instructions – a

216

strong, nautical ring to his voice – and in no time the grumbling post-boy, encouraged with a shilling, had yanked the pony out of the mould and had tied him on with a knot guaranteed to hold a tow in a hurricane, and they were on their way.

Bensley Vernon shot up the sash and sat back, grinning with pleasure.

'I have been to Cookhams,' he said.

'Oh' – she had not been expecting that – 'I see.'

'I confess I am flushed with success. I took a small prize the night before last, sent her to Lynn with my bosun, the only man among my crew I can trust not to offload a barrel or two along the way for his own profit, God help me. It was only a small lugger, a petty little thing, but fully loaded and worth . . . Oh, I have computed it over and over. I would be excessively surprised not to clear five hundred pounds, five hundred pounds, Mrs Fletcher! And if the pump had not broke, who knows how much more?'

'You were off Lynn then when you chanced on the smuggler?'

'No, indeed. I was but two miles from Lingborough, before dark fell I had fixed my position by the church. I had had information through Barnes the riding officer that something big was afoot, enough brandy to float all England and silk for the whole court, so we were determined to stand off and on all night hoping to intercept it. They would not have expected us to be there, not in dirty weather and with the dangers of the coast, but I say you cannot be cautious in affairs of this kind. Battles are not won by caution and nor are barrels of brandy.'

'So the lugger fell foul of you. Only the lugger?'

'They have never, well-found ships, the best seamen this coast can produce,' in a low, musing, preoccupied voice. 'No, no, we caught a glimpse of two others, creeping in, quick and sly as cats. We even got within hailing distance of the French ship that supplied them but she was outside limits, I fear they cocked a snook, so to speak. But one of the other craft . . . a racy little cutter, difficult to see in the dusk when we first spotted her and even more difficult in the dark; she shook out her mainsail – a prodigious big canvas too for such weather – and left us like a greyhound. I would like to meet her master, I would indeed. A devil of a reckless fellow but professional to his boots, Ma'am, to his boots. It struck me he was too competent, too sound in his manoeuvres for the usual common sort of ruffian, there was a *naval* feel about that cutter. And can you imagine the feat of bringing a raking little ship like that on to the beach through such surf? No. Ordinarily it would not bear thinking about.'

The post-chaise proceeded at that pace peculiar to post-chaises, a sort of griping scurry which might on a good road reach ten miles an hour or even more for dare-all travellers but which here in the back of nowhere meant eight miles an hour at best and the possibility of damage to the axles. Lally, looking out as they swung down to the ford, was reminded of her arrival at the parsonage after those many bone-shaking miles from Colchester.

'Could you have sunk the cutter?' she asked, sinking back as they charged the river.

'I could not bring the guns to bear, we were pitching so. I would rather have captured her, far rather. A percentage of *her* cargo and I would have been set up for life! And how I do need it, Ma'am, how I do need it.'

'I do sympathise.'

'Thank you. You know my situation. I'll not bandy words with you. I grieve for that cargo, Mrs Fletcher, for it was worth a fortune, even bearing in mind the number of shares it must be divided into, and the inevitable expenses, and the underhanded way some agents have of going on. Oh, I regret it deeply. For I have been to Cookhams today to ask Mr Brotherton for Kate's hand.'

That must have taken courage; no, he did not lack courage.

'You are so cheerful,' she said. 'Were you greeted kindly after all?'

'Kindly!' he gave a snort, but none the less a cheery snort. 'Brotherton was from home – on purpose, d'you think? I sent a note I would call. He may forbid me the house but he has no stomach for horse-whipping me from it, it seems. But Kate . . . Kate escaped her mother's clutches and came down to see me, spoke to me alone, assured me . . .' and his eyes lit, a vast, profound satisfaction spread over his face, 'assured me she would be my wife at the earliest opportunity, that if she could overcome this damned tangle with her parents she would marry me tomorrow. I told her about the prize. The sweet girl was ecstatic.'

So she might be, thought Lally, but even a lump sum of five hundred pounds was a feeble weapon against Brotherton's objections.

'You did not see Kate's brother, did you?' she asked.

'Bucolic Jack? No, I thank God. What a scrub he is to be sure. Forgive my blunt speaking. He is a sour, dangerous sort, like a damp firework, for you never know when he will go off. I have only met him once and that, strangely enough, was long before I ever met Kate, but I remember then he was calling someone out, ranting about cheats and sharpers quite as if he were not one himself.'

But even the thought of Jack could not damp his spirits. He was brimming with delight, with the blessed certainty Kate loved him. He was afraid of nothing. He laughed, leaned forward. 'And JG? How is JG?'

Lally's sensitive ear detected a pointedness to this question, but the broad weatherbeaten face beside her was still smiling, the eyes shining, and she had no reason to think of him as underhand or cunning. And yet . . .

'I have not seen him for a while. I am afraid I have had adventures of my own.'

'You have not seen him.' It was a statement of fact, and Lally could not help thinking he made it a statement of significant fact.

'Did you know,' he continued after a little, 'that his horse comes to a whistle?'

'I did. So mine used to do when I was a girl.'

'When you played outlaw on the Heath.' Another

imperceptible emphasis? Or her imagination, her guilty conscience? It was nothing sinister to train a horse to a whistle, it was a useful trick – perhaps especially useful on dark nights and in extreme danger.

'And where is the *Snipe,* the lovely creature?' he demanded.

'I thought she lay at Wells.' She was innocent on that score, she had no notion where the ship might be.

'I have not seen her since we returned from our joyous day on board. I was told' – and this with definite, unmistakable emphasis – 'I was told she was back in Yarmouth refitting. JG did not like the rig. I can understand your frown, Ma'am, but it is a tricky business, this business of ballast and canvas, how much and where, what makes a ship sail the sweeter. And if there is an extra knot to be had from that craft he will have it. In a straight run he would show his heels now to every ship along this coast. Even I could not catch him' – he watched Lally adjust the angle of her hat a little – 'there is nothing he does not know about handling ships. Do you know anything of his history, Mrs Fletcher? He is a friend of some people you know in London, is he not?'

Lally carefully settled her brim. It was impossible to meet his mild blue eyes, his blazing smile. It would be next to impossible to deceive him by ordinary means. But she achieved a passable innocence, obliged to deal with some disobliging lace at her throat, and to brush plaster dust off her habit skirt. She stated calmly that she was unacquainted with Mr Lovatt's history, that she had taken him for a naturalist for so he had been first introduced, and that his interest in the sea had only become apparent since he had come into Norfolk. Perhaps Mr Vernon had better ask Sam Uffington, for he and JG were as close as . . .

'Thieves?'

'For want of a better word, Mr Vernon,' she said coolly and dared to turn and look him in the eye. She began to draw on her gloves for they were almost in Lingborough, she could hear the road surface becoming stonier and see glimpses of red roofs and flinty walls.

'I hope you and Kate find a way to be happy,' she said.

They would, he did not doubt it for a minute. He adored her, he continued, taking Lally's bait, his adoration knew no bounds. Of course he would make a poor husband for any woman, the nature of his job what it was, life expectancy not of the highest, etc. He would marry her though, he would marry her or ... Christ, or what would he not do? He immediately asked Lally's pardon for this outburst, looked furious for a moment and then subsided, staring out of the window at the village street as the chaise scraped and squeezed along it, the post-boy yelling imprecations, awful warnings, and what he took to be witticisms at the local population, their dogs, geese, curs, donkeys and cattle, who filled every conceivable foot of space on either side.

'It is like Bartholomew Fair,' remarked Vernon, closing his eyes as an old man avoided the wheel by the grace of God. Lally saw the trace of pardonable temper still in his face, for the wound went deep, indeed it did: a man from a good honest family, respectable, clean living, to be shunned because he was an Excise officer. It was that which barred the door to him at Cookhams, his chronic shortage of money being only a secondary, almost less troublesome complication.

'And Brotherton is a magistrate,' he said bitterly. 'Do you know it would not surprise me to find he was putting up the money to run cargoes ashore? I do not accuse him, mind. I don't believe myself he is the type to commit himself so deep in a risky venture, and he is precious short of ready cash these days, Jack's position is well known. But it has been known. And then he will preach on the iniquities of evading the King's duty to the poor wretches put before him in court for daring to land the goods his money has financed. Such hypocrisy turns my bowels, Mrs Fletcher. I tell you, I may be unjust but I thought of it when I found him from home, I thought perhaps a guilty conscience was the cause of his reluctance to face me.'

The parsonage was in sight. Vernon scowled, looked out, looked back at Lally, tall and grave. He was affronted by the implications, she saw, by the fact that prejudice, politics and double dealing were keeping him from Kate.

'I shall do my best to promote your good name,' she said as they drew up.

'I wish you would. I shall not forget you threw us together. And do you remember how angry you were when I first met you on the beach?'

She remembered. And she felt a sinking of her heart. But she smiled, held out her hand to him, had nothing more than a mildly fatalistic gleam about her eye, a resignation to the ironies of life. It occurred to her as he handed her out that the whole affair probably only went to show how easily good intentions came to nothing.

'You have been very kind to bring me here,' she said, 'I am so grateful.'

'By God,' he exclaimed, bending low over her fingers, 'you don't need to come all formal with me. I am in your debt for ever. I hope we meet again soon. But tell JG' – a swift, sober look, though the sun was in her eyes, she could not judge properly – 'tell him when you see him that there is a saying about a man being known by the cut of his jib.'

'I am to repeat it to him?'

'If you could, my dear. He would take it in better part coming from you, I trust. The cut of his jib, do not forget. Ah, there is a face at the window. Your cousin, I don't doubt. Boy, untie that poor creature and take it round the back.' This to the post-boy who was lounging sulkily at his horses' heads, and then in a sort of aside, certainly not to Lally, and certainly with a wretched air, his joy deflated and all his sparkle gone: 'A cruel necessity, for I like him so. But honour does not permit, does not indeed . . .'

Anne, recovered from her bout of sickness, recovering now from the killing atmosphere of the last two days, met her in the hall. 'Lally, Lally, oh how I have missed you! And was that really Mr Vernon in such a handsome blue coat and a velvet bow on his hair? How he kissed your fingers!'

'You see how I have been corrupted – to let a lowly

Revenue officer kiss my fingers passionately upon the steps of a parsonage!'

'Oh, Lally!' and Anne took both her hands, the misery, the tiredness, the pain all gone. 'How very, very glad I am to see you.'

'If I were a student of physiognomy I would say it was the face of a rogue, small mouth, small sunken eyes, fleshy nose. The debauchery has lent colour and texture to be sure, but dear Jack was born with a mischievous, predatory look,' said JG, turning to yell at one of Sam's dogs with the unreasonable impatience of a man who has already spent three hours tramping damp fields after elusive hares and longs for his dinner and a decent smoke. 'It is the face of a man who might be moved to murder on a whim.'

'There. Poor Wat. We shall not find much for a hare pie on him,' said Sam, dropping their only catch in the bag. 'Shall we call it a day? Look how miserable the dogs are.'

The dogs were aware of having been slothful, cowardly and inept. They slunk along behind, a long way behind, their tongues lolling. Sam's two pointers and a tall greyhound belonging to Mrs Hirtle's son, one of Sam's tenants, a man who farmed less than ten acres and who supplemented this meagre living with his gains from poaching. The whole neighbourhood knew it, but the proverbial blind eye was for ever turned. Brotherton liked a hardy spirit in a rogue, did not mind his game poached in moderation if no damage was done, and in all other respects found Hirtle honest as the day. The dog, a youngster, had accounted for the small hare which was all the afternoon's sport, but he had not distinguished himself and Sam had flayed him verbally several times. For some reason the high fields sheltered by the belt of woodland, Stapleford's land and usually full of hares, were bare and lonely in the sinking sunlight, and nothing had come of the expedition but frayed tempers and chilblained toes. JG was not a hunting man anyway, having done precious little except with his spy-glass and, in former, privateering days, with his ship. He knew he must keep up wind, he knew he must tread softly and steadily, and he knew he must release the dog at the right moment, but practice fell so far short of theory he might as well have gone hallooing out into the fields, said Sam, might as well have let off a blunderbuss.

Their return to The Ship House was greeted by damp and darkness, Rush nowhere to be found and the cat – the yard cat, the mouser – curled up on JG's second-best wig. The dogs howled for her blood, tearing after her into the hall, with much more science and spirit than they had showed in the pursuit of hares. Sam swore at them, almost tripped up, and lit as many candles as he could find. It was barely four o'clock but all that was left of the day were streaks of fiery red and streamers of violet cloud where the sun had set. JG roused the fire, taking the poker to it much as a man might take a stick to a poisonous snake. The room glowed with a pleasant, gentle gold light, a light reflected in the eyes of JG's stuffed birds, whole ranks by now, glaring balefully from the corners.

'So,' came JG's voice between puffs on a cheroot, 'what is to be done about Brotherton? Does anything need to be done about Brotherton?'

'God knows. I am not going knocking on the door of Cookhams if that is what you mean. There is no proof, not one shred. And if it were true, well, that truth would kill the old man. No, there is nothing can be done. I thought perhaps you should know, that is all, since you too ride the Heath at night.'

JG's eyes were bright and thoughtful through the haze of smoke. He knocked off some ash, stooped to thrust another log on the fire, and said: 'How very kind of you to warn me.'

'He has not forgotten you knocked him down once, take my oath on it. He is not the type to forget. If you were to fall foul of him where no one else could see you he would find great pleasure in spitting you through.'

'What do you think I do on the Heath at night?'

'Oh, I had supposed it was something to do with the owls. Owls are nocturnal, you are always telling me so.'

'And do I deduce from this you too are abroad in the dark?'

'I? Oh now and then, if I am troubled about the cattle or I cannot sleep. But Hirtle, well, Hirtle is a poacher and is often out in the moonlight, and he told me recently he had seen you twice walking in the bracken, once on your roan by Tuppeys Hill.'

JG flung himself down in his chair and unbuttoned his waistcoat, and he pulled deeply at the cheroot for a while, watching Sam sink down and down into the twilight before sleep, when he roused him by jumping up and howling at the door for Rush, who did not come.

'Someone else poaching,' he said, returning to the fireside. 'How is Lally? You did not say. How is she taking it? I met Chewton this morning and he asked me was it true, was Mrs Fletcher a scarlet woman and the mother of three bastards?'

'I hope you gave him a nosebleed.'

'I told him he was a fool to believe the rantings of a man disappointed in love.'

'You did what?'

'I told him Lally would have none of Tom Truelove, preferring another, and that he had raked up these calumnies out of grief and mad jealousy.'

The silence was suffocating. Sam tried to look severe but the smile broke through in the end.

'And?'

'And Chewton pondered a little and said the devil he had, moody fellow that he was, and please to tell Mrs Fletcher he, Chewton, was sorry such tales should be put about.'

'You have no sense of decency,' said Sam with a broadening grin, 'none at all. Now you have started a rumour that Tom was in love with her, was after her in marriage – he would not dream of anything else – and with her these mythical rubies, the ones she was, so many gossips ago, supposed to have smuggled from Calcutta under the noses of the authorities, the ones she is now popularly supposed to have stolen. Tom will not love you for it, nor will Lally.'

'Yet you laugh. You do not curse me for making a mock of

your friend.'

Sam shook his head. 'Yes, he is my friend, but I cannot find it in me to forgive the pain he has caused Lally, and may do yet – we have heard nothing from Luffwell Hall. I did not think he had it in him to be rancorous, nor yet so indiscreet, nor, God dammit, so hypocritical. There was more between him and Fanny Johnson than met the eye, and that was when his wife still lived. It is a sad case of beams and motes or whatever. None of us are so pure we should stoop to throw stones. You do not suppose Rush could be found and put to making a pot of the strongest coffee? I shall be asleep shortly.'

But Rush was not in any of his usual haunts about the mill and they were reduced to a capital madeira and some old scones – nothing so old, as JG remarked dourly, as an old scone – and they sat and ate and drank talking hares and pikes, bitterns and backstays. And long afterwards Rush arrived, coming in with the quietest snick of the latch, and he shuffled about in disintegrating slippers and an old woollen hat bringing more drink and more scones and more wood for the fire in front of which, flank to flank, lay the three disgraced dogs. A small boy looked in, a very small, grubby boy with a dead mallard he hoped Mr Lovatt might like for his collection and for which he was given a penny.

'If we knew why it died we might eat it,' said JG wistfully, 'to augment our little hare.'

It had a dull and livid eye. It was a very dead duck indeed, said Sam, could not be more dead without disintegrating.

'As for Brotherton,' he added suddenly two minutes later, as JG helped pull off his boots, 'there is nothing to do about him, nothing at all, I only wish to God there was.'

CHAPTER 19

Almost every afternoon now the little square low-ceilinged parlour at the cottage was full of children, sometimes neat and attentive children, sometimes boisterous, howling children; often the parsonage children and the mischievous gang from the poorhouse bent over their books together. At an appointed hour the poor little boy who was generally considered an idiot would be escorted to Lally by his doubting mother. Dr Milton had declared him deaf, not deranged, but the neighbourhood would not have it, for everyone knew old Hirtle had dropped the child in the hearth at a few months old and it was a wonder the scrap had lived at all. Dr Milton advised Lally to try sign language, and wrote to several eminent men in the county who might be expected to know the latest theories, the newest methods of coping with the deaf.

'You must persevere,' he said to Lally, finding her with the child in her lap and a very great deal of silent and sympathetic communication going on. 'God knows he has been treated like a dog all his short life, kicked here and there, cuffed, spat on, turned out to lie in the straw. His parents have six others to feed and consider him fit for nothing but scaring the crows.'

There were to be more problems, Lally saw, than deafness, more hurdles to overcome, perhaps more thorny and deceptive. Still, scramble across or through them she would.

And when Lally was bold and resolute she was uncommonly bold and uncommonly resolute, and in spite of the rumours Tom Truelove had started, she still struck awe into the cottages where she poked her outrageous hats, singed her wide skirts, and brought presents of tea or sugar or clothes. Her charity was never overbearing, her gifts small and discreet; she made out they came from the parsonage, which they generally did, but no one believed her. She did not appear to be afraid of anyone, and her air of quiet confidence went further than the tea and clothes in gaining her an audience. She cracked her head on several cottage ceilings but came up smiling, waved away assistance, and was not to be put off. If she could press the children to school she would do it, in spite of every practical objection the parents could find, or moral or philosophical ones too.

Then one afternoon the deaf child Daniel did not come.

'Is he ill?' Lally demanded, stopping at his cottage that evening.

'He is not to come again,' was the bleak reply.

'But why not?'

Perhaps she was too regal to leave on the doorstep, perhaps they remembered her past kindnesses or their own native hospitality reasserted itself at last, but they opened the door and asked her in, hoping she would not come.

She came, ducking beneath the beams, a sober, masculine look about her, her hair all gathered up and pinned firmly in place, her firm jaw all the more evident, her eyes aflame.

'Why can he not come?' she demanded. 'He is making such progress.'

'He won't ever be anything but deaf and dumb,' said Mary Wiseman tentatively; who would oppose such as Lally Fletcher? 'What good is it your teaching him to write?'

'A great deal of good.'

'But what is there for him? He can work on the land or be put to a loom. What call for writing, Mrs Fletcher?'

Lally, straight-backed on the settle, her shoes in the ashy hearth, caught a glimpse of three little dirty faces peering at her round the curtain that divided the living room from the sleeping place. One of them was Daniel's.

'And what do you think, Mr Wiseman?' she asked gently, staring across at the child's father, drawing at his pipe and looking mulish. 'What do you want for your son?'

He did not know what he wanted, but he could not say so. Before her light, piercing gaze his own eyes fell to a sad contemplation of the logs in the hearth. He shrugged. He only knew that every hour Daniel spent at Lally's cottage was an hour the child was earning no money, chopping no wood, fetching no water, and hoeing no weeds. He shrugged again, and grunted, and half turned his back.

'Perhaps it is a matter of shillings,' said Lally, not quite so gently.

They tried to look affronted but could not deny it. That was life, their expressions said, life as she could never know it, she who knew what it was to ride in carriages, to wear good clothes. A child of seven must earn his bread.

Lally rose. Even stooped she was formidable when she cared to be. 'Send him to me,' she said, 'and I will pay him as my kitchen boy. Then you will lose nothing.'

They settled it: the hours, the wages. The Hirtles bowed her out as if she had been royalty. Lally hoped, settling her hat more firmly on her severe hairstyle, that she would be able to pay what she had promised. It was little enough in truth, little enough.

'When we have the school started,' she said as she emerged into the cold evening, 'I hope you will send all your children.'

She did not look back to catch their strained, cynical smiles. A little at a time, she thought, walking away, a little at a time. Her crippled sense of purpose returned mended and vigorous, and hope, and the old long-buried joy. She would make something of her life after all, and if she never had children of her own she would have everyone else's, everyone else's between Ledworth and the sea.

CHAPTER 20

The following week Lally received two letters and an invitation to dine at Luffwell Hall, and the highwayman shot dead a bailiff called Higgatt whom he robbed of ten pounds, his ring and snuffbox, and his horse.

Brotherton thundered at Cookhams but could do nothing, only order another patrol, pressed men all of them this time, which naturally enough found the Heath as wild and empty as ever. Higgatt was carried home to his widow, the highwayman was cursed all along the coast and inland some miles, but the highwayman remained a mystery and as far from the feeble grasp of justice as ever. His identity, antecedents, his crime, were the subject of the dinner table at Luffwell Hall where Lally found herself the next evening, in her old cream brocade, the sole guest and made unreservedly welcome, Harriet full of dry wit and little Sir George ready to talk pineapples all night. It was a signal honour. The Staplefords rarely entertained, dining only their very best friends and making up to the rest with an annual ball at Christmas, a local event, to which they had often invited three hundred couples.

Lally had a luxurious, enjoyable evening; it did not matter this was a way of telling the world Stapleford was prepared to overlook her past, that he had no intention of agitating for her removal from the poorhouse. The heady feeling that the poorhouse was still hers, and Eliza Brotherton's school might also be one day, made Lally glow more radiantly than any of the excellent wine. It still left the vexing problem of the cottage, of course. She could not stay in the cottage now Truelove had behaved so badly; he had not been near her, had not had the grace – or the nerve – to write, and yet she knew he must ache to evict her. Truelove's name, however, was not mentioned at Luffwell Hall, with a degree of delicacy and tact entirely due to Harriet, who had drummed into her husband the likely consequences of digging over the past.

'There may be truth in what the man says,' Stapleford had protested, settling his wig on and viewing it glumly all round with a hand mirror; this in the hour before Lally arrived.

'I doubt it. For myself, I do not care one way or the other. I like the girl. And have you noticed she never speaks of Fletcher? Never. That tells me more, far more, than Mr Thomas Truelove with his fourth-hand tales from the London coffee houses.'

Mr Thomas Truelove, however, was holding his course. He *did* write – the letter arrived in the hand of his Holt attorney, a jolly, round, coarse man ill-suited to the darker side of his calling. He had a glass of wine with Lally and hummed and hawed dreadfully over the notice to quit. He was not overawed by Lally, on the contrary thought her a fine-looking woman, admired the handsome way she asked him in and took the bad news. But then, she must have been expecting it, he reasoned, if she was the Jezebel Truelove said she was. He looked at her carefully but he saw no trace of the Jezebel, and he had had to do with a few. He made a leg on leaving, a very respectful leg, and hoped – not without conviction – that he might have the pleasure of meeting her again.

JG was discovered in a greasy jacket, unshaved, and with a clerical hat rammed home over a nightcap. He had been up on the Heath crouching behind gorse bushes peering at, it might be supposed, whatever was the winter equivalent of *Caprimulgus*, and he had wandered down off the heights into Ledworth and along the common towards the poorhouse, making notes as he went.

'If I were not a broadminded man I would refuse to come near you,' cried Sam, overtaking him on his chestnut. 'Where are you off to?'

'To beg a dish of tea from Lally.'

'She is not at home. At this time of day she will be with Peg.'

'Did I hear correctly, that Peg was bought in a halter? How

231

strange to think that scrawny little fellow would buy a great mountain of a woman like that, and yet they are happy, have brought up ... how many children?'

'Six, and three by her former marriage.'

Sam tethered his horse and they crossed the footbridge over the swollen beck. The day was cold though sunny, promised colder yet, and JG jumped up and down and flapped his arms as they made for the door.

'Dear God, why did they make an entrance fit only for dwarves?' he cried. 'Why you who are so much taller never knock yourself cold I shall never understand.'

But within was warmth, yeasty smell, a floury atmosphere, and Peg's effusive, blushing greeting that did not falter even when JG pulled off hat and nightcap together and bowed low. From the back came the sound of female voices raised in contest. There was a dull thud, a muffled cheer, and the door to the workroom flew open and Anne stood there, pink to the roots of her hair, laughing.

'Oh, dear, you cannot imagine ...' she began, but choked, and went off into feeble, exhausted laughter once more, the tears in her eyes.

Sam and JG looked in. A space had been cleared in the middle of the room and in this space Lally was teaching two of the girls to dance amid gales of irreverent merriment, hoots, squeals, salty advice. All the children who were old enough were falling over each other trying to copy the steps, and the very old man in the chimney corner seemed to have laughed himself into a seizure and be beyond human aid.

'Good God!' said Sam.

'A drunken goose,' declared JG, squinting round, 'did I not say so? What is it? Not a gavotte? Surely not a gavotte?'

Lally glared, her cheeks flaming from the exercise and the debilitating laughter, her eyes full of burning defiance. She had been expecting the parson, had been convinced he would try to carry Anne home to the sanctity of the parsonage as soon as he knew she had escaped.

'You are a disgrace,' she said to JG when they had sobered

232

and the dancing lesson was abandoned. 'You have burrs and mud all down your back, and to wear a clergyman's hat with a nightcap is simply eccentric.'

'I have broken a lens of my spectacles,' he mourned.

'I noticed. No doubt it did not impede you, the lack of the lens. What were you spying through your other, much more powerful glass?' and she touched the tip of the telescope that peeped from his pocket.

'Little brown birds.'

'Not white sails out to sea?'

'I must confess that while watching the gulls for diversion I happened to glimpse Mr Vernon's admirable Revenue cutter running for Lynn under her storm canvas as tidily as you like.'

'I suspected as much.'

They had been too long apart, Sam was looking round, and the kettle was boiled, and one of the children – one of Lally's children, her eyes lit up as she watched him, unprepossessing shrimp he was – had come out to play for them on a cheap whistle.

'My love, you have done Anne a power of good. She looks very well,' JG murmured as they joined the audience.

'She is all the better for having something to do. The baby is due in May or June and she is trying to make me promise I will be with her. But what can I say? Now I have been told to leave the cottage what possible answer can I give?'

JG had found a cheroot and he broke it cleanly in half and clamped one of the halves between his teeth. 'You ought to marry again.'

'You, of all people, to say that.'

'We are not all like Francis Fletcher, Lally dear. You must not be afraid, you know. Not you.'

The minute piper finished on an unearthly high note, bowed, and was clapped out of sight. Anne turned a laughing face to Sam, and he, so glad to see her happy, looked very sweetly into her face. He was uncomfortably aware of Lally standing directly behind him, and he wished, rather ignobly, to have been able to overhear her obviously personal remarks

233

to JG. He had ridden over this morning to consult her about the highwayman, but that would have to be deferred now, for Peg was complaining about the range, and Anne was asking something about a masquerade ball in Holt, and JG was jogging his arm and asking him what he intended to do to provide Lally with some suitable accommodation.

'You only have to appear,' he told her when they went out together into the biting cold some time later, 'and quiet and convention are put at hazard. There is not another cottage empty for miles. That probably means you will be invited to move in at Luffwell Hall. *That* would be one in the eye for the gossips.'

'I think I would grow tired of the pineapples.'

They skirted delicately round two small boys, three donkeys and a flock of unfriendly geese.

'You should marry again,' said Sam, knowing it was the most unfortunate remark he could make but making it all the same.

'So I am told.'

'Have you done with marriage then?'

She did not answer for a moment, only looked back to where Anne was straying about happily round the frosted puddles, smiling and saying something low and amused to the attentive JG. She caught a loving look, the most beautiful smile, and saw his gentle drawing of her arm through his, his restraint. Then she looked up at Sam.

'Until I am persuaded otherwise,' she said.

That same afternoon JG, returning to the mill with a basket of fruit from the Luffwell Hall conservatories, met Lally and Anne having yet another difference of opinion with the parsonage donkey at the imposing wrought-iron gates of Cookhams.

'He has taken it into his head he will not go in,' said Lally. 'Nothing will induce him. You may shout till you are hoarse and beat him till you choke to death on dust, but he will not budge.'

Various inducements had been tried, and shouting – it was the shouting had attracted JG – but to no avail. The whip he disdained, having a coat several inches thick and a tough skin under it. In despair Lally had climbed down and taken his head, attempting, against all odds, to turn him round – he would not even do that now, he was struck rigid – in an experiment to restore some kind of momentum at least.

'I fear you are like Cassandra,' said JG, who was still attired in the unbecoming headgear of the morning. 'You will cry woe and woe and none shall hear you.'

Lally, ceasing her efforts, wiped a damp brow and said: 'Was that another of your exceedingly bad jokes?'

'I very much think so. Perhaps' – and here he walked round the donkey thoughtfully – 'perhaps it is a cataleptic fit.'

'My heart bleeds for him! Pray, get up in the carriage and touch him up with the whip. Anne – be ready when I say! Now, pull on the rein! Now!'

The donkey, pulled to the right, crossed his legs and tottered, a look on his large face of one who has suffered much and can suffer much more. Lally said something pithy in Hindu, very pithy indeed; he recognised it too. He wagged his ears. Then he uncrossed his tiny hooves and stood firm again, exactly three inches from where he had been before.

This was why Cookhams was treated to the charming spectacle of Mrs Philadelphia Fletcher riding up the drive sideways on a disgruntled donkey, her lovely skirts in voluminous disarray over what was left of the harness, while behind came JG in his hideous outfit with Anne leaning on his arm.

'Damme, but I like your spirit, Ma'am!' was Brotherton's greeting at the door. 'A dickey's a devil of a creature to ride, and sideways too, quite sideways, in your best clothes.'

He assumed they were her best clothes because she was looking exceptionally dashing, in grey and blue, and a small-crowned, wide-brimmed hat with a rosette of scarlet ribbon. Anne had bought the hat, but he was not to know that.

JG had swept off his own hat politely. Unfortunately this

time the nightcap adhered to his wig, making him look unbelievably disreputable. Brotherton gave him a helpless glance, for he considered him a strange creature, fit only to be confined, and held him responsible for encouraging a romance between his daughter and a very unsuitable, grossly unsuitable, sea-going man. He had an unquenchable respect for his learning though, personal feelings aside; he could not claim distinction in that area, he had a great library of unread books he would one day pass to Jack – who would not read them either. He had stuck half way in *Roderick Random*, could not now recall where he had put it down. He suspected Lally was well read, considered she might not be out of place at a Blue Stocking Club, but then he also considered her as a woman: she was therefore impulsive, could not vote, and was as subject to the weaknesses of her body as any of her sisters. JG being a man, he was more circumspect. It was as well, he had found, not to underestimate the bookish sort. Brotherton motioned him in with a straining smile.

Lally was ushered into the parlour alone, for Anne was decoyed somewhere along the way and given over to Kate and Cecy and JG had been lured to the kitchen regions on the promise of seeing fifty wrens in a hole. The parlour was warm, and elegant, and quiet. Brotherton went to a small desk, groped there a moment, and returned to Lally with a packet of letters still carefully folded in oilskin.

'There are two, sealed, for you,' he explained. 'The other was addressed to me as JP. That is why I sent over to the cottage straight away. A Mr Purley of Calcutta is very eager to be put in touch with you, m'dear. He has writ before, he says, but fears you never received it. See, here, read it for yourself. Gentlemanly, most gentlemanly. He says he is acquainted with the Burneys, they will vouch for him. He says he knew your destination to be Lingborough though he found out you left no name, no place where you might be staying. A damn civil letter, yes, and he is plainly anxious. But here, take it, see for yourself.'

She received the paper between cold, shaking fingers. It

was as if the past reached out and touched her. She strove to remember Temple Purley as she had last seen him, that honest, weathered face anxious only for her safety. Dear God, the man had written off five thousand pounds! Only a rich man or a fool or a very generous heart could have done such a thing.

Yes, it was a gentlemanly letter. He was polite without being unctuous, polite and forgivably brisk. Mrs Philadelphia Mary Elizabeth Fletcher must be found, the matter was pressing, her whole future depended on it. Could Brotherton exert his undoubted influence, could he seek her out? If, by happy chance, he knew the lady, could he put this communication in her hands and give her all the assistance in his power?

Lally broke the seal on the second letter, another in Purley's hand. She walked to the little desk and put down the first. And then …

The dying sunlight striking through the high windows blinded her, or maybe it was tears. She felt her breathing grow shallow, could do nothing, nothing to quieten the beating of her heart; surely Brotherton would hear it even half the room away, lighting his pipe from the smoking embers in the fireplace. She moved at last, walked to the window, held the page up to the light and forced herself to read again, slowly, slowly, drawing deep uncertain breaths.

My dear Mrs Fletcher,

Since my last letter could not have reached you and it has become obvious Price communicated nothing before he was arrested I must lay the facts before you as briefly as possible – and if you will do me the honour of counting me your adviser and man of business, charge me with your instructions as soon as ever you are able to put pen to paper.

Your brother-in-law's widow is dead. Mrs Hester Fletcher was taken with consumption some long time ago but in spite of all – her own constitution, the climate, her dislike of her physicians – she wasted slowly, only sinking to a coma at the last. On her deathbed she insisted you be sent for and it was some time before Dr Porson – whom you surely remember well – could prevail on her to understand you were no longer in India. What she then told him brought him to me, for it was well known I was the last person to see you in Calcutta, and he could find neither Price nor anyone who knew where you had gone.

Some years ago it was made the common gossip that you had taken some jewellery from a drawer in Mr George Fletcher's house in Hooghly where you were staying. The jewels were returned and intervention by members of the Council made certain you were never charged. Mrs Fletcher however, terrified of going to her grave with such an injustice on her conscience, told Porson that she had known all the time her husband wished to make you a gift of those jewels, known, I believe, as the Sarawar rubies. Apparently he had often spoken about them to her, and she had no reason to suppose the story you told when forced to return them was in any way untrue. She acted out of jealousy and unfortunate malice. She disliked your own husband and wished to do him some harm and you and she, of course, had never been on intimate terms. Your feelings, your fate, your public disgrace were nothing to her. Also the jewels were worth a great deal of money, a fact that may not be discounted. She swore you lied to serve her own purpose, deliberately made you out an unprincipled thief.

In her will, which she revised in the presence of Dr Porson, myself, and some other, more notable persons, she restored to you what is rightfully yours: the ruby and emerald necklace, the pendant, the earrings, and a very fine diamond bracelet. In England I should say they would fetch a considerable sum; the individual stones in the necklace are exquisite and besides the piece has an interesting history. I would say that in England you will be a rich woman.

I regret to say Price has been arrested on charges of embezzlement, the least of his many crimes perhaps but one which will end his career at last. He swears you gave him a very rich brooch which was found among an Aladdin's cave of stolen jewels, certificates, and monies discovered at the lodging of his French mistress. The brooch has been identified as one belonging at some time to your late husband, a spray of emeralds and sapphires much like a peacock's tail. Perhaps you would be good enough to write at once to tell me if Price tells the truth, which I doubt, and if indeed your husband owned such a piece of jewellery.

I would grieve to know you were destitute in England for want of twenty pounds when twenty thousand could be yours for the asking and ten times that to follow. I have spoken with Mr Hastings, who has taken a singular interest in this case, and he has undertaken to safeguard your rubies until such time as we hear from you. I enclose a note from Dr Porson, and I remain and hope always to be
your humble and affectionate servant

Temple Purley

'My dear, you are ashen. It is not terrible news? No, no, surely not? Your affairs in India were settled, were they not, tied up?'

'It seems not,' her voice was not her own. Rich, said another, inner whispering: rich, vindicated, acquitted, rich.

Her gaze must have been frightening. Brotherton rushed to her side, took her arm with gruff and clumsy concern, at the same time leaning heavily on the bell-pull and exclaiming: 'Come, m'dear, come. It is no one dead, no one ill? It is no great misfortune of that kind?'

She looked at him, found herself smiling, a strange wild smile. 'No, nothing of that kind. But perhaps, perhaps now, before … May I sit at your desk and write my reply? The matter is pressing, I believe: this good man is waiting for an answer and the sooner he has it the sooner he will sleep with a clear conscience. May I sit here and write?'

But of course, cried Brotherton, dashing out paper, ink, sand, sealing wax. Of course. She must consider herself at home in his house. When Eliza appeared suddenly in the doorway followed by a gaggle of poking, peering servants he waved her away; frowning darkly; Lally, already bent over her letter, did not even look up.

'Is it grave news?' Eliza demanded, when they had shut Lally up alone for a while.

'Can't say. She went white, looked as if she would fall down, and then ... Damme, but then she blazed like ... like I don't know. She looked as if she'd set alight. Leave her. Leave her to it. But you'd best look in after a time, make sure she's not fainted away.'

She did not faint away, she wrote her brief, grateful reply to Temple Purley with a strange, blazing lightness of heart; and with remarkable economy of words, and some kind phrases for the Governor General, Mr Hastings. She also told the story of that night, that terrible night when George, dying, had told her the rubies were her means to escape Francis and sail home. Her description was lucid and bold, ten hours of terror compacted to five lines upon a page. She had never before told anyone about it in detail, neither Francis nor Hester nor Caroline Pascoe to whom she had written at the time.

The sunlight fell across the page. The fire smoked gently. Eleven years ago in this very room she had faced the wrath of poor stupefied Valentine, the blood soaking down her shirt and brown coat and splashed among the ruffles at her wrist. She had felt the same kind of detachment then, a phenomenally clear, cool distance from things, an intense lucidity. She had felt, with an instinctive certainty, that that moment, that hour, was an end to something, that the future would be changed absolutely by her being here, bleeding to death on this brocade sofa.

She stood by the window now, reading Porson's kind, mannered prose. He hoped she was well, he hoped she would be happy. On the desk was her letter to Temple Purley, folded and sealed, awaiting its oilskin covering. It was a long weary way to India and getting wet was perhaps the least of the dangers. She stood and pressed her fingers to the glass, watching the rooks quarrelling on the wind, the tossing trees, the saffron sunshine dying away across the grass. And she knew she did not give a damn about the jewels, that the reason for them was gone, that, as she had told Purley, the ironies of it all were almost too much to bear, and also she did not wish to deprive her nephew Churchill Fletcher, George's simple son, of any part of his fortune. The earrings would be enough, let them give her the value of the earrings. Let Purley take the peacock brooch, surely worth five thousand pounds, and write off the last debt honourably; let the rest, necklace, pendant, diamond bracelet, go for poor Churchill, who was kept from an asylum only by virtue of his father's money.

She had escaped Francis Fletcher, had been acquitted for her crime, and what bitterness was left was not to be annihilated by becoming an heiress.

They were agog to hear her news: Eliza, Cecy, the thin, shadowy-eyed Kate. Their unasked questions, their ardent curiosity burned after her down the passage. No, said Brotherton stoutly when she said she must leave, no, she must sit down, rest, drink a glass of cordial, Anne must persuade her. How could she consider riding back to the common sitting sideways on a donkey? He fussed over her, genuinely worried, and blustered about trying to prevent her reaching the front door.

By now Lally was feeling exhausted, as if she had galloped from Ledworth to the sea and back. She had had great difficulty entrusting her letter to Brotherton without the copious explanation for which he was waiting, had had to say there were some minor problems connected with Francis's estate, that Mr Purley would sort them out to her satisfaction, and how complicated matters became when discussed at a distance of ten thousand miles. Yes, said Brotherton, yes, he would find out when the next convoy was leaving for Calcutta or the next packet, or the next Admiralty cutter, and the letter would be on it, on the first available ship.

JG was bending to brush his lips against her cheek.

'My love, you look ill. You look burned out. Has anything happened? Are you threatened?'

'Far from it. But I feel very tired suddenly.'

'It is nothing you can confide in me?'

She thought a moment. He was so dear to her, so inexpressibly dear, but some things must be assimilated, wondered at, before they may be shared. She shook her head.

'In a while. There must be other letters from India. When they come, if everything is resolved, I will tell you the story.'

'Cecy is going to take you upstairs,' said Eliza, coming to lead her away. 'I have sent for Dr Milton. You must lie down until the shock has worn off, until you are recovered.'

And Cecy was there, extremely tender, smiling encouragingly.

'I do not need to lie down. I do not need a doctor,' cried Lally.

But they hustled her upstairs, Cecy before and Anne behind, and Dr Milton arrived after an hour or so and, taking in her pallor, her haunted eyes, her air of distress, he said: 'Mulled ale. Perhaps a little toast. She looks done up, poor girl. Ah, Miss Cecilia, such a competent nurse. Your common sense is twice as effective as my bag of bottles. Come, come. We shall tuck Mrs Fletcher in bed.'

Anne vanished in search of the ale. Cecy pulled back the bedclothes.

'There is nothing wrong with you at all,' he said in a genial voice as soon as she began to protest. 'Mrs Fletcher, you are as strong as ever you were. Is it shock? Your pulse is fast, a little too fast perhaps. You will be the better for nourishment and sleep.'

She nodded then. Her face looked much thinner than he

remembered it and there were dark shadows about her eyes. And yet, when she raised her eyes to his face he saw a spark, a defiant spark there, as if the nearly-extinguished fires were leaping up already. He asked to see her tongue, laughed, told her to get into bed. 'By God, you are as healthy as any young woman I have ever known. Fainting? Palpitations? It aint possible. But I tell you this, I've never known a woman freckles all over. Damnation, freckles all over!' and he laughed his great round saucy laugh until Cecy scowled and told him he should be ashamed, he presumed too much on his position.

He leaned over the bed. 'I hope it was good news after all,' he said.

'The most welcome news, the most unexpected. I am square with the world again. You cannot imagine the relief.'

He shook her hand, went away. On the other side of the half-drawn bed curtains he consulted briefly with Anne, said he was to dine at Rooks Hill, would give her compliments to Sam. He left then, Lally could hear him clumping away, but then Anne called him back with one last question, her soft, clear voice very eager and shy.

Was Mr Lovatt to be at Rooks Hill for dinner?

Assuredly, came Milton's voice, booming along the landing, assuredly. It was to be a bachelor party, no women at all, thank God. Did not Mrs Glover know that was why he enjoyed Rooks Hill so much?

'No women,' he shouted, descending the stairs at a run, 'no women at all, thank the Lord.' And then, distantly, amid a cacophony of slamming, shouting, doors banging, startled apology: 'Freckles, by heaven, freckles all over!'

CHAPTER 21

There was to be a masquerade ball at the largest inn in Holt, a very splendid affair. Lally was invited to go with the Staplefords, and looked forward to it. It seemed they were first to dine with Sam at Rooks Hill, for this was the custom, and it was to Rooks Hill they trotted that crisp, moonlit evening.

It was very early evening, the moon had scarcely lifted above the trees. Rooks Hill was a blaze of lights, and as they drew nearer they could hear someone singing, a rich tenor and now and again a cheerful bass joining in. At the front door, flung open wide by the combined efforts of Sam, Cushion and the curate, they were greeted with guilty looks.

'We have been merrymaking,' said Sam.

They had; they had been toasting the King, the whole population of Ledworth, and death to the highwayman. Mr Turner and the curate were inclined to involuntary laughter.

'The highwayman!' sniffed Stapleford, having bowed to Mrs Turner and wrung the curate's hand. 'I doubt we will ever catch him. He is like air.'

'It was not air killed poor Higgatt,' said Turner.

'There were always ruffians on the Heath,' put in his wife. 'They most of 'em ended on the gibbet. Ask Sam. He had his horse stolen from under him once.'

There was laughter, teasing, a loud denial from Sam that the horse had been snatched from beneath him. He sounded hearty, almost too hearty, but no one would have guessed he had had a wretched day of it, that several disasters to do with ricks and cattle had punctuated the morning, and that these, allied to a restless, confused state of mind and heart had led to a tension; he was unusually nervous. He had also dressed with care: a mulberry coat, his linen very white, his chin as close-shaved as it could be. The big parlour had been swept and scoured, more candles lit than ever before – they showed up a shabby splendour, glittered in the mild brown eyes of the crouching dogs.

The candlelight also fell on Lally, who had transformed an old red coat of Charlie's, a waistcoat, and an ancient black hat, into a creditable version of an army officer's uniform. The red jacket with its frogging, the hat with its froth of gold lace, the billow of her white skirt, showed her off, made her look athletic, willowy. Her hair was tied back in a large black bow and lay in a single well-behaved curl over her shoulder. How it suited her, thought Sam, how alive, how vital she looked, and how vivid beside Harriet's elegant pale grey gown and Mrs Turner's rather elderly shepherdess.

The meal, like so many at Rooks Hill, was a little watery, but a good piece of beef, as Stapleford remarked later, could not be put down but with extreme difficulty even by someone as determined as Mrs Hirtle. All in all a cheerful meal, and Mr Hayes ecstatic, drinking off glass after glass, for the cold bath project was well in hand and from the advance monies Sam had made a generous donation of fifty pounds. It would rebuild the vestry wall, deal with the troublesome roof – at least in part.

'You know once, years ago,' Stapleford confided to Lally, his neighbour at the table, 'I thought Sam indolent and charming, even a little simple; he worked hard at the farm but at nothing else. Then I discovered he was not to be trifled with, and now my admiration knows no bounds.'

'Well, I'm damned if I would care to splash about in the beck, medical opinion or no medical opinion,' Turner was saying through his beef. 'Cold baths, ha ha!'

And: 'Oh my dear, my dear, what an evening!' cried the curate, just before they left for Holt, coming across Lally in the stone-flagged hall looking about her at the gloomy pictures. 'The hole to be mended and the wall propped up and the hedgehogs safe. I can hardly believe it.' He talked on, aware he had only half her attention. He had swallowed too much good claret, however, to be less than effusive.

Sam was in the doorway. 'They are asking for you, Mr Hayes. There is a spare ticket to the ball and Mrs Turner was wondering if you would care to join us?' And then, after the curate had gone: 'I have something I wish to say to you.'

He crossed the hall to her, one of the faithful dogs at his heels, and to her surprise he cupped her face with one large hand and tipped it so that he could examine it minutely and said quietly: 'You are nothing but a shadow,' and then thought how absurd that was because although she seemed thinner just lately she had appeared to him like a flame, a restless, dancing flame. Whatever had been in that letter from India Anne had told him about had given her a new life, new heart, and had restored with it much of her lost sense of fun and her beautiful smiles. Still, she was thinner, and he sensed she was still vaguely troubled, that the way ahead was not clear yet, letter from India or no.

'Yes,' he said again, 'I have something to say to you,' and turning on his heel flung open the door to an unused room. She walked in and found herself, in the light of the one candle he fetched from the hall, in a large, low, painted room which might once have been, she supposed, his mother's sitting room, for there was a harpsichord half covered by a dustsheet and several elegant chairs and an embroidered firescreen. Sam closed the door behind them and went round lighting more candles until, in a smoky haze, he turned from the side table where he stood and said: 'This is not the time and place, but then I am sick to death of waiting for the right moment. You may think me a peasant, or a fool. But will you marry me?'

Her cheeks slowly dyed the same colour as her dashing jacket. She walked to the hearth, standing staring down at the intricate stitching in the firescreen, plucking at her skirt. She felt the tears prick behind her eyelids, and a wild, tumultuous joy mingled with a dull sorrow. That he should love her was unexpected, wonderful, warmed her through and through, and she knew his desire in action, his kisses, his touch, could

246

never bring her to that high pitch of disgust and degradation she had known with Francis; but would it only bring her a temporary relief from longing for JG?

Her hesitation, her silence, caught Sam unawares. In her new bright mood she ought to have parried him with wit or laughter at the very least, and he had armed himself against a flat refusal, even revulsion. But to find he had made her so forlorn, so very, very thoughtful, moved him considerably and left him at a loss; his mind slipped back with involuntary fascination to her life with Fletcher. This made him angry, with himself, with her. It was a foolish, blind anger but it was very real.

'Marry me!' He moved so quickly she was taken completely by surprise. 'Marry me!' And he caught her up, his mouth against her throat, against the deep freckled hollow where the pulse beat furiously.

'Why not?' into her fragrant hair, and forcing up her face, 'why not?'

His kiss stirred her but it was not his face she saw behind her closed eyes; tenderness was new to her, was overwhelming, but still some part of her remained detached.

'I cannot,' she cried when he let her take breath.

'I shall ask you again.'

'You are a fool then.'

'I shall ask you until you say yes.'

'Perhaps you are mad.'

'Is this madness? Is it?'

A loud voice calling his name let her go abruptly. She stepped back, trembling, against the fireplace. He went to the door, extinguished three candles in one large, unsteady gesture.

'I shall ask you again,' he said.

All the local gentry, every parson for miles, and even a party from Dereham were to be at the ball. There were chairs and chariots coming and going, a great many curious onlookers, lights, lights, everywhere and the distanced, tinny noise of tabors, pipes and French horns. Laughter and the breath of hot, scented air greeted Lally and the Staplefords as they stepped inside.

'Goodness,' cried Harriet, her hand on Lally's arm, 'is that Jack Brotherton? What is he?'

'Othello perhaps,' her husband offered, scuttling away to see if anyone was dancing yet. 'Can't think what else, blacked to the roots of his hair like that.'

The sinister dark face and sumptuous clothes were retreating to the ballroom, a nymph and some unidentifiable goddess in attendance. There, to one side, was Parson Glover in clerical black and several fellow parsons – albeit merrier ones – who gesticulated wildly, a flock of agitated crows. Lally, somehow parted from Harriet in the crowd, found Anne suddenly, a pale and hollow-eyed Titania in a great flow of gorgeous silk, talking to Mr Chewton, who looked crushed and faintly stunned after being crammed in a coach with Good Queen Bess, a shepherdess, an orange-seller and a rose. Lally pressed on to the main room, filled to capacity and abominably hot. She knew her mask did not disguise her, that her dress, so very different from the rest, singled her out in a splash of bright and daring colour, and that the cocked hat with its mass of cheap gold lace was saucy, the millinery equivalent of spitting in society's eye. She did not waver though, for the letter from Temple Purley had healed a terrible wound, and Sam's proposal had made her bold, very bold bearing in mind she had refused him; but then, no one had ever told her he loved her before.

At the far wall she almost fell into the arms of a dark gentleman in a black full-bottomed wig, a capacious elegant frock coat with buttons like saucers, and a sword with a remarkably ornate hilt.

'Who are you?' she asked.

'Charles II?'

'Perhaps there is a passing resemblance. It has nothing to do with the clothes, more with the expression. But I never heard he smoked cheroots.'

They pressed back against the wall to let some ladies by and JG extinguished his cigar with a sigh. 'How they are all staring at you. What a sad place the world is to be sure when a woman's disgrace provides such entertainment.'

'I am not disgraced.'

'I see you are not. You are positively brazen. Shall you dance?'

'I have not been asked.'

'Well, I am not in the mood to remedy that. The hat suits you. Have you seen Sam? Did you not dine at Rooks Hill? He is so often out of temper these days; I have told him he should get Milton to let a little blood. He could only be the better for it. Yes, the hat is very fetching. I admire the angle. It gives you a decided hell-and-damnation air. Now what have I said to make you colour up? If you turn a little, a very little to your left you may see Mr Palgrave – yes, that round, jolly, black-eyed little man, he is a brewer, a very rich brewer indeed – gazing at you quite dumbfounded. He is wondering who you are, not that there is a woman here to match you in height so it should be self-evident. See, he is asking your cousin Maria. Surely that is your cousin Maria in the blue?'

'And she is saying oh, that is Philadelphia Fletcher, to whom we do not speak.'

'It has not put him off. I do believe he is about to gratify your wish to take the floor in a gallop.'

'Don't leave me.' Lally clutched at his sleeve.

'I did not intend to, I only thought you wished to dance. I fear dancing once with you was quite enough for me. Look, dear heaven, look – is that not Bensley Vernon? Come, let's wish him good evening.'

It was Bensley Vernon in defiant mood, dressed in a nautical combination of blue coat and white breeches, his hat under his arm. His hair was in its pigtail, the marks of his rank plain upon his sleeve. He was evidently sailing, JG murmured as he and Lally fought their way back across the room to him, under his true colours and was preparing to deliver broadsides, could she see his gleaming eye? She could. She smiled into it with a genuine interest and warmth. And on the edge of a blur of colour and movement and hot, flaring light she could see the Moor that was Jack Brotherton, and a man in a dark coat who might have been Truelove, and a clutch of perspiring parsons struck silent and staring straight at her.

'You are . . . astonishing,' said Vernon, lifting her hand. 'How you carry it off! And all those tabbies winking and whispering behind their fans. Be damned to them! Will you step out in a gavotte, Mrs Fletcher? Will you do me the honour?'

It was the staring faces decided her. The bubbling happiness, the dark, strong, rosy flame lit within her by Purley's letter, gave her the nerve to curtsey, to say she would be delighted, and to let him lead her to the floor. A stray memory of the uproarious gavotte danced in the poorhouse workroom returned to her, and made her laugh, and so although she did not dance with any more grace than usual, she moved with a swift delight, joy personified. There was scarcely an eye in the room not on her at one moment or another, watching with surprise or fascination or both. The Indian widow – the notorious Indian widow – dancing with the Revenue officer whose quarry was Kate Brotherton, the unprincipled hound!

'There is Kate,' Lally said to him. 'There, at the end.'

A look of profound pleasure crossed his face. Yes, there was Kate, exquisite in pink and gold, another, yet another shepherdess, but surely the fairest. She made the ornate ladies about her look like trollops. She was whirled away with a glowing backward look in the direction of her love, who was clutching Lally's hand with unconscious fervour and missing his steps.

The music ended. There was some applause, a great deal of noise. Lally sent Vernon away towards the seething mass of admirers round his betrothed – for so he thought of her, so he would continue to think of her – and was about to find herself a glass of punch or shrub when: 'How well you look, Mrs Fletcher,' and she swung round bewildered to find the parson bending a dark and anxious eye on her.

He was anxious because he was conscious he had done her great wrong, and he had sat up several nights alone in his study brooding over his wife's passionate accusations and tears and haggard appealing face. He was a pompous, overbearing man, a petty tyrant, but insofar as he could love he loved Anne, though he could no more have told her so in anything but the most dry and soulless conventional phrases than he could have danced a hornpipe; he had never learned how to do it and he could not bring himself to it now. But he loved her, and he had made her unhappy, a fool could have seen it and he was not quite a fool. Sam Uffington, Stapleford, Brotherton, all men of substance and sound mind, had repudiated Truelove's stories as idle gossip; it behove Mr Glover to do the same. He had not been able to find the words to apologise, he had taken up his pen and laid it down several times, but now, faced with this fiery, spirited creature in gorgeous scarlet and white and gold, he was suddenly struck by the thought that if he did not make his peace now he never should. He bowed – he had never bowed to her before – and asked how she did, and if she was having success with the deaf child, he had heard from Anne he was often at the cottage, and then, seeing her shock and her wide staring blue eyes in which, to his consternation, he found there were tears, he said he hoped she was not in want of a roof over her head, she must consider the parsonage her home.

That he did not like her, that he never could entirely approve of her she knew. In view of that, and of the acrimony, the injustices, the mean-spiritedness that had sprung from his dislike, his words were noble, and her gratitude effervesced with her general happiness so that she smiled at him, told him he was very kind, and meant it.

At this point the parson was saved from having to add to – and perhaps spoil – what he had already said by Horace Brotherton charging up and bearing Lally away for a minuet, a dance that suited neither of them and left them both a little sore and shaken.

'Lord,' he cried, clearing a way to the refreshment room afterwards, 'how my feet ache! Lord, is that your cousin Anne talking to my Cecy? Whose arm is that she hangs on? Damme, it's Sam. The silly child should have married him instead of that prosy cleric, I always said so. What a waste to throw away the devotion of a good man not given to philandering, eh? She will live to regret it if she aint already done so.'

And then, coming towards them with some trifle and macaroons balanced precariously with several glasses of punch, was Tom Truelove.

Perhaps a space cleared about them, Lally was never sure afterwards. Certainly it seemed to have gone very quiet in their general vicinity and the flutter of fans was noticeable, some discreet coughing too, and even the orchestra oddly muted. Truelove's poor savaged face went slowly the colour of Lally's coat and then deepened and darkened to a wretched hue. He did not look away, did not try to ignore her, but a man with his hands full of trifle and biscuits cannot hope for unshakable dignity. He could not even bow. He could only face her out, silent, while Brotherton's eyes popped with choleric resentment and unabashed curiosity.

Lally thought they must have stood like that for five minutes, in reality perhaps ten seconds passed. But in that ten seconds she was transported again to India, to routs and card parties and balls and drawing rooms full of smoke from half a dozen hookahs, and saw herself grudgingly admitted, scornfully used, mocked and gossiped over. She had put on her armour of hard pride to see her through, hard, cold but not after all impervious pride. She knew what it was like to be a social outcast. She put on her armour now, drew herself up to her impressive height, and lowered her black mask the better to see him, her eyes brilliant, dancing.

'Good evening, Mr Truelove,' she said, and passed on.

She was a sensation. The effrontery of it! If there was any truth at all in the rumours the sheer effrontery of it! But the rumours were growing less credible by the minute, and several people whom she knew only very slightly and who thought they ought not to know her, remembered how Stapleford had sung her praises over the poorhouse, how she was experimenting with the teaching of deaf-mutes and lunatics, and how very very valuable were the rubies she was supposed to have brought with her from Madras.

'Damme,' said Brotherton, watching her sip her shrub, 'you have 'em by the ears, m'dear. You are the centre of attention. 'Sdeath, if I were twenty years younger, or even ten . . . I know what my brother meant now when he said you was the most devilish, provoking female he had ever had the misfortune to meet, that when you were knee high you'd been beaten on the backside like a lad for snitching one of the squire's hunters, and that in his opinion it ought to be done again; he said he thought it might take a lifetime of good sound beating to make a lady out of you.'

Lally found his kind, bloodshot eye glinting at her over a glass cup of flummery-looking stuff, and she laughed.

Later, much later, the heat unbearable and the perspiration dampening Lally's brow, she found Harriet at her elbow saying something about Kate. 'And I know it is sly and contemptible of me,' she was finishing, 'but I have spent the last half hour casting about from a viewpoint by the musicians – they are roaring drunk, the poor fools, almost too blear-eyed to read their music – and I cannot see either of them, and strange Mr Lovatt has vanished too, and the villainous Moor has only this moment returned, his shoes muddy. You see, I am become a repugnant spy.'

'I am sorry,' said Lally, bending her ear closer, the gabble of voices, much louder and more confused now a general, end-of-the-evening disorder had set in, 'who has vanished?'

'Why, Kate and that square, short, solid-looking naval gentleman. I took it he was the Revenue man to whom she so rashly promised her hand.'

The possibilities rushed in on Lally, bubbling in her veins with the shrub and singing through her aching head. She raised her glass, looked Harriet in the eye, and said: 'To you, too kind to be a repugnant spy; and to them, may they be very happy.'

'I don't wonder you are exhausted,' said Sam, finding her alone in a corner some time later, her hat even more askew and her glossy swathe of hair coming undone. 'You must have danced with every other man in the room. I pity their toes. But how is it we haven't met till now?'

'I have avoided you. I thought you would wish it.'

He took her hand. The familiar warm charge ran up her arm. 'Dear girl, you must think me very shabby. Surely it is I should apologise for my behaviour? But I will not. And I shall ask you to marry me until I have reduced you to accepting me. I will not be put off. I will be as steadfast as Bensley Vernon.'

She was too happy to rebuff him, to withdraw her hand. But she said: 'Let me go, there are people looking. My reputation is still precarious. And speaking of Mr Vernon, have you seen him? And have you seen Kate? I have been sitting here a while and they are not to be discovered.'

His eyes met hers, saw the leaping delight. He thought through the implications just as she had done, and then sat back and dug his hands in his pockets and his smile widened and widened.

'You do not seriously believe they have eloped? She will certainly freeze in a ball dress and with nothing but love to keep her.'

'He has five hundred pounds from his prize.'

'The devil he has! It has made him bold, by the look of it.'

'Are you cross?'

'Cross?' It was an absurd question, his eyes were shining, dark as peat water but shining with merriment.

'You had a *tendresse* for her once.'

'I had nothing of the kind. She was nothing at all to me.'

'You are protesting rather too vehemently and repeating yourself in a suspicious manner. Oh, my head, I have drunk too much wine. And there is the Moor coming this way. He is very fiercely blacked but it is running in the heat.'

Jack Brotherton made a leg, produced a few innocuous

remarks, and asked if either of them had seen Kate, his mother was anxious. Lally, with the aplomb of her airy, disembodied, exquisitely happy state, told him she was sure Kate had stepped outside for some air with Mr Chewton, a plausible untruth since Chewton too had absconded long ago, to sleep off three bottles of claret in an upper room.

'That was a lie,' said Sam, the creases in his thin cheeks deepening. 'I see now even Jack Brotherton is going to be allowed to spoil your evening. Look, there is JG swaggering about with Cecy on his arm. He took Anne from me not an hour ago, made her blush with some whispering or other; she was not sober, she leaned too much upon his arm. If the parson had seen her he would have laid about him with a whip. It strikes me however much a man dissembles a woman will see through him. Who would have thought a man of such odd appearance, not even tall or tolerably good-looking, could draw the women so?'

He looked into Lally's eyes, and in his own the laughter had died away, though his mouth still smiled. She made no reply, and so his smile became rueful, twisting up at the corner, and he said: 'I played cards the other night for his stuffed birds. I do believe we were a little drunk. Anyway, I got along handsomely and won the better part of his aviary, but then he said commute the birds to guineas and play another hand, and of course I lost and had to sign a bill for twenty guineas. I do not say he cheats, he is my friend and in any case that is not his way, but he has a keen, a wicked keen eye, and if I am not mistaken he has played for higher stakes than stuffed owls.'

'So I believe.' A pause. 'Did he ever tell you where he was born?'

'I recollect he said Kent.'

'And nothing else?'

'Oh, that he had been used to fish from a very young age, and mess about in boats, and ride, and that his father was a Tory.' He leaned back again, surveying the scene, the sad, inebriated musicians, almost at their last gasp. 'There are only two dances left. Come, let us make an exhibition of ourselves.

They are all too drunk to give a damn if we fall down.'

Too graceless for the formal dances Lally came into her own in country ones. Her energy, her supple stride, her natural spring, carried her through. She and Sam made a good match, both tall and far reaching, and he was handsome in his mulberry, his own hair tied back, pale as flax. He set her off, she in her scarlet and her brave hat.

'Marry me,' he said.

CHAPTER 22

They were striking up for the last dance, only the French horn and the viola da gamba anywhere near competent, the pipes prostrate and snoring and the tabors and violins long departed. A few carriages had been called, there were rounds of farewells in progress, some drunken scuffling and some bawdy laughter in a corner. Sam and Lally retired, panting, to see if any lemonade, cool reviving lemonade, could be found among the debris.

One of the inn servants side-stepped through the crowd and approached with a scared, sidling motion. Was Sam a friend of a queer old gent in glasses? He must be, for he was the only man in the room with that pale hair. A piece of folded paper changed hands, an extremely small, thin, grubby piece of paper on which were written the words: 'Yard. Now. Depend on you.' The servant, who could not read, looked quite as stupefied as Sam and backed away thankfully, fingering the coin in his pocket.

'It is JG's hand,' said Sam doubtfully.

'I have not seen him since we began to dance.'

'Now what mischief can he be up to?' Tearing the fragile paper across and across: 'We had better go and see, I suppose, since the matter is pressing and he is depending on us.'

'On you, I think.'

But they made their way together through the door to the dim back passages, foggy with the steam from mutton broth and horse blankets and sweating pot-boys. Lally's white skirts did not survive the journey, nor did Sam's immaculate silk stockings, and they came out into the yard and the blessed air looking frowzy and debauched. The yard, a very large one, was the scene of frenzied activity, horses, ostlers, slatternly girls, servants, chairmen, link-boys, milling about and making various caterwauling noises, together with a fair proportion of the revellers from the ball, come out for air or some rather public dalliance. It was an exceedingly dangerous place to dally, for the inn was a staging post, and an overloaded coach and two battered post-chaises were even now competing for room amid the turmoil. It said a great deal for the skill of the coachmen and the steady nerves of the horses that no one was injured; or perhaps it was that the horses were too weary and jaded to mind the shouting crowds.

'I cannot see the fool,' said Sam shortly. 'Come back in, you will catch a chill without a cloak. That is a north wind.'

And then they saw him, flapping his arms wildly from the very farthest corner where there seemed to be some sort of door in the wall that ran along a side street. It took them a moment to recognise the slight dark figure, for he had taken off his wig and was wearing an anonymous, respectable, black three-cornered hat.

'Thank God!' he cried out to them softly as they approached, not without difficulty. 'Thank God. I have been standing here waiting fifteen minutes or more. I began to wonder if you had gone home.' His voice was subtly changed, like his appearance, and now it was something between the naturalist and the captain of the *Snipe*. 'You have your sword of course,' he hissed at Sam, who had not, 'and a pistol? No matter, I have two, the very best, balanced and true, French made,' and he slipped out through the little door.

It was decidedly a side street, a stinking, narrow, stony side street into which the inn obviously slung most of its rubbish, to be rooted about by pigs and the stray lean curs of the neighbourhood. Tonight frost glittered in the choked drain and the water in the deep ruts was frozen solid. And there, slobbering on their bits and shivering their spotless harness, were the parsonage bays.

'My God, you have stolen the parson's coach!' cried Sam as softly as his surprise would let him. 'What are you thinking of! They will cry murder and rape! You are quite mad, I always suspected it. Those blasted owls have turned your wits at last.

Damn you, John, what are you at, pray? Damn you.'

There was no time, JG assured him, no time to stand about in the icy slush arguing the rights and wrongs. At a moment of crisis one must grasp the weapon to hand, and in this particular crisis the weapon happened to be the parsonage carriage. Did Sam doubt his ability to handle two horses on a moonlit road? No. Then let him keep quiet and get in, he would find a drab brown coat, top boots, a cloak and hat, a sword, and the two pistols on the seat.

'Go back in,' he said to Lally, sweeping the reins up over the well-fed quarters of the bays, and preparing to get up on the box. 'If you like you may spin some tale to delay the parson's wrath. The Staplefords will be searching for you high and low. In any case, you will take cold out here.'

He climbed up, had hardly gathered the reins so as to feel the horses' mouths when they started forward, obedient to a touch as to a familiar voice, besides being eager for their warm dry stalls and a late supper. As they broke into a trot, which he checked instantly, for the filth was too deep, the ice too general, and the main thoroughfare too close for antics, Lally wrenched open the door and got a foot upon the step. A timely lurch of the wheels over a great frozen pile of kitchen scrapings gave her the impetus to quell her wild skirts and haul herself inside. She shot up against Sam, who leaned across and slammed the door to just as they took the corner in a sort of bound, the nearside rear wheel scraping the brickwork of the inn and a burst of noise and light and colour in front of them. Sam tore down the blinds and sat back, sweeping about for the sword and the box with the pistols which had been knocked to the floor, and struggling out of his mulberry coat at the same time.

'You will regret this,' he said through clenched teeth to Lally, bundling her soiled skirts out of his way with a groan as he groped and searched in the pitch dark. 'This is no tame adventure with Charlie Windham. I mean to catch that wretch Brotherton if I can.'

'In the parson's carriage? With JG on the box?'

'He will not know it is JG on the box. At any rate, I hope not. It's a damnably clear night, he will see us coming a long way off, will have plenty of time to see anything amiss. Damn you, Lally, why did you have to come?'

He said it brusquely, rudely, aware that her presence was a handicap, that part of his mind, which he needed clear and sensible, would take account of her, would impede his actions. If they met the highwayman, if that highwayman were Jack Brotherton, there would be a bitter ugly scene. He did not doubt it. And now that Higgatt was dead Jack Brotherton must be brought to account, even if the old man died of the shock and shame, even if Cookhams, a whole family's domestic content, must be sacrificed. He hated the thought of it, but murder was murder, and one might lead to another. He had frequently seen how arrogance and power caused, over a period, a gradual, insensible coarsening of the whole man, a hardening, an ever-increasing tendency to callousness; money and ambition accounted for much, the effect of both could be seen clearly in Parson Glover. Guineas, thought Sam, he could stomach the guineas, the loss of property, even the frightening of honest old souls, even turning them out to wander in the dark, chasing off the horses and the carriage, as had happened in one of the first incidents; but to strike a man dead, and for nothing...

'It has long puzzled me,' he said to Lally, letting up the blinds a little now they were clear of Holt, 'why the highwayman kept to the Heath. Now I know sometimes the rogues have their beats, agree among themselves, a sort of unwritten code, not to poach. But why the Heath? There are larger heaths, more lucrative heaths, often infested by three robbers at a time, and long wild stretches elsewhere. Why choose Lingborough Heath? And for what return? I totted it up from the records: not above a hundred guineas in money, say another two hundred in watches and rings, and one horse, say ten guineas. He does not strike me as a man of resource. But he rode an expensive horse; well, he might have stolen that elsewhere; he had good pistols; the same applies. Then there was his voice, disguised yes, but not a bumpkin's voice, nor a gaolbird's.' He fell silent and another mile slipped away as the bays went forward at their peerless trot. Then he sighed, reached up to drag the ribbon off his hair and retied it. 'He haunts the Heath for fun, because it is convenient, because he knows it intimately, and because it gives him great joy to frighten and rob the very people who sit next to him at dinner. How many petty grudges has he settled by those means, I wonder.'

There was a long-drawn-out whoa-oh-oh from the box and the bays were pulled up a little off the road. When Lally looked out she saw a little copse silvered by the moonlight, and a half-frozen pond, and some wastes of fallowed land on either side. Far off the first light of Ledworth winked through the clear dark, and JG was trimming the wicks of the carriage lamps.

'I thought you would contrive to come,' he said. 'How to explain you, God knows. I was going to say Sam and I stole the carriage in a drunken revel, but what part you could play in that without your reputation going to shreds again I dare not think.'

'You believe it is Jack Brotherton?'

'I watched him all evening. I read all his private signals; a man who is greedy gives himself away. I followed him when he went out, and I asked questions where he had asked questions, and I kept my own ears open and lo, there was his horse – he rode over, and did not come with the family – saddled in the stall of an inferior establishment across the street, a tall brown animal with a white blaze. At eleven o'clock, when it looked as if the parson might be becoming restless and thinking of his bed, he slips out, fetches the horse and takes the Ledworth road.'

Lally got down and stretched. The wind struck through her. It was indeed northerly and she shivered.

'This is the only carriage likely to cross the Heath tonight, for the parson was the only person from Lingborough with a carriage. Of course, it may all be fancy. There may be nobody waiting for us by the gorse bushes.'

In five minutes they were under way again, JG cloaked, his hat pulled down, the very image of Bested – the trussed and drunken Bested, snoring in one of the inn's less frequented outhouses – hunched against the cold. Inside Sam sat braced, in the brown coat and plain hat, loading his pistols. When he had finished he handed one to Lally.

'Mind you don't blunder with it, it is not a toy; and it's sensitive, 'twill go off at the least pressure. Don't cock it unless you must, you may blow off your foot.'

She did not reply. It would not do to remind him she had had to defend herself, her staff, her husband – in a stupor, dead drunk – with relays of pistols and muskets fired and reloaded, fired and reloaded, all night and all two blazing days. He would not thank her for it. He would become irritable, and he was already understandably anxious for her safety. So she sat with the pistol on her knee and said nothing, and the carriage swung through Ledworth and rattled on down to The Ship House and made a rousing wake in the ford, the good brave horses going in to their collars and the moonlight glancing off the polished rosettes on their winkers. They had breasted the rise in no time and were up on the level, the call of oats obviously very strong, for the bays broke into a canter at the slightest easing of the reins, and had laid their ears in unison as the bitter wind came singing in off the sea.

There was a sudden single knock on the box above. 'He has seen something,' said Sam. 'Of course. We are nearly to the thickets before the run across to Tuppeys Hill. It is the only sure cover on a night as clear as this.'

Lally felt her heart sink, and in that moment all the dregs of her new-found happiness were gone, and she felt cold and afraid and very, very sober. 'That is where I waited the night I was shot,' she said quietly. 'But it was overcast then. You could not see five yards.'

All she had seen indeed were the twin lamps of the coach looming out of the misty blackness.

'Pull up!' yelled a voice, and the bays swerved and ducked, half rearing, as JG dragged cruelly on their kindly mouths. Such brutality was foreign to them, Bested was a good whip, and they plunged again, trying to turn against the pole as JG deliberately held them up too tight. The man on the horse a little to his right swore, and swore again as his own horse capered sideways. In that second JG drew the pistol from the folds of his cloak and cried: 'Put up your guns,' and Sam, getting out of the far door and running round, drew the man's eye and mind away.

'Put up your guns!' roared JG.

'I'm damned if I will.' A shot, at Sam who was running at the gorse clumps to make a rearguard action; a grunt as Sam fell over, staggered up, fell over again.

Another shot; silence.

Lally got down, casting her pistol behind, her knees weak, her mind numb, no blood at all it seemed but all drained away with fright. She covered the few yards at a sort of crouch, for she was cold, so cold, and her inside ached with the dread of finding him too late. But he was there, stretched out in the heather, one arm flung up, one to the wound in his shoulder; he was stunned, wrung with pain, and helpless, but he was alive. She called out in a cracked, unreal voice to JG, who had had the devil of a task to calm the fractious horses, who not only felt abused but could smell blood. She called again and he did not answer, she could hear his voice – a very distant voice it seemed to her for all that he was ten yards away – hushing and whoaing. And then, pulling Sam's shirt open, ripping buttons off his waistcoat to come at the vital point, straining through the moonlight – not bright enough for this, not bright enough by half – to see how best to staunch the blood, she felt, in some strange slip of time, as if she were calling for herself: that feeble, pleading voice, that cry of the lost, hurt animal abandoned to predators and cruel chance. The black pony had careered off among the bushes, had circled down there by the birch and hawthorn scrub, while she had cried and cried for Charlie in just that voice, dizzy and disorientated and terrified.

And Charlie had not come.

'Help me,' she called to JG, shredding the cleanest part of her silk underskirt for a wad to stop the bleeding; there was far too much bleeding. The wound was only a little higher than her own had been but the ball had gone deep, she could not tell at what angle. She felt the last of her courage going, slipping away like Sam's life slipping out quietly under her fingers. How could she remain calm with nothing to do, no help at hand?

'How is he?' That familiar harsh voice, a hand on her shoulder. 'Alive? Good. Hold his head. We must get him in the carriage.' JG held up the lamp, revealed the mess of linen and blood and all the deep, hard lines of his own face.

'The man . . .' whispered Lally in a voice not her own. 'The man . . .'

'It is Jack Brotherton,' said JG, 'and he is dead.'

Her brave head was not held so high now and she wore no hat set at a jaunty angle. The cold sea wind was in her face and the rustling, haunted woods at her back. She seemed to have been sitting here for ever, Sam's head on her arm and the sound of her own heart loud in the darkness. And then there was a shadowy face at the window, a voice.

'We can start now. I have him on the box with me. You are sure you have the story? We cannot afford mistakes.'

'I have the story by heart.'

'Good. His horse is tied deep in a thicket, I shall retrieve him later.'

'You are so very accomplished at these things.'

'My dear Lally, did you think I have not had to cover my tracks before?'

'And deal with dead men? And lie?'

'All that.'

'Perhaps you deserve to be hung.'

'Perhaps I do.'

'We should hurry,' she said, feeling the weight of Sam's

head. 'Someone will have to ride for Dr Milton.' She spoke calmly now though it was a dead calm, the aftermath of shock and fear. And JG swung open the door and put a foot on the step, leaning in; his cold wet fingers touched her cheek and his mouth brushed against hers briefly, briefly.

'Courage,' he said. 'The worst is still to come.'

They had turned back to Luffwell Hall, from where an eager skinny boy was sent on a thoroughbred hunter for Dr Milton across the parish, and to which eventually came Sir George and a yawning Harriet, an hour late because they had combed Holt for Lally, desperate for her safety.

They found her in their lovely drawing room, her white skirts bloody and her self-control apparently intact; and in their yellow guest bedroom Sam Uffington lay quietly in white and clammy unconsciousness, the bleeding stopped at last; and elsewhere, laid out upon a crimson counterpane, the body of Jack Brotherton, the black grease smeared and streaked across his face.

There was, it seemed to Lally, very little to be said, and, after all, she was word perfect. JG, very drunk, had tied up Bested and made off with the carriage; she and Sam, also drunk, had been cajoled to go for a daring ride around the town. The parson's bays were fresh, however, and JG an indifferent whip: they had drawn along the Ledworth road with inexorable cunning and would only consent to ease up when they sighted the village. By that time JG was thoroughly chilled and growing more sober, would have turned back had he the expertise to persuade the pair against their will, but at that moment Jack Brotherton had caught them up, had been very far from lucid or sensible himself, and had encouraged them to drive the bays home – never mind the parson, never mind Anne, some kindly neighbour would take pity on them.

So to the Heath, the highwayman. The revellers had treated him with disdain, had not pulled up speedily enough for his peace of mind, and one of them – Jack Brotherton – had whipped out a pistol. The rogue had fired both his: Sam was wounded, Jack was dead.

'His horse is found,' said Stapleford, coming in at dawn to find his wife still awake upon the sofa and Lally bolt upright like a statue in a chair. 'It had run back across the common, going home no doubt. There is no sign of the murdering wretch on the Heath, of course, the ground is too hard with the frost. You can see where the two of them lay though, not so very far apart, he must have fired both guns at once; there was the deuce of a lot of blood.' And then, interpreting at long last his wife's terrible frowns and the surreptitious sweeping of her hand, he added: 'I beg your pardon, Ma'am. I run on without thinking.'

Behind him, through the uncurtained window, they saw the sun lift clear of the horizon, red and ochre in the mist. There was a heavy footstep and Dr Milton looked in, said he had the ball out and that everything that could be done had been done, he would return shortly; he would be more sanguine but Sam had lost too much blood, was cruelly weak. He glanced at Lally and she raised her head, gave him a weary, intelligent stare: she should rest, he said, there was nothing whatsoever she could do. He was very far from his usual ebullient self, not half so loud, half so confident, half so brisk. He asked Stapleford to step outside, he must have a word. Harriet rose, put an arm about Lally, urged her to come upstairs, Sam was in God's hands and Mr Lovatt would be back shortly, he had gone to The Ship House for clean clothes and then on to the parsonage to break the sad news there and to make his humble apologies for the drunken folly of stealing the parson's coach.

No, said Lally, she would stay where she was.

She felt numb, or maybe disembodied, nothing seemed quite real, but she was resolute: she did not want to lie down, she did not see how she could sleep. And while people came and went, and the ordinary domestic noises lapped about her, she thought over and over: this is the only way, the best way, the best ... There was no question of it, of course. Let the Brothertons believe Jack died a hero, that his murderer fled –

and that after such a heinous crime would never ride the Heath again. If it was perverting justice still it was kind. The only risk was that Sam, either in delirium or when he woke, would ask some innocent question and unravel the whole carefully knit lie – if he woke. The next day would be critical, for him, for the conspirators. JG had undertaken to ride to Lingborough out of more than honourable remorse: there had been Jack's horse to retrieve and deliver to The Ship House stables where Rush must scrub him clean, so that his broad white blaze once more shone out where it should. And the mulberry coat had been burnt in Rush's tremendous fire, the buttons cast into the mill pond, for in case someone should ask why Sam was wearing a brown one when he was carried into Luffwell Hall they must say his other was stolen in Holt and JG had found him a substitute.

So the short wintry day, the sun climbing hardly at all and sinking away through the mist again, drew on to its inevitable climaxes: the Brothertons in tearful procession – but not Kate, for she had run away with Vernon to God knows where – the parson in a dull, overwrought state, coming in to pat Lally's hand awkwardly and make light of all her tomfoolery, he was only thankful she was safe; and then, in varying degrees of noise and confusion: the Cookhams menservants come to carry Jack home, a constable, another magistrate from Holt, the messengers and grooms bearing letters of sympathy for Sam, and Dr Milton, who passed through them all, a great shambling ox, and looked paler and sadder and more weary every time he did so.

In the late evening Lally, unnerved by Eliza's parting kiss, too motherly and forgiving for her conscience, went up to beg to be allowed to sit with Sam a while. The room was clean and richly furnished, blue damask curtains to the bed and all the basins ranged neatly on the dressing chest; there was a gilded clock tick-ticking on the mantel and the carpet was Chinese. Left alone, Lally sat by the small fire, too tired to think, but every time she looked down she could see the blood on her skirts and taste JG's mouth against her own: 'Courage. The worst is still to come.'

A stirring in the bed drew her there and she looked down into Sam's wide-open eyes, black in his white white face.

'Jack?'

'He is dead.'

He had expected it. He had expected nothing else perhaps since picking up those pistols in the carriage, the pistols of a man who knows about guns, who is a fine shot, who could not miss at such short range . . .

'I must tell you something,' said Lally, putting her face close to his. 'JG and I have been . . .'

He put up his sound arm slowly, with an enormous effort of will, and drew her head down until it rested there in the hollow of his shoulder, her loose hair across his hand.

'Lying?' he asked in a low unsteady voice.

'Lying.' And she told him what she and JG had said downstairs, the whole fragile sorry tale, even to how JG had contrived to restore Jack's horse to its original colour and let it go again.

The hand stroking her hair had stopped. He was asleep or perhaps unconscious again. His breathing seemed more regular, his face not such a dead white.

Lally rang for Phee, Phee who had run over as soon as a servant had been sent to the cottage for Lally's clothes, saying in Hindi: 'I will put you to bed, you must come with me, Mem Lally. Look, I have brought all your favourite things,' pulling open her little bag to show the brushes and combs, the mirror, the bottle of rosewater, the fragrant linen. 'Come, I will brush your hair for you.'

Now Phee ran in that silent, strange way of hers to fetch Harriet and Dr Milton, and to tell them, the light breaking in her huge dark eyes, that the sahib was awake again, that he had spoken.

Time had no meaning. The night passed, morning came and went, the dusk brought sleet and a high wind to scatter it at the window panes; Sam still lay in limbo, mentally Lally accompanied him there. Dr Milton came, looked increasingly

268

cheerful, peered at the wound, at Sam's returning colour, at the life and interest flickering in the brown eyes.

'He will mend. I dare say it to you now, dear girl,' he said, drawing Lally aside. 'The wound is clean, his pulse is strong. There, there. You are surely half dead yourself.'

'It is relief. Only relief.'

'It is want of fresh air and cheerful occupation. Why not walk in the garden? Lovatt called half an hour ago, paid his compliments. You should have gone down to him.'

'He said he would not go up to Sam, he did not like to disturb him. He sent you his dearest love,' said Harriet to her later. 'Why do you not walk down to The Ship House to thank him for the flowers he sent yesterday? How thoughtful, how unlike a man to think of picking roses in November. They are very small, and spotted and frail, I know, and he apologised for them over and over, but still so lovely.'

The following afternoon Lally put on hat and cloak and went out into the wind, some of the old spring in her step. She went across the common and down to the mill where the river was running fast and cold. The sky was clear pale blue flecked by tiny clouds and the river reflected it faithfully, the clouds racing on its current and vanishing beneath the dark arches of the mill.

Sam's two dogs met her, and Rush.

One of the pullets had turned out to be a cockerel, he said, which was rum, he aint never heard the like of it. He had not been born in the country, found it unnerving. He had thought, even with his vast experience of the lower deck at sea, that males and females was males and females. This changing at the last minute was likely to put the whole world arsy-varsy. And please to step in, His Lordship was in the foulest blackguardly mood as ever was, she might sweeten him up, the cunning ruffian.

She stepped in, past the hall table where the eels had writhed that very first time she had come here, in through the low door to the broad familiar shabby room that smelled of cheroots. Through the windows she could see the stripped sallows and blackthorns and the stark maples. A heron was flapping along the river bank and came to rest on the jetty. There was no sun but a brilliant clarity, a frosted dazzle. The parlour was lit by this dazzle, and by a cheerful fire of pear logs. The dogs cast themselves down, panting, their eyes on Lally's face as if they knew she brought word of Sam.

'What did you think of in Madras?' came the unexpected question from the cloud of cigar smoke round the loveseat where JG sat with his notebooks.

'Madras?' She needed a moment to collect her wits. 'I thought of the Heath, and the sea. I used to pretend that next year, next season when the ships left for home, I would go with them, that Francis would let me.'

The notebooks were full of numbers, and initials, and times, and sums of money.

'You have given up the owls then,' she said softly, untying her cloak and letting it fall. 'And the *Buteo lagopus* and the dear *Caprimulgus*. You are leaving.'

'It is long past time.'

'I shall miss you.'

'Of course you will. And when I have time I shall miss you, and think: Ah, there was a girl who might come adventuring the world over, who would not hanker after babies or a settled life or constancy. But it is not true, is it? You would want all those things in the end. You can only play at adventuring.'

He had thrown off his wig and now he stretched, tossed aside the books, considered the angles of her face with a critical intensity. 'You have not been sleeping,' he said, more tenderly. 'All your freckles have faded.'

She was dressed in dark green silk, something lent by Harriet, very formal, very lovely, not at all the dress for afternoon calls; it set off her pale skin, her light hair, and she knew it, she had dressed with very great care. Had she been able to move like a queen she would have looked like one, but she moved with her old elastic stride and looked like Lally Fletcher in a silk gown. It was not fair, she was thinking, not fair she should love this man so deeply when Sam was so dear to her, when Sam's kisses had moved her as she had not been moved before ... But then, JG had never kissed her like that. What if he did? What if he did?

Were her thoughts so plain upon her face?

'My dear, I must maintain a sanctimonious manner, a quite saintly chastity, or I am undone,' he said, throwing his cheroot into the fire and speaking as casually as if he was discussing dinner or the weather. 'And more to the point, so are you. You must ...' His back was to her now as he groped for that wig, the concealing spectacles, all the discarded notebooks. 'You must marry Sam. You must bring Reform and Progress to Rooks Hill.'

And then, as if he would steer them to safer ground, he began to talk about the summer that was past, his fishing trips with Sam or Bensley Vernon, his many excursions with the curate, his birds, his scraps with the improvident Rush who never had anything in the larder. And as he spoke the summer-green river was there, the deep shade beneath the overgrown banks, the sunshot stones at the ford, the drifts of willowherb and meadowsweet, and the dark pools by the mill where the big fish swam silver among the streaming weed. The harsh noise of bleating sheep came back to them, and the haunting cries of the plovers; there were the speckled partridges, the kingfisher, so sour and salt to eat, and the ripple of the soft wind in the ripening barley.

'Do you remember your crossbill,' Lally said, 'your *Curvirostra*?'

And they laughed, quietly and affectionately.

'You have never asked me,' he said, watching her sitting in a spread of green silk, her pliant body bending forwards as she gazed into the fire, 'what I was doing in the Colonies.'

'You were hunting rare birds.'

'I was sentenced to death for killing a Revenue man, just such a cheerful, ordinary, inoffensive man as Bensley Vernon, who challenged me on the beach while I was running barrels ashore. The sentence was commuted to twenty-one years' transportation. And I have returned home with fourteen years still to serve.'

'So if they find you, you will be hung.'

'Just so.'

And then she remembered something: 'Bensley Vernon said I was to tell you a man may be known by the cut of his jib.'

'Did he indeed? How delicate a warning; what an intolerable position I have put him in for sure. Thank you, my love. But it is no matter now. Next week at the new moon the *Snipe* comes for me. And now . . . Now I think you should go.'

But there was something else: 'Who asked you to come here? Who knew of your reputation and brought you to Lingborough?'

He grinned. 'Have you forgotten the exotic fruit?'

'Not Stapleford? Never Stapleford!'

'Well, he is an honest little man in general, loves his pineapples and his gloomy house. If he puts up the money for ships and cargoes as well as poorhouses you must forgive him, he has a great deal of it and it could be worse employed.'

'Of course you speak as a smuggler.'

'Of course. I have sailed and smuggled since I was seventeen. I could no more give it up and live quietly than my friend the pike could turn vegetarian.'

The brilliant light had died away and the dusk was blue and deepening. A silence fell between them.

'You must go,' he said again.

She stood, willowy and proud, her head thrown up. 'Will you not take my hand?'

'To say goodbye?'

'It would be a comfort to know you wished me well.'

'That goes without saying.'

He was reluctant. He looked from her hand to her face and back, and away. He had held out his to her, she remembered, long long ago, and she had taken it, as trusting as a child.

He had walked to the window, stood looking at the river, the last rays of light dying away under the shadow of the mill. 'The passion, were it gratified, would burn out within the year,' he said, but quietly as if to himself, and then: 'You and I

272

are complementary spirits, my dear love, but we were never meant for a long and happy life together.'

Her hand had dropped. She said nothing. In a moment she was groping for her cloak, blinded by tears. At the door where she cast about helplessly for the latch he caught her up, turned her, drew her to him, and his comforting kiss began on her wet cheek but ended on her mouth and his hands slid under her soft hair.

She did not think of peacocks, she thought only that he smelled of soap and cheroots and tar and seawater, and that there was no possibility of resisting him.

'I have nothing to offer you,' he said.

'I have not asked for anything.'

'You should go before it is too late.'

But her back was against the door.

'Mrs Fletcher is leaving,' he said. 'You must light her home.'

'Me feet are drawin' terrible. You don't have to holler. And I only just got in. Look' – and here were disclosed two pheasants dangling under his loose shabby coat – 'a pair of nice birds 'appened to fall my way.'

His beady glance at Lally showed him only a Mrs Fletcher as fiery-eyed, as confident as ever, perhaps a little pale but nothing to signify. He stumped off into the kitchen and came back with his hat on, a green-black, seawater-stained, cockaded hat of dubious ancestry.

'What's that you have under your arm?' asked JG.

'It's the humbrella, the bleedin' old humbrella you said them princesses sat under to drink their julep. I thought Mrs F might like to take it with her, a sort of keepsake like.'

Mrs F's composure deserted her for a moment; he saw quite dintinctly the glitter of tears and the sudden straightening of her warm mouth. He saw the small frown between her eyes.

Ho, Heartbreak Hall is it, he thought, didn't I warn him many a time, didn't I? He watched her take the umbrella from him with a deep satisfaction, though he was shrewd enough to guess it was not the nature of their love to require keepsakes and that if this was a formal farewell it was still not a parting.

'They'll be on the trot with lanterns,' Rush warned them gently, stricken with his new wisdom, 'hammerin' on folks' doors and draggin' the river. Per'aps I'd better put the pony to the trap. It would be quicker.'

But Lally swept past him and out into the young, cold night. 'No,' she said, 'I shall walk.'

Just so had she taken leave of Temple Purley, piercing his kind heart with her defiant courage, her world in ruins about her.

''Ere,' cried Rush, 'wait for me.'

CHAPTER 23

Kate came back to Ledworth for her brother's funeral but left her husband – they had been married by special licence, she still in her ball gown, quite draggled – on the deck of his ship for decorum's sake. She was welcomed at Cookhams without reserve, the shock she had given them wiped out by the greater shock of Jack's murder, and in any case she was dearly loved and had been sadly missed. The inquest had been straightforward, very brief, and Lally had not been asked to give evidence.

Sam, mending strongly now, was carried back to Rooks Hill and his own draughty, smoke-encrusted rooms. Lally, Phee and Mrs Hirtle nursed him, and JG called every day and played him at cards or read to him or sat with a cheroot talking fishing or birds.

'I shall send Cushion to shave you,' said Lally one morning, arriving very early from Luffwell Hall where she was still in uneasy residence, her conscience bewildered by certain inescapable considerations: the smuggling, the real manner of Jack Brotherton's death. Her conscience suffered for other reasons too, entirely to do with JG.

'Cushion's hand shakes,' said Sam. 'Would it be improper for you to try?'

'Most improper. I shall send Cushion.'

They were in the middle of this protracted operation when Dr Milton called, and bowls, cloths, soap and all had to go by the board.

'How are you today? Ha, your colour is excellent and you look uncommon cheerful, even with that froth on your chin. Yes, look, it heals beautifully. I cannot say I am entirely satisfied with my own handiwork but then trying to do a fine job in a hurry and in indifferent light ... You were lucky the ball did not enter *here* and fly across. That would have put an end to you and only for an inch of difference. Remarkable. Dashed lucky. Brotherton now, he took the ball in his heart, clean and true. Yes, clean and true. Mrs Fletcher, pass me that bowl. There, now we shall leave it well alone and God will do the rest. No doubt when you are an old man it will ache like the devil in cold weather. Thank you, my dear. And may I beg a very late breakfast, a plate of eggs and chops perhaps? I have been out all night with a difficult labour on top of dinner with one of those cold bath enthusiasts, one of the eminent gentlemen Sam here is to christen in the beck. Ah well, the money will mend the church roof and build us a school perhaps if it does nothing else, and all the poor wretches who die of pneumonia and shock will keep the gravedigger busy and the curate from his beetles and bats.'

Lally, bringing a basin of clean hot water when Milton had gone, said: 'Am I to understand medical opinion is divided?'

'On the baths? Apparently. I don't give a damn except I receive my rents.'

'What philanthropy!'

Lord, how he wanted to kiss that mouth, he thought, that smiling mouth. He studied her for signs of change. These last few days he had become aware of change, yet he could not analyse it, could not tell if it were in her spirit or her expression, nor whether the one was a reliable guide to the state of the other. She seemed more serious, almost the grave Lally he had first known, but her smile was softer, warmer, and there was a gentle grace about her that had never been there before.

She was by the window now, looking out, and he was conscious of a deep sorrow, a sense of loss, but then her face was half turned away and he had been too long abed and had grown fanciful...

'Will you marry me?'

In view of all she had done for him in the last week, in view of her tender care, her obvious deep affection – he dare not call it love yet, primitive superstition forbade it – he had hoped for more than her quiet: 'Perhaps I am not fit to be your wife.'

An enigmatic, irritating statement, guaranteed to bring him up on his sound elbow, staring across at her.

'Because of JG? I am not blind, you know. There is something between you two, there always has been. I do not know what it is, I do not understand the nature of it, but ...' Was she listening? 'But he is leaving, he tells me.'

Still no answer, no sign. She stood looking out at the white sky and the toiling limes at the bottom of the long-neglected garden, her back to him.

'Are you going with him?' Sam asked, and because the idea had not occurred to him until this moment he felt the small chill of a new fear, and sank back on his pillows.

'No.'

They could hear voices below: Mrs Hirtle with the morning cup of cocoa? Footsteps approached and receded, and Cushion's querulous voice scolded the ever-faithful dogs, on sentry duty at the top of the main staircase. Lally turned round.

'I love him,' she said. 'There is some part of me answers to him, and I will never drive him completely from my heart for all he has done that I regret, for all that he might do yet. I think ... Sometimes I think he is Charlie grown up, grown cynical and cunning. It is the way Charlie would have gone, from childish foolery to petty crime and then to greater folly. And like Charlie he loves courage more than anything, and excitement, and daring. Any woman he took would be ... would be left behind, neglected, disillusioned a hundred times, sickened by the cruel side of his roguery, left to cope and grow resentful, ruined. And then he would come back, sorry she had been reduced to begging the children's bread, and there would be peace and joy again for a time, a very little time, less and less over the years, and then he would throw off his responsibilities and return to action and adventure while she ... She would have the weary round and heartbreak and the bitter end of self-respect.'

Her voice died away. She had rehearsed this argument hour

277

after hour in her sumptuous bed at Luffwell Hall, and by now she neither knew nor cared how true it was. She was only sure that if he asked her to go with him she would go, and that he would not ask her; these certainties left her in a strange, detached frame of mind, the inevitable outcome of facing unpalatable facts with fortitude. She was also deeply aware of the love between them; nothing could diminish that joy.

'You know JG is a smuggler?' she said, as if this might lead them to safer ground.

'I guessed as much a long time ago but did not wish it to be true, so I chose not to be too curious. As you say, love does not change simply because its object is unworthy; one can no more cease to love than breathe,' and he said this last with an urgent, low, appealing emphasis, for her alone, and she crossed to the bed, putting out a hand and then shyly withdrawing it.

'You do not know ...'

'I only know I want you for my wife.'

'You may not when ...'

Mrs Hirtle knocked and entered with the verve of charging cavalry. 'Mrs Glover is below, sir, wondering if she may step up and pay respects. Should I say yes? Or will Mrs Fletcher step down?'

'Tell her yes,' said Sam furiously. 'God dammit, why are the dogs making such a rumpus?'

'Oh, that is because of Daniel, sir. Mrs Glover brought him along with her, he had been missing Mrs Fletcher, and the dogs have taken against him.'

'Then tell Cushion to shut them up in the stables. Lally ...'

But she simply touched his outstretched hand briefly, and smiled, and went towards the door. 'Mrs Hirtle,' she said with all her old royal calm, 'where is the cocoa? I shall have to come down and make it myself.' And she cut short the housekeeper's protests by saying over her shoulder: 'There is a letter under the pillow. It is for you to read. It may please you or astound you or make you never wish to see me again.'

She shooed out Mrs Hirtle, descended to rescue Daniel

from the dogs, to kiss Anne, to make the cocoa. The letter had arrived only the night before, a letter from Temple Purley, much creased and travel-stained, the ink wandering. It told her Churchill Fletcher was dead, though the manner of his death was indecipherably blurred, and that in view of this the Governor General had decided what was left of his estate must go to Lally. True, the legal machinery ground slow but there did not seem to be any objections: there were no other relatives living. Lally would therefore be worth perhaps a hundred and fifty thousand pounds.

'I wish you joy of it,' Purley ended, and she fancied he had laughed aloud at this point and made some remark about the strange, incomprehensibly strange turns of fate. 'I wish you all joy. You are a rich woman. You will be able' – and here his laughter would have startled the boy with the fly-whisk and the bearers waiting outside with his palanquin, and all the clerks in his outer office – 'to marry a duke.'

The moon was a sliver of light above them and down there, a little distance away, the wind fretted across the marshes. The barking of dogs was blown to them, and the hoot of owls. There was sand and gorse and the harsh springy heather and here, just here, they had sat that very day he had brought her home to this beloved place, talking birds and ships, he with his pistol in the picnic basket, she with her skirts bellying in the wind; how long ago.

Now the smugglers' road down, down through the thorns and the banks of gorse, the cold mist thinning as they walked. JG reached back for Lally's hand, her long shapely hand, as she began to fall behind. His own was hard and warm and gripped her fiercely; he made no allowances for her. He made no allowances for anyone, she thought, and then remembered his joyful love-making and all the allowances he had made for her then, she who knew only how to endure and not participate, for whom tenderness and passion had never come together.

The pace was relentless: he must not fail the rendezvous; or was it simply that he had not wanted her to come? Here were the marshes, the reeds rattling and the dykes black and ruffled. In her mind's eye Lally could see the cutter rising and falling, waiting for her master's return, and the way JG would plunge through the surf to the wallowing boat, and the way that boat would pull away for the *Snipe*, lying with all her sails ready to flash out the moment he stepped aboard.

'You will catch your death,' he said now, 'and you have no sense of decency at all, crawling about in the moonlight with your hair down your back.'

It was the last time, she said, the last time she would go adventuring by night. And what, he demanded, if Bensley Vernon had dragged himself from Kate's round white arms just long enough to intercept the cutter? She was unmistakable: that noble spread of canvas, that hugely long bowsprit with its massive jibs.

They did not speak again for a while, thinking of Vernon perhaps and lost hopes and fruitless friendships, and then they had passed the gate where the eel-traps hung and had swung left-handed across the causeway to the sea. Stretches of oily dark water, wind-stirred and cold and fringed with reed, lay either side, and once some duck flew overhead, their wings making a soft, strong beating in their ears. And when they topped the shingle bank the dull continuous roar changed to an enormous depraved howling from where the sea cast itself along the whole straight coast in a line of white foam.

The boat was waiting, drawn up on the beach a little, a man with a dark lantern in the stern who might have been Rush, and all the oarsmen muffled at the bow, knee-deep in surf with every other wave.

'You should not have come,' JG said, stopping and turning to Lally.

'No.'

'You will be chilled to the bone and you have a long walk home.'

'Yes.'

'You will,' and he bent towards her, smiling, 'you will use

the money wisely? Such a great deal of money. You will endow an orphanage, build ten schools?'

'Probably.'

'You will be happy?'

'I hope so.'

'Are you going to marry him?'

'I don't know. He would spend my fortune wisely, and he loves me. But I might wake in the night and think of another man and where he is and whether he thinks of me.'

He took her shoulders, put his cold mouth against hers, and walked away down the shingle quickly, his voice, low, urgent and commanding, coming back to her in snatches on the wind. And out at sea, through the fine blue darkness, she could see the black pointed shape that was the *Snipe*, with her tall raking mast and her huge bowsprit and no light anywhere, everything quiet and sinister and charged with stealth.

But as she looked, the hood of her cloak fallen back and her hair adrift in the charging air, the boat turned against the side of the ship and was lost, a little black bobbing thing against the blacker hull; and the cutter shook out her sails and flew away over the sea, diminishing and diminishing until she was no more.

And Lally threw down the pebbles she had been playing with in her hand, and put up her hood, and walked back over the bank to the kinder air of the marshes and the green smugglers' road to the Heath.